SECOND SON

SECOND SON

VERNABELLE RICE

SCANDIA
PRESS

Copyright © 2013 by Vernabelle Rice

All rights reserved, including the right to reproduce this book or portions thereof in any form whatsoever. For information, address

Scandia Press
PO Box 2222
Poulsbo, WA 98370

Published 2013

18 17 16 15 14   1 2 3 4 5

ISBN: 9-781-936672-67-7

Front Cover Art: "Wash Day" by Vernabelle Rice
Back Cover Art: "Oil Lamp" by Vernabelle Rice
Cover Design by Sheila Cowley
Interior Design by Kiran Spees

To my loving Husband

1
"Leave at Fourteen and Never Come Back"

It was one of those cool crisp mornings that are ordinary in the spring in the Lynden River Valley of Washington.

Near a ramshackle house the river slowly wended its course through the shadowed valley. Cold eddies of glacial water swirled and riffled along, clear and teal green, curling around the roots of the gray cedar stump that clung tight to the bank of rich soil. The sun warmed the moist meadow that lead to the neglected, unpainted house, where sounds of morning had begun.

A tall, gangly-legged boy with red hair stood near the spindly supports of the porch. He stretched and yawned as he picked up a large overturned milk pail. He walked toward the barn, scratching his crotch and called for the two milk-cows. Within moments the cows moseyed out of the willow thicket and likewise headed for the barn.

It was one of those usual mornings for every one except the slim, blond girl who walked down the rutted road leading from the tumbled-down farm. She stood still a moment, head down, a worn satchel gripped tightly in her hands. She heard the sound of the bus grinding its way along the valley road, approaching slowly, rousing robins from the barbed-wire fence along the drainage ditch. The bus came to a halt in front of the mailbox where the young girl waited.

Second Son

Early on a November morning in 1907, Olive Elsa Blaine Jergenson was born to a family of immigrants. Poor, uneducated, they had little to offer a new life except a warm place to grow and enough brothers and sisters filling the small shack to make sure it was never lonely.

Olive was the fourth in line of ten children. The group of red-haired and blond offspring depended on a mother, small in stature, loud of voice, who had an abundant capacity for quick good humor. With the brood she had, humor was a necessity.

The father, Olli, was a tall handsome Norwegian with a smile that "charmed birds out of trees" and used persuasion in the pursuit of making more children whether they be his wife's or the few neighbor's wives who were tempted by his smile.

The daily routine at the Jergensons was one of multitudinous mounds of laundry—hand washed—and steaming pots of soup to ready for meals and tubs of dirty dishes to be cleaned. However busy the day, there always seemed time for the family to flock in when food was cooked and ready to consume.

Play for the young girls was limited to an area close to the house where they could be quickly summoned for chores or when one of the younger children needed help. Though small, Olive's hands were capable. Mostly it was she who was called to assist.

Her oldest sister, Rose, who was unmarried, lived at home. Rose was always out riding the horse over the countryside. She left the care of her two little girls to Ma or Olli or the other sisters, Niva, Eva and Sal.

Year after year the routine crept along in the same cadence, the family absorbing homeless or unwanted children, and friends' children who were in need of help. Each time an addition was made to the family group, one of the older Jergenson children was told a wide world was waiting for them—maybe it was their time to move on. At the ripe old age of fourteen, each was handed a satchel full of clothes, an extra pair of shoes and three dollars, then put on a bus that took each one on the trip to Seattle to make his or her way in the world.

Leave at Fourteen and Never Come Back

At the insistence of Ma and Papa, each achieved a seventh grade education. This would assure them of a better chance for a good self-supporting job; at least a better chance than either of the parents had in the old country.

The only stipulation given them as they left was that they never complain, and never come back to ask for help of any kind, as Rose had done. She had come home with her two babies, had never mentioned to Ma that while the little girls were being cared for, she was out about the countryside, doing the same thing over again. She had tried to abort the third baby herself; she died in the attempt one morning in the hayloft of the barn. To prevent a similar problem and loss, the new policy of no returning was put in force.

The bus door opened. Olli gave a slow tearful glance down the lane toward the house to see if anyone had awaken early to wave good-by to her. The only one she saw was Ted stepping on the porch with the full milk pail. He shielded his eyes from the sun and raised his hand to her in a solitary gesture of farewell.

The driver gave her a cheery, "Mornin' Sis." She boarded the rattly, smoke-filled bus. In the seats were old men and dirty young children, some with sacks of homemade biscuit sandwiches filled with smelly headcheese meat or sausage. These meager lunches had to sustain these kids as they worked in the berry fields for mere pennies.

Olli knew all too well the life given these children, for she had been part of that life last summer and every summer she could remember. In her large family, members were expected to contribute as soon as they were able to work in the fields.

"Morning, Sir," she mumbled, as she sat down directly behind the driver. Her face flushed in shyness as she settled back in the cracked leather seat. The springs squeaked and poked her through her thin cotton dress.

Two unshaven old men in slouch-rimmed hats, sucked on cigar stubs through toothless grins, and looked out of the windows as

Second Son

they mumbled to each other over the roar of the motor. Olli was sure they had made a slur about "That poor damned Jergenson kid" or "There goes another one of those poor damned Jergenson kids, kicked out flat on their ass again." She turned slowly away from the two and stared straight ahead through the windshield of the bus while a shiver ran down her back and tears formed in her eyes.

The driver began a constant line of chatter with his regular customers, as they got on and off at their respective stops. Soon the working crowd was replaced by folks that were dressed in a better fashion and were obviously headed for a shopping day in Seattle or Tacoma. The bus crowd diminished as the shoppers exited. Olli was the only one left on the bus as they slipped into the downtown Seattle bus station. The driver chatted about the weather and every other subject trying to get a response from Olli. He finally asked Olli, "Sis, have you got a job lined up? And a place to stay?"

Olli cleared her throat and smiled. "Oh, yes, Sir," she lied. "I'll be working for a nice family that knows my Ma and Papa. They'll be meeting me here soon." She gathered the handles of her satchel and climbed out of the bus, heading into the fume-filled station entrance.

Olli had never been on a bus in her life, certainly never riding one all the way to Seattle. Entering the vast bus depot, she didn't even know how or where to buy a newspaper, where to go for information, how to find the public toilets—nor which to do first. She had no idea where she was going to sleep that night. She sat on a hard wooden bench, clutched the handles of the satchel, and stared out of the depot's dirty front windows.

Olli sat with her feet crossed beneath her seat. Her hands clutched the bag. The sun streamed in on her plain cut flaxen hair. Hers was a forlorn picture resembling that of a lost nymph perched on the edge of the world.

She was just that. Lost. On the edge of a new life.

The morning dragged on.

Leave at Fourteen and Never Come Back

The depot emptied and filled, emptied and filled, with the daily business of the city. Olli sat lost in her own situation, not seeing, not caring.

At slack times the ticket agent had noticed the quiet, young girl sitting alone on the station bench. He clearly wondered if there were someone coming to meet her.

She remained in the same spot all day looking afraid and dazed. As the time neared for the ticket cage to close, the agent became more concerned. By now he was sure that she planned to stay in the station for the night. He knew well there was an unsavory element in this part of Seattle at night.

The sun had begun to wane.

The driver from Olli's morning bus passed through the station. He began talking to the depot agent in the ticket cage. It was the end of the day's run for him. He was surprised to see the Jergenson kid still in the station. He questioned the agent about it. "Fred, have you seen that girl over there? Has she been there all day?"

"She sure has, Jim, and I think she's got more trouble than a kid her age aught to have." The clerk answered. The driver, whose name was Jim Porter, took a deep breath, and made a quick decision. "Fred, Lucy and I will take care of her for the night, if you'll come over with me and talk to her. Tell her the wife and I are okay and that she'll be safe with our family until she gets her bearings or a place to stay and a job. I think old man Jergenson and his Mrs. really don't do their kids right when they ship them off to town with no experience. You know they've done this thing before to the two oldest boys, and now little Sis. There ought to be a law or an agency that would step in for a case like this."

Fred and Jim walked over to Olli, introduced themselves and asked her about her situation. She, being naive, told them the facts of her situation, then asked them if they could help her. Jim Porter told her that he and his wife, Lucy, would be happy to have her stay with them, and help her find a job.

Olli bent her head. Her limp hair stuck to her cheeks, as tears trickled down and fell from her chin. "Thank you so much," she

Second Son

sniffed. "I really didn't know what I was going to do, and Papa and Ma never told me what to do, or where to go, and I really am afraid." She paused and wiped the tears from her cheeks.

Fred closed the ticket cage, getting ready to call it a day.

Jim gathered Olli's satchel under his arm, and he motioned for Olli to follow him out the back door of the depot to the livery area. There he hitched his waiting horse to a light wagon. He helped Olli up onto the wooden seat, took the reins and clicked the horse to attention, then headed the wagon out into the main street.

Olli smiled her uncertainty at Jim and held tightly to the steel arm of the seat. They began the long trip down the hill toward the Duwamish flats.

Jim chatted about life at home, about his wife and three kids who were waiting for him.

Olli still had no idea of their location, nor of the route, but they soon pulled into a quiet, rutted alley. Jim led the horse into a narrow barn behind a tall clapboard house fenced by a green picket fence. Honeysuckle trailed gently near the fence. Over the top of the fence, bridal wreath and lilac bushes cascaded a fragrant profusion of white and lavender blossoms.

The house seemed to welcome Olli with its warm light coming through the windows. It enveloped her in a quick feeling of *home*.

Three children burst from the door and run toward their father. The oldest, a boy about ten, grabbed the reins and settled the horse in the barn. He smiled at Olli and never questioned the fact that she was with his dad.

One of the children, a little girl, grabbed her dad's pants leg, jumping and begging to be picked up. Jim's jolly chuckle harmonized with a delighted squeal from the raven-haired child who clung to his neck.

The youngest child, about three years old, stood silent and shy, peering from the gate.

"Come here Wally Boy," Jim called. "I want you all to meet Miss Olive Elsa Blaine Jergenson. She is going to visit us for a while." He smiled at them, "She likes to be called Olli."

Leave at Fourteen and Never Come Back

Timidly, each came over to Olli, they shook her hand, and told her their names. Billy, Ruby, curtsied to Olli and Wally Boy mumbled "Hello."

Lucy, Jim's wife, came out of the door, wiping her hands on her flowered apron. She saw Olli standing amidst the children. She glanced at Jim, then at Olli.

A welcome smile broke the serious mask on her face. "Jim, what have we here? Where did you find this young lady?" Jim placed his daughter on the porch as he introduced Olli to his wife. Lucy was slim with long, dark-hair. She smiled at Olli as Jim informed her that Olli was to stay a few days; this fact was not questioned.

As they entered the small living room, the smell of roasted meat wafted from the kitchen. Jim's nose went up, as he smiled and hugged Lucy. "Smells good Hon." He said, as he motioned Olli into the tiny dining room. "Best you have Ruby set another place at the table to make Olli feel more welcome." Olli smiled and thought to herself how welcome she already felt. The feeling surprised her.

After dinner, dishes were cleared from the crisp white table-cloth. The boys sat at the table with Jim who leaned over and turned up the kerosene lamp. Then he took a large book from the shelf and began to read to the boys. Lucy, Ruby and Olli went to the kitchen to do the dishes. They left the dining room door open so they could hear the story while they worked. Olli asked if she could dry the dishes. She thoughtfully listened to the story being read.

Jim's voice pulled the story off the pages with an expressive-ness that made the story come alive, raising and lowering his voice to fit the mood of the story.

This evening was the calmest, most quiet and serene Olli could remember; especially in comparison to the calamity and clamor she knew rang through Papa and Ma's house at this time of evening.

Bedtime arrived. The children quietly said their good nights,

Second Son

kissed Jim and Lucy, and headed for the stairway that lead to the small attic bedroom. Ruby promised to help Wally Boy with his nightshirt.

Jim and Lucy waited until the children were out of earshot before they inquired into the details of Olli's story. After learning the Jergenson family's policy in regard to each of the children's age for leaving home. Olli explained the reasons why the rule had been enforced. As far as the Jergensons were concerned, they had done the best they could.

It was decided that Lucy and Jim would help Olli seek employment by looking in the classified section of the newspaper and drawing a map to help her find the trolley that would take her to downtown Seattle for interviews.

Jim and Lucy's home was in the far outskirts of Seattle, in an area where some of the modern conveniences had not yet extended. Thus they still used kerosene lamps, a wood cooking stove and an outside privy. Jim couldn't afford an automobile, so he drove a horse and light wagon back and forth to his bus driving job.

The neighborhood was heavily wooded and sparsely populated and it was a long walk to the trolley-car line, so it was decided, because of the area, that Jim would take Olli to the trolley where she would wait for the first morning car.

Olli told the Mr. and Mrs. Porter that if she found a job right away she would pay room and board and help with the housework and caring for the children. The plan was agreed to.

Lucy helped Olli clean out a small shed that was attached to the back porch. Jim brought a clean pallet roll, sheets, a wool quilt and a large pillow. Lucy left them for Olli to arrange her small apartment the way she wanted. After all, it was Olli's room—for a while.

Evening fell into the deeper pit of night. This peacefulness and security Olli felt was a new and welcome sensation. The kerosene lamp shed a soft glow of light. Olli looked around at the meager sleeping quarters, with its pealing flowered wallpaper, lack of windows and rough wood floor. But Olli could hardly contain her happiness. Here she felt more cared for than she had felt almost her entire life at Papa and Ma's.

As she finished making her bed she undressed in the weak light of the lamp, brushed her hair, and put on her rough homemade nightgown which Ma had sewn from printed flour sacks.

Olli lay down on the cool sheets and turned down the lamp. She pulled the quilt over her body, feeling herself shiver and not knowing if it was from the chill of the evening or the aftermath of a day like she had never known before. Everything felt new and exciting and every bit as frightening as she could have ever imagined. At the same time she felt more cared for than she could remember. She smiled as she drifted into a dreamless, refreshing sleep.

Olli turned over, as a soft knock sounded on the door. The world came back into focus and she asked, "Who is it?"

With a soft voice, Lucy murmured, "Time to rise and shine, dear."

Olli replied, "Yes, Ma'am, I'll be right there." Olli slipped out of bed and stretched in the unheated room. She shivered, reached for her thin cotton dress.

When Olli entered the warm kitchen she found that Jim had already gone to work, having left without sound. Jim and Lucy had decided to give Olli one day to get her bearings before beginning her search for work.

Olli looked around the kitchen and greeted the three children already devouring a stack of pancakes.

All three smiled and said, "Good morning." Lucy urged them to hurry eating and clean the table, so she and Olli could visit during their morning coffee.

Looking through the paper awhile, Olli had compiled quite a

Second Son

long list of housekeeping positions and jobs along the waterfront, in cafes and fisheries. She and Lucy went over the list eliminating many because of what Lucy described as "being in the wrong area of town".

Both Lucy and Olli agreed that an in-home housekeeping position would be the best thing, because of Olli's young age, plus the fact she knew about caring for children, and was willing, if not adept, at multitudes of household chores. Olli chose four ads to answer the next day and had Lucy help her with a map and trolley-car schedules. Olli then took the three children for a long walk so Lucy would have time to take a relaxing bath without interruptions from the children.

The afternoon went quickly. Olli was excited at the prospect of finding a job, a little stability and making money for a place of her own.

The next few days Olli spent hours riding the trolley in and around Seattle answering the ads for employment. A sudden rain rolled across Elliot Bay and soaked the hills, streets and byways all over town, which only made the long walks and trolley rides more miserable. Olli could not remember her feet being so cold and wet.

The sky's burden of rain lessened but by the time the afternoon rolled into place. Olli felt even more uncomfortable because her wool coat gained weight from the rain it had absorbed. With every step water dripped from the coat hem and ran down her brown cotton stockings into her shoes and made a squashing sound when she walked.

She struggled gallantly to be cheerful, but she didn't realize how, when a door was opened by prospective employers, her appearance presented a pitiful picture—she looked like a drowned kitten.

After three days the weather grew warmer. The rain had done its duty of washing streets, cleaning air, greening yards and helping blossoms make colorful flower baskets of every fenced yard.

Leave at Fourteen and Never Come Back

The evening of the fourth day that Olli had been at the Porters, Jim came home from work wearing a bright smile on his face. He had a slip of paper in his hand and waved it under Lucy and Olli's noses saying, "Olli, Girl, I met a fellow today at the depot. We were talking and he and his wife are looking for a clean, honest, capable young lady to do the housework, and help care for a small child. Mostly he is worried about his wife who doesn't want anyone to know that she is ill and can't care for their child. His mother also lives in the house. She organizes things but needs the help of a younger person to keep the household running the way they are used to. I told him you were looking for a good position of in-home employment. Here is his name, address and directions to get to his home. He wants you to be there by eleven tomorrow morning. What do you think of that, Sis?"

Olli took the slip of paper and looked over the well-penned handwriting. Her face lit up with a cheery smile of thanks and relief. "This is really wonderful, Jim, I'm very grateful."

The children and Olli finished the after dinner chores, so the evening ended with everyone gathered around the dining room table while Jim read aloud from one of his favorite books.

As the story ended, Lucy smiled, " Olli Girl," she said, "You've got to promise to come and see us, if you get this job, and I want your promise to write your folks and let them know where you are and what you're doing so they won't worry."

Noting the Porters' questioning expression on their faces, Olli sat up more quickly than she had intended and cast a surprised glance at Lucy and Jim. Her feelings surged up from a sour pit somewhere below her heart, surprising her with the amount of resentment that was hidden there. She glanced in her lap, her folded hands, and saw her knuckles were white and shaking. Taking a quick breath, she gave a long sigh. "I think it will be a while before I get in touch with them. I would like to write to you, if that is okay. That would make me feel better."

Jim and Lucy exchanged glances. Smiling, Lucy said in an understanding tone, "Yes, Dear, that will be fine."

Second Son

The evening ended. The house became quiet.

Olli lay on her pallet in the dark, windowless room. There was an uneasy feeling about leaving the quiet protected home into which she had been so easily accepted. It was a new world with unknown situations. Not sure whether she was ready to face it, she slept fitfully.

※

Morning. Olli awoke, not really feeling rested.

After breakfast she picked up her satchel, turned to Lucy. "Please give the children hugs for me and tell them I'll write soon."

Lucy hugged Olli.

The children, still asleep, would be disappointed to wake and find Olli gone.

"I'll tell them you said goodbye," Lucy chirped as she gave Olli a final hug. Lucy knew this wisp of a girl was as much in need of good care and a home life as her own children. Instead, she was going to a twenty-four-hour-a-day job.

Jim had the horse hitched and waiting in the alley. Olli climbed into the wagon and arranged her dress, so it would not be wrinkled from a long day of riding the train and trolleys to the address she held in her pocket. The trip to the train depot seemed extra long. Olli was anxious to begin her new life.

It was around six in the morning when Olli arrived at the station. She knew it would be a short wait until the train to Tacoma was scheduled to leave, so she sat on a bench outside in the vague warmth of early morning. The sun had popped over the tree tops, and splashed light down the streets and over the house tops, painting everything with the golden blush.

Jim had given her a list of trolley routes and transfers to take as well as the phone number of the bus station. If she were hired for the position, she could then call and leave a message.

Olli thought, here she was again, sitting alone, waiting for the future to unfold. But this time she knew she had made friends,

Leave at Fourteen and Never Come Back

and had a place to refer to if she ever needed them. She made a mental note and tucked it away into her memory. Friends were of one's own choosing. As for family, you were stuck with them.

Finally, Olli went into the station and purchased her ticket for the train to Tacoma. Generously, Jim and Lucy had given her ten dollars to get to her destination.

Once she got on the train, the trip didn't last that long. She enjoyed the view of Elliot Bay until the train's route started through the low hills and along the tide flats. Olli was headed for Tacoma.

A short, stocky, older man, the conductor had a round stomach and a gold watch chain linked across its expanse. He took the watch out of the pocket in his vest and checked the time for Olli. His manner jovial and good-natured, he chatted with folks as he asked for their tickets.

There was a black waiter that came through each car taking orders for drinks. He stopped and asked Olli if she would like some iced tea. She declined, not having the money for such treats. He was the second black person Olli had ever seen. The first had been an old man who used to help Papa in the barn when he had saws to sharpen for the local loggers.

To Olli the waiter was the color of rich cocoa. His skin glowed like a chocolate bar. Olli thought him a beautiful sight to behold. His manners impressed her. His clean crisp white shirt and black tie made a picture that Olli would slip into her memory as part of her first train ride.

The train soon pulled into the Union Station which looked to Olli like part of great, brick castle. Entering the lobby she looked around and stared at the lovely tiled, domed ceiling. The floor was covered in a beautiful tile pattern that made Olli feel as if she were walking into a fairytale courtyard she had read about in a childhood. She walked confidently through the station. At its entrance, she glanced back through the impressive building, absorbing and preserving the impression the building made on her.

Second Son

Olli's instruction sheet indicated what trolley she was to take. She had to transfer three times before she finally reached the corner marking the end of her trolley car journey. Now on foot, she ascended up Connelly Street, then farther up the hill to Park Street.

It was warm and sunny. Yards were mottled with shade from immense maple trees that lined both sides of the red brick streets. Lawns clipped smooth glowed beside manicured rose bushes and evergreen shrubs which cuddled around the basement windows of a variety of two and three story houses. Each yard was divided by low picket fences or low flowering hedges. The houses were like none Olli had ever seen before, all colors, tan, blue, white, yellow and soft green, with gingerbread trim and carved porch posts. Broad porch steps led to wide verandas and lattice screened porches.

Olli was impressed with everything she saw. She walked up the street, taking in every aspect of this style of living. The picture of opulence that lay before her was beyond her imagination.

She began to breathe unsteadily as she went up the walk to the house where she was expected for her interview.

In the sunshine the elegant three story Victorian shimmered a soft blue. A wide airy porch curved around the front and side. A tower rose up on one corner, stained glass windows shining in the morning sunlight. Back near the kitchen entry, an outside stairway led to the attic area above the third floor.

Olli gulped loudly as she stepped up onto the porch and rang the doorbell. She smoothed her hair and straightened her dress collar. Footsteps echoed inside. The door opened. Olli smiled.

2
A New Life

The man who stood in the doorway towering over her peered down at her through a hedge of black eyebrows.

She tried to speak, but the only word she could muster was a squeaky, "Hello."

The man nodded pleasantly and motioned her into the foyer where a pale young woman, whom Ollie assumed was his wife, stood with a pensive smile on her thin lips. Her large blue eyes calmly scrutinized Olli, noting her worn shoes, cotton shift and natty looking satchel.

The woman led Olli into the parlor. The man gestured for her to take a seat on a carved wooden settee. Plush cushions of deep wine colored velvet seemed too elegant for use, and Olli settled into them very carefully.

At first neither the man nor the woman spoke. Olli sat properly, waiting apprehensively for a reaction from either.

The tall man cleared his throat. "I'm Mr. Gordon. This is my wife, Lettie." His eyebrows formed a V on his forehead. He and his wife seated themselves across the room. "You are Miss Jergenson, I presume."

"Yes, Sir," Olli answered.

Mr. Gordon began again, "Mister Porter told me you are looking for a position as a housekeeper, and you are good with children. Is that correct?"

Second Son

"Yes, Sir," Olli swallowed, knowing in her heart that she had a lot to learn.

Mrs. Gordon spoke quietly, "Clarence, I believe Miss Jergenson feels a bit uneasy. I think if Mr. Porter recommended her for this position, we should hire her." Mrs. Gordon turned to Olli. "Maybe you would like to sit in the back garden, and have a glass of lemonade. It is such a warm day, and you have come a long way today. You might like a short time to relax before discussing your duties." She smiled at Olli.

Mr. Gordon suggested to his wife that Olli first be taken upstairs to meet Mother Gordon.

Mrs. Gordon heartily agreed, adding, "Then Miss Jergenson can have her lemonade in the garden, after which Mother can show her the house and talk over her duties."

Mrs. Gordon stood and walked toward the hallway. "Come – may I call you 'Olli'?"

Olli nodded, rising to her feet. "Yes Ma'am," she added.

They went through the rooms on the first floor, then climbed the open stairway. On the second floor the sun spilled down the hall and sparkled on the polished wood floors.

The door at the end of the hall opened, and a sparrow-like woman stood quietly in the doorway. Although small in stature she had a full round bosom and dainty thin legs. She was dressed in gray from her stockings, shoes, chiffon dress, even her hair was the same tone of gray. As she stood in the light of the hallway, she seemed like an apparition.

Olli looked directly at her and saw that the bright bird-like, black eyes held a twinkle of youth camouflaged by a wrinkled face.

The younger Mrs. Gordon said, "Olli, I'd like you to meet Mr. Gordon's mother, Mrs. Mildred Gordon. She nodded toward Mother Gordon, this is Olli Jergenson. She is applying for the position of housekeeper and helper for baby Louise."

"How do, Ma'am." Olli said. She offered her hand in greeting to the older Mrs. Gordon.

In return, Mildred Gordon extended her hand to Olli. She

A New Life

spoke in a soft voice. "I'm happy to meet you, Olli. We are in need of good help around here." Her flashing black eyes took inventory of Olli, who was very aware of the quick scrutiny.

Mother Gordon took Olli's hand in her bird-like fingers, then turned to the younger Mrs. Gordon. "Lettie, I can take her through the house and show her to her quarters. We can meet in the parlor after she makes the house tour and relaxes a little in the back yard with a glass of lemonade. You can finish telling her about duties and we can discuss her wages at that time."

Lettie gave Mother Gordon a quick glance as if to suggest otherwise, but, agreed, turned and went back down the stairway.

Mother Gordon motioned for Olli to follow her. They looked over the next two floors. Olli learned whose rooms were whose, and what duties were expected.

"Your room," Mother Gordon explained, "is in the attic. There is an outside stairway by the kitchen door. I'll show you to the kitchen, but I'll let you climb up there by yourself to settle in a bit, as it is quite a climb for me to make."

Olli nodded and followed the elder Mrs. Gordon. At the kitchen back door, Mother Gordon pointed outside and gave Olli instructions on how to reach the three story stairway. "The door is not locked, dear. After you've see your quarters and had a lemonade in the backyard, my daughter-in-law and I will meet with you back in the parlor."

Olli thanked Mother Gordon and began to climb the narrow outside stairway, clinging tightly to the railing. When she reached the top of the landing she had a lovely view, looking out over the shade trees below, and off down the hill over the tops of houses and neighborhood shops. Further down she could see the harbor and hear the distant whistles and toots of the tugboats towing their cargo-laden barges cutting V-shaped wakes upon the glassy surface of Commencement Bay.

She opened the door and stepped into a charming room with a low, angled ceiling. Two dormer windows repeated the view she had seen from the landing. There was a stained glass window in the bathroom charmed by dainty flowered wallpaper and shiny linoleum. The bed, though small, looked clean and comfortable.

But the indoor toilet amazed Olli the most. Having never lived with running water, let alone an inside toilet and bathtub, she was not aware that nearly every house in Tacoma had inside plumbing, and that this neighborhood belonged to the town's more affluent families, grand houses considered to be the areas' elite homes. She looked around the room, smiled and whispered to herself, "Olli, girl, I think you'll do just fine here." Thinking of her family, her home, her past, all that gone forever, she felt both sad and excited.

It was a new life she was starting.

Stepping outside once again, she closed the door softly and scurried down the steps. Smoothing her dress, she held her head high as she reentered the house.

Dweena the cook met her with a glass of icy lemonade. Olli took her refreshment to the backyard, seated herself in a lawn chair and heaved a sigh. What a wonderful idea that Mrs. Gordon suggest she relax before coming back to tie up the final agreement concerning her wages.

Finishing her drink, Olli hurried to the parlor. As she approached, she overheard Mr. Gordon's voice booming down the hallway. His laughter was full of pure delight. Olli entered the parlor to find Mr. Gordon sitting on the floor with a chubby little girl about two years old with her arms clinging around her father's neck. She was bouncing and squealing and begging for more piggyback rides.

Seeing Olli in the entryway, Mr. Gordon stood, scooped up the squealing child in his arms, smoothed her little dress and straightened his tie. His voice boomed with good humor as he said, "Come in, come in." He motioned her towards the settee. "Well, girl," Clarence smiled, "Lettie has made a list of duties, but we feel Mother Gordon should oversee your work for a short time."

Olli smiled and answered, "Yes, but I have a few questions

A New Life

about my wages. How much will you pay me and will I be paid every month or every week?"

Clarence Gordon's eyebrows came together again. He said, "For such a wisp of a girl, you're quite a plucky little thing."

Olli swallowed hard. "Yes, Sir, but I have no one else to ask those questions for me."

"You're right," chirped Mother Gordon, "Now Clarence, just tell her for pity sakes."

"Yes, yes, he rumbled, "We think to start you at thirty dollars a month, and after we see how you do, we'll consider a raise. We hold you responsible for being punctual, clean and modest. We will supply you with your work uniforms, room and food. We'll expect you to save some of your wages each month and we'll help you start a savings program at our bank. Saturday will be your day off and we expect you to use it wisely. No senseless running around, and no men—I should say no boys—will be allowed on the premises except with my permission. If all of that is clear, and you agree, we expect you to begin your duties tomorrow morning at six. Lettie will leave your uniform in the kitchen later this afternoon."

Olli had given close attention to all he had said. She smiled, "I feel it's a real pleasure and I hope you'll be pleased with me. I'll do my best. I thank you."

As she walked toward the stairway, Lettie paused and said, "Well, my Dear, I will take Louise up for her nap. Olli, you can have the rest of the day free to go over your list of duties and unpack. We'll expect you to dine with us tonight. Dweena, our cook will be told to put on an extra table setting. From tomorrow on you'll be expected to eat in the kitchen with Dweena and baby Louise." Lettie smiled. The cherub-like child clung to her neck. Lettie started up the stairway. Olli noticed Lettie took each stair step very slowly.

Mother Gordon motioned for Olli to follow her. She started walking toward the kitchen. When the door was closed behind them Mother Gordon sat at the kitchen table. "Olli," Mother

Second Son

Gordon began, "dinner will be at seven o'clock. Cook will ring a bell for you. Please be washed and change your dress. I'll not go up stairs with you. The afternoon is yours. You may want to sit in the backyard, or spend time in your room. It's up to you."

Olli smiled and thanked Mother Gordon and paused to say "Hello" to Dweena before going through the kitchen to climb the outside stairs.

The sun was warm. The breeze caught her hair and carried it in wisps around her face. She opened the door to her very own room. She felt she had moved into a large gingerbread house which had been set on a green velvet carpet. Olli left the door ajar so she could enjoy the birds that were having their afternoon choir practice in the tree tops. She turned on her toes with arms held wide and head tipped back in sheer relief and joy.

She would make it. She would not have to go back home begging for a place to stay, like Rose, her sister Rose with her two little girls.

She sat down on her bed, testing it with a careful bounce or two. Finding it surprisingly comfy, she raised her arms and crossed them behind her head. She lay down and closed her eyes in contentment.

The next thing she knew, a bell wakened her with a start!

She clambered from the bed and quickly washed her hands and face. Fumbling through her unpacked satchel, she undressed and slipped into a clean but wrinkled dress. She tried desperately to smooth the wrinkles, and then brushed her bangs in an attempt to arrange her hair. Carefully she clicked the door shut, took a long slow breath, and descended the stairs.

Entering the kitchen Olli found the cook singing a popular tune. When Dweena heard Olli enter, she turned and again extended her hand in greeting. "Olli, My Dear," she said, in a joyful tone, "I'm happy that you'll be with us and will be caring for baby Louise. The child needs a young person around her."

Olli said, "I'm happy to be here, too, but I have a lot to learn—"

"Oh! I'll be glad to help you with any advice," chirped Dweena.

A New Life

"And I'm sure Mother Gordon will be right behind you every day—for a while—until you learn the routine to her liking. The young Mrs. Gordon, Lettie, doesn't have too much to say about the care of the house. She's not as well as she looks. Mother Gordon is quite possessive about the running of things. I'm sure you'll find that out without me chattering on about things." Dweena spoke softly. Her hands moved swiftly to empty kettles and pans of food into their correct serving dishes then placed the glorious smelling food on a serving cart.

Dweena motioned, saying, "Come, my Dear, and meet the group on their terms and home ground. I'm to feed the baby, Louise, in the kitchen, and get her ready for Mrs. Lettie to bathe her so she can tuck the child in bed after dinner. I'll see you later, before you go up for the night. Come now," she said, as she pushed the serving cart through the swinging door, and into the dining room.

The Gordons were waiting.

Mrs. Gordon indicated where Olli should sit at the table. Olli pulled out the chair and started to sit down, but a quick frown from Dweena told her to wait. They all stood behind their chairs. Mr. Gordon bowed his head. The women did the same. After a quick nod from Dweena, Olli bowed her head and waited. Mr. Gordon's voice boomed out a short grace.

The women sat one at a time, as Mr. Gordon pushed in their chairs for them—Mother Gordon, first, then Mrs. Gordon, then Olli.

Mr. Gordon sat at the head of the table and cleared his throat. "Dweena," he said, "this looks like the results of another of your days of excellence in the kitchen. We thank you very much."

Dweena smiled and bowed slightly, then hurried back into the kitchen, which left Olli rather forsaken. Feeling somewhat out of place, Olli didn't want to make any mistakes.

Olli vowed to herself to watch and learn from the family by doing as they did. She felt this would teach her good manners which she was sure were expected of her. She knew, as an

Second Son

employee of such gracious people as the Gordons, she would be expected to be courteous and have correct manners.

She had never said grace before, as that was not the way Papa and Ma had done. At home everyone sat down in a rush of noise and confusion and reached for what they wanted, or could reach, before someone else took all the food. Olli was determined not to follow any of her old ways. She knew to be socially correct all she had to do was watch the examples set by the Gordons.

Olli waited until Mr. Gordon asked for her plate. He had filled both of the women's plates before hers. She saw it was expected that she wait until Mr. Gordon lifted his fork and knife before she began. The dinner went quietly, with small bits of conversation. Not at all like the hubbub she had known at home. Olli rather enjoyed the dignified environment.

Her mind tumbled into a comfortable fantasy, that some day she might be the owner of such a lovely home. But she was brought back to reality with a brush against her sleeve, as Dweena came from the kitchen with a sweet cake dessert. Dweena seemed aware that Olli had been day dreaming, and gave her a wink and a smile.

Mother Gordon said she'd expect to see Olli bright and early at six in the morning to help her begin her duties. With that, Mother Gordon excused herself and left the room.

This left Olli sitting in the quiet dining room with the rather imposing form of Clarence Gordon. He leaned back in his chair, and unfurled his heavy, black eyebrows. A friendly glance showed a relaxed ease that made Olli more comfortable. His dark eyes softened as he asked, "Olli, are there any more questions you have about your job here?"

Olli thought a minute then replied "Yes, Sir, I have been wondering how it was that Jim Porter came to talk to you about my needing a job?"

Mr. Gordon smiled, brushed his square chin with his hand. "I wondered if you would ask me about that. I guess that Jim is about the most amiable guy I have ever met, and I've known him

A New Life

for ten years. He has been driving the Lynden Valley bus route for a long time. He worked for me. I'm one of the supervisors of the trolley and bus lines here in Pierce County. I also used to work in King County. Jim and I have been good friends a long time, and he wouldn't give either one of us bad advice, Olli. He knew Mrs. Gordon was ill. He found that we were looking for someone we could trust to take care of baby Louise, and someone who would also do a good job around the house. Jim told me about you and your family's way of putting you out on your own." Mr. Gordon paused, as if struggling with such an idea, such a way of doing things. An instant later, he composed himself. "Jim said you were honest, hard working and needed a good start. I talked it over with Mother and Lettie, and we agreed. I met Jim at the station and told him, if you were interested, to have you come for the interview."

Olli sat with her hands in her lap. She glanced down and noticed her fingers were tightly clasp together. She relaxed and thanked Mr. Gordon for explaining his friendship with Jim Porter.

She murmured softly, "Sir, I just hope I can do things to please you. You see, I've never seen a house like this." With her arms outstretched, she gestured at the expanse of the dining room. "I've never had an inside bathroom before, running water, and especially a real room without being lined with beds. I have always had to sleep with one of my little cousins, or my sisters, and I've never had any privacy. I really appreciate all these lovely things. I'll try my very hardest to do good work for your family."

Mr. Gordon pondered a moment Olli's speech. "Well, Olli, we'll all try to help you, as long it's needed, and we'll always be available if you ever need to talk to us about anything. Before I forget, we want you to write a letter this evening to Jim and Lucy and let them know that you will be working and staying with us. I feel that is only fair, as I know they will be concerned."

Mr. Gordon stood and adjusted his tie. "I'll have Dweena get you some writing paper, envelope and stamp. You can mail the

Second Son

letter in the morning. If there is nothing else, I bid you good evening." He turned and left the room.

Olli opted to write, as she wasn't sure about using the telephone, so she stopped in the kitchen and talked to Dweena a few moments and she had writing materials ready for her.

She saw a crisp gray uniform with a white apron and a lace-trimmed hat hanging on a knob of a cupboard. Dweena mentioned that it was ready for her to take upstairs with her.

Dweena said, "From today on, it will be up to you to see that your uniforms are washed and pressed. I did it this time because you haven't started yet. There are three other uniforms coming tomorrow. If you need shoes let Mother Gordon know."

Olli smiled again, "Yes Ma'am, I do thank you and I will need different shoes to match this nice dress and apron. The Gordons seem to be doing so much for me, I only hope they think what I'll be doing for them is worth all they are spending on me."

Dweena nodded, clearly aware of the happy light in Olli's eyes, clearly confident Olli would do just fine.

3
A New Home

Olli awoke to the chorus of birds that breathed in the liquid gold of the morning and expelled crystal songs over the tree tops. She stretched and smiled knowing she needed no alarm clock in her attic room while it was enveloped in the crescendo the birds provided.

She hopped from her snug bed and went to the bathroom to wash in warm water, which she didn't have to draw from the pump or heat on the old wood cook stove. What a treat. If her sisters could only see her in her very own private space, they would be green with envy.

With a sense of caution Olli approached the gray uniform hanging in the closet. She wanted to be sure that she looked presentable. She put the uniform over her head, and wriggled it down over her homemade slip, buttoned the bodice, smoothed the cool surface of the starched cotton fabric over her hips and tied the fresh white apron around her waist. She went back to the bathroom, and vigorously brushed her hair, placed the trim little hat on her head, tied it at the nape of her neck, and momentarily primped in the mirror. She made her bed and gave the room a satisfied glance.

Leaving her room, she again smoothed her uniform, clicked the door behind her, and began the first of many busy days.

The days quickly turned into a delightful routine. Polishing and handling the lovely knickknacks was a joy, and being surrounded by the warm glow of varnished wood and soft cushioned furniture always brought a smile to her face. This pleasure was surpassed only by her feeling of love for baby Louise.

Louise was a typical two year old full of mischief and simple childish questions. With all the modern conveniences available to Olli, it was easy to care for Louise's needs. Olli loved to spend the majority of her time in the nursery or in the kitchen area that was set apart for Louise.

Olli noticed that Lettie hadn't lifted Louise in her arms for the past week. Normally, she would hand Louise to her mother after Lettie had seated herself. Olli knew that Lettie was ill, but she had never asked the cause of the weakness. She felt in time she would be told about Lettie's infirmity. Until then, Olli made herself aware that when any physical lifting or carrying was needed, she was there to help Lettie before being asked.

In the weeks that followed, things went along quietly until one mid-morning after Louise had been put down for her nap. Lettie hadn't come down for breakfast, so Mother Gordon went upstairs to see if she was all right. Olli was busy with the carpet sweeper when she heard Mother Gordon's excited voice echoing through the upstairs hallway.

Dweena came running from the kitchen. Olli and she looked at each other in anxious shock. Mother Gordon never raised her voice, so such a disturbance in the house was unusual. The two dropped what they were doing, and started for the stairway.

Mother Gordon called, "Quick! Dweena! Olli! Call an ambulance! Quickly! Quickly!"

Not being accustomed to using the telephone, Olli let Dweena take it and find the emergency number in the phone book. Olli started up the stairs.

Mother Gordon came to the banister on the second story landing visibly shaken. She whispered, "Hurry! Oh, It's Lettie! It's Lettie! Oh God! Oh God!"

A New Home

Olli rushed forward reaching Mother Gordon just in time to keep her from slumping to the floor.

Olli asked shakily, "Please, Mother Gordon. What's wrong?" Olli led her to the side chair outside of Lettie's room. The older woman refused to sit, holding onto the arms of the chair. She bowed her head and sobbed silently.

Mother Gordon said in a shaky voice, "Oh Olli, it's Lettie. Lettie. She is so ill. I'm afraid—so afraid! Please, where is the ambulance?"

At that moment they heard the shrill pulsing of a siren and the ambulance stopped in front of the house.

A loud scuffle at the doorway was followed by Dweena's voice directing the ambulance attendants. They rushed to where Mother Gordon frantically motioned them into Lettie's room. The two men entered her room while Mother Gordon babbled to them about helping Lettie. They closed the door to the bedroom, and, except for Dweena's puffing when she arrived at the top of the stairway, all became strangely quiet.

Filled with anxiety, Dweena and Olli stood holding tightly one to another, each knowing something terrible had happened.

Tears fell down Olli's cheeks. Flashbacks from that day the previous year when her sister Rose had been found dead in the hayloft. Olli looked at Dweena. "What do you think happened?"

Dweena's head and shoulders drooped. "It must be what they feared," she said, still holding tight to Olli. "Lettie's not been well. You know that is why they needed your help. They never said the word cancer, but I have a feeling that's what her trouble is."

The door opened. The attendants came out carrying Lettie on a stretcher. Glancing at Dweena and Olli, the head attendant said, "We're taking her to the hospital. Please see that Mother Gordon calls Mr. Gordon to go directly to the hospital."

"What is the matter?" Olli asked softly.

"That is to be determined at the hospital," the attendant replied officiously. They carried the stretcher carefully down the stairs and out of the house to the ambulance.

Second Son

To steady Mother Gordon, Olli and Dweena held on to her, again guiding her to a chair in the hall where she sat down. Dweena kept holding the old woman's fragile hand while Olli stepped over to shut the bedroom door. She glanced into the room and a wave of shock rolled over her when she saw the bedding strewn over the floor covered with blood. A frightened gasp came from her throat. She turned to Mother Gordon, hardly able to ask. "What—has—happened to Lettie?"

Mother Gordon looked up. Her wrinkled face was white. Her eyes were brimmed with tears. A look of distress drew her mouth into a thin pencil line.

Mother Gordon voice shook. "Lettie's doctor had told her this might happen. She has cancer." The old woman broke down and sobbed.

Dweena and Olli looked at each other and placed their hands on Mother Gordon's shoulders. The old woman trembled quietly with grief.

After a few moments more, Mother Gordon took a long breath and pushed herself up from the chair. "Lettie has been silently suffering for more than a year—been getting weaker and weaker. Clarence and I had hoped she might get better. But we knew the opposite might also happen. Oh Lord! What will poor Clarence do? And poor baby Louise?" Again she fell to sobbing softly.

Dweena told Olli to go down to the kitchen and heat water for tea, saying, "A hot cup of tea will help settle your nerves, Mother Gordon."

Mother Gordon rose slowly from the chair, gathered her composure, then lifted the ear piece of the phone on the table next to her and dialed Clarence's office. She calmly gave him the message. She told him she would stay at home to be with Louise, but as soon as he found out Lettie's condition she wanted him to call. She slowly hung up the receiver, tears flowing down her cheeks.

Olli set the tea kettle to boiling. Soon the kettle's whistle wafted through the quiet house. Dweena assisted Mother Gordon

A New Home

into the kitchen as Olli prepared tea. All three sat quietly at the table sipping the hot liquid.

The rest of the morning dragged by slow as molasses in winter.

Louise was heard waking. Olli hurried to bring her down to the kitchen play area where she left her for Mother Gordon to care for, hoping it would be a good distraction. Then she and Dweena went up to Lettie's room and removed all of the soiled bedding. The mattress was soaked and would have to be cleaned and aired. Olli scrubbed everything and helped Dweena take all the soiled linen down the back stairs to the basement laundry area: soak in cold water, bleach, launder, hung on outside lines to freshen and dry before late afternoon.

The shrill ring of the telephone jarred the strained nerves of the three women, working and holding their somber vigil, awaiting news of Lettie.

Mother Gordon went to the phone in the front entry, lifted the receiver.

Olli held little Louise and got a hug from the chubby child. Olli and Dweena strained to hear any indication of good or bad news, awaited for Mother Gordon to finish the conversation which, obviously, was with Clarence.

They heard footsteps slowly return to the kitchen. The swinging door opened to show Mother Gordon's ashen white face. "Lettie has passed away. Clarence, he said the doctors did all they could for her. Her condition...was far too...advanced. Lost too much blood—" She slumped down into the nearest chair.

In childish curiosity, patting Olli's face, Louise questioned, "Matter with Gramma?"

Olli whispered in her ear, "Grandma is sad, but she will be fine." Olli decided Mr. Gordon should be the one to explain to the child where her mother had gone. Louise's understanding was so limited. Olli hoped in the days to come the child wouldn't have a difficult time without her mother. Olli took the child out of the kitchen and held her tight to her shoulder as she climbed the

Second Son

stairway. She put Louise in the nursery and stayed with her until Mr. Gordon came home.

It was late in the evening when Clarence Gordon finally came in the door. He looked weary and completely torn, face stern and sallow. He faced Mother Gordon, took her into the parlor and shut the door.

A short time later they emerged. Both and said their quiet "good nights."

Mother Gordon went up stairs.

Clarence went to the kitchen. Dweena met him and patted him gently on his back.

She said, "We are all so sorry, Mr. Clarence. Olli is in the nursery with Louise. We called and had Shoefield's Furniture Store deliver a new mattress. Olli and I have freshened the bedroom, if you wish to sleep there."

Clarence gave a brief sigh. "No, Dweena, not tonight. I'll just curl up on the couch in the study. I have a lot of things to take care of tomorrow in preparation for Lettie's services. Thank you anyway." He went to the study and closed the door behind him.

Dweena trudged up to the nursery to get Olli, who had fed and bathed Louise and tucked her into bed. Olli quietly slipped from the room leaving the child sleeping peacefully.

Olli asked Dweena, "How is Mr. Clarence?"

Dweena replied softly, "He is pretty broken up. He plans to sleep in the study. I don't blame him. It has all been such a shock. Poor man. I didn't ask him, but I'm sure he would want you to stay in Louise's room with her tonight, just in case she should wake and go to her parents' room."

Olli said, "I was wondering what to do about that. I know after the stress of today Mother Gordon needs her rest, so I didn't want to wake her to ask, but I hate to leave Louise alone. I think I'll just run up to my room and get my night clothes. I'll be right back."

Dweena nodded.

A New Home

The next morning was filled with phone calls and front door chimes, as members of the church and small hushed crowds of never-before-seen relatives kept Mother Gordon in a slow whirl of necessity. By ruling with a strong hand she did her best to be the buffer between Clarence's grief and myriad outside interruptions.

Early in the afternoon Clarence called Olli into the parlor where he thanked her for the special care of Louise, and informed her that he had hired a fulltime nanny for Louise, who would arrive before night fall. He told Olli the nanny's being hired bore no reflection on Olli's work. The fact was that a fulltime person should be with Louise now that her mother was gone.

Olli agreed, knowing she didn't have time to do both jobs and it would bring a feeling of normality back to the household.

She told him she understood his concern, but asked if it would be all right for her to continue to spend some time with the child, because she loved Louise and didn't want to abruptly leave her. It would take time for the child to adjust to another person caring for her after the loss of her mother.

Clarence agreed that Olli should spend a short time each day with Louise.

With a strong hand on the helm of the household Mother Gordon made a list of preparations for Olli and Dweena. She advised Olli what bedrooms had to be prepared with clean linens, because during the time of Lettie's funeral a large number of out-of-town friends and relatives would be staying at the house. Dweena was given her own list, and she disappeared into the kitchen to plan the meals Mother Gordon had requested.

The rest of the day Olli busied herself making beds, putting out fresh linens, dusting and polishing so each room would be in perfect order.

Late in the day Olli answered the doorbell for Mother Gordon. The woman who had been hired for the nanny's position stood on the porch. Olli invited her to enter and to please wait in the parlor. The woman smiled, seated herself primly upon the settee, tucking her linen coat neatly over her arm.

Second Son

Mother Gordon asked Olli to escort the woman to the parlor.

After a short time the door opened, and Mother Gordon brought the new employee to the kitchen. She introduced Araminta Schmit to Olli and Dweena, then left with Araminta upstairs to show her the nanny's quarters that were next to the nursery, Louise waking from a morning nap.

Olli was impressed with Araminta. She seemed pleasant, and Ollie hoped Araminta could help Louise, who had begun asking where her mother had gone.

Olli knew it had been difficult for Mr. Clarence. He hadn't yet told child that her mother had died. Maybe he didn't know how to explain such a thing to such a young child. Maybe the new nanny could explain in words the child might understand that her mother was gone.

The dinner bell sounded that evening. Araminta had dinner with the family, as was usual when a new employee began working for the Gordons. Olli and Dweena cared for Louise in the kitchen. Louise's childish chatter filled the room. She talked about the sweet lady who was going to be her new friend while her Mommy was gone.

Immediately after dinner Araminta came to the kitchen. She visited a short while, then took the little girl upstairs for her bath. After her bath Louise had a short play period and story time before bedtime. Araminta was very efficient and clearly showed she had Louise's well-being uppermost in her mind.

After Araminta and Louise had gone upstairs for the night, the front doorbell rang. Olli answered it and opened the door to a tall man whom she did not recognize. He was dressed in a dark fashionable suit and stood casually running his fingers through his blond curly hair. He smiled at Olli. In that moment she felt he looked familiar.

He said, "Hello, I'm Clarence Gordon's brother, Larry. I just heard about Lettie. Is Clarence here?"

Olli apologized, "Oh! No one told me you were expected.

A New Home

Do come in. Yes, Mother Gordon and Mr. Clarence are both at home." She ushered him into the foyer.

He confided. "I'm not expected." He called out, "Mother! Clarence! Anybody home?"

There was a sound of rushing feet. The parlor door opened. Clarence and Mother Gordon rushed from the parlor into the foyer. Larry put his arms around his plucky little mother and lifted her high off the floor kissing her on the cheek. He eased her back to the floor, grabbed Clarence's shoulders and hugged him. The moment slipped from the joy of meeting after a long separation, to a sad unfilled silence that prolonged their brotherly embrace.

Mother Gordon broke the silence by asking Olli to make coffee and bring it to the parlor.

Olli gladly obliged. When she returned with the coffee tray, the Gordons were deep in conversation concerning Larry's possibly staying with the family for a while after the funeral. He'd been gone for so long that Mother Gordon insisted and pleaded, while Clarence seemed to have already accepted the fact that his younger brother would stay the length of time he needed until his new job opened in Alaska.

As Olli left the room, she had the feeling that Mr. Larry would be around for a while.

4
Larry Gordon

The next few days leading up to the funeral, the house was unusually quiet. Araminta kept Louise entertained in the nursery play area. Olli missed the sweet little girl. Whenever her duties took her up near the nursery she would peek in to tell Louise "Hello." Each time Olli visited—Louise ran to her arms, squealing with delight and telling her all the things that she and "Minute"—as she called Araminta—were doing. Olli could see they had become friends, and was delighted to see Louise so happy, but was concerned about the child's not mentioning her mother.

The news of her mother had either not been spoken of, or the child was more resilient than Olli would have expected. Louise continued being her happy self.

Araminta and Louise began having their meals in the kitchen with Dweena and Olli. This gave the three of us women a chance to get better acquainted and gave Louise an audience for her newly learned poems and songs—the child had such a feeling of family. Her father and grandmother were occupied with Uncle Larry and all the people who filled the house during the days before the funeral.

The evening before the funeral there were eight guests, including Larry, who stayed overnight. Events kept Olli especially busy. She was now filling in as a maid as well as doing her regular housekeeping tasks. She and Dweena spoke in whispers about

Second Son

how strange it was that people who claimed to be Lettie's friends had never come to visit while she was ill. They would undoubtedly all be at the funeral and at the later gathering at the house.

"Like a flock of vultures," Dweena observed.

Mother Gordon had asked that Olli and Dweena not attend the funeral because of the large crowd that was expected at the house following the services. They were to arrange the food for the buffet. Setting the table with fine silver and china, for Olli it seemed more of a social affair than a remembrance in honor of Lettie.

After the trip to the cemetery the guests arrived at the house and the parlor filled with a whispered hubbub of voices. Olli observed groups of well-dressed men and women who did not seem there to mourn Lettie's passing as much as to look things over. They kept Mr. Clarence under their monocled glances, watching to see how he was standing up under his loss. Olli thought they looked like small clutches of gawky-necked cranes, ogling and twittering.

Mr. Gordon asked Araminta to bring Louise down to the parlor, which she did. There was an audible gasp from the corners of the room, when Louise ran down the stairway and jumped into Clarence's open arms.

Then shyly she said, "Hello," to her grandmother and Uncle Larry. She looked at all the people from her lofty perch in Clarence's arms and said, "Ooo, Daddy! Wouldn't Mommy love this party?"

Clarence looked at her innocent face, and smiled. "Yes." He said simply.

Louise continued, "My Mommy has gone away on a long trip and she won't be back for a long time." She explained to the crowd. "I'm supposed to be a good girl for Daddy, and Minute, and Gramma Gordon an' everybody, an' I told Daddy I would." She smiled as she wriggled from Clarence's arms, ran to Minute, and grabbed her hand, saying, "May I have some of that pretty cake?"

Araminta smiled, and led the child into the kitchen, with her chosen piece of cake.

The crowd broke into quiet exclamations of "Brave little soldier. Sweet little girl. What a wonderful way of explaining this all to a three-year-old child."

The crowd soon dispersed, except for the eight house guests who had decided to stay one more night. Some had come from back east. Olli and Dweena again cleaned the dining room after luncheon, then began to prepare for the evening meal.

Next morning, after the house guests had gone, the chores were finally finished. Dweena and Olli sat resting in the kitchen, when Mother Gordon came in and announced that her youngest son, Larry, would be staying for at least a month, until his job in Alaska was ready. She then asked Olli to remember to put fresh sheets on Larry's bed everyday. She also asked Dweena to be sure another place was set at mealtimes.

Larry entered the kitchen. "Good morning Ladies," his voice a jovial tone. "I do hope my staying won't make an inconvenience for you, but I guess I didn't remember how much I missed the family, and I need some time to get better acquainted with my niece. I'll soon head to the far north, for another three or four years. I look forward to this time now with my family."

He put his strong arms around his mother's waist. She reached up and patted his cheek, and her eyes danced with pride for her tall, handsome son.

Dweena, and Olli agreed unanimously that one extra person in the house would be no problem.

Entwining her fingers in her son's, cheerfully Mother Gordon led him from the room. On the way out, she asked that coffee and sweet rolls be taken to the parlor.

After they left, Olli said, "When I first saw Mr. Larry at the front door, he looked familiar—now I know why. He looks just like Mr. Clarence, except, Mr. Clarence is dark eyed, has dark hair and is so solemn. Mr. Larry is fair-haired with blue eyes and

Second Son

seems to be of a much happier temperament. He'll be good for the family, especially Louise. He clearly enjoy Louise, and they have become close friends already, even though he has been here such a short time."

Every afternoon during the lovely autumn days of 1922, Araminta took Louise for a long walk. As they left the yard Olli heard the child squeal with delight. She loved scuffing and running through the golden leaves that covered the sidewalks. When they returned Louise breathlessly conveyed all the wonders she had seen. There was always cocoa and cookies to enjoy while everyone within ear shot listened to her tales.

Nearly every day Uncle Larry would come to the kitchen for snack time. He undoubtedly enjoyed Louise's exuberant chatter, as well as the company of all there.

It seemed Mother Gordon was always hovering and fluffing her feathers, bragging about her lovely boy in whom she had great pride.

Dweena would wink at Olli, both acknowledging to the other the fact that Mother Gordon was not only proud of Larry but quite jealous of the time he spent with Louise.

Olli was aware that in the months she had worked for the Gordons, she had, as Ma used to say, "filled out." Her uniforms no longer hung shapeless, on a straight, undeveloped figure. Soon she would be fifteen.

She kept her hair pulled back, held by her lace-trimmed uniform cap, and let the length of her blond hair hang loosely around her shoulders. She used no makeup. She needed none. Her light complexion was accented by natural blushed cheeks. Her mouth had matured to a rosy fullness that relaxed into an easy smile. She was not exceptionally beautiful, but was natural, homespun and attractive which projected the promise of a completely relaxed lovely woman ready to emerge.

Larry Gordon

She noticed that Larry's eyes followed her more and more. She tried to ignore the glances, because he made her very uneasy. But she never said anything about it, not even to Dweena, who had become her friend and confidante.

Larry was at least thirty-five years old, and Olli had just turned fifteen, so she dismissed any thought of anything but friendliness, from him.

One late November afternoon Araminta and Louise came back from a cold, brisk walk. They had their special time in the kitchen, during which Uncle Larry had not appeared. Louise and Araminta went up to the nursery to spend the rest of the afternoon. Mother Gordon was gone to a Ladies Aid Society meeting.

Clarence, of course, was at work. Dweena could be heard humming in the kitchen, as she clattered around with her usual din of pots and pans while preparing the evening meal. No one had seen Mr. Larry all afternoon, so it was assumed he had gone out on business.

Olli made her way up the back stairs, with her arms full of freshly laundered towels and linens. She placed some of the linens in the second floor linen closet and continued up the service stairs to the third floor where Mr. Larry's room was located.

Olli placed linen in the hall closet, and quietly knocked on Larry's bedroom door. She hadn't expected to hear an answer, assuming Larry was not home. However, after she'd rapped on the door, she heard a shuffling of feet. The door opened. She could see Mr. Larry was not himself. In fact, he was quite drunk.

Olli said, "I've brought clean towels for your bath." As she stepped in the doorway he mumbled something about being bothered. She apologized for intruding, "I didn't realize you were at home, or I would never have bothered you."

He bowed and staggered, saying, "Do come in, Sweet Girl. I'm a little drunk. You can see that, but I won't stand in the way of your work—especially for someone sweet as you." He navigated shakily over to the edge of the bed and sat down.

Second Son

Olli quietly said, "Mr. Larry, I'll just leave your towels here on the dresser, and let you get back to what you were doing." She started to back toward the door, depositing the towels on the dresser.

In the instant, Larry somehow managed to get between her and the door and quickly shut it. He staggered back to the bed, and said in an easy manner, "Ah, come on, Olli, I've been up here all day alone. Come on, sit down and talk to me a while. I've just been packin' my things. I'm goin' to be leavin' tomorrow for Alaska. Ya know! Got me a big job. Ya know! Gonna be shippin' out tomorrow. Sit down, Girl." He braced himself, straightened, and patted the bed saying, "Come here Sweet Thing. Sit beside me an' let's talk." He teased, "Come on, Olli."

She felt a tingle go up the back of her neck, a feeling she recognized as fear. Olli smiled shyly and quickly sat on the side chair by the window facing the bed. She was very aware that she had never felt this uncomfortable before.

He smiled at her. Seeming to have picked up the hint of fear on Olli's face, his smile turned to a sneer. His voice changed from the friendly drunken slur to a low threatening growl. His jaws tightened. His eyes flashed. Before Olli could move he jumped from the bed and grabbed her by the shoulders. "I told you, Sweet Thing, to come here!" He hissed in her ear, as he dragged, a now struggling Olli, to the bedside. She started to scream, but his large hand slapped her face and covered her mouth. "Shut up!" he demanded, as he pushed her down on the bed, where with his other hand he tore at her clothes.

Olli couldn't believe what was happening to her. Frantically, like a small animal caught in a trap, she flailed and turned trying to escape his forceful attack. Her world split with pain and throat-wrenching fear. She knew he had become a predator, a beast that had been hidden behind the jovial smile of an easy going, beloved son and brother.

When he finally finished with her, he rolled over on the bed, pulling her on top of him. Still in his drunken stupor, he shook her by the shoulders. She twisted like a rag doll, in shock of what had just happened to her.

He hissed through his teeth. "Girly, if you ever tell anyone about this, I'll be back, and we'll really have a good time. Ya hear me? You remember. If you ever utter one word, I'll be back, and fix you good. I'm too drunk now, but remember...I'll get you." He sat up and threw her to the floor.

She lay, shaking, not uttering a word. She looked around the room. It seemed as if she was someone else. She lay with her face on the cool shiny floor where she stared under the bed and realized she hadn't dusted there. Her mind floated away seeing the dust balls. She thought to herself, I must remember to do that. The dust balls moved slowly from the draft in the room. They tumbled along the bright reflection of the wood flooring. What a crazy thing she thought.

Larry pushed her with his foot, demanding, "Get up! And get out of here!" He growled, "Leave, now, unless ya want more. If you ever tell, remember what I'll do to you."

Olli snapped back to reality and slowly rose from the floor. She stumbled from the room shaking and broken in spirit. She crept cautiously down the hall to the service stairs and slowly made her way down past the kitchen into the basement laundry area without Dweena hearing her pass.

She slumped to the floor and began to sob. She knew what had happened, because while living at home with Papa and Ma in the same bedroom with all the brothers and sisters and cousins, she had heard the sounds in the night. But that was different. It was not the same for her. Fear, pain and gripping disgust swept over her. She knelt on the cold cement floor and tried to compose herself. She could hear the sounds of people moving around upstairs and knew Mother Gordon and Mr. Clarence must be home.

Her clothes were rumpled. Her hat was missing. The hair around her face was matted with tears. She stood, found a washcloth, and went to the laundry tubs. She ran cold water, and

Second Son

washed her face and hands and cleaned her legs. She straightened her clothes.

Rather than go through the kitchen and have to explain her appearance to Dweena, she went out the basement door and along the outside yard then climbed the outside stairway to her room. Once inside, she put her arms around her waist, bent over and sobbed openly. She did her best to pull herself together and took a hot bath to scrub off the filth she felt covered her.

Then in a form of emotional escape she slipped into bed.

Olli heard the dinner bell and knew by the darkness outside she must have dropped into a deep exhausted sleep. She quickly dressed in a fresh uniform and combed her hair, looking at herself in the mirror. This time she saw not only her image but the shadowed image of her inner self—*screaming! screaming and clawing in fear!*

She quickly shut off the ceiling light to eliminate the sight of herself. Turning on the porch light, she hesitated, then turned and locked her door. Starting down the stairs to the kitchen, she prayed others would not see the horror and the shame that lay behind her eyes.

5
Shame

The next morning Olli made herself scarce by quietly moving from room to room, cleaning, dusting, staying out of sight as much as possible.

She heard Mr. Larry's voice, as it boomed around the downstairs rooms in his preparations to leave.

Mr. Clarence had stayed home that morning in order to take his younger brother down to the docks to catch the ship that would take him to Alaska.

Olli could hear little Louise's laughter and chatter as she waved goodbye. She heard the tramping of small feet as the child noisily climbed the stairs yelling at the top of her lungs for "Minute."

Mother Gordon was very quiet after her two sons had left the house. She asked Olli to bring coffee to the parlor. When Olli arrived with the tray Mother Gordon asked her to sit down, she wanted to talk to her.

Olli hesitated, then did as she was asked. She could hardly look Mother Gordon in the eye, but she smiled, wondering what the talk would be about.

Mother Gordon began. "Olli, I will miss that youngest son of mine now that he has gone to his important government job. He's a smart, handsome and loving man. Of course, Clarence is too," she added. "But Larry is the light in my life. I feel he will do great things, and has a wonderful future. That is why I'd hate to have anyone do anything to put a question in people's minds, or think

43

that he ever stepped out of his level of social acceptance for anything, or anyone. Do you understand me?" She questioned Olli in a near sinister tone of voice.

Olli didn't understand her meaning. She looked down at the older woman's thin hands from which dangled a gray lace-trimmed hat. Olli knew it belonged to her. It had been missing since yesterday after Larry's attack on her. Olli looked with a questioning stare at Mother Gordon's face and saw in her bright bird-like eyes a glint of disgust. Her wrinkled face had hardened.

Mother Gordon began again. "I was up in my son's room this morning to see if he had forgotten anything and I found this on the floor behind the bed. Can you explain how it got there?"

Olli swallowed. A flash of fear went through her as she remembered the growling threat that had been whispered in her ear after being attacked by this favorite son. She glanced at her white-knuckled hands clasped in her lap, then looked at Mother Gordon's accusing stare. She lied, "No, Ma'am, I can't tell you how it got there. Maybe I lost it when I was cleaning upstairs earlier this week."

Mother Gordon grumbled, and dropped the hat on the side table. "Olli, I want to know why that hat was where I found it."

Olli took a deep breath and said, "Maybe you should have asked Mr. Larry that question."

Mother Gordon snapped to a stiff sitting position and whispered in a fierce, hoarse voice. "What should I have questioned him about? He wouldn't have done anything to warrant my questioning him. I have a feeling that it is *your* morals—or lack of them—that need questioning, My Dear."

Olli stood up and stared down at Mother Gordon stating softly, "You may think that your son is perfect, that I'm too low on the social scale for the likes of him, but I did nothing wrong. I will talk to Mr. Clarence, and if he wants me to leave my position, I will. But if he wants me to stay on, I'll do that." Olli started from the room.

Mother Gordon stammered, "Oh, Olli, please, let's not be

unpleasant. I may have spoken out of place. I don't think we should bother my son with this misunderstanding. We wouldn't want any accusations about you or Larry. Clarence so adores his brother, and we wouldn't want Clarence to question him, or you, now would we? Let's just forget this conversation, and let this unpleasantness pass. Shall we?" Mother Gordon cooed.

Olli so wanted to tell Mother Gordon about her precious son's assault on her, just to hurt her the way her accusations had hurt Olli's already wounded pride. But even now that he was gone, she still remembered his threat to attack her again if she ever told. Instead, Olli softly answered, "Yes, Ma'am, let's do that."

The uncomfortable feeling that had generated like an electric spark between Olli and Mother Gordon slowly dispersed, so after but a week they could easily speak to one another. In fact no one in the house had known there were ever any harsh words between them.

Olli began to notice that every morning it was hard for her to make herself get up early. By the time she had begun her daily routine of work, she had a terribly squeamish stomach. She mentioned this to Dweena. One morning she barely made it to the bathroom before she was violently sick. After emptying her stomach she went to the kitchen, white and shaking, positive she had a dread disease. She put her head on her arms on the table and sat in silence.

Dweena noticed her come into the kitchen. She put the kettle on for tea then sat down beside Olli. A look of concern came to her face.

"Olli, My Dear," she began, "I've noticed you've not been feeling well lately. Your symptoms lead me to believe something I never thought possible, especially with you, Dear. I wonder if you are not pregnant."

Olli looked at her as if she hadn't heard clearly.

Dweena continued. "Olli, I think you are going to have a baby. God only knows how a good girl like you would have such a problem." Dweena patted Olli's arm, looked straight in her face and asked, "Tell me, child, how did this happen? Who have you been seeing? I know you've not been out running around on your days off. But tell me, didn't you know that going to bed with a man could lead to this? Didn't your mama tell you anything about sex or babies?"

In shock Olli stared into Dweena's eyes. She had seen her sister Rose before she had her two little girls, and she hadn't been sick a day. She had been there when Ma had been pregnant with the last three babies and Ma never had a sick day before the babies came. How could Dweena say that just by knowing Olli had been sick in the mornings that she was going to have a baby? Olli dropped her head to the table top. Her shoulders shook as she quietly sobbed.

"Dweena," Olli said, "I can't tell. He said if I told anyone he'd hurt me more. I can't tell. Please don't ask me. Please don't tell Mother Gordon or Mr. Clarence," she pleaded.

Dweena asked her, "How long ago did this man do this to you? You know a thing like this can't stay a secret for very long, don't you?"

"Yes! I know that," Olli said, struggling to compose herself. "But what can I do? If Mr. Clarence finds out he'll fire me and I'll have no place to go. Papa and Ma would never allow me to come home. And if Mother Gordon finds out she'll want to kill me."

Dweena thought that was an odd statement for Olli to make, but pushed it out of her mind, thinking the statement was just the rambling of a desperate girl.

She took Olli's hand and said, "If you want, I'll go with you, and we could talk to Mr. Clarence, together. You don't have to tell him the man's name, unless you want to, especially if the man said he'd hurt you again. But Mr. Clarence should know. I think you'll find him more understanding than you think."

At that moment Mother Gordon came into the kitchen and hearing the last statement Dweena had made, she questioned them about what Clarence would be so understanding concerning.

Shame

The old woman saw concern on Dweena's face, the ashen face of the tearful girl.

When Olli lifted her head and looked straight into Mother Gordon's eyes, she saw the old woman had been calculating time and circumstances, and in near disbelief, Olli could tell the old woman knew! *She knew!*

Mother Gordon immediately put the pieces together. The hat she had found in Larry's room, the time since Larry had left for Alaska, and now this broken looking girl full of despair. She knew it hadn't been Olli's fault at all. Her own sweet Larry had done an unthinkable thing to this child in her and Clarence's own house, then he'd left for Alaska, without blinking an eye.

Dweena quietly told Mother Gordon of Olli's dilemma, that someone had done her this terrible wrong, and that he had threatened her with harm if she ever told.

Mother Gordon took a deep breath that filled up her round bird-like bosom, then slowly exhaled as she made a silent decision, that she would hold fast—come hell or high water. No one must know it was Larry. Olli could stay, if she kept out of sight of the social circle. Mother Gordon would see that she was cared for, but when the child was born it must stay with her and Clarence. Olli could continue on in the household only as insurance that Larry's child stay with her.

Mother Gordon spoke very slowly. "Olli, I'll talk to Clarence about this. No need of your upsetting yourself any more. He'll listen to me. You must tell no one else, not even Araminta, We don't want this problem to get out, now do we?"

Dweena thought it odd that the old woman had been so understanding. She didn't know that Mother Gordon had planned in her heart to control the baby's future. That was yet to be learned by both Dweena and Olli.

Over the next months, there was not another word spoken to Olli by either of the Gordons about the expected child. Mother Gordon was highly protective, calm and understanding. Olli

Second Son

feared the old woman's attitude. She felt as though a soft cloak was smothering her and she was unable to shake the feeling from her shoulders.

As Christmas drew near there were days when Olli felt so ill she barely completed the simplest chores.

Araminta, and Louise began a campaign to celebrate the Christmas season. They made sure Clarence brought a tall green pine tree home. A noisy, happy tree trimming session ensued.

Louise placed the shiny ornaments on the lower branches, and with Clarence's help she held the candle holders and the shiny star until the tree trimming efforts were completed,

Little Louise was learning to sing a few simple carols. She hopped and skipped like a happy bird. Her clear voice chirped from room to room.

Louise had just had her fourth Birthday and was convinced she could do everything that big folks could do. She asked Araminta if they could go on the streetcar down town to shop like big folks did at Christmas. She was promised the two of them would go the week before Christmas. This promise made Louise skip and dance with happiness.

Araminta truly loved the little girl and was constantly with her, teaching her all that a bright four year old could absorb. Louise had been asking why Olli had been sick, and Araminta told her she didn't know. Araminta didn't ask questions. She was not blind or uninterested, but she knew if she waited, the problem would in time become evident. Besides, she figured it was no business of a four year old chatter-box.

Olli had saved a small sum in the bank and was quietly excited. At lest she could afford Christmas cards and a few small gifts. She didn't have anyone except Jim and Lucy Porter to send a card to. She had no longing to get in touch with Papa and Ma, especially, now that she was expecting, even though it was the result of being attacked against her will. She was quite certain they would not welcome her home again.

The weather had turned bitter cold, and the north wind

whipped the bare maple trees causing them to whisper and moan. Olli walked the few blocks to the neighborhood markets. Mother Gordon had told her it was all right to go because her pregnancy didn't yet show.

Olli's eyes filled with wonder at the sight of the street decorations and the brightly decorated store windows. She purchased a colorful kaleidoscope for Louise and a lapel pin for Dweena. She bought three Christmas decorated postcards and a little tin box of watercolors. The butcher gave her a small roll of white meat paper. With these last two items, she planned to make hand painted wrapping paper.

On her way back to the Gordons, the wind finally brought with it tiny biting snowflakes that stung Olli's face and hands. She was glad to reach the warmth of the kitchen, where Dweena had a hot cup of tea waiting for her.

Dweena smiled and paused from her cooking. She sat down to enjoy a cup of the steaming brew with Olli. She heaved a long sigh, happy to see that the hollow look in Olli's countenance was gone. Olli's face pink from the cold, her eyes glowed with the excitement of her secret purchases. She was feeling better and had resigned herself to her situation.

It was two days before Christmas. The doorbell rang and in the waning light of the winter afternoon Olli answered the door. It was a telegram. She quickly took it to Mother Gordon in the parlor. As Olli shut the parlor door she heard a scream—it was Mother Gordon. Olli ran back into the room. She found Mother Gordon had fainted and fallen to the floor. She shouted for Dweena while patting the old woman's face and hands.

Mother Gordon opened her eyes as Olli knelt beside her. Dweena came and bent down to hold the old woman's head in her lap.

"Mother Gordon," Dweena said. "It's Dweena. What happened, Dear?"

Mother Gordon lifted her hand. Clutched in her fingers was a

Second Son

telegram. Dweena took it from her grasp, read it, and passed it carefully to Olli. Shock as of a lightning bolt hit them both.

The telegram read, "To Mr. Clarence and Mrs. Mildred Gordon. We regret to inform you that on the date of December twenty-first, while on a business assignment in the Gulf of Alaska, Mr. Lawrence R. Gordon was drowned. Body not found. For more information contact the Seattle office. Our Regrets."

Dweena's head bent in sorrow.

Olli's head seemed to spin. She took a deep breath. She stood up, and walked to the window. Tears filled her eyes. She didn't know if the tears were for Mother Gordon, for Clarence, or from her inner relief that the fear was gone that had filled her heart. The fear of Larry faded from her mind leaving a strange, dull blank. Was it relief? Whatever the feeling was, it made her nearly blind to the soft blanket of snow that filled the yard. The white mantle produced a somber, gray etching of bare trees lining the street. A cold chill fell on Olli's shoulders. The fear of Larry was gone. The relief left her weak.

Dweena had been watching her. Suddenly, for Dweena, the unanswered question of who Olli's attacker had been was answered. *Larry.* Dweena had always been convinced it had not been Olli's fault. Now she knew.

Dweena helped Mother Gordon from the floor to a large armchair, and made sure she was stable before leading Olli away from the window.

Olli felt faint, hot and cold as if feverous. She was in a state of shock.

Mother Gordon began babbling, "My lovely Boy! Gone! And him so young, so full of promise for the future. So much to live for." The babbling soon became the heavy breathing of disbelief, despair.

The daylight had gone. Dweena turned on the lamps and porch light knowing that soon Mr. Clarence would be driving up the driveway.

Because of the crushing news of Larry's death, the glow of

Shame

Christmas was dampened except for Louise's wide-eyed anticipation and enthusiasm. She was a true believer in the magic and mystery and was convinced her every wish would be granted. It was the first real Christmas Louise could comprehend what was happening, the gifts and the sweets. She was on cloud nine, and she didn't let the quiet sadness of the adults in the house diminish her excitement. Except for the ray of joy that shone from Louise's little face, there was no other sign of the holidays in the Gordon house.

Christmas came and went, as a matter of practiced repetition.

The New Year 1923 was entered into with a feeling of relief that the old year had gone. The Gordons had seen the loss of both Lettie and Larry, which greatly saddened Clarence and Mother Gordon.

Mr. Clarence had contacted the company office in Seattle for more information about his brother's death. He was told Larry was lost overboard in an unexpected storm in the Gulf of Alaska. The government would honor the insurance, as there had been a number of crewmen who had seen the huge wave crash over the deck and sweep Larry into the twelve foot seas. The information of the circumstances of his death didn't lighten the burden of sorrow for either of the Gordons. Mother Gordon had slipped into a depressed state of mind that kept her on the edge of awareness and hung like a dark cloud over her every moment.

Olli was going through a complicated mix of feelings. Now that Dweena knew about Larry's attack on her, Olli felt she could openly discuss her feelings about what she should do. She talked to Mr. Clarence about what they wanted her to do after the baby came. Clarence and Mother Gordon had talked it over and agreed Olli could stay on her job. Olli was told she needn't worry, because Araminta would take care of the new infant, as well as Louise.

The months passed quickly. When spring came Olli's pregnancy was very evident. Louise, in her childish curiosity was told Olli was just getting fat. This seemed to satisfy the child's questions.

Second Son

In the meantime, Larry's life insurance was paid to Clarence and his mother. A portion of it had been set aside in an account to cover needed costs for Olli, and the new baby's care.

On June twenty-first, 1923, the weather was extremely hot for the first day of summer. Olli woke early with a terrible backache, which made her anxious, because she had been told what to expect as signs that her labor had begun.

She literally rolled out of bed and felt the weight of the baby within her pull on her already aching back. She went into the bathroom to relieve herself. As she sat down on the toilet she immediately felt a rush of warm water and knew her water had broken. She put a towel between her legs. In her robe she went out on the small porch outside her attic room and pulled the cord that had been installed along the stairway down to the kitchen. She saw Dweena quickly appear at the back door and wave. Olli gave the signal for Dweena to call the midwife for whom Mother Gordon had arranged. It was so planned that a doctor would not have to be called in.

Olli knew Dweena had been on alert for over a week. Dweena had told Olli not to worry, that she'd get help as fast as she could when Olli needed it. Olli knew the time was here. She was filled with a mixture of fear and excitement. Suddenly a crushing pain made her knees feel weak. Slowly she stepped back into her room where she lay on the bed, softly moaning as waves of pain swept over her.

The door opened and Dweena escorted an older woman into the room, introducing her as Grandma Thomas. She was large-framed, with a shock of white hair, a silky smooth complexion, and a reassuring smile. She had a small bag of equipment, and carried a bundle of clean towels and linens. She placed them on a chair.

She walked over to Olli and took her hand. She smiled and said, "Olli, I have to examine you to see how the baby is doing. First, I have to feel your tummy, then we'll have a look to see about your water breaking. Okay?"

Shame

Olli nodded timidly as the old woman placed her hands on Olli's swollen abdomen.

Grandma Thomas quietly massaged Olli's abdomen and smiled as she said, "You're in good shape there, my Girl. I can't feel any complications. The baby is in a perfect head down position. Now let's have a look at your other progress."

She had Olli lie on her back, bend her legs, and spread them. Just then, another pain washed over Olli and she began to perspire. She began to moan in a high pitched tone. Grandma Thomas waited for the pain to pass, then finished her examination. Olli turned her head as a tear slipped down her cheek.

Grandma Thomas asked Dweena, "What time did she ring for you?"

Dweena answered, "About seven this morning." Grandma Thomas said, "I can hardly believe that. She is nearly ready to deliver." She turned her questions to Olli.

"My Dear, you say your water broke shortly before seven?"

Olli nodded yes. "How many pains have you had?"

Olli loosened her clenched hand, and put up four fingers. She was smothered by another wave of pain and she began to moan in agony.

Grandma Thomas spoke sharply to her. "We've got no time for your feeling sorry for yourself, so stop whining and put your mind on getting that baby out of there. Do you understand?"

Olli began to cry.

Grandma Thomas said, "You're wasting energy with that behavior. Settle down, and let those pains come easy. Don't fight them."

Another hard pain engulfed Olli. She perspired profusely and started panting again, but she was nonetheless able to quiet herself a little. The pain had gone faster than the one before, so she knew the old woman's advice had brought her back to reality. She must work with the pains. They were coming harder and longer with less time between them. She shifted on the bed and felt a terrible urge to push and strain. She nearly became frantic again, as the pressure increased. Olli wanted to get the heavy, ripping, tearing thing out of her. She knew that only then would the pain go away.

Grandma Thomas examined her again, and said quietly to Dweena, "This one is coming very fast. Can you hand me some towels?"

She wrapped Olli's legs and stomach area with clean towels and watched the girl grasp the ornate iron headboard of the bed, as another pressure pain passed.

The old woman said, "All right, Girl, this baby of yours is wanting to get out of there, so let's help it. When the next pain begins, I want you to push easy at first, then as the pain really hurts, push with all you've got. We're going to have a baby here if you do it right."

Olli felt the crushing agony begin to roll over her again. She began to push. She gripped the headboard and pushed so hard that she saw black spots floating in the air. She soon felt a spreading, then a heavy lump form between her legs.

The rush of pain rolled over her again. This time when she pushed a scream tore from her throat and she felt a slippery rush, then the loss of weight where the baby had been.

"Good Girl." Grandma Thomas said as she lifted a slippery, mucus-covered baby high in the air and patted its bottom.

Olli heard a shrill, wavering cry. She looked down to see her baby take his first breath of life. She began to shake with relief, exhaustion and joy at the sight of the healthy, squalling boy.

Grandma Thomas finished the care of the infant, wrapped him in a towel and handed him to Dweena, who took him to the table and washed the tiny wailing infant. Dweena wrapped him in a soft blanket and placed the crying child in Olli's arms.

Dweena had tears in her eyes. The emotion of the moment overwhelmed her.

The wonder of birth also overtook Olli, who lay smiling with tears running down her face. She was aglow with the wonderment of the baby she held.

Shame

Olli said, "I'm going to call him Cal. Cal Jergenson." Then she turned to Grandma Thomas and asked, "Could you or Dweena take him for a while? I'm awfully tired, I think if I can rest a few minutes I'll be able to hold him longer." She handed the soft warm bundle to her friend, who had helped bring this precious baby into the world.

Dweena said she was confident that the baby would be safe even as Olli fell into an exhausted sleep.

When Olli awoke she heard soft whimpering, and saw Grandma Thomas in the rocking chair holding baby Cal. Olli said, "If he's hungry I can let him nurse. I asked Mother Gordon about it, and she thought it would be best. She said I shouldn't mess with bottles, when I could give him the best food myself." Olli hadn't been aware that, while she had been sleeping, Mother Gordon had actually climbed the stairway and held her tiny grandson.

Grandma Thomas brought the baby to Olli and placed him in her arms. She placed his face to her breast, and he began to nuzzle and search for his source of strength. He found the nipple and began to nurse.

"He is so precious and sweet, isn't he?" Olli asked Grandma Thomas, who had turned away, knowing she had seen a rare moment of mother love.

6
Motherhood At Fifteen

As was customary Olli spent the next ten days in bed. Baby Cal was cared for, fed and kept completely content—as was Olli. She loved her sweet baby boy. She was enchanted to sit and watch him sleep. His lips would pucker as he dreamed of nursing. Her hand cupped over the silky, golden hair that curled around her fingers. She played with his soft, petal-like fingers and counted them over and over.

The perfection of the child astounded her.

When Olli began to feel stronger, she took the baby downstairs so Dweena wouldn't have to bring her meals upstairs. Olli planned to have her meals in the kitchen. She bundled Cal in a soft blanket before she made her way down to the kitchen. On this first trip she was rather shaky, but quickly recovered when she reached the bottom of the stairs. She placed Cal on the table, as Dweena, wiping her hands on her apron, came over and peeked inside the soft cocoon and smiled at his tiny yawn.

Mother Gordon came into the kitchen. She seemed happy to see Olli up and about. She picked Cal up, and unwrapped his head to better observe the tiny bundle. She touched his gossamer hair. A faraway look of remembrance came to her face, as she thought of her own fair haired boy child. She smiled and as she handed him back to Olli she said, "He is the image of Larry, you know." Her demeanor changed as she continued, "I think you should reconsider eating down here until next week, after Louise has been told about Uncle Larry's baby boy coming to live with us. You should bring him to the nursery and Araminta will begin caring for him. I think you should resume some of the easier household chores." She paused, taking a deep breath, as though she had something very weighty to relate.

The old woman slowly began speaking again. "Louise will be told that the child that is coming for Araminta to care for is her Uncle Larry's baby, and you are not to tell her any differently, under any circumstances, especially that you are the baby's mother. I've already told her the reason you've been away is you had a vacation, and went to see your folks. Louise has been told Cal's mother, Larry's wife, died. She understands about dying, you know. She has been told that is the reason for the baby coming to live with us. This baby will be baptized...Cal Lawrence Gordon. Do you understand?"

Olli looked, first, at Mother Gordon, then at Cal.

Dweena stood at the sink, with her back to them, head bowed, scarcely believing what she had just witnessed.

Olli's eyes narrowed in disbelief. Why should Mother Gordon tell such a lie? Olli became angrier and angrier. Why should she give up her baby to such a lying old woman? *Cal was her own child!* She knew Mother Gordon just wanted to keep up appearances? To hide the Gordon family's *dark secret*?

Olli stood up and asked in a hard flat tone, "What do you mean? Does everyone believe that I'm not his mother, because of your filthy lie? You'd rather have me give up the right to my own son to cover up for Larry, for social appearances? I don't believe you honestly think I would go along with such a story and let you take my baby."

Mother Gordon, glared with an icy stare, her flashing black eyes filled with menace. "My Dear, may I remind you that Cal is my Grandson. He is Larry's child, and the only thing I have left of my son. I've made sure you had a place to stay before this child was born, and kept any hint of scandal from you, and I'll see that your job is secure. Cal will have the best of everything that we can provide for him, as long as he is raised as Larry's son. The story of his wife dying, it won't be hard to convince people—as long as you keep your mouth shut!"

The old woman turned to Dweena. In a threatening tone she added, "That goes for you, too. Not a word of this is to ever leave this room, or I'll see you don't work in this or any other town for as long as you live."

Mother Gordon turned back to Olli. "I happen to know you can't go home with this child, and you can't find another housekeeping job with a newborn baby to care for. Your next choice would be giving him up to the state for adoption, so you see you might as well agree to my terms and let us give him our good name, then you'll have him around you, to care for as long as you never tell anyone who his real mother is."

Mother Gordon watched Olli's reaction. "I tell you this, if he is raised as my grandson, there will be no barriers between us, but cross me and you'll never see him again." Again Mother Gordon's eyes locked on Olli's. "I need this child as much as you do. No harm will come to him if you abide by my story."

Olli was still in shock after such a proposal and sat quite speechless. She wanted to say a hundred things, but could think of no more words, no more reply.

Mother Gordon began again. "Don't think you can take Cal and go for help to the Porters either. I went to see Lucy a few months ago. She agreed, after I paid her a considerable sum of money, she would never mention this to anyone. She could see you and Cal would be financially better off with us."

Olli clutched Cal tightly. "It seems," she said, "that you have my life and Cal's pretty well planned haven't you? I suppose you think I'll just hand Cal over to you. Well, I'll just go see Mr. Clarence about this and see what he says."

Mother Gordon smiled, "I'm sure you'll find I have his complete approval, because the money is mine that will be used to raise Cal. Clearance has nothing to do with it.

Second Son

"Besides, he has been so busy at work and so engrossed with the new lady in his life, he'll do anything I ask, and he's already agreed we've been lenient enough with you. He feels as I do. The child should stay with us as Larry's son. You see, Clarence is ready to ask his lady friend to marry him. She belongs to a very discreet circle of influential people and he doesn't want Larry's name scandalized. So we insist you and Cal stay, and you must live with the agreement I've proposed. You give it some sensible thought and let me know what you decide, after dinner." Her eyes narrowed again. "And don't let Louise see you with the child unless you tell me you agree with everything I've said."

In shock after this long and frightening proposal, Olli sat speechless, then took Cal and quietly left the kitchen. She held him close as she climbed the stairs to her room. She placed the sleeping baby in his basket and sat in the rocking chair, staring out the window. She felt trapped and helpless. Love for her child welled up in her throat. She tried to make some sense of the old woman's words and knew that she must have had this plot in mind from the very first. All her care and concern had been with one thing in mind, to make sure the baby stayed within her grasp.

Finally, Olli cried. She knew it wouldn't give her a solution to the problem, but she let the tears cleanse away the hurt of being used and helpless to stop it.

Louise had been absent from dinner in the kitchen that evening. Araminta had taken her, under Mother Gordon's instructions, to the neighborhood park for an early evening picnic. Olli was sure it would give her the chance to have Cal in the kitchen with her and Dweena during the meal until the old woman received the affirmative answer to her proposal.

There was nothing Olli could do. She was beaten.

After dinner the old woman came into the kitchen, and Olli agreed to let the Gordons raise Cal as their grandson and nephew. Mother Gordon, gushed, preened and cooed over the child in such a way she reminded Olli of a gray bird trying to regurgitate nourishment to its young.

The newly acquired status of Mother Gordon as grandmother turned Olli's stomach, but she kept a firm grip on herself and smiled, showing none of the disgust she felt toward the conniving old woman.

The weeks and months passed in swift succession, and Christmas approached once again.

But, this year, the holidays were not darkened by bad news. Instead, there was a large gathering of friends. All were excited over the precious baby boy of Larry's that the Gordon's had so graciously taken in after the death of his mother. The group thought this a wonderful gesture on the part of Clarence and his mother.

The topic of conversation among his friends was Clarence and his fiancée who were to be married on New Years Day, which made the holidays doubly exciting. Sophie Thornton had always been considered a real catch for someone. She came from Chicago, from old money and a family of high standing. She had known Clarence only a short time, but was accepted with open arms in Clarence's group of friends.

Mother Gordon didn't like her. "She's too bubbly and chatty to please me." She whispered to one of her overdressed cronies as they stood and watched the impromptu dance that had begun in the parlor.

Olli was sure that Sophie would add a touch of life to the house, and it was truly needed. Sophie was a vision of the latest fashion trends and that evening she was dressed in a wine-red velvet dress, with a chiffon shoulder scarf. She looked as if she had stepped from the pages of a fashion magazine.

Christmas slipped by in a clutter of gift paper, ribbons, glitter and noise. The house was decorated for the holidays, and the wedding which was planned for New Years Day. Large bouquets of red poinsettias and white chrysanthemums were shipped from

Second Son

California. Long stemmed roses bedecked the dining table, green cedar garlands looped up the stairway and across the second story banister.

The guest list for the wedding was small. The food was to be catered, so Dweena and Olli had little to do. This meant while Araminta had Louise down stairs, acting as her father's flower girl, Olli and Dweena went to the nursery with baby Cal. Olli saw he was beginning to roll over by himself, and was trying to sit up, even pulling himself to stand unsteadily in her lap.

Downstairs, the newlyweds danced, ate and laughed, raising such a din that when Clarence and Sophie left for their honeymoon in a hail of rice and good wishes the following atmosphere of quiet was a relief.

Clarence and Sophie had a long honeymoon planned in San Francisco. They left by ship directly after the ceremony.

Mother Gordon was in charge of household affairs for at least a month.

The day after the wedding the household had returned to the regular routine. That afternoon, Mother Gordon asked Araminta to meet her in the parlor. Olli was glad to stay in the nursery with Louise, so Mother Gordon and Araminta might have a private talk.

After the period of an hour, Araminta returned to the nursery, red-eyed and very upset.

Louise was napping. Olli asked in a hushed tone. "What is the matter?"

Araminta, who was always reserved and calm, was now shaking and wringing her hands. Sobbing quietly she said, "Olli, they've fired me. Mother Gordon has given me notice to find another job, then I'm out. I haven't any idea what to do or where to go. What about Louise? She needs me. I thought I was doing so well." Araminta sobbed.

"Mother Gordon said that when Mr. Clarence and Sophie return, Sophie will be taking over the job of mother for both, Louise and Cal. I have become attached to him too. I hope I haven't stood between you and your baby. I understand all the hurt that the old woman has caused you and I really feel bad for you, but I will miss that sweet little Louise so much it breaks my heart." Araminta couldn't stop crying.

Olli was sympathetic because she knew Araminta's job meant the world to her. Her attachment to Louise was very evident. Olli told Araminta, "I know how bad you feel, that you'll miss Louise—you're such a wonderful nanny!" She tried to be encouraging. "You'll be fine. You'll soon find a good job in a better place."

Olli hugged the sobbing woman.

Araminta had presumed from the first about the baby belonging to Olli and the circumstances of her pregnancy, but she had never spoken of it.

Olli wondered if Mother Gordon's lie about the baby had been mentioned during the conversation with Araminta. "Please tell me if Mother Gordon said anything to you about Cal. Did she threaten you about being quiet about him, or did she threaten you about working anywhere in this town in the capacity of a nanny if you ever spoke to anyone about him?"

Araminta looked startled, and said, "Yes, she did. Olli I don't know how you can put up with *that old witch.*" She paused, caught herself. "I only hope and pray for your sake that you never cross her or change that awful story she has told everyone. If you ever tell the truth, I have the feeling that, to save the memory of her "golden boy" son and keep herself in the high position in her circle of friends, she would do something drastic to the person who uncovers her lie."

"You don't have to worry about me," Araminta promised. "I'll keep quiet. For your sake."

Olli guided Araminta to a chair. She brought another chair and sat down beside her. They looked at each other knowing there was nothing either could do to help the other but accept their futures, as the old woman had so cleverly manipulated. The bond of sympathy for one another had welded in them a friendship that had been absent until Mother Gordon's lies changed their lives. They had become comrades and friends.

Second Son

Olli and Araminta sat in the quiet nursery.

Olli remembered her initial plight: leaving home, her position here at the Gordon's, the death of Lettie, her rape, her son's birth and how much she loved him. She recalled the old woman's unending pressure to completely take over Cal's life with an elaborate lie to save the family name. And now—getting rid of Araminta. What would the old woman's next control tactic be? Olli wondered.

Araminta's mind wandered as she looked out of the window, seeing only the bleak leafless trees that surrounded the second story room. She had watched the manipulative process that Mother Gordon had pursued since the day Larry Gordon left for Alaska, especially since the death of the "beloved son." Araminta knew that Olli's pregnancy had something more behind it, probably involving Larry. She had noticed how his eyes had followed Olli whenever he was near her. She thought at the time he was not to be trusted.

She had also wondered how Mr. Clarence felt about his mother fawning and gushing over her spoiled youngest son when it was Clarence who put up with the old woman's domineering ways. It was Mr. Clarence who took care of her in the way she seemed to be accustomed. She supposed the old woman controlled the family money.

Araminta spoke softly. "Olli, I hate to leave you and the children, but it will be like a breath of fresh air to be away from Mother Gordon's overbearing ways. When I find a new job, I promise I'll write to you."

Louise awoke, so Araminta, now more composed, took the drowsy Louise down to the kitchen.

Olli sat rocking her baby when Mother Gordon came into the nursery carrying a box from the pharmacy. "Olli, I'm so glad to find you alone. I've bought you a breast pump." She handed the package to Olli. "The pharmacist said it's the best way for Cal to still have breast milk while Sophie is caring for him. You'll pump your breasts every morning, then put the bottles in the icebox.

Motherhood At Fifteen

That way you can continue your duties and Sophie can feed Cal. You see, as far as she knows, Cal is Larry's son. She must never know anything else. Clarence has agreed to leave the story of the death of Larry's wife the way it has already been told. Do you understand?"

Olli spoke with a deliberate sharpness in her voice. "Aren't you designing this deception a bit too far? I agreed to your demands earlier, but have you considered Sophie's feelings in all this? The fact of her being a new bride, she may not want to be strapped with a four year old and a six-month-old baby night and day. Have you thought about that? Then, what happens to baby Cal? Haven't you got enough of the world at your beckon call? Must you now begin on Sophie, without her opinion in the matter?"

Mother Gordon raised her eyebrows. She smoothed her gray hair into place. "Olli, my dear," she cooed, "Sophie and I have already discussed this and she is eager to help due to Araminta's being so ill she can't continue working for us. So you see things will work out fine. Sophie has been told we really need her help with the children, and we don't want folks to think Araininta has deserted her responsibilities, now do we?"

Olli snapped at the old woman. "When do all the lies stop, Mildred? Will you keep weaving them until they topple upon you? I think you are a wrong to rearrange everyone's life around yours, making them do what you want so you look like the guardian angel of two motherless children. You are no guardian angel. *You are a hovering vulture!*"

Mother Gordon spoke slowly, choosing her words carefully, "Olli, as long as you are allowed to stay in our employ, you are never to speak to me in that manner again. And you are to never, ever, use my given name when you address me. Do you understand? For as long as you are employed here. Do you understand?"

Olli became quiet. She understood well the threat. As long as she was allowed to work here she had best toe the mark or lose any chance of being near her son. She was sure the old woman had an answer to that tucked up her sleeve, too.

Second Son

Olli smiled a quick, false smile and edged away from the gray, hovering, old woman and mumbled, "Yes Ma'am, I understand you very well. I apologize. Please forgive me for being so outspoken. It won't happen again. Now I must be about my duties." She slipped out the nursery door and disappeared down the service stairway into the kitchen.

When Olli came near the kitchen she could hear Araminta and Louise having an afternoon tea party with Dweena. She smoothed her apron and pinched her cheeks to give them color. She knew that when she was upset her face turned pasty white and she didn't want anyone to notice.

Olli opened the door and gave a happy, "Hello." She poured herself a cup of tea, trying to maintain her composure, glanced down and saw that her hands were still shaking. She sat down at the table and pretended, for Louise's sake, that everything was fine. In the back of her mind she knew life had become a complex game of covering up lies to appease a crafty, social climbing old woman who had no one in mind but herself and her dead son's good name.

Two weeks passed quickly.

The newlyweds returned in a rush of gala wrapped gifts for the children. For one day an air of ease drifted through the house.

Sophie made a real attempt to charm Louise. She knew Araminta would be leaving the next evening and she wanted to ease Louise's loss of her friend and teacher. Getting very little response from the little girl, she turned to baby Cal, who, supposedly had recently been brought to the Gordons for her to care for. She spent much time in the nursery enchanted by his genuine squeals of delight because of the special attention Sophie lavished on him.

On the evening Araminta was to leave, Mother Gordon kept Olli busy in the basement and laundry room with meaningless chores, just to make sure the two friends would have no chance to say good-by.

Motherhood At Fifteen

Araminta came down the service stairs, stopped to say a quick farewell to Dweena, then left through the back door.

Mother Gordon had suggested that Louise have dinner with the family, so she wouldn't see Araminta leave the house.

Dweena had given Araminta a warm hug and told her she and Olli would keep in touch. Araminta put on her gloves, pulled her coat collar up around her throat, picked up her suitcase and with her prim felt hat perched squarely on her head and marched out of the house on her way to the trolley stop.

The next few months went by under the authoritarian rule of Mother Gordon. She was working her wiles on Sophie who scurried around to please the old woman. Sophie wasn't yet suspicious of Mother Gordon's domineering ways. Mother Gordon was an expert at deception, when it served her own purpose. But Olli and Dweena knew that eventually Sophie would see the light. Presently, however, Sophie was delighted to please her husband's mother by doing little favors for her.

Sophie took special pride in the fact that she had finally won Louise's affection.

After Araminta left, Mother Gordon bragged to everyone about how well Sophie was doing with the children. She explained that Araminta had been too ill to remain in their employ, and those facts were accepted as gospel.

The social groups that frequented the house were all delighted with Sophie and her charming ways, as hostess and as loving mother to the children. Visitors were heard saying how lucky Clarence was to have found someone who truly cared for his mother and children.

On Cal's first birthday the Gordon's had a big party. There were presents and a cake with one candle. Cal was victorious over the candle with his first exuberant puff.

Second Son

Olli stayed in the background as an observer. She never let the hurt show, but in her mind she could picture him in a much more relaxed setting in the park. There they would sit on a soft blue blanket she had made for him—just the two of them. That would have been best, but as things were, she wasn't allowed to even acknowledge him as her son. She was caught in her predicament of forced deception like a fly on sticky fly-paper. She could think of no way out.

After the party everyone went out to the backyard. The evening was warm as the sun eased its way down toward the rim of the Olympic Mountains. Guests seated themselves in lawn chairs and began the quiet buzzing that would turn into conversation.

In the soft evening air Mother Gordon rose from her chair, raised her glass and said in her clear commanding voice, "I want to make a toast, first to our birthday boy. Our happy one year old, Cal. I have a small token of love for our precious baby boy." As she spoke she took a gold baby's ring from a blue velvet box and placed the ring ceremoniously on the little finger of baby Cal's right hand.

Everyone cheered.

She continued. "And to the proud parents of our sweet Louise, and soon to be adoptive parents of baby Cal. Clarence and Sophie have see their lawyer and have legal rights to adopt my youngest son Larry's child. Since the death of both parents we all feel he needs to be an official member of the Gordon family."

Everyone cheered again.

Olli stood in the kitchen doorway in shock. The tray of lemonade glasses she was holding crashed to the floor of the porch. She turned and ran into the house.

Clarence rose quickly and excused himself telling his guests he'd see what the trouble was.

Olli sat at the kitchen table sobbing as Clarence came up to her. He asked, "Olli, why are you so surprised at Mother's announcement? She said you had agreed to the adoption. So what is this big display all about?"

Olli looked straight up at him, livid with anger. She spoke through clenched teeth. "Your mother is not going to get Cal so easily. You can't see that all along she'd been planning this. She wants me to give up all claim to my baby. He's *mine!* And *mine alone!* Larry may have been his father, but only by *raping me*, then being coddled by having his mother cover up that fact."

Olli caught her breath, wiped her eyes on her sleeve. "I let myself be hood-winked, and maneuvered by your mother to keep the town from knowing what a villain Larry was. Well, let me tell you, I'm not letting go of my baby to appease your mother. Not now, not ever! What kind of man can you be to go along with all this? *Cal is my son!*" Her voice began to quiver, and take on a high, hysterical tone. "You can't have him!" she shrieked.

By that time Sophie and Mother Gordon were in the kitchen, making sure the outside door was closed. "My guests!" Mother Gordon sputtered. "Olli, you have to stop this. Hush up! Girl! What will my guests think?"

Sophie stood, transfixed, with a questioning look on her face, not understanding why the housekeeper should create such an uproar because she and Clarence wanted to adopt that darling orphaned child.

Olli turned and burst from the kitchen into the back yard. She saw one of the socialite women holding Cal. She put her hands over her face, turned, sobbing and ran up the outside stairway to her room.

The guests looked on in surprise, wondering what on earth had just transpired. Why had the hired girl broken up this lovely party? She must have a reason, but who could explain it.

Clarence came out and said that the housekeeper had become ill after receiving bad news about someone in her family, so they had excused her for the day.

One by one, the guests excused themselves, leaving Cal in Sophie's arms. They said their confused good byes with questioning glances toward Olli's upstairs retreat.

Clarence and Sophie went into the house with Cal and the chattering four year old, Louise, who kept asking about what had happened to Olli.

Second Son

Mother Gordon sat in the kitchen muttering to herself about how her friend's questions in the days to come would force her to explain something about her housekeeper's strange outburst.

After a short while, Clarence climbed up to Olli's room and quietly knocked on the door. Olli rose from the rocking chair to open the door. She looked as though she were sleep walking. Clarence entered the room and motioned for her to sit down again. As if in a stupor, she seated herself, then sat staring out of the window hardly aware of Clarence being there. She didn't see the sunset beginning to blush the sky. She didn't hear her bird chorus in the tree tops, nor did she feel the breeze wafting through the door.

Olli seemed to be in an uneasy state of shock, her hair matted with perspiration and tears. Listlessly she awaited for Mr. Gordon to speak his mind.

Clarence cleared his throat. "Olli, Mother wants you to know she is appalled at your behavior," he paused, frowned. "That's her opinion. I too have been lied to by Mother—about your approving our adoption of Cal. I understand the hurt you feel about her actions. And I apologize."

Again he paused, as if to collect his thoughts and measure his words. "Mother, she can be very conniving at times. No one knows this better than I. Again, I'm sorry this whole thing seems to have gotten out of hand, Mother's...lying. She has been so intent on keeping Cal in our family. To her, well, Cal is her last connection with...her favorite son.

"Indeed!" Clarence glanced almost sheepishly at Olli. "I am quite aware of my younger brother's status in Mother's eyes. He was always the favored one. Maybe it's because she could see how weak and no good he was, she overcompensated for it by coddling him and covering up his mistakes." Clarence shook his head sadly. "Who knows why she did it, but I'm here to tell you I'm truly sorry for this whole mess."

He was clearly agitated, Olli could see that, as his words began to sink in.

Motherhood At Fifteen

"I have to confess," Clarence continued, "Sophie even now doesn't know that you are Cal's mother. She truly loves Cal—and my Louise. She is willing to help me raise them both, but I must have your okay on this. I want you to think about what you could give him in the way of education, other opportunities and every aspect of his future. I hope you see that Sophie and I could do so much for him. We would be a real benefit to that little boy. Why don't you and I strike a deal, a deal that has nothing to do with my mother?"

Mr. Gordon looked intently at Olli. "You may stay on and work here and you can care for Cal as long as Sophie or I are alive. You can have complete care of him. You can give him love and all the attention he will need," Clarence cleared his throat, "but when it comes to outings, schooling, doctor's care, and education, Sophie and I will provide that."

He studied Olli's reaction. "If you will agree to let us call him our son. We will not ask to adopt him. But please, let him be called Cal Gordon." A note of pleading softened the commanding tone of his voice. "Then I won't have to explain to Sophie why I let such a terrible lie get started in the first place. You do know Sophie can never have her own children, that's one reason she has tried so hard to become a mother to both Cal and Louise."

Clarence paused a moment, then added, "Mother needn't know of our arrangement, and I couldn't have this done legally on paper, because she would interfere. It will be a verbal agreement between us. Eventually things will smooth out. Who knows, Mother may be pacified just by having a son to carry our name." Clarence continued, "You will also take all your household duty orders from Sophie from now on, for she *is* the Mistress of this house. Think about what I have offered and let me know your decision tomorrow?"

Clarence rose, left the room, and started down the stairs, then turned, and called back. "Olli, I'll do my best to quiet my mother."

Olli went to the door and watched as Clarence reached the bottom of the stairs and disappeared into the house. What a

Second Son

difference in the two brothers! How lucky Sophie was to have a man so understanding. Olli knew what he had suggested to her was sensible and would ease feelings on both sides. She was sure he had Cal's and her futures in mind.

She sat down on her bed, thinking she too could see into the future and a chill passed over her. What if Clarence died? No one but Olli would know of their secret bargain. Sophie would do her best to keep Cal, thinking he truly was their son. Then Mother Gordon would take complete control again. On the other hand, if Olli took her baby and left the Gordon's, where would she go? Where would she find another job that would allow her to keep her baby with her and work at the same time? She worried as she paced the floor trying to come up with an answer to give Clarence in the morning. If she stayed—she felt afraid of the consequences for the future.

Then, as if a light turned on in her head, a solution sprang out of nowhere. She could take the baby and go to Araminta. Dweena and Olli had kept in touch with her since she left. She had mentioned in her letters more than once that she was working at a twenty room estate on Whidbey Island, caring for eleven children ages two to fifteen years. Araminta's employer had mentioned that he needed to hire an extra housekeeper.

She knew what she must do. That very night she had to Cal and leave. They would go see Araminta and hopefully be accepted to the position of housekeeper. There, at least she would know someone. She must take Cal and leave as soon as the house was dark and quiet.

She waited.

And waited.

And as she waited, she planned the details of her escape. She pulled her thoughts together considering what she would need to take with her. Only that which was easy to carry onto the boat to Whidbey Island.

The dinner bell rang below.

Olli held her breath and waited.

But she didn't go down. She had some more planning to do. Because after dark, when everyone was asleep, she was going to sneak down the stairway, up the back service stairs, make a duffel of Cal's things, quietly lift him out of his cradle and escape down the back stairs. They would go to a place where there was no lying, no deception, and no chance of her losing her child to that scheming old woman ever again.

The street lights came on when it turned dark. Olli had her satchel packed with her few necessary belongings. She made sure her cash and savings book were safely tucked in the satchel's bottom, under her clothes.

The downstairs and second floor lights were out and the house was silent.

Olli eased out of her door and edged her way down to the kitchen door. She entered the house quietly. Because of her familiarity with the floor-plan, she slowly made her way up the back stairs and inched her way along the dark, second-story hallway. She entered the nursery happy that Sophie no longer stayed the night with the children. In the dark she found a crib blanket, diapers and other items she knew she would need. She put them in a tight bundle, and tucked it under her arm.

She tiptoed over to Cal's cradle. She could hear the soft easy breathing of her sleeping baby. She bent over and eased his plump little body to her and pulled his blanket with him, tucking it over his soft hair. He cuddled on her shoulder. She backed away from the cradle and turned to leave.

Then in a flash all the lights were on, nearly blinding her. Standing near the closet door was Mother Gordon. Olli knew in a split second the old woman had never gone to bed, but had waited to pounce like a cat. Olli was her prey. The old woman had suspected Olli would come for Cal.

Mother Gordon had the look of someone who had won a prize and intended to flaunt it.

Second Son

Olli was undaunted, "I should have known you'd be lurking about like an old lioness ready to pounce. But you'll not stop me. I'm leaving this place and I'm taking Cal with me."

Mother Gordon burst out laughing. "Olli, my Girl," she said, "You can't take that baby anywhere. You can't even prove he is yours. You didn't have a doctor. The midwife has been paid to keep her mouth shut. In fact, she's gone from the state." Mother Gordon paused dramatically. "You didn't sign his birth certificate, did you? No. I filled it out and put Larry's supposed, dead wife's name on it as if the mother had it recorded. You are such a trusting, ignorant child. I'm afraid you can't afford a lawyer to settle all of this. Besides, I have the original certificate in my safety deposit box, and until I die you'll never get it." Her voice lowered. "You have no legal claim on Cal, except your word, and who will believe such a poor ignorant girl as you, especially when someone with my standing in the community claims you're lying? If you try to leave this house with Cal, I'll have you arrested for kidnapping and you'll be put in prison. You see, I have connections in this town."

Clarence, having been awakened by the loud voices, came to the nursery with Sophie close behind. "Olli, what is this? I thought the offer I made to you would be the safest and best way to handle this whole affair. Is your attempt to take the boy your answer to my offer?"

Olli's nerves were spent. She held tightly to Cal, who had now awakened and was beginning to fuss. "Mr. Clarence, I must go. I can't let Cal stay." Olli's voice broke.

Sophie turned to Clarence to question why he didn't have Olli arrested for trying to kidnap the child they were going to adopt. Clarence told her to calm herself and let Mother take care of the problem.

Sophie, with a puzzled expression and exasperated glare at Clarence, turned and left the nursery. "You and I are going to talk about this when you come back to bed, Clarence. Do you understand me?" With that, she stomped off.

Motherhood At Fifteen

Olli glared at the old woman and Clarence. She held tightly to her crying child. Clarence left the room, carrying Louise, who had been awakened by the loud voices. This left Olli standing alone in front of the old woman.

Mother Gordon said to her. "Olli, you might as well put Cal back in his bed and go to bed yourself, because you'll never take him from this house."

When she finished speaking she left the nursery and went to the telephone in the hallway, dialed for the operator, and asked for the police department.

Olli couldn't believe her ears. The old witch was going to accuse her of kidnapping her own baby.

Her legs seemed to give way. To keep from dropping Cal she went to Cal's crib and laid him down. Olli cried, "Mother Gordon! Please hang up. Don't do this!"

In the hallway, Mother Gordon turned. With a smile on her face, she dropped the receiver back into place. Her wrinkled face shone. Her black eyes flashed with victory.

She spoke harshly to Olli. "Alright, Girl, I accept that as your answer. The child is mine." She glowered in triumph. "Now you get yourself out of this house at once! If you ever take your story of what has transpired here to a lawyer, or tell anyone about it, or come back and try sneaking him from me again, I will surely have you charged with kidnapping!" Her voice was menacing. "And I swear, you will be convicted and you will spend all your years in prison. I told you I have connections in this town, and I can promise you your life will be ruined! *I never want to see you again!* Now grab that paltry satchel of your junk, and get your ass out of this house!" The old woman's voice was high pitched and as near hysteria as Olli had ever heard it.

Mother Gordon grabbed the bundle of Cal's belongings from Olli and tossed them onto a chair.

All the while Olli looked at her small son who was once again peacefully sleeping. She tried to fuse a picture in her mind of Cal's soft mouth, turned up nose and golden curls covering his ears. The infant was the picture of contentment. Olli turned away from the old woman, unable to think of anything to say. Her head bowed to her chest, hot tears rolled down her face. She reached down and touched her precious child's hand. In doing so—her fingers touched the small gold ring Mother Gordon, just hours before, had placed on Cal's chubby finger during his birthday celebration.

Olli tucked the soft comforter over Cal's cherub-like hand, and in the same movement nimbly slipped the ring from her baby's finger and raised her hand to her face as if in an attempt to wipe away her tears—and thus, unnoticed, she secreted the ring into her mouth under her tongue while her body was turned away from Mrs. Gordon.

Olli's fighting spirit had withered.

The old woman had won, having coerced Clarence, confused Sophie, and completely devastated Olli.

Exhausted and broken, Olli's only thought was to get away from the vicious old woman and her mad house. She would have to trust that Clarence would keep his word and see that Cal was cared for, as he'd promised to do, and insure her little boy a normal life. She didn't have enough money saved to hire a lawyer. She had no legal proof that Cal was hers. She knew the old woman had taken advantage of her innocence and ignorance.

Olli turned and picked up her satchel. She was sobbing so hard she nearly stumbled down the stairs and almost swallowed the ring hidden in her mouth. She went through the foyer and out the front door into the night—leaving the door wide open.

In a trance like state Olli walked down the street toward the trolley stop.

It was midnight on her son's first birthday in the year 1924, and he had been taken from her. It was indeed, a dark night.

7
Cafe Beyond The Dark Night

The sun bounced against a cracked mirror that hung in the shabby hotel room. The light glared in Olli's eyes. She turned over on the hard mattress of the squeaky iron bed. For a moment she was completely lost and confused—then the reality of what had taken place the previous night hit her like a bucket of ice water.

She remembered the reason she had made her way toward the waterfront and why she was in a shabby hotel room. She shook her head to clear it enough to think what she should do.

First, she thought she would find a telephone and have the operator connect her long distance to Whidbey Island. She wanted to talk to Araminta. If she could contact Araminta, and if the job there was still available, she would take the freight and passenger boat out to the island and ask for the position. She could be assistant housekeeper for Araminta's employer.

Olli climbed out of bed surprised to find herself still completely dressed. She tried to pull the wrinkles out of her cotton dress to no avail. She gathered her meager belongings and left the tacky room determined never again to stay in a place like that.

When she descended the rickety stairway into the smoke-filled lobby she found a grimy telephone booth. Inside, she hesitated to sit on the seat covered with cigar ash. She lifted the receiver and asked the operator to connect her by long distance to the Westinberg Estate on Whidbey Island. After paying the correct change, she waited until the operator instructed her that the contacted party was waiting to talk to her on the other end of the line.

The maid inquired in a courteous voice to whom she wished to speak.

When Olli asked for Araminta she heard the maid call for Araminta to take the upstairs extension. A moment later Olli heard Araminta's familiar voice and began to cry.

Araminta, realizing who the caller was, finally calmed Olli down enough to make sense of the sobbing babble that had burst from the receiver.

Olli steadied herself enough to explain where she was and that she needed a job. She asked if the job Araminta had mentioned in her last letter was still available. However, to her dismay, Olli was informed the job had been filled earlier in the week.

Araminta tried to sound hopeful. She gave Olli the only advice she could. That was to buy a Tacoma newspaper and search the classified section. She urged Olli not to give up. Olli was a good worker and she would find something in town.

The operator came on the line and informed Olli that her time was up. Olli dropped one more dime in the phone giving her time to say goodbye to Araminta. She promised to write as soon as she found work.

Sitting down now in the dirty phone booth, with her head hung in shame trying to gather courage enough to step out, someone standing outside rapped noisily on the smudged glass door and growled loudly, "Come on, Girly, there's more of us waitin' to use the phone."

Olli looked up, gathered her wits along with her belongings and stepped out of the booth. She went to the hotel desk clerk, bought a newspaper, and sat in one of the dusty velour chairs near the door. There, she scanned the classified ads for a job.

The need for day laborers in the raspberry fields in the Puyallup Valley near Tacoma, was quite apparent. There were also jobs for housekeepers. She decided neither would do. Besides, Mother

Cafe Beyond The Dark Night

Gordon would expect her to look for a job in housekeeping and Olli didn't want the old woman to find her, know what she was doing, or know her whereabouts. For as the old woman had said: "She had connections."

At that moment Olli—born Olive Elsa Blaine Jergenson—decided to change her identity. She would use her middle name, Blaine, and shorten her last name to Jergens. She left the paper lying on the chair in the lobby and began to walk down near the waterfront and along the docks before the sun heated the sidewalks. It would soon be too hot to tread the streets.

She walked for nearly two hours, up and down the hilly streets near the waterfront, her mind dancing with the stress and loss she had lived with the past months.

She nearly walked right by the "Waitress Wanted" sign in the window of a small, clean cafe.

Hesitating but a moment, she opened the door to *Walt's Cafe*, nonetheless knowing that she must look a pitiful sight. She still wore the wrinkled dress she had slept in, but at least her hair was carefully combed. She held her head high and asked for the manager.

A chunky, dark-haired man behind the counter replied cheerily, "My Girl, you're talkin' to him." Then questioned, "Are you askin' about the waitress job? If so, have you waited tables before?"

Olli smiled and said, "Yes, I'd like the job, but I've never worked a cafe. However at home I used to wait on ten to fifteen people in my family for three meals a day." She added, "I also did dishes and cooking. Nothing fancy, you understand, just good home grown food.

"I'm also good at butchering and dressing out rabbits and chickens. I've done housekeeping for some folks, too, so I think I could do a good job here."

The man smiled, "Tell ya what, Missy, I'll let ya work the lunch crowd. If ya do okay, ya got the job. Wages are four dollars a day, plus tips. I've got a fresh apron for ya, an' I'll show ya how ta' write up your orders an' count change back to the customers. Then you'll be ready ta' go. Okay?"

"Oh, yes!" Olli was excited. "Where can I put my things?"

He led Olli through the kitchen to the back room of the cafe. He gave her a clean apron and a locker of her own in which to keep her things. She turned and said, "I don't even know your name, Sir. Would you like to know mine?"

Walt smiled a broad warm smile. "Ya, my name is Walter, Walt's Cafe—and yours?"

Olli smiled and extended her hand. She paused after deliberating for a split second then she said, "My name is Blaine Jergens." This statement seemed only half a lie, but as per resolve, it was best to keep secret her full name, which was the name by which Mother Gordon could locate her. So for a fresh start she felt it would be best for her to use this bit of deception. Suddenly she felt more secure from Mother Gordon's all-seeing connections.

Walt said, "Okay, missy, Blaine it is. When you're finished puttin' your stuff away, come out front and I'll give ya the complete whirlwind tour of the waitress business.

When Walt had gone back into the cafe, Olli looked around and found that the back door opened to a wide deck that overhung the tide flats. The tide was out and she saw clams squirt and little rock crabs scurry around in the shallow tide pools. She thought the deck would be a pleasant place to come when she wasn't busy. Maybe she would sit at times and dangle her feet in the cold water as the tide came in. She smiled and went back inside—to begin again.

Olli learned quickly, so Walt went back to the kitchen saying, "Just ask me if you need help. The noon crowd is due any minute. They're a bunch of great guys, so don't worry. Just keep things movin' until after the rush. Then things will slow down the rest of the day."

As Walt finished speaking the bell above the door jingled and a crowd of noisy dock workers filled the lunch counter and booths.

Cafe Beyond The Dark Night

Over the noise of the rough and tumble sounds of the customer's voices, Walt yelled, "Hey Guys! The new girl is Blaine Jergens. Give her a break, okay!"

In unison, they shouted, "Hi, Blaine!"

Surprised at herself, she answered in a confident voice, "Hello, fellas."

When lunch time ended, the tables were cleared and Olli, aka Blaine, pulled the change from her pocket and counted out two dollars and twelve cents in tips. Quietly she ask Walt, "Where do I put the tips?"

Walt laughed heartily and told her the tips were hers. Olli-Blaine's face lit up with a big smile. She decided to save tips for something special. She began cleaning the counter tops.

Walt chuckled, "I see you're quite a scrubber. Well, that's what this place can use. If you see anything else that helps the looks of the place, feel free to do it. By the way, you've definitely got the job here for as long as you want it. I have a small spare room upstairs if you need a place ta stay. I'll charge ya twelve dollars a month which includes lights and water, and if ya can stand my cookin', your meals will be free."

Olli-Blaine thanked him and said she accepted the whole package, on his terms. She felt a heavy weight lift from her shoulders. The rest of the afternoon she busied herself mopping floors. And one other thing she did, she removed the "Help Wanted" sign from the window.

There was a different type of crowd for the dinner meal: a few plainly clad couples, some older gentlemen, and a few tired dock workers. They sat quietly, ate slowly and dawdled over many cups of coffee, as if they needn't hurry, because there was likely no one waiting at home, wherever home was. They let the closeness of the cafe fill a void in their work-a-day existence.

At seven in the evening Walt finished cooking the last order, turned the sign on the front door to closed, and sat down to enjoy a leisurely cup of coffee while the last few customers finished their meals.

Olli-Blaine bustled around the kitchen and behind the counter, cleaning where needed.

Walt looked over the cafe and smiled broadly. "Ya know, Missy, you've only been here for half a day and you've got this place lookin' pretty darn presentable. I thank ya."

Blaine smiled and sat down to have a cup of coffee while she waited for an elderly man to finish his meal.

She fought her mind, forcing her thoughts to stay away from the reason she was working at the cafe. She pushed her mind to recognize the fact that she was lucky to have found work, a place to stay, and the new feeling of a *job well done*. She secretly smiled at the fact that the first day of her new life had been a success.

After closing the cafe for the night Walt walked Olli-Blaine around the cafe building to the wooden deck behind the cafe. He gave her a key to the door opening into a hallway which led to the stairway leading to her second floor room over the cafe. She picked up her bundle of belongings, bid Walt good night, and began the climb to her room. She paused at the top of the stairs and shouted, "Thank You."

Walt had already disappeared around the corner of the building.

The room was snug and clean. It had a small bay window overlooking the harbor.

At high tide the setting sun threw sparkles across the water and scattered reflections on the walls of her room.

The rosy glow of the evening sky accentuated the smile on Olli-Blaine's face. She eased down in the large cozy chair and closed her eyes. For the first time in a long time she was completely relaxed and felt contentment encompass her—a feeling she had forgotten existed.

She began to believe, just a little, that maybe things were going to work out. The fact that she had given Walt her newly assumed name, Mother Gordon would not be able to find her, and that gave her a feeling of security. She forced her mind away from the events of the past two years. She focused on the present and the future. She knew keeping herself looking ahead was the way she would be able to survive.

For the next few weeks her routine kept her bustling from morning until late at night, but she loved it.

Working with the busy breakfast crowd, the rush of customers at noon, and the easy, quiet dinner crowd combined to bring her a touch of excitement, of which she never tired.

Blaine—though she still thought of herself as Olli—became acquainted with the regular customers. They called her Missy. She knew it was their term of endearment for her.

Mr. Magruder, who owned the corner grocery, came in at exactly six every morning, ordered the same thing, and liked his coffee waiting for him in the back booth. Mr. and Mrs. Crawford, who owned the clothing store across the street, ordered only toast and coffee. Chung Lu and his sons came and went nearly unnoticed, always ordering tea before going to their laundry in the same block as Walt's Cafe.

Taxi drivers, Joe and Clyde, dropped in for a quick cup of coffee between calls. Perkins, the local policeman, was as regular as clockwork for coffee.

Daily the dock workers, longshoremen and some crew members from the ships that were in port, filled the booths.

Blaine was more particularly aware of one group of customers: the ever present down-and-outers. Their coffee money was usually all the money they had. Sometimes Blaine would take her tips and put them in the cash register to cover the cost of a doughnut or pastry. This was her small gesture of kindness to these men when she refilled their coffee cups. She'd smile, and in return she would get a hat brim touched in thanks from a grateful recipient.

Some merchant marine crews made Walt's a favorite hangout when they were in port. They were in and out—usually in a joking noisy gang. The sailors loved to tease Blaine. She had learned to give them a good natured reply, but always kept her distance.

Second Son

By the end of August, Blaine had been asked out on dates by a few of the longshoremen and merchant marines. She managed always a gracious "No thank you." She began to realize she had a real fear of men in general. She had no idea of how she should act or what to expect if she were out with a man. Her only experience with the opposite sex had been utterly frightening.

One afternoon as a lull came in the day's work, Walt and Blaine sat in the back booth to enjoy a rest and chat as they drank their coffee.

Walt, jolly as always, said openly, "Blaine, I see a couple of the fellas askin' ta' take ya' to a movie or go for a walk with 'em an' ya keep turnin' 'em down. What's wrong? Ya don't have any kind of fun on yer time off, an' yer such a pretty little thing. I don't see anything wrong with havin' a few boy friends. They might be a way to keep from bein' lonesome."

Blaine blushed, answered, "Walt, I've really never had a date. I wouldn't know how to act or what to say. Besides, I like to have my evenings to myself. I relax and sit out on the back deck and watch the gulls fly over the water, and that's just fine for me right now."

Walt smiled knowingly and drawled, "One of these days the right guy will come along an' ask ya' an' you'll know what ta do an' what ta say. If ya need any help in the ways of the heart, just ask me an I'll help ya just like I was yer dad. Okay?"

Blaine smiled sweetly and thanked him, thinking all the while of her Papa and the feelings she had for him. She remembered how he had made her leave home at fourteen, because he felt she was old enough to be on her own and take care of herself. This policy had been forced on each child in the family and took the burden off Papa, making it possible that he had more time for fiddle playing and would need less money to feed the remaining siblings cared for.

Blaine couldn't remember Papa sitting down with a purpose of giving advice, showing concern or even speaking directly to her. He never used her name except to order her to do a chore, or reprimand her for some action that hadn't pleased him. At home she had been a nonentity, one of the many he had spawned.

She felt Walt was more concerned about her and was more of a father to her after the short time she had been working for him than Papa had ever been. She told Walt that she was fine, but if she ever needed his help she'd be sure to come to him for advice. She couldn't begin to tell him of the heavy load of sadness she carried, so she patted his big rough hand, smiled and picked up the menus for the two sailors that had just come into the cafe.

The evening clientele began drifting in. She took Walt's and her coffee cups into the kitchen and set to work on the dinner routine.

Late August was hot. Blaine spent the evenings after work out on the back deck reading the paper or watching the boat traffic on the bay. She had acquired a pet seagull—or he had adopted her—she didn't know which, but it seemed a mutual agreement. She needed his haughty companionship and he had picked her as an easy mark for a nightly hand out of scraps which she brought from the cafe.

She named this fearless gull Herman. When she called him, Herman would sail down from a near-by piling, then walk in a sophisticated waddle along the deck railing, cock his head and demand the collection of the day's delicacies. In return for the food he'd sit on the railing to preen himself. With his ever watchful eyes alert, he'd listen as she spoke of things that were on her heart.

One evening Blaine was sitting on the deck with her back against the rough cedar shake siding, her legs bent and her arms encircling her knees. She was cooing and talking to Herman. The tide was high, and the waves softly lapped at the base of the pilings under the deck.

Blaine heard footsteps. Thinking it was Walt coming from the cafe for some reason, she turned and smiled to see the bright young face of one of the regular merchant marine customers. In fact, she remembered serving him lunch that day.

Second Son

Blaine swiftly jumped to her feet, and brushed off her skirt. "Oh! You startled me." She said sharply.

The young man tipped his hat brim, and flashed a handsome grin. "Sorry," he said. "But I didn't expect to see you out here on the deck. May I sit down? It looks as though I've interrupted your conversation with your humble bird friend."

Blaine smiled and gestured for him to sit down on the edge of the deck, as she sat down again, dangling her feet over the edge. She glanced briefly at his profile while he looked out over the bay. "What brings you out here behind the cafe this time of evening?"

He looked at her. "Well," he began, "Walt told me you lived back here, and I've wanted to talk to you for the past few days, but you always keep so busy I haven't had a chance. Name's Dan Scarbrough. I crew with the freighter, Webber. We usually ship out of Tacoma to Sitka, the Orient and back to Tacoma again, so I'm on the water more than I'm in port, the sailor's life."

Blaine smiled. "I thought you seemed new around here, but I guess it's just that you've been at sea. By the way, I'm Blaine Jergens." She laughed. "Not Missy, as everyone calls me."

Dan reached over and shook her hand. "I'm glad to meet you, Blaine. How long have you been working for Walt?"

Blaine replied, "Been working here nearly eight weeks, and I love it more everyday."

Herman, the gull, flopped his way from one piling to another, then again, bravely landed on the deck railing twenty feet away from where Blaine and Dan talked. He tipped his sculptured head and with a critical eye, looked Dan up and down, then made a little clucking sound in his throat. He proudly waddled his way toward them, his bright orange feet grasping the railing.

Feeling the bird's scrutiny, Dan turned to Blaine and asked, "Does your feathered friend always inspect your guests this thoroughly?"

She chuckled, "Well, just the unexpected ones. Herman is quite the fellow, you know, and he's very demanding when it comes to snacks that I bring from work. But he's a good listener.

He's even let me pet him a few times. He trusts me and he's good company."

The bird dipped his head and emitted a shrill gull screech that sounded over the waterfront. Then he silently lifted himself from the railing and flew down the bay, leaving the two young people to their conversation.

The sun was down and twilight painted the water, tide flats and shabby waterfront buildings with blended lavenders and blues. This helped night pull the shade on what was left of the day.

Blaine stood and put her elbows on the railing, as did Dan. It was a simultaneous motion. They laughed at their identical movements. She told Dan it was time for her to go because she had chores to do before it got too late.

The sky's last light eased into darkness, as Blaine started toward her door, turned and said good night to Dan. "I'm glad that Herman and I had company to watch the sun go down. I expect I'll see you in the cafe again before you ship out on another trip."

Dan nodded. He walked around the corner leaving Blaine to unlock her door to the stairs that led to her room.

She lay in her bed, her mind flitted over the smooth conversation and pleasant meeting she'd enjoyed with Dan. The vision soon faded away into a restful cloud of sleep.

Dan became a daily customer. He was always counted among the coffee drinkers that lingered after the crowd was gone. Courteous and jolly, he was quite a conversationalist. He knew all the longshoremen, shop owners and merchant marines who frequented the cafe.

They all liked Dan too. There was always a happy mixture of laughter wrapped around the booth or table where he sat. Blaine especially enjoyed listening to the joshing and camaraderie that filled the cafe at such times.

One evening Dan was the last customer to finish his meal.

Second Son

There was a twinkle in Walt's eye, as he watched Blaine finish her end-of-the-day routine.

Walt had a hunch that Dan would ask Blaine to take a walk after work. He was right.

Blaine waited for Walt to close the kitchen so they could walk out together.

Dan sat dawdling over his coffee. He put his cup over the counter into the sink, stood with his hat in his hands, cleared his throat and called to Walt in the kitchen. "Hey! Walt. How'd it be if I walk Blaine around to her place tonight? It'd save you the walk, and she'd be just as safe with me as she is with you."

Walt answered back. "Ya gotta get permission from Blaine, not me."

Blaine smiled at the obvious maneuvering by the two men. She chuckled out loud. "All right you two, I'll let Dan walk me home. It's such a long way." Blaine laughed, "But only if he promises to help me feed Herman tonight. That darn bird has become completely attached to me. I don't know if it's the snacks or my good looks that keeps him hanging around."

Walt called from the kitchen, "It's got ta' be the snacks and bread crumbs. Don't ya think Dan?"

Dan smiled, opened the door for Blaine and said, "To each his own, but if I was a bird I'd choose the good looks over the snacks every time."

They bid Walt good night. They could hear him laughing as they went around the corner.

Blaine had a sack of bread crumbs for Herman. The bird was prancing one foot to another, impatiently walking the railing waiting for the hand out.

Blaine handed the sack to Dan and in the process the sack dropped from the deck to the tide flats. Immediately it was swooped upon by a flock of gulls that appeared out of nowhere. Blaine laughed at the bird's antics. She turned and saw a soft mellow look on Dan's face—which had nothing to do with the birds.

Cafe Beyond The Dark Night

    Dan took her hands in his and lightly touched his lips to her forehead. She was surprisingly calm and completely at ease. He put his hands on her shoulders and gently pulled her to him. She didn't resist. It seemed so natural. He kissed her on the mouth.

    They stood on the deck in the early evening glow, embracing into one silhouette. The gulls flew near them in a noisy chorus—which neither of them seemed to hear.

8
Dan

During the next two weeks Dan and Blaine showed the obvious affection that had sprung up between them. Blaine was surprised at her feelings for Dan. It really pleased her that she had found it so easy to care for someone. This feeling was entirely new and pleasingly comfortable.

The trauma and heart chilling fear she had of physical or emotional contact with men had evaporated. Her new attitude was clearly due to the patience, understanding and friendship—dare she even say love—which Dan showed her. Every word, every thought, every touch made her feel that she was a treasure in his hands.

She didn't realize that Dan was afraid if he said too much, held her too close or let his feelings show too much, he feared their precious closeness might burst like a bubble. For her part, she had no such doubts.

August lost its sweltering days to the color and crispness of early September as the trees began their autumn show of red, yellow and gold, and the year 1924 waned toward winter.

Every evening after work Blaine and Dan scuffed through the leaves which danced along the streets. The leaves musky fragrance filled the air. Blaine placed those special evenings in her secret memory. Their hand-in-hand wanderings always ended at Blaine's door with a few kisses, and a prolonged parting.

Dan would have preferred to end in a more intimate manner,

Second Son

but he would not pressure her. He felt if he insisted on a more intimate relationship, Blaine would likely flee as a timid bird. Dan did not want to lose her. He told her, "Honey, I'm having a terrible time."

She looked concerned, and asked, "What is wrong?"

He held her hand and looked out across the bay, said, "Something has happened."

Blaine looked troubled and she put her head on his shoulder and asked, "What is wrong, Dan? Tell me."

Dan whispered into her hair. "I'm in love with someone and I don't know what to do."

Blaine pulled away from him looking shocked and hurt. "What do you mean, *someone*? Do you have another girl somewhere? Have you just been spending time with me until you get back to her in some other port? Alaska? The Orient?" Her eyes flashed fire.

Dan held her at arms length and gave a hearty laugh that echoed out over the waterfront. "Blaine, honey, it's nothing like that. *It's You!* You funny sweet girl. I love you! And I'm having a terrible time trying to find this," he said, as he fished around in his jacket pocket and brought out a small velvet box, opened it and removed a small diamond ring.

Blaine sputtered, "What? What is this? Dan, what have you done? What did you say to me? You love *me*? Is this true?"

Dan quickly took her left hand in his and slipped the ring on her finger. "Yes, dear God, I love you! And I want you to consider this a firm proposal. I want you to be my wife, Blaine Jergens. I love you."

Blaine's eyes filled with happy tears—despite the shadow of foreboding that haunted the moment, which she would allow into her consciousness.

She threw her arms around Dan's neck and kissed him. Drawing away she shouted loudly across the bay. Her voice echoed against the shabby waterfront buildings. "It's True! It's True!" As she spread her arms and danced in a wide circle. Coming back to

Dan

Dan she held his hands and looked at him in a way that promised a great many things. She quietly said, "Dan, I love you too. From the very first time I saw you. Oh, I do love you, and I accept. I will marry you."

Dan's smile was as bright as the moon glow that glittered across the water. He held Blaine and placed a soft kiss on her smiling face. He pushed her toward the door, and said in a husky voice, "Enough of this. You better get behind that door and lock it, or I can't guarantee how much more I can stand."

She agreed, knowing by the wave of emotion that rolled through her, she'd better do as he said. She let go of his hands, threw him a kiss as she went in and locked the door behind herself.

Blaine could hear Dan's footsteps as he sauntered around the corner. She stood behind the door at the bottom of the stairs for a long moment, then slowly walked up the stairs looking at her hand where the tiny diamond twinkled in the warm glow of the ceiling light.

Again, the shadow of foreboding lurked on the edges of her consciousness.

The next day Dan didn't come into the cafe. Blaine shared her news with Walt and all of the regular customers. She nervously kept watch on the door all morning. After the noon crowd had come and gone and still Dan hadn't dropped by, she began to worry.

At two in the afternoon a large bouquet of yellow roses was delivered. It was from Dan. The note said he'd see her the next day. Blaine held the roses in her arms and buried her face in the blossoms' spicy fragrance. These were her first flowers. She cried openly.

When Dan arrived the following afternoon he told Blaine he wanted to get their marriage license as soon as possible.

Blaine was uneasy about the rapidity events. Walt had told her she may need her parent's consent because she had only just turned seventeen—not being eighteen, of the age of consent. She would also need her birth certificate. She knew she had neither of the items, and how to get them was a complete mystery to her. The fact that she had shortened her name and never told Dan or Walt the reason for her deception also worried her. She feared Dan's questions that would follow. She told Dan that she needed her birth certificate, and he told her all she needed to do was call the records office in Olympia and have them send her a copy by mail.

Walt said he would sign for her if she couldn't get in touch with her folks.

Before the dinner crowd arrived, Dan left the cafe feeling content that all the required preliminaries for their license had been taken care of. They could be married within the next two weeks before his next three month trip over seas to the Orient.

He told Blaine that the trip was a usual route the ship took at the end of every September, returning to Tacoma just before Christmas.

Blaine was upset by this revelation, and Dan tried to console her. "You have your work at Walt's Cafe, and your upstairs apartment. There will be times when I'm in port from ten days, other times for two or three months at a time. You'll get used to it."

"I know you say I'll get used to this life, but you'll be so much. I still don't have to like it."

※

The next day, Walt felt the need to question Dan's and Blaine's rushing into wedded bliss. "Where do you kids plan to live? It will be fine with me if you want to stay on in the room Blaine has now, if you think it won't be too small."

Then he asked, "Will you have a justice of the peace or will you be married in the church up the street? Or your family church, Blaine? Surely you've made some plans."

Blaine said quietly, "I didn't give all those things much thought until now. I did call Olympia and was told that if a copy of my

Dan

records wasn't available they would send me a notarized letter containing everything I needed to apply for a marriage license."

Blaine cleared her throat and decided this was the time to give both Dan and Walt an explanation about having changed her name. "I have to tell you both, when I was sent away from home at fourteen, as my folks do with all my brothers and sisters, I felt I needed to change my name, to start a new life on my own. I don't need...don't want my folks to know about my life anymore. I didn't want them to ever find me."

She said nothing about having worked at the Gordon's, about her rape, her baby boy.

Dan and Walt both indicated they understood her motives, her desire to disappear from a bad home life, and accepted her explanation. Dan asked, laughing, "Do I still call you Blaine? Or would you like me to call you Olive?"

Blaine smiled. "Blaine is fine. And thank you for understanding. I love you."

In her heart, Blaine told herself that someday she would confide in Dan about her past. But for now, it still hurt too much to even think about it. Her violation. The loss of her sweet son. These were deep wounds in her heart, their memories still churned her stomach.

In the middle of the week a registered letter came from Olympia addressed to Olive Elsa Blaine Jergenson.

The letter had the needed information. Blaine was excited to receive it so quickly without having to contact her parents. Since she had left Papa and Ma they had never tried to find her or contact. She certainly wasn't ready to let the old feelings of rejection be rekindled. All she felt for her parents at that time was emptiness. A dark blanket had fallen over her childhood memories of home. The only thing she could remember was the loneliness she had felt as she sat in that old bus three year ago, as she let it carry her from the only home she had ever known.

Her mood quickly changed when Dan came in the cafe that evening. She showed him the letter, and he grabbed her around the waist and twirled her around, laughing and telling her, "Tomorrow, baby. Tomorrow we get our legal, honest-to-God, marriage license."

Caught up in his excitement, Blaine let her laughter blend with Dan's, while Walt and the dinner crowd cheered them on.

The next afternoon Walt gave Blaine time off during the usual lull at the cafe. After Dan arrived, the young couple, ran hand-in-hand to the trolley that would take them uptown to city hall.

It took a short time to fill out papers. When asked if she had written permission from her parents, she told the clerk that her folks were no longer around, but if he needed someone to sign as guardian she would call Walt and have him come and sign for her. The clerk gave them a quick wink and signed his name as a witness, collected the two dollar fee and handed the license to Dan. The clerk reminded them of the three day waiting period, then gave the couple a broad smile and wished them a happy life together.

Blaine was nervous as they rode the trolley back toward the dock area. She began to fidget with her handkerchief. Dan reached over and enclosed her hands in his firm grasp and reassured her with his broad smile. Blaine sat close to him, put her head on his shoulder, and sighed.

He whispered, "Are you happy, honey?"

Blaine looked up and nodded her head yes.

They discussed what day the following week they could plan to go back to the city hall and have the Justice of The Peace perform the ceremony. They agreed Tuesday would be best.

The trolley came to a noisy halt. They clasp hands as they stepped into the street. It was raining as they ran down the sidewalk in a frantic sprint. They were soaking wet as they turned the corner, and in spasms of laughter, entered the door of the cafe.

Walt was sitting alone, having a cup of coffee in the empty cafe. The rain seemed to have discouraged the usual afternoon customers. Dan and Blaine excitedly told Walt they'd like to be married the next Tuesday and asked if Walt would give Blaine a few days off.

Dan

Walt wryly pulled at his chin, and looked at the young couple. "Well," he drawled, "I suppose I could get along by myself for three days, being the weather has turned so bad and it looks as if you two just won't be patient and wait a while." He smiled his broad warm smile. "Sure, kids. Ya' need a few days, so go ahead Blaine, take off Tuesday, Wednesday and Thursday next week. That should give ya' one day to get married, and a couple more to settle in that little room, but I guess when you're young and in love ya' don't notice things like small rooms. Blaine I'll expect ya back on Friday."

"Oh, Walt!" Blaine squealed, "You're such an ol' sweetie." She gave him a quick kiss on the cheek. Walt's face turned pink with embarrassment. They all laughed in excitement and friendship.

The rest of the week plodded along in its usual manner. Dan and Blaine had finally taken time to talk about where they would live. As Walt had suggested, they decided to stay in the room in which Blaine was already established. It was small, but adequate for two, especially when Dan shipped out. Blaine would be working, too, and would spend only her mornings and evenings there.

Dan brought two sea bags full of clothes, books, and accumulated trivia that only a seagoing man would have gathered. They had fun storing them in the closet. Blaine wanted to know the story behind each item. In that way she learned about Dan's job and the many adventures of her seafaring man.

Dan, for his part, did not speak of wanting to stay in the room with Blaine before they were married, though it had crossed his mind. He figured that neither Blaine nor Walt would think it a good idea. So he continued to bunk onboard ship until their wedding day.

9
A Bride-To-Be

Autumn 1924, Tuesday morning, Blaine woke to the sound of rain on the roof.

Clouds hanging over the bay looked dark and stormy. Wind whipped the rain against the windowpane. Blaine thought it a gloomy day for a wedding. She jumped out of bed and took a quick bath, powdered her body with perfumed talc she had bought at the drugstore, then brushed her hair until it was dry and shiny as silk.

She had washed the sheets and pillow cases the night before and hung them on a temporary clothesline that swooped from the bathroom door to the opposite corner of the room. After the sheets dried she quickly made the bed. As a romantic touch, she sprinkled some of her talcum powder under the pillows.

The rest of the room was tidy and she glanced around and smiled to herself, knowing this small room would be her and Dan's home. She was satisfied knowing she would finally have someone she could love and count on, whatever happened.

Deciding against buying a new dress to be married in, she ironed her light pink georgette dress and slipped it over her head. Looking at her reflection in the mirror, she tipped her head critically and decided she presented a pretty decent picture of a bride-to-be.

Walt had promised to meet her and Dan at the city hall at ten A.M. sharp to be a witness.

Second Son

It was nine-thirty when Dan knocked on the door and told her to hurry, he had a taxi waiting. Blaine picked up her coat and tied a scarf over her hair. They dashed down the stairs and out into the drenching rain, around the corner the taxi was waiting. The two bundled inside, laughing and wiping the rain from their faces.

Dan gave the driver the destination and they settled back in the seat. Both were a bit nervous. Dan reached up to the shelf behind the seat, where he had previously placed a clear celluloid box. He placed it in Blaine's lap. In it was a corsage of three creamy white gardenias entwined with gold ribbons. It was the only corsage she had ever received. She was convinced it was the most beautiful and fragrant gift she could ever receive. Dan gently kissed her and pinned the corsage to her coat lapel.

They sat holding hands until the taxi stopped in front of the city hall.

They waved at Walt who was waiting inside the main entrance of the building out of the rain. When they got inside, they grabbed his hands as the three walked down the marble-floored hallway toward the office of The Justice of The Peace.

There was another couple ahead of them, so they sat and waited. Dan squeezed Blaine's hand and smiled reassuringly at her.

As the other couple left the office, the frail looking secretary asked how she could help them.

Dan cleared his throat and said quietly, "We've come to be married, Ma'am."

The thin-faced woman asked for their license and motioned them to follow her into the inner office.

The room was gloomy due to dark paneling that made the room appear scrunched and stifling. There were dark green shades at the windows. One shade was torn and the other shade was rain-stained.

The Justice of The Peace stood behind a desk piled high with reams of paper in disarray. He introduced himself to the couple and to Walt.

He was a red-faced little man whose vest stretched over a

A Bride-To-Be

tremendous paunch. He looked over the papers that the secretary handed him and asked the couple to hold hands. He cleared his throat, and in a monotone that edged on boredom, he droned a few sentences, then asked, "Mister Scarborough, do you take this woman to be your lawful wedded wife?"

Dan looked at Blaine and quietly answered "Yes."

The monotonous voice plodded on, and Blaine picked out the words, "Do you, Olive Elsa Blaine Jergenson, take this man to be your lawful wedded husband?"

Blaine pulled her mind out of its near hypnotic state and looked at Dan. Finding his eyes riveted on hers, holding so much emotion she could hardly answer "I do."

Dan was told to place the ring on her finger, which, with shaky hands, he did.

The old man was puffing as if he'd been running, as he pronounced them man and wife.

Dan kissed his bride, and Blaine responded with a quick kiss in reply.

Walt hugged them both. To Blaine, "Honey, you are now Mrs. Dan Scarborough." He smiled broadly. "Congratulations!"

They were then dismissed so they could sign the wedding certificate at the secretary's desk. The Justice then sat down behind his pile of papers.

Blaine saw him pick up a half finished sandwich and he began to munch on it as though they had interrupted him with a bothersome waste of his time.

Blaine felt dirty as they left his office. She felt like they had barely been acknowledged by the lackadaisical manner in which the short ceremony had been conducted. She had the feeling of wanting to escape from the dark, gloomy room and dusty hallway.

Dan felt the same, so they hurried from the building. Walt followed them, and threw hands full of rice that surprisingly appeared from his large coat pockets. Their laughter, broke the melancholy spell the gloomy Justice of The Peace had thrown over them.

Second Son

Dan hailed a taxi. Walt yelled at them saying he'd see them on Friday. The newlyweds took the taxi uptown, which was a surprise to Blaine, as she had expected to just go back to their room.

They entered the Golden Tower Hotel, where Dan had luncheon reservations for two. He ordered the Maine Lobster special. Blaine was thrilled! She had never tasted lobster before.

There was no disguising the glow on their faces. Soon many of the other diners were whispering about the newlywed couple.

Blaine had no idea that Dan had reserved a room for them for their wedding night. He told her during their lunch. Blaine gave a hushed, excited squeal. She had never been in such a lavish setting; nor had she had the privilege of spending the night in such a lush room. She could not hide her excitement as the elevator took them to the fifth floor.

Dan unlocked the heavy oak door and carried her over the threshold into a green fantasy. Blaine had never seen such a lovely room.

The windows were draped in regal satin, as was the bed. The deep oriental carpets were soft as eiderdown. She took off her shoes and ran across the room and jumped into the cloud of feather comforter and large pillows.

Laying her coat on the chair beside the bed, Blaine was careful that she didn't crush the gardenia corsage.

Dan joined her in a tumble of comforter, satin sheets, and pillows. They lay touching each other, openly laughing, and kissing as the floor became littered with a striped tie, starched shirt, trousers, and a pink georgette dress that smelled of talcum powder and gardenias.

The newlyweds spent Wednesday and Thursday in their room behind the cafe, never noticing the weather was cold and gray. They went out for dinner both nights, but not to Walt's Cafe. With so many things to talk about, dining in an anonymous setting seemed easier.

"I wish," said Dan, "I didn't have to leave next Monday for our Alaska and Orient run."

A Bride-To-Be

"I will learn to live with your job." Blaine smiled the best she could. "I will miss you terribly, but I will also always be waiting for my sailor to come home."

Friday Dan and Blaine woke extra early. They made love, listened to the rain on the roof, dozed off, awoke, and made love again. They bathed and dressed quickly, realizing the time had slipped by and it would soon be time for Blaine to go to work.

At the cafe they had coffee with Walt before the breakfast crowd came in. Dan and Blaine let their wonderful morning slip into the back of their minds making way for the day to fall into its old routine.

Dan left for the ship telling Blaine he'd see her early in the evening after work.

Saturday night Blaine went directly to their room after the cafe was closed. Dan was already home. He had one of his big duffel bags out on the bed, cramming it full of his wool jackets, hats, heavy pants and sweaters.

Blaine entered the room and leaned against the door jam.

Dan looked up, stopped what he was doing and came over and kissed her.

She turned away from him saying quietly, "I'd do anything if you didn't have to go."

He held her at arms length. "Now pumpkin, you know this is the way I make my living. I don't want you to fuss, okay?"

She smiled and shrugged her shoulders. "I know," she said. "I'll be okay. You can count on me."

He took her hand and drew her to him. They sat on the small sofa. Patting her hand, he said, "Honey, we get underway early Monday morning, so I'll have to spend Sunday night aboard ship. I'll be gone about three months. I should be back by Christmas." At that news she drew away from him and began to weep quietly. "Now, honey," he begged, "please don't do this. I hate to leave you too, but I've got to go. Walt will watch out for you just like he did before we met. You will keep busy so the days won't be so long and the time will go by quickly."

Second Son

Blaine sighed and wiped her eyes, took a deep breath and, as her Ma used to say, she mentally pulled up her bootstraps. She smiled at Dan, nodding her head, saying softly, "I know I'll be fine, but we've only been together such a short time. I'll miss you so much. But I will think ahead and plan for a lovely Christmas with you. Maybe later this winter your trips will be shorter and you can be in port more often." She questioned bravely, "Do you suppose?"

Dan hugged her and told her he hoped that's the way it would work out.

Their last evening together was spent in hushed conversation interspersed with tender lovemaking that lasted far into the night.

Sunday morning when they awoke the rain was still hammering on the roof and the wind threw sheets of rain against the window, Blaine made the bed and got ready to go to work. They went down to the cafe to have coffee with Walt.

Dan hung around for a while. They had a leisurely breakfast. Then he kissed Blaine and told her he'd be back before he left for the ship.

Blaine smiled bravely and gave a quick wave as Dan walked out of the cafe.

Near closing time Dan walked into the cafe and leaned his duffel bag against the wall. He and Blaine drank coffee together. Blaine kept a sunny smile on her face, but the bleak look in her eyes gave her away. Dan kissed her and held her close before he grabbed up and adjusted the sea bag on his shoulder, turned and walked out the door.

Blaine retained her composure as Walt locked the cafe door and walked her around the corner to her door. He gave her a quick, fatherly squeeze, and told her things would be okay. He left Blaine standing outside her door.

She fumbled for her keys trying to unlock the door. Her hot tears mixed with the cold rain.

10
Waiting for Her Sailor to Come Home from the Sea

The next few months Blaine worked every day that the cafe was open.

No one could tell she also had become a bit pale—a little makeup took care of that. And once in a while she'd serve a customer, then casually go to the rest room where she would be sick, wash her face and return to work, never complaining or explaining her actions.

Blaine knew what the trouble was, and it stirred her heart with feelings of true delight. She held a treasured secret that she could hardly wait to share with her dear husband. In fact, it would be his Christmas surprise. She would tell him she was carrying his baby. The secret she held made her miss Dan more everyday.

As Christmas drew closer Blaine had Walt buy a small Christmas tree to put in the front window of the cafe. She strung cranberries and popcorn on long strings and looped them from limb to limb. She had been saving cardboard milk bottle caps which she painted in bright colors. She glued glitter on them and hung them from thin threads on the tree bows creating the illusion of glass ornaments.

Walt said it was the first time the place had been decorated for the holidays, and he felt it really put his customers in a festive mood, who hesitated not to complement him on the new decor.

Second Son

As Christmas drew closer, Blaine tried to keep herself from being too excited. Her happiness grew from day to day in anticipation of Dan's return. She planned special shopping trips. She had saved money so they could get each other gifts.

Three days before Christmas, during the afternoon lull, the cafe door swung open and Dan walked in, head high and a big smile on his face. He dropped his duffel bag by the door and grabbed Blaine up off her feet, swinging her around.

Squealing with laughter, she squeezed her arms around Dan's neck.

Walt bellowed from the kitchen a hearty, 'Hello.'

Finally, Dan carefully set Blaine back on her feet, looked her in the eyes and said, "I'm home." Then he took a seat at a table and sighed. "Ma'am, I'd like to order a cup of coffee, please."

Soon the three sat together over coffee. Dan related his latest adventures. Walt and Blaine filled Dan in on the mundane happenings at the cafe.

Excusing himself, Dan said, "I should stow my gear." He got up to take his things to their room.

Blaine fidgeted but, needing to finish her day shift, said, "I'll be there soon, honey!"

At the end of the dinner rush, she blew Walt a kiss and sprinted up the stairs bursting into their room.

Throwing her coat on the sofa she quietly yielded to Dan's arms as he held and kissed her. During their embrace Dan reached over and touched the light switch throwing the room into half light, making shadows of rumpled bedding and young lovers.

Later, lying together. "I'm going to have a baby."

"Then, we're a family."

"Yes," said Blaine. "A family."

Christmas 1924 came with a flurry of laughter and unwrapped gifts.

Blaine, once called Olli, had never known such happiness at

Waiting for Her Sailor to Come Home from the Sea

Christmas as she felt with Dan and Walt and all the friends she had made while working at the cafe.

Alone and snuggled in bed, Blaine talked with Dan about the expected baby. He was so thrilled and made a teasing remark about her being a fertile little flower, because they'd only been together five days before he boarded ship.

She told him she thought the baby would be born in June. She hadn't been to the doctor yet, but promised she would go now that Dan was home.

The doctor told Blaine her guess of when the baby was due was correct and he assured her that her physical condition was excellent, she should have a normal pregnancy and had nothing to worry about. He scheduled four more visits closer to her delivery date and dismissed her with the promising outlook that 1925 would surely hold a real change for her and Dan.

Dan was on a short work schedule of ten days at home and ten days at sea. Blaine continued to work at the cafe until March when her condition was more than obvious.

"Walt, I think I'll need to take off from work for awhile. Dan and I would appreciate continuing to rent your room. Would that be okay? I feel safe here."

"Of course, dear," Walt replied. "For a time, anyway."

While Dan was away on one of his ten day tours, Blaine having learned to crochet when she was very young, began crocheting hats and booties and soft baby blankets.

As the child grew within her, Blaine was completely engrossed in every aspect of its being. She was thrilled with the motion, the weight of it, the feeling of stretching and growth. This feeling was an elation she hadn't known when she carried Cal, and she knew it was because of the circumstances being so different. She was cared for by those around her, not being hidden away in shame as Mother Gordon had done to her.

When Dan was in port he doted on her every need and was

amazed at the movement of their child within her belly. Its movement seemed its way of protesting the crowded environment it inhabited.

Blaine felt her child was getting ready to face the world.

The end of June approached. In the middle of the afternoon of the twenty-fifth, Blaine was suddenly aware of the pressure. By the low pain, she knew what the next few hours would bring.

Dan, happily home from duty, ran to the telephone at the cafe and called the doctor.

Dr. Collins told Dan not to get too excited, because it would likely be a few hours before Blaine would need him, but he'd drop by to check on her within the hour anyway. Meanwhile, Dan was to collect clean towels and sheets and have them ready for use. Dr. Collins advised Dan to make Blaine comfortable.

When Dan returned to their room, Blaine was lying on the bed and visibly in pain. He paced the floor, then came to the bed and lay down beside her and held her in his arms. Each pain seemed worse than the previous one. Blaine knew it would not be long until the pushing urge would be more than she could control. She became frightened that the doctor would be late and Dan wouldn't know what to do. Dan held her and soothed her with soft words giving her quiet assurance that the doctor would arrive very soon.

A knock sounded at the door and Dr. Collins pushed his way into the room, followed by his nurse. He placed his black bag on the side table. The nurse, seeing the distress Blaine was already in, took a can of ether out and prepared to administer it. The doctor examined Blaine. He asked Dan to leave for a short while. Reluctantly, Dan went below and stood outside leaning on the railing of the deck.

The examination took only a couple of minutes, but the pains had changed and Blaine knew she had to push. The doctor gave a signal to the nurse and Blaine saw a small screened apparatus filled with gauze being placed over her nose and mouth. After taking a few deep breaths of the acrid odor the pain floated away.

Waiting for Her Sailor to Come Home from the Sea

Her ears began to buzz. She couldn't hear anything but whispers on the outskirts of her world of pain.

She heard her name called and it roused her back to consciousness.

The doctor was saying, "Alright, my dear, give us a couple of big pushes here and we'll see that this baby gets out into the light of day where it wants to be."

Blaine did as she was told and after four wrenching pushes she heard a quivering wail that changed to a hearty cry, even as the doctor's hand slapped the soft flesh of the baby's bottom.

Dr. Collins exclaimed, "Blaine you've got a husky healthy baby girl!"

The nurse wrapped the baby in a towel and put its foot imprint on the birth certificate, then washed the firm little body and rewrapped it in a clean flannel blanket. Blaine's daughter was placed in her arms.

Blaine looked at her precious baby daughter and believed she was one of the sweetest baby she had ever seen.

Dr. Collins said, "This was one of the quickest deliveries I have ever seen. Was it easier than your first?"

Blaine looked at him in stark disbelief. "Why do you ask that?" She stammered.

Dr. Collins said, "Well, Blaine, I've always known this was not your first pregnancy. The presence of stretch marks and old scar tissue were evidence of another birth. What happened to the first child?"

Blaine felt numb. She hadn't even spoken of baby Cal since she had left him at the Gordon's house a year ago. Hot tears filled her eyes. She softly whispered, "He was taken from me."

Dr. Collins clearly interpreted Blaine's reply to mean the child had died. He patted Blaine's arm and said sympathetically, "Well, let's hope this little sweetie will fill that empty place. She is healthy and strong." He signaled the nurse who went to the door and called down the stairs.

"Mister Scarborough, your baby is ready to meet her father."

Second Son

Dan sprinted up the stairs and hesitantly crept into the room. Quickly a feeling close to fear came over him when he bent over the bed where Blaine lay holding a moving, living little being. When he asked Blaine if she was all right, a small pink hand peeked out of the soft blanket.

Blaine smiled and told him, "Your daughter and I are doing fine. A little tired."

Dan turned and thanked Dr. Collins and the nurse, and after the doctor had given him some basic care instructions Dan escorted them down the stairs to bid them good bye. He hesitated as if he were a bit afraid to be left in charge of the small vulnerable family who waited for him upstairs.

Dr. Collins congratulated Dan, adding, "This child is good and healthy. I'm sure there shouldn't be any problem like there was with the first baby."

Dan looked at the doctor with a puzzled expression on his face. The doctor and nurse started to walk away when Dan grabbed the doctor's arm and sharply turned him around. "What are you talking about? First baby...."

Dr. Collins saw the questioning look on Dan's face and realized Dan hadn't known about the other child. The doctor asked Dan to take a short walk down the dock with him.

Dan followed. In an angry voice, he asked again, "What the hell did you mean—the first baby? This is our first baby."

Dr. Collins spoke softly. "This is something you and Blaine will have to talk out between yourselves. All I know is that I could tell that she has had at least one other pregnancy which she apparently has never disclosed until I asked her about the other child right after I delivered this baby. She implied the child was dead. At least, I assumed that's what she meant when she told me the child was taken from her. I could tell this was her second pregnancy, and I just expected that you knew. I am sorry you have had to learn of this...situation in this manner. I think you deserve an explanation from Mrs. Scarborough. But I'm asking you, from a medical standpoint, that you not press her about it for a few days, because this was a hard, quick labor and she needs lots of rest."

Dan, still in a state of shock and disbelief, thanked the doctor. With hesitant steps he ascended the stairs not knowing quite what to do with the revelation that had just been thrown at him. He decided, as had been advised, to postpone any questioning about it for a few days. He hoped the waiting wouldn't fester into anger in him and burst out against Blaine. She could explain to him later. He would wait. He must, he told himself.

He went back in the room and closed the door on the late summer evening's glow that softened the light in the room.

Blaine had unwrapped the baby and was gently examining the soft bud-like hands, counting toes and fingers.

Dan reached down and touched the soft flaxen fuzz on his daughter's head.

Blaine looked at Dan with an expression of controlled emotion. Dan wondered if it was love, or a hidden fear that forced tears from Blaine's eyes.

Dan held her hand, sat beside her and quietly asked, "What should we name her?"

Blaine heaved a sigh like a heavy load had been lifted from her shoulders. Her face brightened. She looked down at the tiny bundle in her arms. "I think Jenny Danielle would be a nice name," she answered.

Dan spoke the name, "Jenny Danielle Scarbrough. I like her being named after me. Yes, I think that is a fine name for our daughter. Jenny. Yes, that's who she'll be."

Dan knew he was scheduled to ship out again in five days, so he decided to wait until he returned from the next ten day trip. Then he would ask Blaine for an explanation about her first pregnancy.

He still couldn't make himself believe what the doctor had told him, because there had never been the slightest hint from Blaine. Had she been married before? He knew after their wedding night she wasn't a virgin. But he never questioned her because he hadn't been white as the driven snow himself. He was able to forgive Blaine, but a previous child, that was a different matter.

Dan was in and out of the house during the days before he was due to leave again.

Blaine felt that he had been quite cool and off-ish toward her, but she couldn't pin the feeling down. It was as if he had something he wanted to talk about, but was hesitating.

Blaine brushed aside the cloud of uncertainty when she watched him pick up Jenny and hold her. The tender look on his face showed his feelings when he held his baby daughter. She knew he loved their child.

Dan had feelings of pride and responsibility, that fact alone eased Blaine's mind. She was silently grateful he was such a good daddy for Jenny.

The day Dan left for his ship, he softly kissed Blaine and Jenny.

Ten days passed quickly as new mother and daughter learned in the intimate way only an infant and mother can know of closeness and dependence.

Dan returned ten days later. He didn't really wanting to bring up the subject of Blaine's other child, yet he had to know before the uncertainty festered in his gut and divided them.

On the first night he was home, after they had finished dinner, and Blaine had fed and changed Jenny and tucked her into her basket, Dan motioned for Blaine to come over to the couch and sit by him. He said he had to talk to her about something very important.

A stab of fear struck Blaine's stomach. She knew this conversation had something to do with Dan's attitude he'd shown before he'd left on his last trip. The fact was he had acted strangely since the day of Jenny's birth. For some reason she felt frantic.

Dan said, "Blaine, I have to know if what the doctor told me is true, the day Jenny was born."

In a shaky voice Blaine asked, "What did Dr. Collins say to you?" She twisted her fingers and clenched her hands.

Waiting for Her Sailor to Come Home from the Sea

Dan made her look straight into his eyes. "Honey, I have to know if you've ever had another baby like the doctor said. I promise I'll listen and do my best to understand, but I've got to know the truth."

Blaine stood up and began nervously pacing the length of the small room wringing her hands. She was trying to gather strength to force the words out of her mouth. She began to tell the whole story. As the words tumbled out, she couldn't stop. She told Dan about how she had been raped and become pregnant, and why out of shame she'd never told anyone—not even him. She explained why she had shortened her name, not so her parents couldn't find her but rather so Mother Gordon couldn't find her. She feared the old woman and knew she could never stand to see Cal again unless it was with mutual agreement on the Gordons' part. She knew that would never happen as long as the old woman was alive. In a manner of speaking, she had hidden out, and hoped that all but the memories were behind her. But Dr. Collins had reopened the wound. In a way she was relieved that the facts were now out in the open, at least between her and Dan.

Dan listened patiently while Blaine paced up and down pouring out her story. She ended by nearly collapsing on the couch quietly sobbing. In this condition of anxiety and stress, she buried her face in her hands waiting for Dan to yell at her, condemn her, or just get up to leave. She didn't know what to expect from him. And deep down she knew she couldn't blame him.

Dan lay down on the couch and firmly pulled her to him and made her lie down beside him. He cradled her head on his arm and soothed her by whispering soft endearments, stroking her hair and telling her how sorry he was that he'd ever doubted her or questioned her after all she'd been through. But he had just needed to know.

He found it hard to believe she could continue day by day keeping such a happy outlook on life after silently suffering as she had done.

Blaine lay in his arms for a long time softly sobbing until she

Second Son

dropped into an exhausted sleep. Dan rose from the couch and put a blanket over her. He wanted her to sleep until it was time to feed Jenny, feeling he had caused this anguished disclosure. He was sorry she had been hurt so badly in relating her story, and by the past which she had hidden for so long.

For the next ten days Dan became acquainted with, and very much attached to, the sweet little infant he had fathered. He held her and hesitated to break away from both his daughter and Blaine when his next ten day tour arrived.

The summer of 1925 passed quickly and the beginning of October arrived too slowly for the Scarbrough family.

When Dan arrived home again, he immediately showered love on Blaine and Jenny. The infant had begun developing a sweet, happy personality. When Dan picked her up her way of communicating was kicking happily and cooing softly. She clearly loved her daddy, a fact for which Blaine was very thankful.

Dan's attitude toward her and Jenny was that of a perfect husband and father. He was so kind to Blaine and loved his baby daughter so openly that Blaine fell more in love with him every day.

The night before Dan was to leave on his next trip, Blaine tossed and turned in the dark, her thoughts darted around the events of the previous year. In flashes of memory she saw Dan's face, his smile, and felt his strong, gentle hands on her body. She lay awake listening to his warm, easy breathing. She wanted to touch his mouth or weave her fingers in his course chest hair; to hold his slim strong waist and hips. Instead, she rolled over close to him and cuddled to his smooth back, tucking the blanket over his shoulder. She couldn't bear the thought that the following night, after his departure, she would lie alone in their bed with only her own body heat warming the sheets.

Fearing her tossing and turning would wake him, Blaine slipped out of bed, tiptoed shivering across the cold linoleum,

Waiting for Her Sailor to Come Home from the Sea

and turned on the small gas heater. She checked the baby, cozy and sleeping with the contentment known only by a healthy and much-loved infant.

Blaine switched on the light in the kitchen, quietly prepared the coffee pot for their early morning breakfast, then slipped back into bed. Thinking with a gnawing pain of regret, it would be their last morning until after Christmas. She put her arm over Dan's waist as he lay on his side. Her feet were icy cold. She thought any other morning she would have playfully put her cold feet on the back of his legs and hugged him awake. In the past when she had done this, he would wake and lock her in a bear hug. She would feign a desperate struggle which would end in the quick, urgent pleasure of happy lovemaking, leaving them in a state of invigorated exhaustion, the feeling that comes only from two people who become mentally, physically and emotionally one being. Instead, she quietly moved closer to him and fell asleep.

With the coming dawn, Blaine awakened to the sensation of Dan's hands on her breasts. She smiled, opened her eyes to see his face in the half morning light gazing at her with an unmistakable look of desire. With his hands he was expressing an urgent need which aroused her. She turned, arched her back and openly accepted the tender, then savage rhythm.

Blaine grasp the iron bedstead above her head, moaning in both pain and pleasure as they together reached the pinnacle, a oneness in a trembling crescendo.

The lovers lay quietly until they were both breathing easily.

In a hushed tone Dan said, "Hon, you are my best and only sweet girl. I hope I didn't hurt you. It's going to be a long time before I can hold you again. I love you Blaine. You know that, don't you?'

Blaine smiled, nodded yes.

In a husky voice full of emotion, Dan said, "I've been dreaming of you all night, so when you cuddled up cozy and warm I had to have you one more time before I left. God, Girl, I don't know if I

Second Son

can stand to be away from you for the next three months. I love you more everyday."

Sunshine peeped in the window. They lay quietly in each other's arms mulling over their own thoughts; hating to break the spell they had cast on each other.

Baby Jenny stretched making her morning squeaks and groans. Dan smiled as he heard her tiny rosebud fist find her hungry mouth as she began a soft sucking sound warning of protests to come if she wasn't fed.

Blaine rose from the bed and lit the stove under the coffee pot while Dan bathed and shaved.

After changing and cleaning the baby, Blaine cuddled her to her breast to nurse while Dan and she sat at the small green kitchen table having their usual coffee, toast and jam. This was their favorite time of day.

Dan gazed out of the window saying in an earnest tone, "Hon, I do hate to leave you. I really hate to go this time. I know it will be difficult for you—all the chores, the baby." He paused. "I hope you'll be okay. I'll write you from every port," he added. "You won't be able to get letters to me. That's the way things are. In case of an emergency you can contact the shipping office. I've written the address and phone number down on the bulletin board by the sink."

Blaine said sadly, "I miss you so much when you're gone. But this time it's even harder because of Jenny. I've always done well with babies, but now, being alone with such a wee one for such a long time, and you being so sweet and good with her." She shook her head. "I worry too." She got up, laid the baby in her bassinet, and returned to the table where she lightly sat on Dan's lap. She put her arms around him, lay her head on his chest. "I promise you," she whispered, "I'll take care of everything while you're away."

Dan gave her bottom a playful pinch.

The conversation became spaced and hushed until Dan moved toward his duffle bag. He glanced at the clock and put on his seaman's jacket and cap. The sun rose higher splashing gold light on his baby's head. He bent and kissed the sleeping infant, then held Blaine, kissed her soundly, opened the door, hurried down the stairway and was gone.

The first day of October, 1925.

Dan shipped out on the Webber for his usual three month trip to Alaska and the Orient. He hated to pull himself away from his wife and baby now that they were firmly linked in a love-bound bundle known as Family. It took a great deal of strength on his part to pull away, knowing his job was essential to their livelihood and survival.

Blaine and baby Jenny were comfortable in the small room behind the cafe and felt safe there, but Blaine hoped they might look for a larger place after Christmas when Dan returned.

Dan had been at sea for two weeks when Blaine became ill. She had a temperature and began vomiting. A terrible headache raged and she was convinced she had a bad case of the flu, but in a few days she broke out in a swollen red rash.

Walt came by to see her and the baby. Finding Blaine in such a condition he called Dr. Collins and asked him to drop by.

The doctor came and examined Blaine. His diagnosis was measles. Blaine was concerned about Jenny contracting them, too. Dr. Collins ask if she had ever had any such illness when she was a child. Blaine couldn't remember, so the doctor told her to watch Jenny just in case she had no natural immunity. There was a possibility Jenny could get the measles too, which in infants can be dangerous, and if she did Blaine was to call him. On the way out, Dr. Collins put a sign on the door stating the inhabitants were quarantined.

Blaine struggled out of bed and hung a blanket over the window to keep the light at a minimum. The doctor said bright light could affect her eyes during the following days of illness.

Recovery was slow. Every day Blaine watched Jenny carefully to see if any symptoms appeared. Finally she was convinced that the baby was going to be fine. Then one morning she woke to put Jenny in bed with her to feed her. Jenny was fussy and wouldn't eat. Blaine felt the sturdy little body and found it very hot. Blaine had been so careful, yet clearly Jenny was ill. Blaine put the baby in a warm blanket and then in her basket. She hated to leave, but dashed down stairs to the phone in the cafe.

Walt asked what the trouble was and Blaine told him she was afraid that Jenny had the measles. Walt told her he'd call the doctor and she should return to care for the baby.

Dr. Collins told Walt he'd be there as soon as he could. Walt passed along Dr. Collins message, finding her sitting in the rocking chair holding a very sick baby. He tried his best to reassure her, then returned to work.

After what to Blaine seemed hours, Dr. Collins knocked on the door and entered to find Blaine sitting in the rocking chair still holding the hot, listless baby. The doctor made a quick examination of the child, checked her mouth, and recorded her pulse, respirations and temperature. "Blaine," he said seriously, "Jenny does have the measles. If we can get her fever down now, and you can keep it down all night by treating her with cool baths and alcohol rubs, I think it may help the rash to break out on the skin. The presence of the rash in her mouth indicates that she already has the rash internally. She needs to be watched carefully. Can you do that?"

"Yes," Blaine replied, holding back her tears. "Should I take her to the hospital?"

Dr. Collins told her that wouldn't be necessary if she would treat the baby in the manner he had explained. "Don't worry," he reassured her. "I'll be back in the morning to check on things. Jenny's a strong baby." He put a warm blanket over Jenny, picked up his coat and black bag. "Take good care of her, she'll be fine."

The rest of the day and through the night, Blaine cared for the feverish infant, often forcing cool water into her tiny mouth. The baby protested and sputtered each time. After midnight she seemed to rest slightly between fussing and being washed with cooling alcohol.

Waiting for Her Sailor to Come Home from the Sea

After two in the morning, Blaine lay the child down beside her on the bed and fell into a cautious, sketchy sleep. Jenny's sleep began fitfully, but soon quieted.

The light of the cold gloomy morning awakened Blaine. She'd been asleep for hours!

Blaine reached over and felt Jenny's forehead. It was cool. She heaved a sigh of relief, got out of bed, wrapped the baby tighter in her blanket and picked her up. Jenny didn't move. Blaine turned the light on and held the quiet, still baby close to her breast. She didn't feel Jenny breathing. In a frantic gesture she put Jenny on the bed and stripped the blanket from the baby's cool body.

The early morning air was split with the scream which tore from Blaine's throat.

It was nine o'clock when Dr. Collins and Walt rushed up the stairs. They knocked on the door and entered the dimly lit room.

Blaine sat cross legged on the bed, rocking slowly, humming to herself. In her arms lay Jenny's blanket-wrapped corps.

11

The Great Loss

Dr. Collins turned to Walt and said, "We've got to get the child out of her arms so I can examine it." Walt and the doctor approached Blaine.

The woman clawed, screamed and roared at them like a wild animal. Her wild eyes communicated she would not let the two strangers touch her baby!

The outgoing, happy Blaine the two men knew so well had vanished, and in her place sat a bewildered, mentally broken woman.

Dr. Collins held back and prepared an injection of a strong sedative.

Walt approached cautiously, grabbed a hold of Blaine forcibly while the doctor administered enough medication to ease the grip with which she held the dead infant.

Slowly Blaine's body relaxed, her eyes blurred, and after a few minutes the sedative did its work.

The doctor took the still infant, unwrapped and carefully examined the tiny bundle to diagnose cause of death. It was, indeed, the measles. Tears formed in his eyes and ran down his cheeks. Seeing that Blaine was now in a deep narcotic sleep, Dr. Collins asked Walt if he knew of any way to get in touch with Dan aboard ship.

Walt said he thought the ship's freight office would be able to contact Dan, but he hated to do that, because there was no way Dan could leave before it returned to port. "Such horrible news," he whispered to the doctor, "to receive such news and be powerless to do anything about."

The doctor thought a moment. "How about her parents? Do you have any way to contact them?"

Walt had only spoken with Blaine of her parents once since he had known her, just before she and Dan were married over a year past. Walt opened the drawers in the dressing table and fumbled through a folder of papers. He found the wedding certificate and Blaine's birth information, but the parents' name and address were not listed. He gave the papers to Dr. Collins. "Call the records department in Olympia. They should be able to get you the correct information."

"And," added the doctor, "I am thinking we should admit Blaine into the hospital. I will contact local authorities about mental health commitment. Just in case." He shook his head sadness spread across his face. "Walt, we must notify Dan of his baby's demise. And Blaine's condition. There's no way around it. I will try to find her parents...to sign the papers for her mental health care. She's still only seventeen. Especially if Dan remains unavailable in the interim."

Walt and Dr. Collins left the room together.

Outside, Walt said, "I agree with you, doctor. Her mental condition—I worry about her. And Dan."

Downstairs Dr. Collins called for an ambulance.

Attendants placed Blaine, in her sedative-induced sleep, on a stretcher and carried her to the waiting vehicle.

Dr. Collins wrapped the small baby's body tightly in her blanket and carried the still form with him, climbing into the ambulance. Calling Walt over, he handed a quickly scribbled note to him with instructions about where they were taking Blaine and the baby's body. The note also informed Walt to lock the room until the police came to take down any information they might need. He told Walt that he would contact him later to let him know if he had been able to locate Blaine's parents.

The Great Loss

The Whatcom County sheriff drove down the weed-covered road that led toward the ramshackle house near the Lynden River. He had received an emergency call from a doctor down in Tacoma, who had needed to reach the Jergensons. Apparently, one of their daughters was in the hospital, and due to her underage status, and the fact that her husband was at sea, the doctor needed the parents' consent before admitting her to the state hospital.

After stopping his car at the door, the sheriff watched as a short thin woman came out on the porch. A tall handsome man took his place beside her and asked if there was a problem.

The sheriff explained the situation.

When he mentioned Blaine's name, Mrs. Jergenson slowly realized it was Olli the sheriff was talking about. In a reflex of shock, her hands flew to cover her mouth and stifle a gasp.

Mr. Jergenson grimaced before asking, "So, now, where do I have to go to see the doctor who thinks my girl is crazy?"

"Now, that's not what I said," the sheriff objected. "The doctor, Dr. Collins, simply said your daughter needs appropriate treatment...after the death of her baby. That's all I said."

The Jergensons looked at one another realizing they knew nothing about Olli's life since she had left home nearly four years past. They didn't know where she had been, or that she'd changed her name, had married, or that they were grandparents twice over. Their daughter, as was the family custom, had never written to them.

"Here's the hospital address, and the doctor's information," said the sheriff, handing them a piece of paper. "Olli's married name is Blaine Scarbrough. Husband's name is Dan." He wished them the best and drove off, leaving the older couple to act on the information he'd given them.

The next day in the hospital, Dr. Collins met the Jergensons. At the front desk Mr. Jergenson asked to see their daughter, Olli Jergenson.

Second Son

"I'm sorry," began the receptionist, "there's no one here by that name. Maybe—"

Dr. Collins quietly reminded them that Olli now called herself Blaine and that her married name was Mrs. Scarbrough.

Mrs. Jergenson broke in, "Our daughter's name is Olive Elsa Blaine Jergenson. I have no idea why she has decided to use her middle name."

Dr. Collins told them she would be in the hospital for a short time, after which, he felt she needed to be transferred to the mental facility for a period of treatments. "I'm confident that her time at the mental facility will help her cope with the terrible loss of her child. I am also confident that such treatment is essential for her mental stability."

Mr. Jergenson, even before seeing Olli, signed the required papers to treat her. "Doctor," he asked, "where is the child's body? We will want to give a proper burial." He stared at the doctor. "And I should think Olli will want to attend the service. Do you know when she will be released?"

Dr. Collins was somewhat startled by the utter lack of emotion in the parents. He was thus determined not to let them see their daughter until they promised not to speak of funerals or burial services. Finally directing them to the ward where Blaine was, he warned them not to expect much response from Blaine. "She had been through a tremendous shock. You must take special care not to upset her. Do you understand what I am saying?"

The Jergensons both nodded in the affirmative as they entered the hospital ward.

Blaine lay unmoving in the iron bed. Face ashen white. Eyes closed as if quietly hiding in a place far removed from emotional pain. Hiding in the recesses of a gray fog bank which no one else could see. Hearing only the echoes of a familiar voice calling a name she knew from another life. *Olli. Olli. Can you hear me? Olli, it's Ma.* She couldn't make her eyes open. Someone took her hand. A slight smile formed at the corners of

The Great Loss

her mouth. Then she slid back into the twilight refuge. Keeping reality at bay.

Two days later Blaine was transferred to Western State Mental Hospital outside of Tacoma. She remained in a frozen posture wherever she was placed, whether in bed, sitting in a chair or standing. Eyes fixed, she stared at her hands in her lap, or stared at the glare outside the window. Farms surrounded the hospital and supplied food for the staff and patients. But Blaine could perceive nothing of the outside world, only the frosted glass in front of her face, cold and gray to her staring gaze.

She hadn't seen the fallen maple leaves turn from gold to a brown mush where the automobile traffic had ground the jewel-tone leaves beneath their tires, to be frozen white with the first heavy snowfall.

Autumn died into winter.

At night the halls echoed with agonized wails accompanied by the constant babbling of patients in the beds nearby. Daylight hours filled with sketchy shadowed figures. She found them easy to ignore, her mind folding the safe gray fog around her. There she was protected in a tentative peace.

The Jergensons made arrangements for the baby's funeral service and burial in a small country cemetery about a mile from their house in Lynden Valley. Ma had insisted on pictures being taken of the sparse winter flowers and the tiny white casket, so when Olli came home, they could show her the nice service they had provided for their grandchild. Papa mentioned that it would be only proper if Olli's new husband would reimburse them for all they had done, for the out-of-pocket expenses incurred to bury a grandchild they had never seen—or even known about.

Three days before Christmas, Dan returned from his tour at sea. He had been contacted aboard ship three weeks earlier and told

Second Son

of Jenny's death and Blaine's mental state and commitment. He hurried to the café. He would need to call Dr. Collins right away.

Walt saw the haggard sailor rush in the door and through the empty dining room. The older man grabbed Dan by the shoulders and folded the emotionally broken young sailor in his huge hairy arms. He held him like he would hold his own son. Walt felt the sadness move through Dan. He held him until Dan took a deep breath and pulled away.

"I know," said Dan softly, "I know Jenny is dead, but I'm so worried about Blaine. I have to call Dr. Collins. Have you seen Blaine? Did you find her folks? Did they go to see her? Do you know if her folks had the services for Jenny? I'd hate to think that because I was gone they'd have buried our baby in an unmarked plot somewhere."

Dan looked to Walt for answers. Walt told Dan what he knew, that Blain's parents did in fact have a service and buried Jenny proper in a local cemetery. As for the rest, Dr. Collins would have to give him the details about Blaine's condition and treatments.

Dan asked Walt if he had the address of Blaine's folk's. He owed them a visit and wanted to thank them for all their help while he was at sea. He felt it was good for Blaine to finally get back on speaking terms with them, not realizing Blaine had no idea that her folks had been to see her, nor that they hadn't come to see since the funeral; what with no sign of response or recognition from their daughter, they soon ceased visiting altogether.

Dan called Dr. Collins and made an appointment to meet him the next day at Western State Mental Hospital. Dan needed to talk to him before going to see Blaine.

After hanging up the phone, Dan wondered why Blaine's condition would be so bad that she'd have to be put in a mental hospital. The Blaine he know was a strong, independent girl. He had never considered that his being at sea when she'd been ill with the measles could cause her to become mentally unstable. Jenny being ill, then the death of their dear child, all while he was gone to sea. Maybe it was the loss of her first baby, Cal. And the rape.

The Great Loss

Now Jenny's death. And who knows what else going back as far as when she had left home years before. It seemed everything had combined and clustered into an unbearable load that landed on Blaine's shoulders and finally broke her down. She was unable to pick her self up by the bootstraps now.

According to Dr. Collins, Blaine had closed the door on her harsh reality and wrapped herself in a safe world somewhere inside her head. The doctor explained what he knew about such problems and possible treatments. Then he led Dan to the ward-room where Blaine lay.

There were seven beds other than Blaine's in the sparsely furnished ward. These beds were empty, their occupants in the day-room, hallways or treatment rooms.

Blaine sat in a straight-backed chair near a window. Dan scarcely recognized the thin, white-faced woman who sat staring blankly. Her hair was unkempt, tangled and hanging in lusterless strings around her expressionless face. Her posture and demeanor were those of a caged animal. She slouched in complete oblivion, with no hope of escaping the invisible, self-induced cage in which she sat trapped, motionless and unaware of Dan's presence. Blaine's youth and free spirit had fled from her eyes, leaving dark holes in her white, mask-like expression.

Dr. Collins saw the cold shock hit Dan as he approached his sick wife. The doctor stepped between Blaine and the window, and quietly spoke to her as he held her hands. "Blaine, Olli, This is Dr. Collins. I have a surprise today. Look who's here to see you." He motioned for Dan to come forward, softly coaxing Dan to speak to her.

In an uncertain voice Dan said, "Blaine, Baby, it's me, it's Dan. I'm home."

There was no sign of response.

"Dan, tray again," said the doctor softly. "Be positive. But explain to her about how her family had had a wonderful funeral service for baby Jenny. Be encouraging."

Dan knelt beside Blaine. The young woman sat unmoving, as

Second Son

Dan spoke to her. He held her hands and wept quietly between words—still, Blaine showed no response.

Dr. Collins motioned for Dan to get up. He placed his arm around Dan's shoulders. In disbelief the young man sobbed quietly. His jolly girl, his vivacious, self-reliant, loving Blaine was gone. In her place sat an unblinking statue, totally unaware that he was beside her.

Dan and Dr. Collins left the room and went to the office where Dan tried hard to collect his confused thoughts and ragged emotions.

Dan leaned toward the doctor. "Have you seen any improvement since she's been here?" He sobbed, "I can't imagine life without Jenny!" Calming himself with great effort he added, "She was such a sweet little baby, Jenny. But with Blaine in this condition, I don't think … I can…. How long will she be here? Will she ever get well? God! I'm so scared for her. How can I go back to work and leave her alone here? What am I going to do? I love her, but that person isn't my wife!" He slammed his fist against a wall, knocking askew a small framed picture.

Dr. Collins took a deep breath. "Well Son," he began, "I think we'll have to give Blaine time to wash this shock out of her mind. We'll just have to be patient and see if we can find the key to help her unlock herself from this self-induced prison." He paused. "My suggestion is for you to have patience. Come in to see her every day you are in port and talk to her as if she's alert. Take her hand, make her aware that you are with her, maybe she'll push the wall away by herself, if she realizes you are there for her. On the days you're out on the ship, the attendants and I will work with her to get her to face reality. If there's more about her past you can tell us, that would help a lot. I'd appreciate any information you can give—anything."

Before leaving, Dan told Dr. Collins what Blaine told him about the past few years of her life, every detail he could recall to mind.

Dr. Collins' face showed concern, hearing all the difficult times Blaine had faced, with no real support, whether from her parents, siblings, or friends. These traumas and tragedies no doubt left their make upon her, thought Dr. Collins, and lead to a crisis point with the death of her second child, Jenny. There was a good chance Blaine's recovery might be hastened with the information Dan had given him. But predicting the length of time it would take to cure her remained to be seen.

12

Cry of the Child

As the new year of 1926 began, Dan seldom had time from work to return to his sick wife's side at the mental hospital. When he could get away to visit, Blaine continued to be completely lost in her own world, shutting him and everyone else out. He left the hospital despairing and broken-hearted.

Dr. Collins and the hospital staff worked with Blaine to help her recall and come to terms with the trauma she'd been through. The key hope she was constantly reminded of was that her loving husband Dan would soon return; that was a reason to get well, to continue her life.

Dr. Collins tried to convince her parents to visit their daughter more often. But every time they did get by, they found no response from Blaine. Mrs. Jergenson ended in tears while Mr. Jergenson left with the same words on his lips, "Olli, pull up your bootstraps."

Soon Dr. Collins asked the Jergensons not to come again until he called them, though he had asked them to consider allowing Blaine, when even moderately recovered, to go home with them for a short time where they might care for her. And the Jergensons had agreed to the doctor's recommendation. He was nonetheless a bit hesitant about this arrangement for Blaine's post-hospital care. He couldn't rely on Dan, given his work schedule and his distraught condition. Dr. Collins had become more and more concerned about Blaine. Everyday he searched for a key that would help bring her back to reality and the beginnings of mental health.

Winter turned to spring with no change in Blaine's condition.

But a strange quirk of fate was preparing to bring an about-face in Blaine's life.

It was Sunday. Blaine was seated in the dayroom near a sunny window. She sat unmoving, as usual, in her straight back chair.

Visiting hours brought guests and visitors. Family members of patients began arriving, filling the dayroom with a pleasant buzz of quiet conversation.

An older woman came into the room carrying a blanket-rapped infant. She was the child's grandmother, the child's mother being a patient. Knowing the hospital rule that no children under the age of twelve years were allowed in the visitor's room, the older woman had secreted her grandchild in by entering when the nurse was looking the other way.

The three, grandmother, mother and child, sat together in a corner. The younger woman was holding her baby when the child began to cry. As the baby's wail became more intense, in a lightning flash, the infant's cry pierced Blaine's mental shield. It crumbled the walls and broke the bars of the invisible cage in which Blaine had imprisoned herself. Gripping the seat of her chair, Blaine shook her head, turned it from side to side, looking for the source of the crying.

The attending nurse entered the room spying the illicit baby. She stalked toward the young patient, ready to ask the grandmother to take the baby and leave, then stopped when she saw Blaine slowly rise from her chair, turn and walk toward the crying infant. The nurse, being well familiar with Blaine's condition, stood very still, tracking Blaine's animated movements as she slowly approached the baby. Blaine bent over the young mother's shoulder where the baby lay crying in its mother's lap.

They all watched as Blaine gently reached down and touched

Cry of the Child

the downy soft head. She smiled and showed a desire to gently pick up the child.

The young mother didn't object. Both she and the grandmother, having noted Blaine's near-comatose condition, were in awe of the change they saw take place in Blaine.

Carefully rocking the baby in her arms, Blaine cooed softly to the child. Soon the child calmed down and stopped crying, finally sucking on its thumb, contented. Blaine stood holding the warm, sweet-smelling baby. Suddenly she looked around the room. The nurse came up to her, and quietly ask if she could hold the baby. Blaine carefully handed the baby to her. The nurse gave the baby back to its grandmother, and turned her attention to Blaine, who was standing with a puzzled look on her face.

"Nurse, where am I?" Blaine asked. "I don't recognize this place. Where is my husband...Dan Scarborough?"

The Nurse took Blaine by the arm, put her arm around the thin girl's waist, and asked her to come to the office with her. She assured Blaine that she was safe and everything was fine.

They went into a small office where Blaine sat in a soft chair. The nurse smiled to reassure Blaine, then went to the phone and asked the operator to connect her with Dr. Collins' home.

Within an hour Dr. Collins appeared at the office. Blaine recognized him, greeting him with the question. "Dr. Collins, could you tell me where I am?"

Dr. Collins was amazed, but answered in an even voice. "Blaine, you've spent some time here with us. You're in a hospital. You needed a good rest after Baby Jenny passed away, but I can see you are much better. Dan will be here soon. Your being better will make him happy, I can assure you that."

Out in the hallway the nurse quietly related to the doctor the happenings with the baby in the dayroom. Dr. Collins realized the key for which he'd searched to help Blaine recover was indeed an infant's cry of distress.

Later in the afternoon Dan rushed into the hospital and found

Second Son

Blaine sitting in a chair self-composed and calm. Before she turned to look at him, her posture and appearance told him that she was back from the dead, from the inner sanctum of her lost inner world.

Dan slowly walked to her, coming around her chair to stand in front of her. Without hesitation, Blaine stood holding out her arms. Tears of relief and joy rolled down her face. She had so many questions to ask. She wanted to know everything that had happened during her lapse of memory.

From that day forward Blaine held tight to reality and worked with Dr. Collins' prescribed regimen. She came to accept Jenny's death, began to plan for the future, hers and Dan's.

For his part, Dan was inwardly ecstatic with Blaine's recovery. But outwardly he showed restraint. Blaine didn't even notice Dan's caution, because she was so wrapped up in the fact that she had overcome her dark tragedy. She had climbed over the top of sorrow. She could cope with life, and she hope for tomorrow.

The time came for Dan to ship out again. He would be gone from late spring to mid-June. "I'll write as often as I am able, honey!" he assured Blaine. "Don't worry. The time will pass quickly!"

Blaine waited five days, then ten, for a letter from Dan. She heard nothing. She waited anxiously for his return. Days, then weeks went by. She questioned Dr. Collins to find if Dan had been in touch with him. But the doctor had heard nothing.

After almost three weeks, at Blaine's request, Dr. Collins phoned Walt at the cafe. Walt related to the doctor that Dan had come to the couple's rented room two weeks previous, just before setting sail. He boxed up all of his belongings, leaving Blaine's things behind, and told Walt he was leaving for good. Walt said the most surprising and upsetting part of it was that Dan had taken the baby's clothes, even the bassinet, and thrown them from the back deck into the bay. Then without another word, Dan had just walked away, not looking back.

Cry of the Child

Walt was sick at heart about Dan's actions, but hadn't told anyone because he couldn't understand the young man's behavior. He couldn't bring himself to think that Dan would not return at the end of his voyage, to start again his life with his beloved Blaine.

Dr. Collins was equally shocked, but never mentioned any of this information to Blaine. The doctor wanted to find and speak with Dan, if for no other reason than to ask about his change of attitude toward Blaine, especially now that she would be able to leave the hospital and return to her normal life. Dr. Collins was afraid of what another loss would do to Blaine if Dan had truly gone, never intending to return. If Dan deserted Blaine at this juncture, all her progress toward mental health might crumble.

The doctor thought Dan may be having his own crisis in a different form. He wasn't facing the loss the same way that Blaine had. Grief takes different forms—hiding, running, complete desertion from relationships—therefore avoiding the need to look grief in the face. Dan may have chosen what his livelihood easily provided, an escape. It gave him a place to hide. He could just walk away or sail away and leave all the hurt behind. Dr. Collins was afraid this was the path Dan had chosen. The doctor decided Blaine could wait to be told what he suspected to be true; at least until Dan's ship was schedule to come back into port.

After another week of no news from Dan, Dr. Collins wrote to Blaine's parents and asked them to come for her. She was ready to leave the hospital.

Dr. Collins promised Blaine that if Dan came to the hospital he would leave instructions to direct him to Blaine's parent's home.

❋

End of May, 1926.

The Jergensons arrived the next Monday. Their son Orin had driven them to the hospital. He showed no emotion nor concern for his younger sister.

Second Son

Blaine hadn't seen him since she'd left home. She remained quiet and distant, but thanked him for taking time to come and drive her home.

Ma hovered and fluffed like she always did when she was nervous. "Oh, Olli, I'm so glad to see you back to normal."

Ignoring her mother's insistence on calling her Olli, Blaine didn't really understand Ma's nervous concern. It seemed a bit out of character for her. If Ma had shown an inkling of caring a few years before, Blaine's life might have taken a different turn.

Blaine had decided when she left the hospital to resume her original identity as Olli, letting the family address her as they always had. For a time she had been safer using her middle name. She had become Blaine. This person had been her new identity. But in her mind, Blaine had not been her true self. She had been hiding—not only from a segment of her past that would always be a fragment of tissue torn from her heart, but she had hidden even from herself. She vowed to leave Blaine behind and let Olli move on. She told herself she would have to discuss this "identity thing" with Dan when he returned.

Blaine-Olli had become a stronger person, master of her emotions, able to carry the losses and able to make room for new gains. Olli left the mental hospital, erect and feeling a new confidence.

As the car pulled away from Tacoma and headed toward the Lynden Valley, Blaine—Olli!—felt the weight of the past few years lift from her shoulders.

Her eyes were busy taking in the sights that spring had playfully tossed along the roadsides. Marsh areas blossomed full of lush green skunk cabbage leaves growing in the ooze of the swamps. She noticed the wild red flowering quince bushes, fluffing their lacy red flowered dresses where they stood beside the roadside pussy willow bushes. Gray willow kittens clung tightly to every twig of the pussy willow branches.

As the journey neared its end, the familiar sights of the valley brought back to Olli—she was Olli now—a combination of feelings. She was happy knowing contented cows browsed along the fences. She shook with a quiet joy as the car rumbled past old farms, the quick flash of flocks of small meadow birds rising from roadside fences.

The lane that led from the valley road to the rundown house had not changed. It was still rutted and edged with last year's matted grass. The house remained the same as if frozen in time past. The emotion that welled within surprised her. The soft sigh from her lips slipped out in both awed remembrances and shadowy misgivings. She swallowed hard to keep salty tears from filling her eyes. The tears squeezed themselves from hidden places.

When the car came to a halt—the porch of the house immediately filled with the youngest Jergenson sisters, Eva and Sal, along with Olli's two nieces, Elise and Bernadine. They climbed and clambered over each other, half a dozen cats and a few porch dogs. The noise was a mix of happy greetings, cats meowing, dogs barking and Papa's booming voice demanding quiet. Ma began her busy clucking, like an old bantam chicken trying to organize a brood of turkeys.

Olli hugged each family member while trying to answer multitudes of questions thrown at her from every direction. "Yes, she was staying a while. No, she wasn't sick anymore. Yes, she was happy to see them and of course she'd noticed how they had all grown."

Her homecoming was a much more exalted affair than her departure had been four years before.

That afternoon the family enjoyed a simple meal together. The table, devoid of luxury, wafted full of warm conversation—and a feeling of home. Strangely, maybe more feeling of home then she had ever felt before, even as a child.

After dinner, the muddled routine mixed with voices and filled the small house. It was as though Olli had stepped out of the room a minute to return and find everything the same despite the passing of years.

She learned that one more brother, Kyle and her younger sister Niva, had left home in the same manner as she. They had

Second Son

remained in the valley choosing part-time employment and seasonal work to stay close to the family. Ma said they still stopped by regularly.

Olli was given the same bed she had occupied years before. It still had the handmade crazy quilt that Ma had sewn so long ago. Olli smoothed her hand over the colorful, rough fabric in a manner that said a familiar "hello" to an old acquaintance.

She unpacked her meager belongings, wishing she had her nice things that were still in her and Dan's room in Tacoma. Dan was on her mind constantly. Once in a while, when some specific thought of him crossed her consciousness, she would pause momentarily, puzzled at his absence. Confused at his silence. Old anguish and questions about his whereabouts and his unexplained reasons for leaving came tumbling down around her like children's wooden blocks, leaving her mind and soul feeling bruised.

Ma asked Olli to go for a walk with her down by the river. Olli threw an old sweater over her shoulders as she stepped into the cool spring air of early evening. Two of the young nieces started out following Ma and Olli, but Ma told them she needed to talk to Olli alone, and sent the gangly-legged youngsters back to the house.

Olli had a feeling the walk was two-fold in purpose. A pleasant walk. And, Ma had something serious to discuss. Olli didn't know if she was really ready for anymore stressful news, but Ma never did read people close enough to ascertain underlying feelings. To Ma everything was an open book, even if opening the book was painful.

Ma was in her cotton house dress and apron. Olli tightly hugged the old sweater around her shoulders as she strolled toward the riverbank in the wet spring grass. The ground was saturated from an earlier rain shower. Dandelions edged the field and riverbank, their yellow flowers were closing for the night.

Ma stopped at the river's edge and sat on the roots of the huge cedar stump that years ago had lodged itself in the riverbank. For years this spot had been Olli's refuge from the tiny storms in her

Cry of the Child

growing-up years. She felt at ease when she climbed up the gray weathered root mass where she found her favorite seat.

Olli could see Ma was having a hard time beginning the conversation. She nervously wrung her hands, staring over the dark glassy surface of the river.

Olli reached over and gently touched Ma's shoulder. She waited a moment then spoke. "Ma, I know this whole thing has been hard for you and Papa, but it's been difficult for me, too. You know a few things that have happened to me, but you don't know all of it. Right now I'm not ready to talk about everything."

Ma took Olli's hand off her shoulder and placed it on her cheek. Olli could feel the tears.

Ma replied, "Olli, we know about your baby girl 'cause me and Papa saw to it she had a Christian burial. She's down in the little valley cemetery about two miles from here. The same place as your sister Rose. Papa will never go with us, 'cause he figured Dan done you wrong by leaving without a fare-thee-well. Papa also thought Dan should have helped pay to bury that baby, so he won't even talk about it. I'll go with you to the cemetery when you're ready, 'cause I want you to see where part of your flesh 'an blood is laid."

Squeezing Ma's hand she said, "Ma I appreciate you and Papa taking care of things the way you did. I wasn't able at the time, but I'm better now, and I want you to know I'll repay Papa from my savings. If he has bad feelings about Dan I can't help that. I, too, have a heavy heart about Dan. I still love him as much as life itself," she choked back the tears, "and I thought he loved me and Jenny. But I didn't have a chance to talk to him much while I was in the hospital. After the first day, he came to see me so few times and for such short visits he never really gave me a chance to tell him how it all happened. I guess I was unresponsive for quite awhile also."

Olli paused, shifted her seating so she could look out over the river. She glanced back at Ma, then continued. "I guess he couldn't face me. He probably thinks if Jenny got the measles

Second Son

from me that it's my fault she died. But, Ma, I was so sick myself and so tired. I guess he'll have to work it out in his own way. If he comes back I'll take him back in a flash, but if he never comes back, I'll accept that, too. You see, Ma, I've grown up a lot."

The older woman nodded her head, seeming to agree with or at least accept everything Olli told her.

Olli added softly, "Give me a few days. One warm afternoon you and I will walk up to the cemetery. I'd like to see where my Jenny is laid to rest."

Ma rose from where she'd been seated on the cedar root. She said, "Olli, I'm not going to pussy-foot around because I know you're a woman full grown, and you can take the other news I have to tell you."

Olli drew in a deep breath. She knew there was more than one thing on Ma's mind.

Ma stated flatly, "Your Dan has moved to the East coast. Dan's working out of New York City. He works on ships that go to Europe. He won't ever be back."

Startled, Olli looked at Ma, knowing what she'd said must be true. She asked, "Ma, how do you know this?"

Ma lifted her head sadly, then defiantly. "I told Papa not to open the letter. It came last week. I told him it was your business, but he said it was from an eastern law firm, and he had to know what it was." Ma continued, "Pa said Dan hired this lawyer and he's sent papers for you to sign. He wants a divorce. He claims you're mentally unstable and an unfit mother, because you didn't take good care of Jenny—so she died."

For a flashing moment Olli saw gray fog form around her. She sat stone cold and still, then brushed her hand over her eyes. Things were clear and in focus again. Ma's head was bent, and Olli saw tears in her eyes.

She said, "Ma, in my heart I knew he'd never forgive me. In my gut I knew his going without saying goodbye meant he'd gone for good. The sad part is he left never caring that I was getting well."

Olli sat up straight, confident of her feelings. There were no unanswered questions left. Her face softened into a slight smile. "Dan has made his decision. He'll have to live with it. I'll sign the papers if you'll have Papa mail them for me."

Ma held Olli's hand a second longer, and said, "Papa will be glad to do that for you, Olli Girl."

Olli asked Ma to leave her with her thoughts for a while. She promised to come up to the house before dark.

Ma agreed, turned and trudged up the field toward the house, leaving Olli perched on her childhood castle of tree roots and staring at the dark river.

In this quiet environment Olli took a close look at her life, comparing it to a many-faceted stone. She now had the ability to turn the stone so it would only show the dark side, or turn it in a direction that would catch the light and flash brightness and color on every faceted surface, making it shine. She determined that every time she faced a problem, from then on, she would be wiser, and she would become a more valuable person because she was now able to shine.

Olli was thankful for her new found ability to accept life in the manner dealt her. And she knew Papa, in his old way, would tell her he was glad she had pulled herself up by the bootstraps.

13

By Her Bootstraps!

June 1926.

For the next three weeks Olli enjoyed having her two younger sisters, Eva and Sal, follow her around the house each day after they'd come home from school. It made Olli happy to have their good-natured chatter filling the corners of the rooms.

Since she'd been gone from home, her nieces, Elise and Bernadine, had grown from toddlers into elementary school aged children.

Ma seemed to enjoy having Olli puttering around the house. Ma was relaxed more than in the years before when the house had burst with her ten offspring and two nieces. The numbers had lessened to five which put Ma more at ease. Conversation grew easier between Olli and Ma. A comfortable kinship of mother and daughter sprung up between them as each learned day by day more of the other's sorrows and joys.

Olli realized Papa was no longer the stabilizing factor in the family. He may have laid down the law in years past, but his wandering eye and sporadic work pattern had kept neighbor women either flirting or gossiping, and as usual he barely kept the family table supplied with basic necessities.

Ma never complained to Olli, but the stiff stance of her tiny frame, her firmly set jaw and a quickly raised eyebrow at appropriate times exuded the authority needed to keep Papa from making roaring inflexible restrictions on the family, as he had done in the past. Olli could see all was not roses and buttercups between her parents, but she overlooked the uneasy static because she was so happy they had allowed her to return home to recuperate.

Olli felt stronger each day. She knew this was a springboard to health for her. A time that was readying her to go another step up the staircase of life that rose before her.

The month of June showed itself in the rose bed and fields, as well as on the pages of the calendar.

Olli became restless with only the rhythm of the family around her. She knew the time was right. She must look for a job. She needed to replace the savings she had used to pay her folks for Jenny's funeral expenses. No money had ever come from Dan, nor would Olli ever receive anything more from him than the divorce papers that had just arrived from Dan's lawyer. The State of New York hadn't denied Dan. What he wanted was Freedom. Her illness which in the end hand not broken her had nonetheless, somehow, broken Dan's love for her.

Olli scanned the Tacoma newspaper—Papa's one monetary extravagance. She was hoping to find a job close by, so she could keep in touch with the family. She answered a few ads only to find they were for part-time employment. She knew if she was going to better herself she needed a full-time position.

There was a job listed for a hotel maid and waitress at a mountain lodge near Mount St. Helens in the southern part of the state. This appealed to her for two reasons. First, she wouldn't need to buy an automobile. She didn't even know how to drive. Second, the job included room and board because the lodge's mountainous location was too far for a daily commute.

Ollie walked two miles to the local valley store and phoned the lodge. When she talked to the manager he wanted her to come for an interview the next day. She thanked him and said she'd be there. She knew the bus trip would take four or five hours, with the combination of slow buses, miles involved and unpaved roads leading from the main highway up to the lodge.

At dinner that evening, Olli told Ma and Papa she was leaving the next morning to see about a job. There was little response, dinner was quiet. The younger girls, her two nieces, and Olli's youngest brother Orin hated to see Olli leave just when they had begun to know her again. Olli realized family ties had been reconnected. Yet she also knew it was time to let go and move on.

Olli excused herself from the table, went out on the porch and sat down on the steps. The family, one at a time, joined her and they talked of everyday things until the curtain of sleep hung heavy around them. It eased everyone from the porch and into their beds.

Soon the family was asleep, yet Olli remained restless. Morning couldn't come fast enough for her. She lay in bed hearing the even breathing of those sleeping around her. Olli suspected it would be the last time she would sleep under the same roof with her family. Her mind raced in a jumble of thoughts until she felt sleep would never come. Nonetheless, finally sleep snuck in upon her, leaving her three hours to rest before waking and readying herself for her long bus trip.

Olli sat with her mother, drinking a cup of coffee. Ma insisted Olli tuck a sandwich into her suitcase. Knowing the trip would be a few hours in duration, Olli was obliged to accept Ma's gesture of concern.

The younger children were still asleep when Olli left the house to catch the early bus. Olli was surprised to see that Jim Porter was no longer driving the valley route. The bus soon arrived at the main depot in Seattle where Olli transferred to one heading south to Portland.

It was about three hours to Castle Rock. From there she would transfer to the tour bus that took vacationers up the rutted, dirt road which led to the Mountain View Travel and Hunters Lodge.

After Olli had boarded the lodge bus she sat as quietly as she could. The primitive conditions of the road caused the small bus to rattle and bump through mud, mire and rocky sections of the road. This made it difficult for Olli to maintain her seat as she slipped and slid on the smooth leather.

Second Son

Two other couples were making the trip up to the lodge. The driver told them that most passengers took the earlier bus so they would have time for hiking or horseback riding before the late bus returned them to the highway junction at Castle Rock.

The closer the bus got to the lodge, the more Olli was amazed by the beauty of the surrounding country. One of the women assured her she would love the old lodge. She and her husband were familiar with all parts of the area, it being their favorite vacation spot.

The weather was quite warm, but there was evidence of an earlier rain shower. The water in roadside ditches ran in muddy rivulets. Alder and maple trees formed a green tunnel over long stretches of the road, filtering sunny warm patches with dappled coolness from the overhead arch.

The road followed the Toutle River from the highway junction to the lodge. There, a more primitive road continued up the mountain to the river's source, Spirit Lake, which nestled at the base of the majestic cone of Mount St. Helens. The Mountain View Travel and Hunters Lodge perched on a rocky vista overlooking the crystal clear river.

The panorama, including the mountain, foothills of the Cascades, river, lodge were as Olli had pictured them in her mind, only the real wonders were on a scale Olli could not have imagined. The lodge was a huge log structure with gray river stones around the base and up the full height of one end of the building ending above the roof in a massive stone chimney. A wide covered veranda surrounded three sides of the main building. River stone formed porch pillars giving a feeling of permanence and rugged grandeur. Vacation cottages were scattered amid huge hemlock and fir trees a short distance from the main lodge.

Olli picked up her meager luggage and made her way toward the office door. She took a deep breath, then stepped inside with new confidence.

14
The Lodge

The place first impressed her with a mixture of odors, varnished wood and wax, the smell of warm cinnamon buns baking in the kitchen, scents of pine and fir following her inside. As Olli entered the office, the manager appeared and asked if he could help her. Olli introduced herself.

The manager introduced himself as Mr. Fred MacGruder, and asked Olli to sit down. The interview was short. Mr. MacGruder asked very few questions, seeming to have convinced himself by Olli's attitude that the slender-figured young woman was capable of the job. He gave her a short tour of the facilities, upstairs rooms, dining room, kitchen, then explained that she would of also care for the cabins.

Returning to the office, Mr. MacGruder said, "Olli, if you think you can handle both the housekeeping and the dining room, you're hired. I may have to hire more help later in the season."

"It should be no problem to coordinate room care duties with the dining room hours," Ollie replied. "I'm available to begin work this afternoon if that suites you."

Olli was shown her living space—a cozy room behind the kitchen. There she stowed her luggage. A dark green uniform hung in her room. It looked a bit too large but after she put it on she tucked it around the waist and went to the kitchen.

Olli talked a while with the cook, who was very happy to find that she had worked as a waitress before. Studying a menu, she asked about the table setup. She didn't want to get confused during peak serving time, which was between five and eight P.M. During the summer season breakfast was served at eight A.M., but during hunting seasons breakfast started at five A.M. Olli was told the hunters from Portland liked to get up and going before sunrise.

The cook clearly enjoyed chatting, but Olli soon excused herself, giving the cook a warm smile. In the office she asked Mr. MacGruder if any upstairs rooms needed her attention.

"No, that's fine, Olli," he replied looking up from his work. "Mrs. MacGruder took care of them earlier today."

Olli turned to leave when Mrs. MacGruder entered the office. She had a happy face. Round as the moon and pink as a rose.

Mr. MacGruder paused from his bookkeeping and introduced his wife. "Ah, here she is now. Olli, this is my wife, Gabriella. Gabby, this is the young woman I hired for the housekeeping and dining room job, Olli Scarborough."

Gabby smiled as she shook hands with Olli. "Glad to meet you Olli. I hope you won't find this place too lonely, or the work too demanding. The girl that worked here before didn't mind the job, but she grew to hate the solitude up here. I hope you'll stay with us for a while."

Smiling, Olli assured Gabby, "I enjoy hard work. And the natural beauty here in the mountains, it is just wonderful!" She excused herself and left the office for her room.

Olli was so happy about everything, she had completely forgotten to ask about wages, pay days and days off. She didn't care—she felt good about the place and herself. She was at peace. There were two hours to spend before the dining room opened for the evening meal, so she decided to explore a bit. Wandering behind the lodge, she walked the short trail to the river. There a hint of moisture combined with the smell of moss drifted from the thick-forested lands across the river.

Olli sat on a smooth gray boulder and looked into the clear, icy water. Lazy speckled trout moved from the riffles to a deep

The Lodge

pool, flashing silver in the sun's rays. Overhanging branches of fir, cedar and hemlock edged the far side of the river—a scene worthy of a painter's canvas.

From her spot by the river, Olli took in the impressive blue cone of Mount St. Helens, the crisp azure sky, and the thickly wooded foothills of the Cascade Mountains. As her vision spanned the huge panorama before her she was convinced she had found the perfect place for a new beginning. She heard voices coming closer as a group of weary hikers returned to the lodge from an afternoon trek along the rugged trails which knitted through the nearby foothills.

Olli left the river bank, hurrying to the kitchen, knowing the dining room would soon be filled with tour bus passengers, hikers, and other adventurous individuals.

As summer lazed into July, it took only a short time for Olli to adjust to the daily work routine. She found there was little time for leisure. As the days passed the tourist crowds increased. With the seasonal boom in full swing the work load was also more demanding.

The weather continued warm and clear. The unpaved road that led to the lodge and continued up the foothills toward Mount St. Helens became a continual cloud of fine gray pumice which settled over every tree branch, fern, window ledge and porch step. Dust was tracked into the lodge and cabins. Olli took the dust as an affront to her neatly-kept rooms and waged a daily war, removing the gritty substance from everything. And by the time the dining room filled with people demanding her full attention, Olli was exhausted.

Gabby MacGruder busied herself helping with the housekeeping chores when she could, knowing that the increased number of guests was an unexpected boon to the business. But she could see Olli would never complain even when swamped with work.

One day Gabby came into one of the cabins where Olli was plumping the last pillow on the bed. She plunked her pumpkin-shaped body down onto a chair where she sat puffing because of the heat. "I'll be glad," she said, "when this weather cools. Even here by the river it gets pretty unbearable doesn't it? I don't see how these foolish people can stand to hike the trails or ride those blamed horses all over the mountainsides in this heat. I wish it would rain real hard for a day or two."

Olli smiled as she began the inevitable wipe down of tables, window ledges and floor.

Gabby noticed how methodically and efficiently Olli completed each cabin in succession but knew Olli would have no time to rest before she went to the lodge for the noontime meal. Another tour bus was due soon, and the guests would want dining room service before they left for the last hike to the waterfall up river.

Polished wood flooring reflected sunlight filtering through side windows of the dining hall. A rustic glow invited travelers into a comfortable room where they could enjoy their meal in an atmosphere of leisure.

Gabby followed Olli into the kitchen. The good-natured older woman knew the two jobs were becoming too much for one person.

Olli was the best help the MacGruders had ever had. But the load of summer traffic to the mountain had become more than expected, especially due to the modern trend of people driving their own autos on trips instead of taking tour buses.

Gabby knew how busy they would be in late September when the added traffic of hunters began their yearly invasion of the lodge area. The reservation book for the lodge was full, including trail campsites. At least one more fulltime person was needed—Olli simply couldn't handle it alone, though she worked valiantly and never complained.

Fred MacGruder hugged his round rosy wife when she entered the office.

Gabby plunked down in a chair, wiping the perspiration from her brow. "Boy oh boy!" she sighed. "It has really turned hot out

The Lodge

there today. Olli is running in tight circles to get everything done. I'll say this, she is the most efficient little thing for her size. But I know by the time the hunters flock in here she won't be able to handle all the work. I've been puttering a bit to help her, but Fred, we've got to hire another girl."

Fred, being on the conservative side, shrugged, saying, "She'll be fine. Don't worry so much. Olli's a smart girl. She can handle the job."

Knowing her husband's priorities, Gabby replied, "Yes, I know Olli is very capable. But I wouldn't want badmouth advertising to spread that we are understaffed. Or that our regular customers feel the service isn't up to the standards they expect when they come here, come here to spend precious time and good money, all because we refuse to hire more needed help."

Fred glanced up from his bookkeeping, put his chin in his hand, thinking about Gabby's last statement. After a minute he admitted, "You're right Hon. We've always had the best service of any of the local lodges, plus we are twice as busy already this year. I'll look into hiring more help."

After the evening rush finished, Olli was arranging chairs in the dining room when Gabby entered to help wipe tables and put on clean tablecloths in preparations for the morning meal. When they were finished, Gabby seated herself at a table by the windows overlooking the river. With a gesture she indicated Olli come and sit beside her, which Olli did happily. Olli leaned back in the chair, exhausted, smiled and closed her eyes letting a soft sigh escape her lips.

Both women relaxed in silence, feeling new friendship and the satisfaction of another day's work well done.

The sun had gone down leaving a rosy purple aura round the mountain top. The rich color reflected from the river's surface making the water appear a purple satin ribbon flung among the granite boulders. The same color eased into the lodge, spreading the fading mauve light gently across the polished dining room floor.

The chairs had been handmade by a craftsman who had formed them from small peeled, varnished tree branches. The tables were of the same material and design. Crisp white table linen accentuated the polished tables. Olli smiled at the peacefulness she felt when she was in the room. The huge peeled log beams arching over the dining room's expanse were upheld by log pillars which supported the second story of the lodge, as well as the stairway and a half dozen rooms off the open balcony.

The stairway treads were eight foot logs which had been sawn in half lengthwise, rounded side down, making an impressive rustic staircase.

At the far end of the building a massive river stone fireplace covered the entire end wall of the lodge and extended upward past the balcony to the roof.

After a short time, Olli smiled warmly at Gabby. "This is the best part of the day."

Feeling comfortable with Olli, Gabby returned the smile. "Yes, it is as peaceful here this time of evening as anyplace I've ever known." Gabby replied.

A moments later the older woman got out of her chair, and with her stout little duck-like waddle went to the sideboard and poured two steaming cups of coffee. She brought the cups back to the table giving one to Olli, then unceremoniously plunked herself back down. After a few sips of coffee, she said, "Olli, Fred and I are really pleased with you and the work you're doing here, but we feel that the rest of the summer will be busier than usual, so Fred is hiring another girl to help out, at least through the hunting season. She will work along with you, but you'll be responsible for assigning her to work where you feel she'll be the most help."

"Thank you," said Olli, pleased at this news. But she confessed, "I'm not sure I'm very comfortable telling people what to do. I don't know if I'll be very good at giving orders."

The Lodge

Gabby said. "We feel you're the best person to detail the work, because you know the routine. It will make your paycheck bigger, added responsibility should be rewarded. So, if this is agreeable to you, we'll hire the new girl next week, and you'll have time to train her before late summer and the rush of hunters this fall."

Olli agreed to the idea, being especially happy to hear she would get a raise after working on the job just over a month. On her way out of the dining room, she cleared the table of coffee cups then went to her own room. She closed the bedroom door and quickly eased off her shoes, removed her clothes, and ran a tub of warm water for her evening bath. She was so happy that the MacGruders appreciated the efforts she'd put forth since she'd come to the lodge. Whoever the new worker turned out to be, the help and companionship would be greatly appreciated.

Olli had been thinking lately that one thing she had never had, outside of her immediate family, was a woman to be her friend, to share little odds and ends of chatter at the end of the workday. Of course there had been Dweena and Araminta, but they seldom wrote to her anymore. She felt their paths would likely never cross again. She anticipated finding a friend her own age.

The next week was the last week of July. Olli couldn't believe that summer weather could be so cold, windy and rainy.

The heat everyone had enjoyed the proceeding week disappeared. In a few short days the roadway became a quagmire. The tourist bus arrivals and personal autos filled with mountain enthusiasts, dwindled to a few vacationers who had made previous reservations and decided to endure the bad weather. They stayed in the lodge playing table games, billiards and swapping hunting and fishing tales.

Olli loved to walk in the rain and did so in her free time. She loved the sound of it. She loved the earthy smell of the forest when the moss was soaked and the river rumbled white with foam and pumice silt. As she wandered the trails near the lodge—rain pelted her legs and rattled the top of her red umbrella.

Second Son

    Returning from a short morning walk one day, Olli noticed the Wednesday tour bus arriving at the front of the lodge. Only three passengers emerged: two older ladies dressed in heavy hiking togs, both carrying rain gear; the third passenger, a tall young woman with jet black hair wound in a long braid that hung nearly to her waist. This distinguished young woman walked with a firm, arrogant stride directly to the office.
    Olli went quickly to her room and changed out of her rain spotted clothes into a clean dry uniform. She brushed her hair carefully and went to the dining room to help Tommy, the cook, prepare for the evening meal. Even though the group was small, due to the rainy weather, Olli knew the dinner guests would linger far beyond staff quitting time—which was the way things went when the guestrooms weren't fully booked.
    Olli was about to stop and chat with Tommy, when Fred and Gabby came into the dining room followed by the stately young woman Olli had seen get off the bus earlier that afternoon.
    Fred announced, "Olli, this is sheriff sheriff. Lena, Olli."
    Olli smiled and shook Lena's slim, firm hand. "Hi! I'm Olli Scarbrough. I'm very happy you're here."
    Lena appeared to be nervous, replying with a barely audible "Hello."
    Fred and Gabby left the dining room to give Lena a quick tour of the lodge. A short while later the three returned, and Gabby asked Olli, "Would you please show Lena her duties, Olli?"
    The evening went surprisingly well. Lena was a quick learner. The only thing that troubled Olli was Lena's approach to the customers. She kept her face and her eyes cast down, never looking anyone in the eye, giving scant response to their friendly conversation toward her.
    After the room had emptied out and the cleanup finished for the night, Gabby came in, poured three cups of coffee, and sat down in the quiet, darkened room with the two younger women to chat over the events of Lena's first night at work and inquiring of Lena how she felt things had gone her first evening.

The Lodge

Olli offered a quick reply. "Oh! Gabby, things went much better tonight. Lena learned quickly and will be a great help."

Lena shifted in her chair, still shy and quiet, but clearly pleased with the praise from Olli.

The conversation eased into a well-played question and answer game with Gabby as the leader. Early in the conversation, Gabby and Olli learned that Lena was from a regional Indian tribe, though Lena gave little detail and said little of what that meant.

Lena was aware that Gabby was trying to get her to open up and talk and feel at ease, but it seemed difficult for her to open up to the other women. She admitted that as a child she hadn't been expected to engage in women's conversation, or express her own opinion on anything. Her mother and grandmother had taken care of any talk with other women, as was her family custom. In her home, young women, until they were married, remained silent helpers. Mothers or grandmothers held the place of importance in the care of the home in Lena's Indian family. But only the sketchiest of her family life was expressed to Gabby and Olli.

Gabby asked. "Where are your folks, dear, and what town are you from? I don't believe Fred asked that during your interview."

Lena's gaze instantly became cold and distant. "I'm from Eastern Washington," she flatly stated, hoping a curt answer would let the two women know she didn't like being questioned. She made no other comment. She felt as long as she did her job it was none of their business where she had come from; nor the circumstances that had brought her to this job.

Olli asked, "Did you live on a farm or in a town?"

Not answering, Lena quickly rose from her chair, took her coffee cup and walked into the kitchen. She left without even a "Goodnight."

Olli and Gabby glanced at each other. Gabby shrugged her shoulders, turned to Olli and asked. "What did we say? She is very touchy. I guess we should leave well enough alone and just talk to her about her work until whatever is bothering her passes."

Olli agreed that might be the best policy for the present.

15

The Lodge, Part Two

From that day, work went routinely.

Olli, in her gentle way, tried many times to talk to Lena about trivial things beyond the boundary of work. But, more and more, Lena closed within herself, becoming sullen and distant. Being around Lena gave Olli the feeling of having a pebble in your shoe that wore a sore spot with every step you took.

Lena's work was excellent. She was clean, neat and efficient, but never assumed more than she was directed to do, never asked favors or time off, yet she refused to communicate. Eventually she didn't even exchange small cordialities with dining room customers.

During the summer tourist rush Olli had looked forward to the added help, but she had anticipated having a friend her own age to confide in, laugh and chum around with. But Lena didn't make herself available to closeness of that sort.

Olli didn't understand Lena's attitude. Lena was reluctant to talk of her family or anything she had done before coming to work at the lodge. Olli couldn't distinguish if the girl's sullen attitude came from shyness, a feeling of shame, unworthiness, or haughty pride. And how to respond to Lena's peculiar attitude became a burden to Olli.

Olli would have loved to have had Lena's good looks, tall and stately with a beautiful figure and a warm gentle face. Olli was short, thin, flaxen haired, and she thought herself quite plain.

Second Son

Lena seemed unaware of her own graceful movements, and regal appearance. The strange woman remained completely enclosed in her own uninvolved world.

Many of the local customers noticed the two girls' opposite appearances and attitudes. Olli, because of her open friendly manner, was by far the favored. Lena, lovely though she was, approached the customers with lowered eyes. A dark aura, like a heavy blanket, hung about her shoulders and dampened the atmosphere when she was in the dining room.

Fred and Gabby noticed Lena's attitude, so Fred decided to have a talk with the girl, to see what caused her sullen behavior. Therefore, one afternoon before the dining room opened, Fred called Lena into his office. He and Gabby were intent on finding out if they could help her in some way, or at least better understand what was bothering her.

Fred sat in his usual spot at his desk. Gabby lounged in a chair across from the office door, to one side of Fred. Lena sat stiffly in the chair across the desk from Fred.

Fred picked up his fountain pen, set it down, leaned back in his chair. "Lena, if working with the customers in the dining room is hard for you, makes you depressed somehow, short tempered or irritable—well, you know we can't have our costumers uncomfortable." He thought a moment, continued. "That can hurt business, you know. Lena, is there something we can help you with?"

Lena was in the office for over an hour. When she came out, Olli noticed her step was more sure and graceful, her stride showed a marked uplift of pride. Her face held the faint hint of a smile, which was something Olli had not seen before.

Lena entered the dining room, came to the service area, took the menus to the hostess area, and started walking back to where Olli was wiping tables. She started to say something, but was interrupted when the door opened and some local customers came in waiting to be seated.

Three of the regulars were the Brauer brothers. They were

The Lodge, Part Two

laughing and playfully slapping each other's shoulders, raising a small ruckus as they waved and boisterously, called "Hello" to Olli and Lena.

With a broad smile on her face, Lena took the menus, and showed the three happy-go-lucky brothers to a booth by the windows.

Olli was so surprised at the change in Lena's demeanor, she nearly dropped the coffee pot.

The three brothers instantly commented on Lena's smile. Their comment brought another broad smile from Lena, while she took their dinner orders.

Olli wondered at the remarkable outward change that had come over Lena. She decided to talk to her after work to see what had brought on the metamorphic emergence of the charmer Olli had just seen working her wiles on the vulnerable Brauers brothers.

The brothers lived miles from the lodge, but had been making their appearance at dinner time every Friday for the past few months, so by now she knew them on a first name basis.

Whenever Lena came near Ben, the red haired, younger brother, his eyes followed Lena with the look of someone smitten. The smile on Lena's face had made his face light up like a beacon, and it also seemed to have rendered him speechless. Olli was surprised and continued to wonder about the change in Lena's behavior.

Fred and Gabby smiled as they stood observing the results of their earlier talk with Lena.

Olli wondered what magic had been wrought by her employers when they had talked to Lena in the office. Whatever had transpired, Lena was better for it, and for that Olli was grateful.

That evening the three Brauer brothers, Ben, Cole and John spent a long time in the dining room dawdling, and casting more than a few glances at Lena and Olli.

As the two older brothers headed out, Ben lingered little awhile longer, quietly talking to Lena. Olli smiled to herself knowing the good natured, red haired, younger brother would be back soon, because anyone could see he was interested in more than the Friday night meal at the lodge. Olli hadn't notice one of the brothers had furtively glanced at her all evening, as he'd been doing for many Fridays. Olli hadn't noticed, because Cole was the quiet one of the three.

After closing time Olli casually said to Lena, trying to make conversation, "I noticed you have a red-haired admirer."

But Lena smiled politely and told Olli to mind her own business.

It appears, thought Olli, that Lena's dramatic change in behavior was for on-the-job only. She would do what was expected of her by her employers, but once off work, she was the same Lena, closed, aloof, a loner.

Having the feeling of being well told off and not understanding Lena's double personality, Olli said goodnight and went down the hall to her room. After bathing and brushing her hair, she tried to forget the disappointment she felt about Lena. She took out her stationery and finished her lonely evening writing long overdue letters to Ma, Papa and her young niece Elise. She wrote her annual notes to Dweena in Tacoma, and Araminta who was still working on Whidbey Island. She seldom wrote to them anymore. But she felt lonely and wanted to keep in touch with the past, at least the better parts of it.

16

Fire

Olli slept uneasily and woke in the morning with a feeling of foreboding, which to her seemed strange, because she usually had a positive outlook and a happy attitude starting each new day. But for some reason she dressed in a hurry and made her way to the kitchen to start the coffee pot. Sipping the first cup, she gazed out of the dining room's side windows, watch the sunrise touch the tops of the trees. The river and cabins behind the lodge were splashed with a soft golden glow.

The sun, for August, seemed to be struggling through a heavy haze settling over the hills and canyon areas near the mountain. The usual blue cone of Mount St. Helens was lost in the oppressive denseness of the ever-increasing haze. Soon the sun was no longer visible. The heavy black haze increased.

On the other side of the river a breeze began to whisper through the cedar and fir trees. When the air began to move down the valley from the mountain, Olli became aware of a smell that frightened her. She smelled smoke! Not the sweet wisps from the lodge fireplace, but caustic, acrid, pitch-filled billows that began to filter into the yard and the lodge.

Tom, the cook, came into the kitchen, and in an anxious tone of voice announced, "It must be the logging camps southeast of the mountain. They must be burning slashing."

(Slashing was debris from cleaning up after recent logging activities.)

Second Son

Fred, Gabby and Lena appeared from different directions, all with anxious looks on their faces.

Olli knew such a heavy concentration of smoke was not likely the result of slash burning. With a questioning glance she looked at Fred and Gabby, then Lena. Olli forced a smile, and commenced to pour each a cup of fresh hot coffee.

"I called the logging company," said Fred. "Asked them about all the smoke. They told me there were no fires connected to any logging operation in the area." Fred also said he'd called the sheriff. "Asked him. He said there were reports of game-poachers camping on the East slope of Mount St. Helens, and apparently they'd left an unattended campfire resulting in a small forest fire in the foothills. An easterly wind's pushing the fire down a canyon approximately twenty miles from the here. He assured me there should be no reason to worry about the lodge unless the wind changes."

Within a few minutes, the lodge doors flew opened and the sheriff and two deputies burst noisily into the lobby calling for Fred.

"What?" exclaimed Fred, as they all gathered around the coffee service, pouring coffee into mugs.

"We have a situation, Fred," began the sheriff. We're going to need your lodge—as a base camp from which the firefighting crews can work—just until they have things under control."

"I understand," said Fred tentatively. "We'll do what we can for support. I'll assign our staff in shifts to work the kitchen, dining room and cabin maintenance during the emergency."

The sheriff looked relieved. "You know we appreciate this, Fred, Gabby."

In the afternoon forty to fifty firefighters unloaded firefighting equipment from trucks and buses in the lodge parking lot.

Local loggers, concerned farmers and unemployed men, finding not only an opportunity to help, but a chance to earn a few dollars, added to the busy confusion in the surrounding area.

Fire

One of the trucks parked in the lot belonged to Cole Brauer. He and four of his brothers arrived ready to do what was needed.

They unloaded supplies consisting of axes, saws, picks and bed rolls.

The five Brauer men were very much aware of the potential danger to fire fighters, and to the surrounding forest from which they made their living as loggers and florist evergreen suppliers. They were also concerned about the lodge, its owners and staff.

Cole also could not hid his anxiousness for his brother Ben whom everyone knew was smitten with dark-eyed, mysterious Lena. Neither had Cole hidden his keen interest in a certain vivacious young lady whose earlier glances had sparked a warm, unquenchable glow inside him—again a fact unhidden to no one. Cole chose many ways to be around Olli without being obvious, even though he had barely spoken a word directly to her.

Olli, too, had become aware of the tall quiet blond, Cole Brauer. She noticed his blue eyes following her as she went about her busy routine in the dining room.

Having just be assigned her support duties by Fred, Olli felt a blush heat her cheek when she saw Cole's truck parked in front of the lodge; not wanting to admit his appearance at a time of possible danger warmed her heart and fired her emotions with feelings she'd not had for quite some time.

Evening came with an increase of wind that filled the air with acrid smoke. The sky darkened to inky black, but for an orange glow that grew brighter behind Mount St. Helens. The glow transformed the cone-shaped mountain into intricate silhouetted rock ridges where individual trees were outlined by the ominous vermilion reflection from the forest fire. The fire was raging and devouring the timberline terrain beyond the majestic mountain.

Fire crews made their way over the lower foothill ridges and cut a fire break in the underbrush as they edged their way uphill toward the flames. This was an attempt to retard the incessantly creeping, low growth fire. A hungry roaring menace, that when touched by an up draft wind, flared into the upper limbs of the ancient hemlock, fir and cedar trees, and making it impossible to control the crackling, crunching of the fire's appetite.

When dawn broke, the lightened sky revealed to everyone not only the glow and smoke of the fire but the flames that had broken over the brink of foothills but a few canyons away from the lodge.

The morning winds increased. Smoke, filled with gray ashen fir needles, whipped in ghostly threads through the tree tops around the lodge.

In the office the sheriff counseled Fred, "I'm afraid, if the wind didn't diminish and change to the southwest to slow the advance of the fire, Fred, we will have to consider evacuation of the lodge—before darkness makes things more difficult." The sheriff turned to Gabby, "I'm sorry. You know we'll have no choice."

The sheriff's news shocked Fred and Gabby. Their livelihood—their life savings!—was all wrapped up in the lodge. Even with the insurance that should cover the property loss, to lose all the years of hard work that had built the business would be more than they could stand.

Fred cursed. Gabby prayed. They then notified the staff to do their best with the busy work load; but to be prepared to leave if the order came through from the fire marshall.

Olli had been so busy with morning dining room duties, when a lull came in the rush, she realized she was very weary. She poured a cup of coffee and sat exhausted on a stool in the kitchen. She watched Gabby bustle about the kitchen helping Tom prepare the meal to feed the next group of fire fighters due in from the fire lines.

Olli sighed, finished her coffee.

Gabby turned and gave Olli a quick understanding smile. "I guess you should park your bottom while you can." Gabby said. She turned back to the stove to stir the huge kettle of bubbling beef stew. When she spoke again her voice held a tone of disappointment.

"I suppose by four o'clock we will know the outcome of this

Fire

whole mess. Fred and I are still hoping the wind will change. The sheriff said the weather forecast from Portland predicted rain was on the way. We hope that's true."

Olli noted the tension and worry Gabby showed was out of place on the usually happy woman's face. But Gabby and Fred, all of their married life, had invested in making the lodge a successful, well-established business. That they might lose it to this fire, all their hard work of the past years destroyed, it would break Gabby's heart.

At noon the dining room quickly filled with weary men voicing hopes for a change in the weather. Some optimistically insisted they could feel a change in the air. Everyone hoped for rain.

By three o'clock the wind had sharply turned to the southwest bringing with it a bank of water laden clouds blowing in from the Pacific Ocean.

By four o'clock rain fell in a steady downpour.

Nature, at the last, had brought its own fire brigade.

The fire crews began straggling out of the crew buses. They were soaking wet and covered with ash. The men who had been on foot trails working near the lodge joined the group.

After a few hours, to be sure that all of the crews and volunteers had been safely accounted for, the sheriff asked the rangers to choose a clean-up crew to remain on duty in case the rain diminished and also to begin monitoring the remaining hotspots. Local men and volunteers could go home with thanks for the turnout and for all their help.

After four days the fire was completely out. The danger to the lodge was over.

Everyone was exhausted but jubilant that the threat to the forested area and the lodge had passed. No lives had been lost, no properties damaged.

Before twilight seeped into the valley, the lodge parking lot was nearly empty. The only remaining vehicles were those of the rangers, the sheriff, Fred and Gabby's truck and a pickup belonging to Spirit Lake.

Cole, Ben, Carl, John and Wes Brauer, who had continued on with the rest of the fire crew, were muddy and ash-covered as they sat in the lodge dining room. They had come in with the last of the firefighters and remained behind after the others had left. Ravenously hungry, they ate loads of freshly baked bread and steaming bowls of Gabby's famous beef stew.

Lena and Olli were both working in the dining room when Ben got up to leave. Quickly, Lena met him at the cash register, where, for a short time they spoke in low tones. Then Ben left to wait in Cole's truck until the other four brothers had finished their meal.

One by one the men left the table, paid at the cash register and went to the truck.

Cole, being the last, stopped Olli as she cleared the table.

He smiled in a quiet, assuring way as he spoke. "Olli, I know the past few days have been hard for the fire crews as well as you folks here at the lodge, and you are probably as tired as my brothers and I. But I wonder if on your next day off you would let me take you for a drive up the mountain? The fire didn't damage any of the area around Spirit Lake. We could hike the trail to Harmony Falls. Maybe we could take a picnic lunch, spend the day and do some trout fishing. I think you'd like it. It's so beautiful up there. We could climb up the east ridge and see where the fire stopped. A person can catch trout right from the lake shore, too. I would really like you to come, and if you'd feel better about it maybe Ben and Lena could join us. Whatever you decide." He smiled. "You'll let me know, won't you?"

Olli was surprised, but pleased, because she was very aware of his glances, good manners and quiet smile. She felt warm and shaky as she told him she'd be happy to go.

He went to the truck with a smile on his face.

Olli wondered if she shook from the long hours on her feet, or was it Cole's closeness, and his interest in her, Could it be that her thoughts about him had risen to the surface so she could face the

Fire

fact he was no longer just one of the brothers, but someone whom she thought about more than she wanted to admit?

Hunting season was soon to begin. Both Olli and Lena would be back to a seven day work week with no time for days off. So the next evening, when Cole came to the lodge for dinner, Olli suggested the following Wednesday, before the first hunters arrived, would be a good day for the outing up the mountain if the weather cleared.

Cole told her Ben and Lena had already talked about the trip to the lake and had said they'd be happy to come along.

Cole's quiet "Goodnight," left Olli in a state of elation. But the longer she thought about it the more she felt Lena's manipulating force likely at work on Ben, which she was sure had led to the whole idea in the first place, leading Ben to talk Cole into taking all of them in his truck. The longer she mulled it over in her mind the more she wondered if Cole really wanted her to go, or if Lena had wanted to be with Ben and knew there was no privacy at the lodge. Ben didn't have transportation so had he influenced Cole to invite Olli on the fishing trip? Maybe she was just being overly self-critical. It was not normal for her to be negative, but she couldn't help it.

Olli finished the clean up work and slowly walked to her room. Her thoughts of Lena's possibly contrived planning, mingled with the long-awaited spark which Cole had flicked into her boring routine, filled her with mixed feelings.

After she bathed, Olli sat curled up in her nightgown. She cuddled deep in her overstuffed chair. She could see the moon peeking its lovely face out of the dispersing clouds that had miraculously saved the lodge by drowning the threatening forest fire.

The moon's silver glow glittered and danced on the surface of the river that riffled and surged barely within its banks. The night grew quiet. The wind covered everything with a warm whisper.

Second Son

Olli brushed her hair and pressed her head against the back of the chair. With a look of complete exhaustion, yet expectant pleasure, she fell asleep feeling as though wrapped in sturdy safe arms of one who wanted to be her friend—maybe more.

17
Incident On Mount St. Helens

For Olli, the anxiously awaited day arrived, clutching in its breathtaking sunrise the promise of a glorious early autumn.

Cole and Ben, in Cole's truck, drove into the lodge parking lot at seven to find a glowing-faced Lena and a shy, smiling Olli sitting on a picnic bench where the girls had barely spoken to each other because of Lena's continued standoffish attitude.

Olli had a large basket. She had prepared a lunch of sandwiches and iced tea.

Cole helped Olli into the middle of the front seat, then put the lunch basket in the back bed of the truck, and climbed in the driver's seat beside Olli.

Lena became quite animated and cheerful. She jumped in the front seat and sat on Ben's lap wiggling and giggling as Cole started the engine. Away they went up the muddy rutted road toward Mount St. Helens.

It was a bumpy drive until they reached their destination in the rough parking area near the water's edge of Spirit Lake, a beautiful glassy surface at the base of the majestic, blue and silver mountain. Cole parked the truck. The two couples strolled to the lakeshore amid the primitive landscape filled with immense quiet.

When she was a child Olli had thought there could never be another mountain scene that would thrill her or stir her heart like the sight of Mt. Baker as it loomed over the family home in the Lynden Valley. But she had been away from the homestead long enough that she breathed in the pristine blue of the towering mountain before her. She placed her hand on her forehead shielding her eyes against the silvery sparkle of the glaciers which lay in crevices on the shoulders of the massive visage before her. It made Olli's breath catch in her throat. She whispered to herself, "It's so solid, clean and peaceful."

Cole glanced at her and smiled, knowing what she felt by the look in her eyes.

Ben and Lena chattered as they separated the fish poles deciding what gear they would use. Making their choices, the couple walked toward the lake's edge near the outlet where the Toutle River started its slow, shining descent away from Spirit Lake.

Ben cast his fish line into the crystal clear water, and Cole and Olli saw Ben's fish rod suddenly bend in an arch, showing a trout had found the bait. He struggled as he landed a twenty-four inch rainbow trout. At the same time, Lena reeled in another trout of similar size.

Cole and Olli picked up their gear and Olli followed her guide down the forest trail that led to Cole's favorite spot. Cole called to Ben and Lena, who waved them on down the trail, as they both were coping with large trout splashing on the ends of their lines.

A few miles of hiking led Olli and Cole to Harmony Falls. It was a pristine area where a high mountain waterfall plummeted into a pool, then into a clear stream that trickled into the lake. Cole told Olli the fishing was perfect near the falls, where the view of the mountain was mirrored on the surface of the lake. The two walked at an even pace, where Olli let Cole take the lead up the narrow shaded trail.

Olli stopped abruptly when Cole raised his hand, making a hand signal for her to be very quiet. He pointed towards the lakeshore where three deer drank at the edge of the water. Olli smiled in delighted pleasure. The trio raised their heads in unison, looked at the hikers, then resumed their drinking.

Cole and Olli heard the sound of the waterfall, as they rounded a corner of the trail. Olli stood stark still, completely enthralled

Incident On Mount St. Helens

when she saw the clear mountain stream tumbling from a moss covered rock cliff. Spray and foam floated across the deep pool at the foot of the falls.

Near the base of the waterfall Cole clasped Olli's hand firmly in his, helping her to step gingerly on large smooth stones as she crossed the narrow stream. On the opposite bank the young man held Olli's hand. She gave a short jump from her foot hold and began to slip. Cole's grip tightened as he pulled her up the creek bank holding her very close to his chest.

Olli looked up into Cole's smiling face. Her eyes looked directly into his and she felt his easy hold on her shoulders. She glanced away, but he touched her chin to bring her gaze back to him. The tender look in his eyes stirred her. He bent over her and pressed his lips firmly on her surprised mouth. Pulling back slightly, he held her gently and took a deep breath, as though he had run a long distance. He held her only a brief moment before releasing her. His easy smile filled her heart with a warm contented feeling. She felt a little dizzy, but happy.

Cole handed her a fish pole, then sauntered down the trail toward the lake. She noticed a satisfied swagger in his step. She quietly followed him, feeling a spark of hope within herself. She now knew that he cared for her. Her cheeks warmed as a satisfied smile brightened her eyes.

The morning sun climbed an invisible stairway over the lake and marched along the arch of sky into early afternoon. Cole and Olli sat side by side fishing and talking in an easy, lazy rhythm. Their fish creels were full of trout when they stood and prepared to hike back to the truck. Occasionally Cole helped Olli when they reached parts of the trail where she had earlier needed assistance. She again accepted help at the stream near the waterfall. Cole's touch was easy. Her response was warm, but not once did he touch her with the emotion they momentarily had shared that morning.

When they entered the parking lot they saw no one near the truck or the lake shore, so they began shouting and calling for

Second Son

Ben and Lena, telling them to come and see some REAL fish. Receiving no answer they went to the truck and honked the horn. Still there was no reply from them.

Olli waited while Cole scouted around the hemlock trees near the parking lot—calling for Ben.

Olli spread the blanket on the ground where she arranged the picnic. Then she waited for Cole, Ben and Lena.

Cole was out of sight up the wide trail which led toward the mountain when Olli heard soft giggling mingled with gruff laughter coming from a nearby clump of wild salmonberry bushes.

Olli walked slowly down the road toward the bushes when Lena came running toward her stumbling drunkenly and laughing. She was stark naked! Ben followed closely behind Lena stumbling and soused. He too, was naked as a jay bird.

Ben grabbed Lena around the waist and threw her to the ground, where, in the dust of the road they began a drunken orgy. They writhed, screaming and laughing, completely unaware that Olli was running from the scene in disgust.

Olli arrived at the truck just as Cole came jogging down the trail from the mountain. He dashed passed Olli and grabbed his brother by his red hair, pulling Ben off of Lena's brown form. Both of them smelled of cheap whiskey and screamed and shouted at Cole for breaking up their drunken tryst. Cole punched Ben's chin which landed him in a heaped pile of torso, legs and arms. As Ben fell and sprawled in the dust, Lena jumped on Cole's back and began beating him with her fists, all the while drunkenly cursing him. Cole grabbed her by her long black hair and slapped her face. In response, Lena screamed and clawed at Cole's face.

In disgust, Cole pushed her to the ground, stepping back from the two and turning to head back to the truck.

Ben haltingly stood to his feet, shook his head. He seemed sobered up enough to run to Lena and pull her to her feet. He dragged her back to the screen of the bushes as she screamed obscenities.

Cole came over to Olli who stood by the truck. She had

gathered all the picnic things in the red blanket and had tossed them in the truck bed. Cole kept his eyes averted from Olli's face. He apologized about his brother, telling Olli that as soon as Lena and Ben sobered up and dressed themselves he'd get them back to the lodge.

Olli was silent, ashamed and angry at Ben and Lena for spoiling a previously, marvelous day. She felt their actions were crass and shameful, and wondered why they hadn't found some other time and place for their drunken revelries.

After a few minutes, Lena came staggering clothed but dusty and climbed silently into the back of the truck. She hung her head, not speaking a word. Ben, with his pants on and his shirt slung over his shoulder, climbed likewise into the back of the truck. He grumbled, stammered, telling Olli he was sorry. He lay down near the picnic blanket using the basket as a pillow.

Cole put his arm around Olli's waist and helped her into the cab of the truck. He buried his lips in her rumpled blond hair. His warm whisper was meant to comfort her, "Forgive and forget them, honey. This won't ever happen again. I promise you that."

With a silent affirmative nod of her head, Olli settled herself in the truck seat so she would be sitting close to Cole. He climbed into the cab and started the engine.

It was nearly sunset when Cole stopped the truck in the parking lot at the lodge.

Lena staggered out of the back of the truck without Ben offering to help her.

Cole opened the passenger door of the truck, and took Olli's hand, keeping it in a gentle but firm grip while he led her to the back door of the lodge. His quiet speech and manner showed Olli how bad he felt about his brother's and Lena's behavior.

He closed her in his arms and gave her a brush of his lips on her cheek. "Good night," he said.

Olli understood by his manner that he wanted more than these loving gestures, but was gentleman enough to know the time wasn't right.

Second Son

After Cole left, Olli went to her room, showered, dressed, and then realized she was starved. She went down the hall to the kitchen and dished up a large bowl of beef stew. Choosing a piece of pie and a glass of milk she took them back to her room where she curled up in her large overstuffed chair. Closing her eyes she tried to erase the disgust she felt for Ben and Lena.

That night Olli lay in bed a long time before falling into a realm skirting sleep. Like a slow motion movie, she ran the days events behind her eyes. A calmness crept through her when she recalled the warmth of Cole's closeness as he kissed her. She didn't remember the conversation they had exchanged all day, but felt a calm connecting of ideas and goodness emerging from Cole, which she needed deep within. A seed of much more than friendship had sprouted in Olli's heart.

As the day's events rotated in her head, a flash of heated shame over the drunken scene with Ben and Lena, changed her attitude and brought an unwelcome tightness to her sleepy brow.

She tossed and turned until the cloak of weary sleep fell over her tired body.

The following weeks passed quickly. Fall hunting season had begun.

The lodge and cabins filled to capacity with guests from Portland, Seattle and out of state.

Olli and Lena seldom spoke except when Gabby was near, so Gabby wouldn't realize the rift between the two young women.

Guests' meals were prepared and served in an efficient, unhurried atmosphere. But away from the eyes of the patrons, the lodge crew worked double time to keep things moving smoothly.

Lena had given Gabby and Fred notice that at the end of hunting season she would be leaving her job at the lodge, saying she had found a job in Toledo, which was closer to where Ben lived.

Gabby and Fred weren't unhappy about Lena's leaving, because they had felt the static between Lena and Olli. And they would rather lose Lena with her temperamental ways, than lose Olli, whose temperament was cheerful and pleasing to the customers. Besides, the tourist season would be over and customers would dwindle to the local people through the holiday season.

There was a murmur on the local grapevine that Ben and Lena planned to be married before Christmas, but Gabby had learned not to pry into Lena's affairs. So Gabby didn't ask Lena about it, though Gabby had noticed the curly red haired Ben Brauer at the lodge frequently. He and Lena spent short hidden times together kissing in the back hall during Lena's breaks.

Gabby saw their romantic relationship had, indeed, become very serious.

In early November of 1928, when her employment ended, Lena didn't say goodbye to Olli. One day she was there, the next day she was gone. In fact, it was as if she'd never been there, except for the stressed, unspoken tension between Lena and the crew that had been so apparent. Her absence made everyone feel as though a fresh breeze swept through the place.

18

Cole Brauer

Ben brought Lena to the lodge occasionally on Friday nights. He seemed boisterous and happy, as always, but Gabby called Lena's attitude, "snobbish."

Cole came for dinner two or three nights a week, but never on Friday when Ben and Lena were there. He always arrived for the late dinner hour, and stayed until Olli was off work, so they could sit and talk.

Olli would sit with Cole in front of the stone fireplace in the far end of the huge lobby. Sometimes they would stroll by the river, if the late night hour was not too cold.

One night the moon was so bright that the shadows of the tall tree silhouettes stretched across the new snowfall making the yard look like black lace. Olli felt it was just too lovely outside not to be walking in the enchantment of it all. With warm rubber boots and her tweed sweater and long woolen coat pulled around her slim frame, she met Cole at the back door of the lodge.

They walked in the moonlight beside the river where it was solemnly quiet, except for the water as it flowed whispering near their path. When their breath condensed in soft clouds around their faces, they could tell the temperature was becoming too cold. So Cole took Olli by the hand and led her to his truck where they climbed in and cuddled in a wool blanket. Cole pulled her close to him and kissed her soft mouth. Her body yielded to his embrace, and she laid her head comfortably on his shoulder.

Olli removed her gloves and touched his face, feeling his high forehead and smooth clean hair. She traced her fingers around his ears, across his eyebrows, down his nose, to his chin and gently stroked his lips. She knew his face so well.

In the moonlight she saw him smile. His face was kind and strong; not truly handsome, but firm and honest, which made her feel secure. His smile continued as he cupped her little chin in his large hand and traced her delicate facial pattern in the same manner that she had touched him. When his fingers touched her lips he felt her smile. He pulled her slowly to his chest, kissing her with such intense feeling she yielded to him.

Olli's emotions roared in her ears. Her breasts were warm, and a thrill trickled down her slim spine, activating a yearning she had resisted for a long time.

When a sighing whimper escaped her lips, Cole knew he could go on until he reached a place where he wouldn't be able to control his longing for her. And he knew she was nearly at the point of giving herself to him with a fever that would burn itself into his soul. With all the fervor he could muster he pushed her soft body from his arms. He took a deep breath and whispered, "I think we should stop before we can't."

Olli started to protest and clung to him, but he held her at arms length and said in a deep emotion filled voice. "I need you Olli, but I want it to be right. I love you and I want you for my wife. Not just for your body. I want you for my wife forever. I want the whole, sweet, happy, loving woman you are. I need you in my life everyday, Olli."

Olli drew a quick breath, and looked into Cole's moonlit face, as she held his face in her hands.

"Cole," she whispered, "You really know nothing about me. We haven't known each other that long, nor dated enough for you to ask me to be your wife. I had some things happen to me a few years ago that I need to tell you about before you ask me to marry you. You may change your mind."

Cole straightened his head and started to tell Olli that whatever the problems had been they would never make a difference in his feelings for her. But Olli dropped her chin, and Cole could see glassy tears forming as she searched for the right words to say.

"Cole," she began, "I have waited for someone as kind and good as you to care for me. Lately my mind carries you with me nearly every waking hour, and I would love to be your wife. But you need a good, pure woman that has no heavy garbage from the past. My past has had a lot of that. You need a woman you would be proud of, not someone like me. We've really never spoken to each other of the past," Olli whispered, "and it makes me afraid. Afraid that you wouldn't or couldn't forgive me for things that happened which weren't my fault. But they happened, and Lord knows I have tried hard to forget."

Cole turned her by her shoulders so he could look straight into her large tear-filled eyes, took a deep breath and pulled her gently to him. He pressed her head to his shoulder, and his mouth murmured warmly consoling words. "Olli," he whispered in a voice husky with emotion, "I can't make my mind think of anything you could have ever done that would change my mind, or my heart about how I feel for you. Whatever it was that happened, I'm sure God has forgiven you, so I have no recourse but to do the same. And anything you tell me will be like fog in the wind—blown away and forgotten—because I think the love I have for you is stronger than you know. Olli, in my heart, even down in my gut, I know you're the one I need. Let's worry later about anything in your past, or in mine. Right now let's think of what we need now. Olli, I need you."

In a muffled voice that caught in his throat, Cole whispered, "Please, Olli, Please marry me."

Olli held Cole's strong hands in hers. In his gentle face she saw a man she knew would never leave her. A man who truly wanted her, to live their lives together and share with her until they died.

She kissed his cheek, then his firm mouth, until she felt, in that act alone, she had become one with him.

When she breathlessly drew her face and body from him she

whispered, "Yes." Then she said it louder. "Yes." Then, she threw open her arms and shouted in a loud voice, which rang through the moonlit night. "YES! YES! YES! Cole, oh, Cole, YES!"

Her widespread arms encircled his chest. The quick embrace triggered a pleasant tingling sensation in her spine. Her heartbeat quickened, breaking down the walls of uncertainty, leaving her with a need she wanted Cole to fill. Now! Now, before her good sense flashed her back into the sanity of control.

Cole could feel her body move and knew she was vulnerable. As difficult as it was, he held her gently and rocked her in his arms while he murmured, "Soon, very soon, Olli, soon. Not here. Not now. Soon."

The next few weeks Cole and Olli didn't see each other due to an early, heavy snowfall that made it impossible traveling the road to the lodge. At the end of the two weeks, three feet of snow covered the parking lot. The surrounding terrain took on the appearance of a hand painted Christmas card.

The county road crew finally acquired the use of a motorized snowplow and, in a matter of a few days, the road was cleared from Toledo and Castle Rock up the river to the lodge.

Thanksgiving 1928 was just a few days away, so preparations for the lodge's annual Harvest Dinner kept everyone busy. Thanksgiving dinner at the lodge was one of the well-attended functions of the year—not only for local patrons but also for important clientele of hunting and fishing organizations from Portland and Seattle. Due to weather conditions, group reservations from areas such as Spokane and Yakima were few.

Gabby and Olli decorated the banquet and dining rooms with cedar boughs, orange candles and large pumpkins. They also made forty table centerpieces with colored maple leaves that had survived the snow fall. They added moss and local evergreens collected along the forest edge. The results of their efforts were lovely, and Olli was especially pleased since she learned of one reservation from the local area which surprised everyone. It was for the entire Brauer family. This was the first time that more than a few of the brothers had included the lodge in their holiday plans. "And," exclaimed Gabby, "about time, too!"

Fred had always admired and respected Preacher Brauer, and he felt it would be great to see him and his tiny, proper wife Mattie, their eight strapping young sons and their daughter Margaret.

Olli was secretly delighted, yet a bit uneasy about the upcoming meeting, because of the fact she had not yet met Cole's parents or the other three brothers and Margaret. Nor had she met brother Wes's wife, Mary. The reservations also included Nanny Anne, the black woman who had been a member of the family since Cole was a child. Cole had always spoken of her with the same tone of respect in which he spoke of his mother. There would be twelve in all.

Work was hectic on Thanksgiving Day.

Though the roads were still slushy and full of holes, the dining room was busy even before the Brauers arrived. They came in three cars and Cole's truck. Olli greeted them and showed them to the banquet room where they were seated at a long table specially prepared for the large family gathering.

Cole's father, Cole Sr., a tall, bald, somber-looking gentleman sat at the head of the table. Petite Mrs. Brauer, white haired and not quite five feet tall, was dressed properly in a small flat-brimmed black hat and a dark maroon dress with a lace collar. She carried herself with the surety of one who had not only given birth to these tall, jovial men and their large ungainly red-haired sister, but was capable of seeing to it that all acted with some decorum, merely because she and their father were in their midst. And the family of a minister must fulfill the correct expectations of their diminutive mother and tall, properly-poised father.

Cole stood beside Olli, and as he helped seat each person, he introduced her to each of the family members whom she hadn't met. Wes's wife, Mary, was a tall dark-haired woman whose pregnancy was evident. Nanny Anne had an unlined face for a person of her years. A calm beauty shone in the aura of her smile and her kind, all-seeing eyes. She clearly saw the looks upon Cole and Olli's faces, and she winked at Olli.

The three younger brothers seated themselves near to Nanny Anne. Carl was nineteen. Liar was sixteen, Jess was fifteen. Olli wondered why such big healthy young men still needed a nanny. Then she realized the truth of it, that the round, jolly, buxom black woman was as much a member of the family as any of the Brauer's children.

When everyone was seated Olli noticed an extra place set at the table, so she asked Cole if they were expecting another member of their party. As she asked, Gabby came from the kitchen and nodded to Cole. He pulled the chair out and motioned for Olli to be seated. Startled, she looked at Gabby, who smiled and indicated with a nod for her to sit and enjoy the meal with the family.

Only at that moment did Olli realize that Cole and Gabby had planned this surprise. She could not help herself but to become shy. Everyone was smiling at her, clearly each knowing she had been expected to join them.

Before the meal was served the family joined hands. Olli was included in this expression of unity and reverence. They bowed their heads and Cole Sr., in a solemn voice, prayed that blessings from God be placed on the food and the family.

The gesture filled Olli with a feeling that she had missed something special in the clamorous rearing she'd received at home with Ma and Papa. She had never felt family closeness—not like this—because she had never been introduced to the calm pleasure of a family praying together.

The dinner went by pleasantly. The conversation flowed from jovial remarks and jesting among the brothers. The family atmosphere put Olli completely at ease, and she felt accepted and comfortable interjecting small talk with Mattie Brauer, Mary, and Margaret, and even Lena.

After Gabby had served warm mincemeat and pumpkin pies, an after-dinner quietness settled over the family.

Finally, Ben cleared his throat and made a short announcement. "Lena and I got married, in Portland, last week."

Cole Sr. stood, not wanting to seem pious or condescending, he walked over to Ben and shook his sons' hand, and leaned over his new daughter-in-law's shoulder and gave Lena a fatherly kiss on the cheek, welcoming her to the family.

After a short applause Mrs. Brauer raised her voice and stated clearly, "Benjamin, I think you two could have let your father officiate at the ceremony."

Cole Sr. said calmly, "Now Mother, that would have been lovely, but these children are old enough to know what they want."

"I still think they should have come and asked you, dear." Mattie reiterated.

"Let's hear no more about that, Mother." Cole Sr. said in his characteristically firm tone.

After his father was seated, Cole Jr. stood, taking Olli by the hand, and urging her to stand beside him. "Dad, Mother, everyone," he began, "I haven't seen Olli for a couple of weeks—as you know the snow made that impossible—but before the snowstorm, I asked Olli to marry me."

Olli looked around the table at the large happy group, then looked at Cole, even as the family broke into exuberant applause. She stood speechless.

Cole turned and looked into Olli's face and speaking only to her, he said "Olli, I want to ask you, again, in front of all the people I love. Will you marry me?"

Olli lowered her eyes, then looking straight into Cole's tender face, she took a deep breath and said, "After I speak with your father about some answers for which I need counseling. Then, if your father will perform the ceremony, I will be proud and happy to marry you."

Everyone looked at Olli as if she held a terrible secret that couldn't be shared with the rest of the family. Ben rose to his feet, held his coffee cup high in the air and broke the silence with a hearty, "Here's to Lena and me, and to the next bride and groom, Cole and Olli! Hip hip hooray!"

All the brothers stood and slapped Cole on the back as they cheered. They raised such a ruckus Mother Brauer frowned and tried to shush them, while Cole Sr. simply nodded his head and smiled.

Cole Sr. stared off into the distance, clearly pondering the young woman's words; what would be troubling Olli so much she felt she needed his counsel, even before accepting Cole's proposal. His second son was quite smitten with the slim, blond, young woman, and Cole Sr. knew well enough that once Cole Jr. had made such a serious decision it would take strength-to-move-mountains for anyone to change his mind.

Mother Brauer was also secretly puzzled about what Olli would have to talk to Father Brauer about. But she also knew, whatever Olli felt she needed to discuss with Cole Sr., it would never be divulged to anyone, including herself.

Cole and Ollie were still standing together. Cole pulled a small velvet box from his pocket, took out a gold band displaying a small diamond. He placed the ring on Olli's finger, then proudly gathered her in his strong arms and planted a very serious kiss on her surprised mouth.

Again, the family cheered while Olli blushed profusely.

The other dining guests in the room were local patrons. They too clapped when Cole and Olli made a swift retreat from the banquet room into the lobby.

Cole laughed heartily as he held Olli's hand. Breathlessly happy, Olli was overwhelmed by all the attention showered on their engagement in front of the local customers and the whole Brauer clan; she could tell they all approved of Cole's selection of his blushing bride-to-be.

After Thanksgiving business at the lodge eased up, and for Olli the days passed slowly as she awaited Christmas and New Year.

She would no longer be spending her holidays alone, for the rest of her days, for she would soon be Cole's wife. They had set the wedding date for January 1st, New Year's Day 1929.

Olli had set aside a day during the following week to travel down the mountain to Castle Rock to talk with Cole's father. She felt she should talk to him about the incidents in her past. She wanted to go into her marriage to Cole being truthful, as well as feeling she could achieve a peace within herself. She hoped Dad Brauer would understand her past—and her love for Cole.

The week before her engagement, Olli had written a quick note to her dear friend, Dweena, telling her that if Cole asked her to marry him, she would. At the same time she would tell him about her life at the Gordons, child and all. And she would talk over her past with Cole's father, Pastor Brauer, so they would know everything about her. She would hide nothing.

Olli received a return letter the day before she was to speak with Dad Brauer. Dweena's advice was to let the old heart aches lie and for Olli to start over new and clean within herself, and not tell about her being raped and the loss of her son to the Gordons. On the other hand, Dweena suggested, Olli should tell them about her marriage to Dan, her divorce, the death of her baby, Jenny, and her hospital stay, all of which were in the public record and could be found out. The incident at the Gordons, she felt, wouldn't be as readily accepted by Cole's family, or the church, especially a rape that had never been reported, or a child taken from her by the child's hateful grandmother.

So Olli struggled with indecision. Would telling the whole truth be best? Or should she reveal only half the truth? The letter from Dweena troubled her because of her loss and due to the fact Dweena was still in the household where her son was growing up—without his real mother. Dweena saw baby Cal every day, and she clearly believed her reports to Olli about Cal's welfare were appreciated; she kept Olli up to date on young Cal's growth and the family's care of him.

Olli mulled over Dweena's advice and decided to do as her old friend suggested.

The day Cole drove to the lodge to take Olli down to the quaint logging town of Castle Rock to talk to Dad Brauer the road was icy and in terrible condition. It took nearly two hours of careful maneuvering before they reached the trim-steepled church building.

Leaving Olli at the church, Cole walked over to the parsonage to visit with his mother until his dad rang the bell, a signaling device which Ben had installed between the parsonage and the church. The bell saved Mrs. Brauer many extra steps with messages for Dad Brauer.

Olli knocked on the heavy double doors at the front of the Church. Dad Brauer immediately opened the doors in a wide sweep. He greeted Olli with his warm smile and ushered her inside.

He asked her to be seated. She chose a stiff hardwood armchair near the desk. Dad Brauer moved his creaky swivel chair from behind his desk and placed it in front so he and Olli could have a more informal conversation.

Olli felt more at ease, though she was still hesitant to know how to begin.

Cole Sr. was very tall and lanky with a shiny bald head and long facial features. His appearance gave Olli the impression he had been the model for a famous story book character, Ichabod Crane. But, unlike the ungainly storybook character, Dad Brauer had two characteristics that distinguished him far and above the story book description. Those were his wonderfully gentle eyes and his quick broad smile.

Olli took a deep breath and began to fidget with the handles on her handbag. Cole Sr. sensed her anxiety, reached over, patted her hands and looked her straight in the eye. "Olli—or would you rather I call you Olive?" He smiled, "Whichever you prefer."

Olli took another deep breath to relax her mind and replied, "Olli, would be fine. Should I call you Pastor Brauer, Father, Dad, or...."

Cole Sr. flashed his quick smile. "I rather like Dad Brauer," he said.

"Well, Dad Brauer," Olli began, "I guess I should tell you about myself and see if you still think Cole and I should marry." She paused, "I love Cole, and I know I could be a good wife. I'm willing to work beside him in anything he chooses, and I'll stay with him through the worst and the best. But right now I need your approval, and the church's, concerning things that have happened to me in the past seven years, which I have as yet to speak fully about with Cole."

Dad Brauer waited. "Where would you like to begin, my dear?" He asked.

Olli cleared her throat, then began quietly.

"I was married a few years back. My husband deserted me after our baby girl died. I was admitted to Western State Mental Hospital outside of Tacoma for a while, because of the nervous shock of it all. When my husband left he moved to New York. He sent divorce papers saying because of the baby's death, I was an unfit mother. I signed the papers shortly after I was released from the hospital. It's all I could think to do. At the time I didn't have a job and couldn't fight it."

Olli paused. Dad Brauer noticed Olli's knuckles were strained white where she gripped her handbag tightly. He knew the telling of the past was a difficult task for her, but because she had initiated this consultation he felt she needed to confide in him. Not only as a minister, but as a future father-in-law.

Olli began again. "I'm fine now, my work up at the lodge goes well. I am fully able to carry on with my job and responsibilities. But I have never had any religious training or instruction, and I want to know if there is anything in your church rules that would keep Cole and me from being married in the church. I know it would mean a lot to Cole for you to perform the ceremony. And it would make me feel more a part of a real loving family if you would accept me after knowing these things about me."

Olli glanced down as she fidgeted with her handkerchief. "I've been told it is a sin to be divorced, that I would be committing adultery if I remarry. I need to know if this is true. I don't want to hurt Cole, or any of your family, so I need to know if you will marry Cole and me and accept me as your daughter-in-law?"

Dad Brauer touched Olli's shoulder. "My Dear," he began, "Due to the fact you were not married in the church before, and that your ex-husband deserted you, and you signed those papers when you were still not mentally stable, these are things that must all be considered. I will study and pray on these things according to the church, and with the help of God, after I talk to the elders of the congregation and contact a few legal sources, I can give you an answer by late this afternoon. Of course that will mean you won't get back to the lodge until late tonight, but it is the best I can do. Will you wait?"

"Of course." Olli agreed.

Dad Brauer told Olli that Mother Hattie expected Cole and her to stay for lunch. "Then why don't you and Cole spend the afternoon in town. It would give you a chance to do some shopping."

Olli thanked him and left the church feeling a bit dubious about Cole's father presenting all her past circumstances to a board of church elders. But she felt he was a fair man and would honor her story to protect his son and herself.

Olli and Cole had a leisurely lunch with Mother Hattie, during, which Olli's attention was on the elder's meeting rather than the delicate sandwiches and tea. She was less concerned of what she had in confidence told Dad Brauer then of what the church elders' decision would be.

She had said she would marry Cole only if his father would perform the ceremony, but, thinking about it now, she truly meant it. Olli didn't want to step into a family as devoted and close as Cole's without the full social and religious approval of everyone involved. However, she knew Cole would insist on their marriage whether or not the church or his family approved.

Dad Brauer called two of the church elders and asked them to attend a meeting with him early in the afternoon. But before those calls, he phoned The Maritime and Longshoreman's main offices in Portland, asking for information about Dan Scarborough, his whereabouts and any other pertinent information about him that was held on file.

After shopping and walking around town in the sharp, chill wind Olli and Cole returned to the parsonage with a number of packages of items Olli needed to take back to the lodge.

At four o'clock Olli left Cole at the parsonage with his mother, and walked across the frozen grass that separated the buildings. Very tense, she fretted about the decision reached between Dad Brauer and the elders concerning her being married in the church. Olli softly tapped on the door and was asked to enter. She found Dad Brauer waiting at his desk. It surprised her that he was alone. She, again, sat in the stiff armchair feeling quite apprehensive.

Dad Brauer told her the presence of the church elders was not necessary. They had reached a decision. With his soft, caring eyes—so much like those of his son—Dad Brauer looked at Olli in his all-seeing fashion. "Olli, first I have bad news," Dad Brauer stated bluntly.

Olli drew a sharp breath in anticipation of a negative decision and waited with her heart beating rapidly. "What?" she asked in a near panic, gripping the arms of the chair.

Dad Brauer again reached over and patted her hand to reassure her. "The bad news which I speak of, my dear, concerns your ex-husband, Mr. Scarborough. After checking through the correct channels I have found Dan Scarborough is deceased."

Olli sat upright in the chair. She was paralyzed with shock, grief—and truthfully, she admitted to herself, even a feeling of relief. "What happened?" she stammered. "How do you know this? Where? I don't understand."

Dad Brauer said in a voice meant to reassure her, "I made some inquiries into his records at The Maritime and Longshoreman offices in Portland. His death was recorded as a shipboard accident last June. And because of the records showing his divorce, no effort was made to contact you. I suppose the New York office, being bogged down with paperwork, just recorded the death in its files and went no further."

Olli sat with her head down for a few silent moments then raised her eyes to look into Dad Brauer's deep-set, wonderfully familiar eyes and knew he could see her sadness, as well as the feeling of relief and release she felt. Her mind whirled giddily, clutching at the information and trying to steady her acceptance of it all.

"The good news is mingled with the bad, my Dear." Dad Brauer reiterated, "Due to your ex-husband's demise and the mitigating circumstances you spoke about; after much prayer and consideration, the elders and I have looked into God's word. Through our understanding, there is no reason why you and Cole shouldn't be married as you've requested. We'll help you contact your friends and family and anyone else you will want to inform about the ceremony."

Olli straightened her back, and struck a thoughtful pose. She hadn't heard a word from Ma or Papa since she had left Lynden Valley for her job at the lodge. They knew where she was. She had written to them, the only one who replied was her niece Elise.

Olli had been in touch with Dweena at the Gordon's in Tacoma, but that was a page of her life she hadn't flipped back to and felt it better to leave that early chapter closed. As for her sisters, brothers, and parents, it seemed they felt she had evaporated into thin air. They treated her much the same as they had when she had unwillingly left home seven years before. The next instant Olli blurted out, "No there won't be any one to contact. I'll write my family later. I'd rather have just the Brauer family and my local friends. Yes, that's what I'd prefer, a small Brauer family gathering is what it should be."

Dad Brauer thought it strange for such a loving young woman to have this sharp edge to her voice when speaking of her family. He felt in time he would talk with her and try to gather a better understanding of the underlying feelings he had seen flash by when he asked about her family. He would also advise Cole to get to the bottom of the problem, if there was one.

Cole and Olli left the church and parsonage at five P.M., leaving Cole's parents waving goodbye in the gathering early darkness of the chilly winter evening.

Dad Brauer felt perplexed about Olli, but true to the code of his pastoral calling and as a future father-in-law who had been entrusted with confidences, he didn't mention to Mother Hattie anything except that the wedding date was set.

Mother Hattie, being the understanding wife of her loving husband, knew better than question further.

The drive up the Toutle River toward the lodge was more miserable due to freezing road conditions than it had been earlier in the day. The road was rutted and frozen into ridges, making it very difficult for Cole to steer the car. It began to snow.

Olli was very talkative, and Cole thought it was because she was so happy about the wedding date being set.

But Olli's constant chatter was more to cover the nervousness she was trying to cope with concerning Dan's death. In her mind she reviewed the confidences she had shared with Dad Brauer. The things that had happened to her before she had met and fallen in love with Cole, she knew would have to be dismissed from her mind. It would take time, but there would be time, and she could overcome the past as long as she had Cole's love to support her.

It was after nine P.M. when they arrived at the lodge. Cole felt it was dangerous for him to travel back down the river, because of the cold and bad road conditions. He rented a room for himself. Then Olli and he went to the deserted dining room where they sat at the back corner table.

Gabby laughingly told them the place was closed, as she set two steaming cups of coffee on their table. "I've got some baked pork chops and mashed potatoes, if you two are hungry."

"Thanks," said Olli. "That sounds wonderful."

Second Son

After finishing their meal they sat quietly holding hands across the polished table top.

Cole touched the small ring he had placed on her finger the night of the engagement. "Olli. I know I'm doing the right thing wanting you for my wife. I just hope you believe you're doing the right thing by accepting me. I'm not a handsome man, Olli. I'm not a rich man. But I love you as much as life itself, and I'll do the best I can for us. I promise. I'm really happy you talked to Dad today about things that have been on your mind. Some day maybe you will talk to me about some of those past things, but only when you're ready."

Olli smiled and squeezed his hands, and promised that one day she would indeed tell him about a lot of unspoken incidents from her past. But for now she needed only his love and trust.

They told Gabby goodnight, and Cole walked Olli to her door, kissed her and returned to his room.

Soon after climbing into her bed Olli dropped into a dark, exhausted sleep, wrestling with eerie shadows from the past. She had flashes of brightness in which she saw Cole's calm, loving face and felt his caresses on her hair and face. Then a gray fog of uncertainty faded Cole's image and she awoke with a stark feeling of fear that Cole had gone. Her breath came in short gasps and her heart pounded so hard it frightened her. Lying there in the hushed darkness of her room she became aware that the images had been a muddle of mixed feelings drifting past her eyes like a parade in a silent movie.

Cole's sleep came slowly as he lay recounting the business of the day. He wondered about Olli's visit with his Dad, and her reluctance to talk to him about some of her past. He felt in his heart that as time went by that she would trust him enough to tell him. He knew somewhere there had to have been some things that had happened to Olli to make her care so little about her family. He had yet to meet them and didn't know why he was apprehensive. Drifting off to sleep, a smile tickled his lips as he remembered that in less than two weeks he and Olli would be man and wife. This gave him a great feeling of peace and security.

Unbeknownst to Olli, Cole had been making plans for their early days of marriage. He wanted her to quit her job at the lodge. They would move to Castle Rock where they could rent a small house until spring. When the weather warmed a bit, Olli and he would use his large tent to camp along the scattered creeks in the area. His brothers Ben, John and their wives could join them. They would finish the summer and fall picking ferns, salal and huckleberry brush in the nearby hills to supply the evergreen florist supplier they worked for in Portland. Cole knew they could make good money if they were frugal. The work would give them a nice little nest egg before the winter's cold rain and snow brought an end to their camping.

Cole knew how hard the work was, but he felt Olli would enjoy the chance for them to be outside working side by side in the woods where, at least during the day, they would be alone. He could hardly wait to tell Olli his plans. She might have a few ideas of her own to impart to him, but he had a few things about himself and future plans to tell her too. He felt his plans would be a great way to start a new year and a new life together.

Being the second oldest son in a line of eight siblings, whose father was a straight-laced minister, was not the easiest position for a man like Cole, who had his own code to live by. His code was tempered by good sense, trust and a bit of boisterous good-natured mischief.

He and his brothers had never done anything illegal in their growing up years. They just loved hard work mingled with pranks and good times. In truth they were like a group of frolicking, oversized raccoons with an insatiable curiosity and stamina to cause mild havoc when out from under the watchful eyes of their father.

Cole had outgrown most of the pranks, as should be expected of a man nearing thirty. He had spent time in the army, but never fought in a foreign campaign as had his older brother Wes.

Cole was more adapted to the quietness of the woods and the

easy pace of an evergreen supplier. He had logged a bit, but very soon decided that logging was too dangerous a vocation for him. Until only a few years ago, he had lived at home. Then his brothers Ben and John and he had rented a small place in Toledo. It was close to the high timbered country of the Cascade Mountains where ferns and other marketable evergreens were plentiful. Cole loved the outdoors.

The next morning everyone at the lodge woke to the driving wind and rain. The weather had changed during the night. A Chinook warm weather front had blasted its way up the river and the frozen world outside was melting into a sea of ankle-deep mud.

During breakfast Olli and Cole discussed the wedding. "Olli, I think it would be best for you to quit your job here at the lodge the week before the wedding. We can move down to Castle Rock, stay with my folks until we're married. Then we'll rent a place of our own until spring. How does that sound?"

Olli agreed with a simple, "Yes." And a smile.

Cole happily left the lodge early, confident that he was in charge of all plans for their married life.

19
Christmas 1928

The weekend that would be her last as an employee at the lodge, Olli gladly helped trim the lodge for the Christmas festivities. These were annual events that were anxiously awaited by the local customers and the usual groups from Portland. The clientele from Portland made their way up to the lodge to spend their holiday in the splendor of the pristine Mount St. Helens area.

Olli and Gabby draped the balcony with fragrant cedar boughs, and large red velvet bows were attached to the banister and down the log stairway.

A huge pine tree stood proudly beside the massive stone fireplace in the main lobby. It was trimmed with blown glass ornaments. Silver tinsel dangled from each branch making the light from the fireplace and the hundreds of white candles that were attached to each bough send myriads of mirror-like reflections to glitter festively around the room.

With all the trimmings finished Olli became misty eyed. She did not know if it was because it was the most beautiful Christmas tree she had ever seen or the fact this would be the last Christmas she would spend with her friends at the lodge. Maybe she was just caught up in the excitement of her upcoming wedding and future with a stable, loving man—and finally being included in a respectable, loving family. Whatever it was caught the tears in her throat, and she knew her outlook for the future was brighter now than anything she had ever hoped for.

Olli told Fred and Gabby she would stay through Christmas Day to help serve the gala dinner so they wouldn't be short-handed. It was a gesture both Fred and Gabby appreciated, knowing Olli was such a good-hearted person she would never leave them at the busiest time of the winter season.

As she looked around the banquet room, Olli felt the place was dressed in its finery to bid her a fond goodbye. She would miss this stabilizing piece of patchwork in her life that had introduced her to the future.

Christmas Eve Cole came up to the lodge and rented a room so he could spend the later part of the evening with Olli after she had finished serving in the dining room. He watched the local and Portland patrons arrive despite the mud and slushy road conditions.

As the night progressed it happened that Cole spent half the night helping friends get their cars and trucks pushed out of the knee deep mud that spilled out of the parking lot and down the rutted, unstable roadway. The road had thawed dramatically after the arrival of the holiday crowd, leaving huge mud pits as thick as pudding in the road.

After dinner some of Cole's friends asked him to help push their cars down the muck filled road so they could get home for Christmas Day. Cole, wanting to accommodate his buddies, spent no time with Olli because he was out in the black of that miserable night wallowing in the mud until nearly two A.M.

At two-fifteen in the morning Olli heard a soft rapping on her bedroom door. Thinking it was Gabby she opened the door to find Cole standing in the doorway soaked to the skin and covered with mud. He had a broad grin on his face, but his eyes had a blurred glaze that startled Olli.

"Olli Girl, can I come in? I'm really cold and I need a bath and somebody to get me warm. Olli, I need to lie down." He said with a slur.

Olli saw his drunken manner, smelled his breath. She inadver-

Christmas 1928

tently took two steps backward—more in shock of Cole's apparent drinking than from his muddy appearance. He took two steps inside the doorway and fell in a drunken heap onto the floor.

Olli ran past him and down the hall to the cook's room. She knocked loudly, "Tom, can you help me?"

There was a mumbling behind the door asking her to wait as he shuffled around putting his pants and slippers on. Opening the door, Tom, scratching his head, came to alert attention when he realized Olli had an anxious look on her face. "What's the trouble Girl?"

Olli explained as quickly as possible that Cole had come to her door, apparently drunk, and had passed out on the floor and she needed help to take him to his own room.

Tom went with her to where Cole lay on the floor. He checked him over declaring, indeed, he was drunk, and said, "I suppose his buddies gave him drinks to thank him for spending the whole damn evening shoving their stupid butts around in the mud."

Tom had known Cole quite well for many years and told Olli that Cole used to have a drinking problem, but he hadn't known him to drink a drop for years.

Tom left the room and went to get Fred to help him maneuver Cole back to his own room and sober him up.

Fred shook his head in disbelief. "I haven't seen Cole in this shape for years," he stated disgustedly. "But don't worry. Tom and I will take care of him and get him cleaned up and into bed before he even remembers where he is."

Tom and Fred left, supporting Coles' tall lanky frame between them, leaving Olli with a puzzled look on her face. The drinking problem was a detail Cole hadn't mentioned to her. One of many details neither had talked about. One of the many details that would soon have to be addressed. They each had skeletons rattling around in their closet.

Olli wasn't angry, just in a mood of uncertainty as she crept back into her cold rumpled bedding, curled into a fetal position proving inwardly she was more troubled than she wanted to admit. Lying in the cold she wondered how truths of her past would affect Cole. They indeed needed the week ahead to talk, and hopefully learn to forgive and forget before they could promise to love, honor and obey.

Christmas morning dawned gray and rainy. Olli thoroughly cleaned her room and packed her belongings before carrying her baggage down to the lobby. She went to the dining room to help Gabby serve breakfast to the storm marooned customers who had rented rooms the proceeding night rather that face the dreadful muddy road conditions.

Midway through breakfast, Cole sheepishly walked into the dining room and seated himself at the farthest corner table and waited for Olli to take his order. She finished with two other customers before she made her way to Cole's table. She was carrying a large mug of strong black coffee. She told him she would talk with him when she finished with the other customers.

Cole sat sipping the scalding brew, knowing it would clear the mossy feeling from his mouth and brain. Cole nodded a greeting to Fred when he entered the dining room. Fred came straight over and sat down at the table across from Cole. They talked briefly. Fred left for the office when he saw Olli making her way toward the table. She was carrying a pot of hot coffee and a cup for herself. Fred knew the couple had some things to talk over after seeing Cole's condition the previous night. Olli had asked Gabby if she would mind if she took her last coffee break so she could talk to Cole.

The dining room was nearly empty. Olli and Cole sat talking in hushed tones. Olli kept filling their cups with the hot, strong elixir, then she held Cole's hand briefly before taking the empty cups into the kitchen.

Cole decided to wait in his room during the afternoon while Olli helped serve Christmas dinner. Her work was over at seven o'clock. The dinner had been another success but hadn't ended any too soon to suit Olli. She told Cole she was ready to leave.

Christmas 1928

Olli was on the brink of a new life, being married and finally having a home of her own to share with someone she truly loved. Even with his faults, she was ready, from that day on, to make the best of her life.

Cole told her during their brief coffee talk, that she would never see him take a drink again. By the earnestness and solemnness in his voice, she believed he was telling her the truth; besides, Olli knew she must forgive him his frailties because when he learned of the parts of her past that she should tell him, she hoped in his heart he would find the strength to forgive her.

They both had some slate cleaning to do, and they would work things out together as man and wife.

Cole put her baggage in his truck, then went with Olli to say their goodbye to Fred and Gabby. When Fred handed her pay check to her she noticed a sizable bonus had been added. She thanked them and gave them each a big hug. She asked them to come and see them whenever they got the chance. Waving farewell, Olli and Cole ran to the truck through the pelting rain.

Olli blew kisses to her good friends as the truck pulled through the muddy parking lot away from the lodge. Cole gently pulled Olli across the seat so she was sitting very close to him. He slipped his arm around her shoulders. She looked into his smiling face, feeling the warmth of this closeness, and returned a smile as she lay her blond head on his shoulder.

When they had driven down the road, around the first curve out of sight of the lodge, Cole pulled the truck to a stop. Without saying a word he pulled Olli roughly to him and kissed her soundly. Still silent, he held her shoulders. His face was a firm, serious mask that spoke of love, shame, a plea for forgiveness and promises to keep. He released her, gave a quick boyish smile and turned the truck back onto the road.

In silence they traveled toward their future, their minds filled with happenings, behind and ahead of them—also filled with small doubts and large expectations.

20
Toward The Future

Cole had rented a small house which, when they arrived, Olli found he had sparsely furnished. He gave a viable excuse that he wanted her to choose some of the things, nothing brand new because of the spring and summer plans when they would be camping out in the near-by forested hills. While camping, less furniture would mean lighter packing and moving problems when they were finished for the season.

Olli was happy to see that Cole had used his head in the purchase of a good used wood burning cook stove. It was light green and cream colored enamel with chrome warming oven and trim. Cole's other purchases consisted of a large air-tight wood heater, a small wooden table and two matching kitchen chairs. Cole had also purchased an iron bedstead which held a new cotton filled mattress. There was a pile of colorful woolen blankets and two goose down pillows—all which pleased Olli very much. The kitchen shelves were filled with canned food and staple items, plus an assortment of cooking utensils for their upcoming camping venture.

Olli was thrilled and told Cole that this was the first time she actually could call furnishings and homemaking items her own. Cole promised to buy her new things after the camping trip was over. Turning to him she kissed him warmly and told him how well he'd done. "You'll never know," she exclaimed, "how much having my own things means to me!"

Second Son

Cole smiled and said, "Hon, now I don't want you to get too tied up in fixing up this dump. It won't be long before we'll be packing it all up and moving to Chehalis where Ben, John and I have found our camping spot. I know you'll love it there. We'll be camped right beside a small creek. You wait and see. Ben and Lena, John and Hilda, and you and I will have a great time out in the woods."

Olli patted his face and cheerfully replied, "I just know I'll enjoy the change. I love you, Cole." However, deep in her soul, Olli could not deny her misgivings about the large tent they would share with at least two other brothers and their wives, especially Ben and Lena.

Cole continued, "Hon, I know we'll make a lot of money. The evergreen business will always do great because it seems there will always be a marry'n or a bury'n. As long as that goes on we will have work. We are our own bosses. We work when we want, where we want. So no matter where we move in Western Washington we'll be able to work."

Cole lifted Olli off the floor and gave her a quick whirl and a kiss. "You're going to love this whole set-up, I just know it. The work won't be that hard, and you'll learn to love the peace and quietness of the woods. I'll teach you all about the forest. I'll teach you the good mushrooms from the poisonous ones. The herbs and medicines, the edible plants and the tree names. It will be like going to school every day."

Olli wriggled from his arms and laughingly assured Cole, "I can hardly wait!" But to herself she thought: *first things first*. What she could hardly wait for was her wedding day—and wedding night. After that she would be able to handle all the new ideas and cope with the added in-laws and adventures of her new life. Yet, with the brothers and their wives around, Olli wondered if she and Cole would ever have any time to themselves after they moved into the tent. She'd just have to wait and see.

"Cole," Olli asked quietly, "do you suppose we should get a warm fire started in the heater before it gets any colder in here?

Toward The Future

You'll end up with a cold if you still plan to stay here by yourself for the next few nights. Or I could stay here to keep you warm," she suggested jokingly.

Cole's face turned solemn. "Hey! Don't talk like that. You know I've got to be a real good boy and make sure I take you to my folks place to stay for the next few days. I've got to keep in mind how they look at us and everything we do, out of respect for them—and for you. I'll stay here until the wedding."

Olli smiled and began collecting the things she needed to take to the Brauer's. She put them in a small satchel and set it by the door.

Cole took her suggestion and started a small fire in the heating stove to take the chill off the room. Later he drove Olli through the quiet, quaint logging town to his parent's house.

Olli told Dad Brauer she felt she was imposing and should have stayed at their new little house and let Cole stay with them, but neither Mother Mattie nor Dad Brauer would hear of it. So Olli was shown to a tiny attic bedroom high under the eaves.

After dinner, and Cole had left for the night, Olli said goodnight to her future in-laws and climbed the steep steps to her cozy sanctuary above the murmuring voices of her new family. In her mind some things were very unsettled, but here, right now, she felt cared for and completely safe.

During the next seven days Olli shopped for things she needed for the wedding. She found her dress in the only dress shop in town. Fortunately the shop was owned by an older lady who was an excellent seamstress. Olli chose a soft blue-gray georgette shift and an ivory colored lace collar with a matching cloche hat. She was told it was the latest style of the day. After all, the year ahead was 1929, and she wanted to look her best for her wedding.

Mother Brauer gave an afternoon tea to help Olli become acquainted with close family friends. It was a quiet, rather stiff affair, and it made Olli very conscious that she had no close friends or family to attend. But it was a kind attempt to acquaint her with in-laws and the Brauer family circle friends.

Nanny was clearly pleased with Cole's choice for a bride. She smiled and patted Olli's hand when she felt the conversation drifting away from familiar topics. She understood well Olli's feeling of sometimes being overlooked in festivities.

The three new sisters-in-law to be were in attendance and soon brought up the subject of the men's spring and summer plans to camp and work in the woods. All the ladies fluttered and twittered about what fun that would be for Cole and his bride, his brothers and their wives, to spend the summer working together in the great outdoors.

The conversation dwindled and the afternoon grew long. Soon the ladies began to excuse themselves and bundle up in their winter finery before wishing Olli good luck in her wedded life. Each one thanked Mother Mattie for the lovely party before they scurried off into the cold winter day.

Olli was pleased with what she had feared would be a dreadfully boring afternoon. She hugged Mother Mattie and told her how much she appreciated the time she and Nanny had spent preparing the sweets. She was happy they had made the effort for her.

Olli told her new sisters-in-law goodbye.

The husbands came to the house and honked their truck horns in a good humored clamor of noise, knowing that breaking up one of their mother's tea parties with a wild abandon from propriety would lead to a good-natured scolding. This was what her big boisterous brothers loved to do. The Brauer boys, all over six feet tall, loved to tease their mother who measured four-foot-eight. But she never backed down when it came to reminding her boys of their need for good manners.

That evening, being not only New Years Eve, but also the eve before their wedding, Cole and Olli decided to go for a quiet drive instead of mingling in the crowd at the community hall. It was the usual gathering place for all New Year festivities. Both Cole and Olli felt the need for time to talk and do a bit of catching up on things that been left unsaid, so they drove out the icy road that lead to The Jackson House. The Inn had been the pioneer residence of the Jackson Family. Over the years their farm became a half-way stop for road travelers from the Cowlitz River landing to Tumwater and the state capitol of Olympia.

Cole pulled the truck into the parking area of the Inn and left the engine running so the heater would keep them warm. Huddled in the cab of the pickup, they talked for over an hour.

Cole confided that he'd been in the army, but had never been sent to Germany. He was still in boot camp when the war ended, leaving him with an honorable discharge without ever having to fire a shot. He had come back to Castle Rock and became entangled in a group of unemployed, rough-and-tumble school chums. They began a drinking spree that lasted over three years. Cole only worked long enough to earn more whiskey money before going on another drinking binge. Despite pleas from his religious parents, his erratic behavior continued until on a drunken fishing trip two of his best friends drowned in the Cowlitz River. The loss of his friends was because of Cole's inability to respond to their cries for help due to his drunken condition. That rude awakening ended Cole's drinking days, and he even considered becoming a minister like his dad. His dad and he had many career discussions. Cole finally decided to go to school to become a mortician. He tried his best at that profession, but failed miserably.

Much needed solitude drove Cole to the natural surroundings he loved, where he began gathering florist evergreens and found the work satisfying and soothing, as well as profitable. Work in the woods was a healing tool for Cole and fit his disposition well. He found he was his happiest when the solemn whisper of wind and tree boughs in the woods made him forget his self-imposed guilt at the loss of his friends.

Cole seemed to have exhausted his ability to bring up any more things he felt he should tell Olli. He sat holding the steering wheel and was silent for a long moment. Then he turned and looked at Olli. She cleared her throat.

"Well," she began, "I guess I should do some catching up on some of my past too. I've already talked to your dad about all of this, so I guess it's only fair you hear my story also. You could say, for someone only twenty-one years old, you'll likely think what I'm going to tell you didn't happen to me, but it did." Olli, told Cole of her having to leave home at the age of fourteen. She omitted the part of her life that included her life at the Gordons and the child she had been forced to leave, but she did tell him about her marriage, the death of her baby girl, her husband, Dan Scarbrough, divorcing her—then, finally, the news of Dan's death, which she had heard by way of Dad Brauer's investigations.

Olli intentionally omitted that whole part of her life at the Gordons. She kept those details to herself, as her old friend, Dweena, had advised.

Cole listened intently. He showed neither surprise nor distrust. He drew Olli into his arms and pressed her head onto his shoulder. "Hon," he murmured, "my life didn't really have a purpose until the day I first met you. Do you think dragging our old chains behind us will do any good? I think not. I'm happy we cleared the air on both sides, but we're going to leave all the chaff behind. Tomorrow will be our chance to start fresh and new. From this day on I will be a one-woman man, and you'll be that woman."

After their long talk thy both felt better because of the bond of understanding they shared.

Olli boldly asked Cole if he wanted to go to their own little house and spend the night.

Cole grasped her shoulders and kissed her firmly. "I'd love nothing else, Hon! But, well, I owe it to my folks to honor their wishes that we wait until after we're married. It is after all only one more day."

Toward The Future

On the drive back to town bells and horns began to blow to herald in 1929.

Cole and Olli knew time would pass very slowly until the family gathered, the vows were said, the license was signed and family social graces were performed before their love for each other could be satisfied.

21

A Big, Short Wedding

New Year's morning Olli woke early. She lay there looking out of the attic window of her cozy attic room. She knew the cold and dampness on the outside would never penetrate this comfortable attic chamber. She felt safe and contented as she lay listening to the hushed tones of conversation below. The clanking of pots and pans announced the preparation of a large family breakfast to honor of the bride and groom.

Mother Mattie had said yesterday that instead of a big dinner they would all celebrate at breakfast. Because the wedding time of eleven o'clock would then give Cole and Olli the rest of the day to begin their short honeymoon in their own house across town.

Olli quickly dressed and went down stairs. Cole had already arrived. She could hear his low happy voice as he talked and teased his mother, while she fussed and fluffed around in the kitchen preparing something that smelled delicious. Olli realized she was famished.

When she entered the kitchen Cole gave her a smothering hug and an unashamed kiss, at which Dad Brauer laughed heartily.

Mother Mattie said, "Good morning Olli," while she rattled the implements where the great-smelling food was being prepared. "My Dear," she said, "while things are being readied, it would be a good time for you to bathe and get dressed in your good things before the rest of the boys and their wives get here. There is plenty of hot water and you can take your time. We'd love to see you in your pretty new things before the ceremony."

Olli thanked her and went back to the attic and brought her satchel that held all her finery and took it into the bathroom. She drew a tub of warm water, undressed and slipped into the soothing suds. She used lavender soap—and rubbed its fragrance over her body making her feel quite like royalty. When she was out of the tub she rubbed her body dry with a rough towel until her skin was pink and glowing. She dressed in her new lacy underwear—a luxury to her. Then, in a manner close to reverence, she slipped the simple blue-gray georgette dress over her head and smoothed it over her firm breasts and slim hips.

After donning her silk stockings, she stepped into her lace covered shoes which made her feel as if she could take a prize for the best dressed bride of the year. She gathered her things, combed her hair and picked up her lovely matching cloche deciding not to wear it until the ceremony.

When she entered the living room she saw that the rest of the family had already arrived. Everyone gave her a standing or boisterous "Hurrah," which embarrassed her. She ran to Cole and he laughingly held her to him tightly.

Mother Brauer announced, "Breakfast." The family seated themselves at the festive table.

They all bowed their heads and waited for grace to be said, then they devoured the huge feast that Mother Mattie and Nanny had prepared.

The day began to slip closer to eleven o'clock, and the women helped Mother Mattie clear away the meal. Cole and Olli visited quietly with the rest of the family. Cole's sister Margaret and his three youngest brothers filled every chair in the living room. The other brothers and their wives arrived to standing-room only.

Before it was time to go to the church Cole gave Olli a large cellophane box. Inside was the loveliest bridal bouquet Olli could have ever imagined. The bouquet was yellow rose buds mingled with baby breath which formed a huge nosegay from which

A Big, Short Wedding

streamed blue-gray and yellow satin ribbons. Olli was speechless. Her eyes filled with tears. Cole knew how happy she was. She gently kissed him and whispered, "These are the only flowers I'll ever want."

Dad Brauer looked at his gold watch. He called to the women in the kitchen telling them it was time to get over to the church. Then, in one jovial group, they all strolled across the yard from the parsonage to the quaint little church building. They entered the church and Dad Brauer went to a small room behind the pulpit. Wes's wife Mary seated herself at the pump organ in the front of the church and began softly playing The Wedding March.

The rest of the family seated themselves.

Wes held Olli's arm and waited at the back of the church until Cole and Dad Brauer were standing at the altar. Then Wes, whom Olli had asked to give her away, motioned for Olli to walk toward Cole. Her feet nearly refused to move until she saw Cole's broad smile

Olli looked angelic as she put her hand in Cole's. They exchanged vows. Dad Brauer gave a short message, asked all to bow for prayer and then pronounced Cole and Olli man and wife.

After the ceremony a brief reception was held at the parsonage.

Within the hour, Cole and Olli escaped from the jovial, boisterous, clutch of loving brothers, sister, sister-in-laws and parents. They headed out of town with strings of rattling cans and old shoes tied to the rear bumper of their truck. After they had driven into the countryside Cole stopped and removed the rattling conglomeration from the truck bumper. He drove the back roads until they reached their tiny house.

The brothers knew better than to bother the newlyweds. Cole had threatened his brothers, if his wedding night was interrupted, after waiting nearly thirty-one years for the right woman, he'd skin them—one by one. Then he'd hang their hides on the fence if they planned any monkey business. Not a soul disturbed them.

Cole carried his bride over the threshold. He closed the door with one foot; never breaking his careful stride as he strode to the

Second Son

cozy little bedroom. He walked directly toward the ornate iron bed and gently placed Olli on the soft mattress.

Olli lay very still as Cole eased down beside her, still holding her and stroking her shining crown of blonde hair. He kissed her face. Her neck, even with her wool coat between his mouth and her body she could feel his warm breath on her.

Cole slowly stood up and pulled her to stand close beside him. "I hope you are ready to be loved for a long time Girl, 'cause, my sweet lady, we're about to be so busy we'll never get out of this house for a week. I'm going to love you until we're both weak with pleasure, or hunger."

Olli removed her coat and tossed it on the foot of the bed. She held his hands and pulled Cole to her.

"Olli," Cole whispered, "I want to undress my bride, if it's all right with you?"

A tremor of excitement shook Olli's slim frame. She answered his question with a smile and an affirmative nod of her head as she sat, then eased down on the bed.

Cole knelt beside the bed not noticing the chill of the linoleum floor. His interest was on Olli's softly clad body that stretched out on the bed before him.

He removed her shoes, more by feel than sight. His gaze never left Olli's eyes. She watched as he reached her hosiery tops, gently lifted her dress until her thighs were in view. He smiled when he saw her garter belt and the clips that held up her hosiery. His breath was heavy with emotion as he smiled and said, "This is getting complicated."

Olli lay very still while Cole uncoupled the fronts and backs of the garter belt and slowly rolled her stockings down to her knees, then further, until each stocking slid off her toes. He touched her ankles, letting his hands move up her legs stopping short of her lace panties.

Olli reached up to unbutton the front of her dress, but he took her hands away from the dress saying, "Please, Hon, let me do this. I want to be the one who opens this pretty package."

A Big, Short Wedding

Cole slowly unbuttoned her dress front, pulled her to a sitting position and peeled her dress bodice down to her waist. He drew her close and kissed each shoulder while he reached behind her and lifted her camisole, letting it fall in her lap.

He sat back on his heels and stared at Olli's rounded, petal-soft body. He breathed deeply. "Oh, God," he murmured, "I knew you'd be this beautiful.

Cole gathered her in his powerful arms and kissed her soundly on her soft responding mouth, then he completed the task of completely disrobing her. It seemed strange to her, but she felt no shyness in the act. She knew only a pleasant feeling of completely belonging to someone and that knowledge filled her with excitement that led to complete ecstasy.

Cole covered her with a warm blanket, removed his clothes and slipped into bed beside her. The urgency of their love making turned the afternoon into a fervor of movement, and touching, making their love complete. More precious than a priceless gem, more grand and fulfilling than a million exploding stars.

Olli knew, at last, she had found the rest of her life.

Cole held her in his naked embrace, marveling at the fragile softness which kept their lovemaking growing from crescendo to crescendo until a peaceful exhaustion overtook them.

For the two lovers, New Year's Day faded into a chill starlit night outside the insignificant house on Fir St. But inside the fire burned bright, though no eye could see it. In the lovers hearts, a flame had been lit that would keep out the cold of the whole world.

Cole and Olli warmed each other with love in body and spirit.

22

Mr. And Mrs. Cole Brauer, Jr.

The months that followed were filled with Cole working everyday and cherishing evenings with his bride in the tiny house. Olli busied herself with routine chores. She hand sewed two-pieced quilts like the ones she'd seen her Ma make.

In March the planning began for the long-talked-about campout that Cole, Ben and John had been anticipating.

At the last minute their oldest brother Wes decided if there was room enough in the big army tent, he and his wife Mary would join them. It was a chance to make a good sum of money in a short time, as they were expecting their first baby, and Wes wanted Mary to have the best care he could afford.

The four brothers selected a campsite near Chehalis in a wooded fern and evergreen-laden valley beside a creek. The tent had a canvas roof, a wooden floor and wooden panels half way up the walls, with four windows on each side. They divided the bedrooms by hanging sheets as four room dividers, leaving a communal kitchen and small living room area.

They built a privy at a prudent distance from the living quarters, and erected an open-sided tent for evergreen storage a short way from the creek. The picnic table was established near an open pit for outdoor cooking. On warm summer days, meals could be cooked and eaten outside.

All the plans, and the execution thereof, were completed when Wes's wife Mary went into early labor and delivered a frail, baby

Second Son

girl. It was decided that Wes would still work with the men, but Mary and the baby would go back to town and stay with Dad and Mother Brauer, close by medical help if it was needed.

The other sisters-in-law were expected to work in the woods with the men and do the rest of the daily chores as well. This was quite a change for all of them. Olli and John's wife, Hilda, never complained, but, as Olli had expected, Lena was constantly whining and finding other things to do instead of helping as she had promised to do.

Ben made excuses for her which didn't bring much harmony, but when Lena was in her "room" camp life was easier. So Hilda and Olli decided to leave Lena there and do the chores themselves rather than have conflict.

Each brother and wife kept an accounting of their own earnings by tagging the evergreen bundles they picked everyday.

By April they were involved in the hard task of supplying evergreens to several wholesale florist warehouses. Their work was beginning to pay great rewards, not only from the florists in Portland, but also in Seattle.

The summer passed quickly. Their bank accounts grew, which made the men even more enthused about the working arrangement. However, underlying tensions grew among the women. Some of them fussed about having to wash clothes in the creek. There was contention about the cooking schedule. All but Lena were too tired to enjoy the picnic area by the creek.

Olli worked up schedule so she and Hilda worked four days and took three off. Any day they were ill or worked too late, it was Lena's turn. On those days Ben helped Lena in the kitchen. This schedule seemed to work more smoothly—for a while.

By the end of September Olli had picked and canned wild raspberries, blackberries, mushrooms and trout, that is, on the days she was free from working in the woods.

She and Hilda collected two buckets of red and white agates from the creek bed. They found them as they washed clothes in the shallow pools. They were determined to make something decorative for their houses when camping days were finished for the season.

One afternoon Hilda was working in the woods. Olli was cleaning the kitchen. She took a dishpan of soapy water out beside the tent intending to dump it in the grass. She bumped into Lena, who, at the same moment, came sauntering around the corner of the tent. Reacting to avoid splashing Lena with the warm soapy contents of the pan, Olli dumped the water down the front of Lena's dress and all over herself as well. She looked at Lena and herself, and, seeing the hilarity in the situation, began to laugh.

Lena on the other hand let out a loud squeal and instantly became angry.

Having dropped the dishpan, Olli apologized as she attempted to brush the bubbles from the front of her own dress and apron. She reached out to brush the suds from Lena's dress. Lena swung her hand to ward off Olli's attempt to help her. By mistake, Lena struck Olli on the chin. The unexpected blow knocked Olli to the ground.

Shocked at the consequences of her quick temper, Lena dropped to her knees to help Olli and see if she was all right. Lena clutched Olli's shoulders assisting her to rise.

Olli, looking directly at Lena, saw her face go blank, then twist as if in pain.

Lena gave a childish whimper. Glassy tears formed in her deep brown eyes, and she hung her head as though in great shame. Lena hunkered down, head bent, hands holding her knees. A shudder of sadness shook her body. She began to sob. She was showing a side of herself Olli had never seen before. Lena's cloak of superiority and irritability had dissolved.

To quiet her, Olli crawled over to Lena and gently patted her shoulders to console her sister-in-law. "Please Lena," she said, "I'm okay. And I'm sorry about getting you wet. I didn't see you coming. It was an accident. I know you didn't mean to hit me. It was all just a silly accident."

Lena watched Olli struggle to her feet, watched the water and bubbles stream down the front of Olli's dress, down her legs, into her anklets and overflow into her shoes. From somewhere behind Lena's tears a giggle raised itself through her chest and up her throat and she burst into uncontrolled laughter. She grabbed Olli's arms, struggling to stand amidst peals of laughter. Olli caught the infectious humor as she looked into Lena's face and began laughing too. They clung to each other for quite a long moment, until both were breathless from laughter.

When the incident was over they brushed the bubbles from their clothes and looked at each other in a manner that had never before passed between them. An understanding or camaraderie had immerged.

Olli had first met Lena at the lodge over a year ago. During the interim Lena had kept Olli shoved away, often showing open hostility. For the short time at the lodge after Fred and Gabby had talked to her, Lena acted like a happy, gracious person, especially with the customers, but her attitude toward Olli had always been hostile. She had never been what Olli could call her friend. After Lena and Ben were married, Lena hadn't been friendly with any of her sisters-in-law. Even when their combined camping venture started, Lena had detached herself and hadn't done what was expected of her. Olli and the other sisters-in-law felt it best to leave Lena alone, hoping in time things would work out.

Olli picked up the dishpan and walked toward the back door of the tent. As she started to go inside Lena made the first attempt at conversation.

"Olli," she said quietly, "could you sit out here with me for a minute?"

Surprised, Olli replied, "If you're not too uncomfortable in your wet clothes, I guess we could sit a minute." She indicated the picnic bench near the door.

Lena looked at Olli again showing signs of tears in her eyes. She spoke in a quiet manner. "Olli, I know for all the time I've known you, you've tried to be kind to me. I guess I haven't wanted kindness from anyone. I apologize for the trip to the mountain when

Mr. And Mrs. Cole Brauer, Jr.

Cole and Ben took us fishing. I got drunk and acted pretty stupid. I was sure after that embarrassing incident that you thought I was just a drunken Indian. I was ashamed, so I stayed away from you. Gabby and Fred saw I was unhappy. They called me into the office and made me tell them all about my background, to see if they could help me change my attitude at work. If I didn't change, they said they would have to let me go."

Lena paused and seemed to take a cleansing breath before going on. "I really needed the job," she continued. "I told them how I was raised and where I came from. They gave me good advice. I took their advice on the job, but, other than Ben, I couldn't make myself be friendly with anyone. You see, being a member of an Indian tribe is a tough thing to be when you leave the reservation where you were raised, especially for me. I am the daughter of a chief. I wasn't expected to do woman's work. We lived on a reservation in eastern Washington. I was told I held a position higher than other women, so I did as I pleased."

Lena chattered on as though she had opened the lid of a long closed box and was bent on emptying all the contents in one big heap, as if to clean out long-held cobwebs. "When I became a nuisance at home I went to town and got in with a bad crowd, drinking, and carousing and causing trouble until my father took me before the tribal council. I was told to find a job and care for myself away from the tribe. I had become an embarrassment to my family. If I tried to go home I would be sent to an area in Puget Sound where undesirables were sent. So I ran away and went to Chehalis where I saw the ad in the paper for the job at the lodge."

As Lena continued, Olli could see Lena's life hadn't been easy and she could relate to that. Lena went on. "Fred and Gabby gave me a chance. They told me I was pretty. They told me I could improve myself by being charming with the customers—that part of their advice worked. I did well for myself. The tips showed me that."

Her demeanor saddened at her next statement. "I always felt I was ugly and would eventually end up toothless and bent like many of the older women I'd seen when I was a child. Then I met Ben, and he liked me, and I liked him. I never had a women friends, so I didn't know how to act around you or Hilda or Mary, or even Mother Mattie. I pushed you all away."

Lena's face began to light up as she said, "But I think it's about time I joined this family of brothers and sisters-in-law. Especially now that I know we'll always live close and work together and have children that will know each other. I'd like to start by being more friendly to you, if you'll forgive me for my earlier mistakes. Maybe Hilda and Mary and the rest of the family will accept me too, if I change my attitude and my ways. What do you think?"

Olli took Lena's long lovely hands in hers, smiled and quietly answered, "Lena, we have all had our troubles and we've all made mistakes. You are not queen of the hill in that respect. I know I'll do my best to be your friend, as will all the family. Even without your life story or explanation, I think everyone will be happy to see a change in your attitude. Your new outlook is already pretty evident to me."

The two women stood up and walked to the door. As they reached the door each felt their soggy, wet dresses and again began to laugh until they got hiccups. A simple thing like a pan of soapy water had broken down an old barrier.

23
October 1929!

Once a week Cole brought mail from Chehalis to the camp. Olli received letters from Dweena, her sister Eva and her niece, Elise. Eva had recently turned fifteen and was still at home. This situation did not sit well with Ma and Papa—who were quite clear about the rule of leaving at fourteen—as observed by the previous siblings, including Olli herself.

Opening the lavender envelope that she knew to be from Eva, Olli smiled to herself. Eva was so romantically-inclined she never wrote on a plain piece of paper. Neither was her handwriting plain. She wrote in curls and flourishes making her letters immediately identifiable. Olli scanned the short letter and found it was a request from Eva to move to Chehalis and stay at the camp sight with her and Cole and the others. It was not merely a request, she begged and pleaded that they let her come, as things at home were not going well.

Eva promised to work with them in the woods and do her share of chores—anything to get away from home, and away from the unhappy situation of having Papa's constant haranguing about Eva not working and paying for the privilege of a roof over her head.

How well Olli remembered the feeling of not being wanted, the feeling of helplessness, and the fear of being out in a world about which she knew very little. She saw that Eva's letter was a plea for a way out.

Second Son

Olli spoke to Cole about Eva's request. Cole felt that having one of Olli's family near her would make her happy, so he agreed Olli should write and ask Eva to take the bus from Lynden to Chehalis where Olli and he would meet her the bus station.

After talking to his brothers and sisters-in-law about the addition of Eva to the group of Cole's family, all were in agreement that another pair of hands to help with the work would be an advantage. Besides, everyone could see Olli was excited at the prospect of her favorite younger sister's arrival.

Olli wrote a note to Eva telling her which bus to take. She tucked enough money in the envelope to cover the price of the ticket. In the note she told Eva that they would be working and camping until October. After which they planned to move to Shelton, a small logging community out on the westernmost reach of the Puget Sound. There the brothers had found new territory from which they could harvest a variety of marketable evergreens. Olli told Eva she could live with her and Cole. If she found she didn't like working in the woods, there were many other opportunities for work in town.

A week went by before she received a letter back from Eva asking Cole to pick her up at the bus station in Chehalis on the following Wednesday.

Eva arrived and Cole let her know there would be only a few more weeks at the camp. The fact that they would soon be moving didn't seem to disturb Eva. In fact, she quickly blended into the family group and took a large burden off the women by doing all the cleaning. She was a welcome asset and a real scrubber.

The weather turned from sparkling gold and green days, to what Olli called, the glooms, winter just around the corner. Having Eva with her she found herself in a happier mood, despite the rain and fog in which they worked. The leaky tent, the chill and dampness were all easier to adjust to when Eva's clear sweet singing voice tricked like warm sunshine over the drab walls of the tent.

The week they packed their belongings to move to Shelton,

October 1929!

Ben came back from town calling to everyone to gather 'round. "I heard it on the local station!" he said out all in a rush. "Blasting the news all morning! All about the crash of the stock market on Wall Street! Men loosing fortunes! Jumping from office building windows! Plunging to their deaths! The financial loss of millions of dollars in a few hours! In just hours!"

Cole tried to calm everyone, reminding them they were lucky, having taken all their hard-earned money out of the bank the preceding week in preparing for the move to Shelton. Each had their summer earnings in cash. "It sounds like," he added, "we'll all feel very fortunate in the coming months."

Thus Cole, Olli and Eva moved to Shelton, followed by John and Hilda. John had three carpentry jobs waiting for him. Wes and Mary, with their ill baby daughter, had decided to move to the thriving town of Wenatchee over the Cascades, where they purchased a furniture store and a small house in the apple-growing region of the state. Ben and Lena planned to stay in Chehalis until they could decide how to invest their money. Cole was fearful that it might be invested in a saloon—not to own it but to frequent it. He didn't however feel it his place to comment.

Cole and Olli rented a house at the west end of Shelton. The backyard had a wide sunny spot for a garden which they would plant the following spring. At the far end of the yard a wide creek tumbled aimlessly, murmuring through cottonwood and maple trees. Eva was given the loft bedroom that overlooked the creek. She told Olli she felt like a queen to have her own room. After being crowded sleeping with two of her sisters in one bed at home, the quiet was a luxury! Eva knew Olli and Cole were giving her the room at Olli's urging. For Olli was well aware since her experiences at the Gordons, how important a person's privacy could be.

Eva was far more fortunate than Olli had been at her age. She had a place to stay where she was wanted and had become part of Olli's family. There was no time to feel the homesickness Olli had suffered. Eva knew she was lucky that she was with her kind sister.

Cole helped Eva lift her luggage, mattress and bed frame up

the narrow stairway into the attic. They wouldn't allow Olli to help because Olli discovered the week before the move, she was pregnant.

Cole began treating her like fragile glass. He was obviously very happy and protective of her. Olli had never had anyone give her such care and show such concern. She loved it. And she was excited having her very own home. She had so many things she wanted to do to fix the house inside and out. Cole told her she should let Eva do most of the painting and wallpapering and flowerbed gardening. He would spade the garden spot.

Olli felt a bit helpless in the following weeks while Cole and Eva hustled and bustled every spare minute accomplishing the tasks that needed to be done.

Cole was such a soft spoken, happy man. He loved Olli very much. He whistled while he worked in the yard. Olli and Eva could tell where he was by the happy tunes that floated through the garden and echoed through the house.

Eva knew Olli was fortunate to have found such a good man, especially since Eva knew the sad times Olli had been through years before. Eva had felt she was the luckier of the two sisters—until Olli found Cole. She hoped that she would be as lucky when she found a husband. Eva's thoughts traced back a few months and remembered how impressed she had been with the handsome young bus driver who talked to her all the way from Tacoma.

Eva had taken the bus from Tacoma to Chehalis, when she came to live with Olli and Cole. The bus driver, Kurt, asked if he could write to her and asked for her address. He promised to write soon. Since that time she hadn't heard a word.

Cole started using small terms of endearment for Olli, which, given the circumstances of the somewhat cramped domicile, embarrassed her. She told him she wasn't used to being pinched, teased, kissed and nuzzled in front of anyone, let alone her sister Eva. So Cole chose a nickname for her which amused her. He called her Muzzy. He said it was short for Little Mother.

Olli always smiled when he whispered in her ear the

October 1929!

endearment "Muzzy." Olli began calling Cole by her own term of endearment, Tatta. "It means 'Daddy'," she said.

It made Eva happy to see Cole so much in love with Olli.

Cole wouldn't allow Olli to work in the woods gathering evergreens, so Eva worked in Olli's place.

Cole wrote to Ben and Lena and asked them to move to Shelton and work with him. The orders for evergreens were piling up and two people couldn't work hard and fast enough to fill them. Cole told Ben that even with the depression in full swing it seemed the florists always needed evergreens. Ben and Lena soon moved close by to labor with Cole and Eva.

The four worked everyday in rain, snow, wind and sun, filling the multitude of orders from Seattle and Portland. They made a comfortable living despite the fact that many of their friends and neighbors were out of work.

Eva was a great help to Olli. Even after working all day, Eva's energy seemed never to lag. The sisters had a happy time making baby clothes and blankets and crocheting sweaters and booties in the months awaiting the arrival of Cole and Olli's first child.

Olli had a wonderful doctor who cared for her during the pregnancy. The doctor knew the baby was not Olli's first, so told her the second or third delivery would likely be faster and easier than the previous one.

August 1st, 1930. The day arrived for the baby's expected appearance. Cole called the doctor who came to the house. He arrived just in time to deliver a healthy baby girl, whom they named "Tess." She was endowed with curly red hair and a lusty cry. Cole was amazed at the short time Olli had been in labor, as apposed to the long difficult labor that Ben, Wes and Johns' wives had suffered.

When the doctor called Cole into the bedroom to see Olli and the baby, he was clearly taken aback at the infant's small size. He gently kissed Olli before lifting the flannel blanket from the baby's face. His first glance showed the wonder he felt. "Such a delicate little creature!" he exclaimed. "Her hands are so tiny, yet every finger is perfect." He smiled at Olli as he touched the delightful silky halo of curly red fuzz which covered the baby's head. He knew his mother would be especially happy to know his first child had hair this fine color, a true Brauer and Ogden redhead.

Cole's mother, Mattie, had been a Welsh redhead when she was a girl, but by the time she had nine children her hair had turned snow white. "No doubt from the stress of nine offspring," she had often stated. Cole's brother Ben's red hair had carried on the Ogden tradition, but Cole and Olli's baby was his contribution to the family legacy—the Welsh blood line. This made Cole very proud. He was not aware that Olli's mother and two sisters also had red hair, so, he felt totally responsible for the child with the golden-red hair. Olli didn't discourage his enthusiasm by telling him differently. Tess was a delightfully happy baby. And why not? If Olli wasn't answering her every whimper and whim, Aunty Eva or her daddy Tatta cared for the child's needs.

Shortly after the baby's arrival, Eva received a post from Ma containing an opened letter from Kurt, the bus driver she had met months before.

The letter had been returned to sender, then sent to Cole and Olli's old address in Chehalis and on to Eva's old home address. The letter was months old. No doubt Ma had received it and put it aside or decided to not send it to Eva, then changed her mind. Clearly Ma had read the letter. Eva knew Ma didn't respect any of her children's privacy, but Eva was happy nonetheless, despite Ma's meddling, as she read the short missive. Kurt was a perfect gentleman—a fact born out by the brief note. In the envelope containing Kurt's letter, Ma had included a scrawled note informing Eva she'd be well advised not to write back to Kurt, but to pay attention to helping Olli. Eva folded the note from Ma and tossed it in the wastebasket.

That evening Eva confided in Olli about the letter. "I want to reply to Kurt, but Ma says I shouldn't."

"Eva," said Olli, "you must start thinking for yourself. Ma and

October 1929!

Papa no longer control your life. Why don't you invite Kurt here for dinner sometime."

"That sounds great! Oh, Olli, thank you!"

So Eva wrote a return letter inviting Kurt to come and meet her sister's family.

Three weeks passed, marking the end of August, before Eva heard from Kurt. His letter informed Eva that he had three days off beginning next Monday. He made reservations at the largest hotel in Shelton, so that he and Eva could have dinner two evenings together, after dining with the family on his first night in town. Tuesday and Wednesday he planned to take Eva on a few scenic drives: one out to the coast to walk along the ocean and one north to Hood Canal.

Eva was overjoyed! With Olli's help they began planning for the family to meet Kurt.

Eva chattered excitedly about what she should wear and asked Olli if she should plan a boxed lunch to take on their trips or should she expect Kurt to buy lunch?

When Cole came in from work that evening Olli told him the plans to meet Eva's friend and the invitation that had been sent for him to have dinner with them. Cole said, "Good. About time Eva made some friends. She's too young to be isolated with only family members. I've been giving some thought about her. If you don't need her to help with Tess as much as before, I feel it would do her good to find a job in town. That way she'll be meeting new people, and the work would not be as hard for her."

"I agree entirely," said Olli.

And so did Eva. "You have been so kind to me, both of you," she told them. The prospect of working uptown in a store would give Eva a chance to wear some of the stylish clothes she had sewn for herself.

The day finally dawned for Kurt to come to dinner. Eva was in a flurry of scrubbing, ironing and fussing so she would look her best. Olli prepared a wonderful meal. Cole came home from work early. "Lord forbid," he quipped to Olli, "that I shouldn't look good to impress your little sister's new suitor."

Before Kurt arrived, Eva asked Cole and Olli to tell her if they liked Kurt by just giving her a nod of approval, which they agreed to do. Cole, with a wink directed in Olli's direction, said, "Eva, you can bet if I think he's not good enough for you I'll boot him out on his ear, so he better watch himself."

Eva laughingly replied, "Oh Cole, I just know you and Olli will think he's great. Even though we've met only once he seemed so nice. He's funny and handsome too. I can hardly wait until he gets here." She fluffed her hair and asked, "Do I look alright?"

Cole and Olli assured her she looked very grown up but was acting like a giddy school girl. They all laughed together. Cole looked out the window and announced, "I believe he has just driven into the driveway." He immediately went to the door.

Kurt knocked and Cole open it, inviting him in. "Name's Cole." Indicating Olli, "My wife, Olli."

"Howdy," nodded Kurt. "Mrs. Brauer."

Olli and Cole were immediately impressed with Eva's friend, and as Cole had promised, he gave Eva an approving nod as he lead Kurt into the living room.

The evening went well. Kurt thoroughly enjoyed the food and conversation. The two couples played cards for an hour or so, laughing and joking amiably, enjoying the new found camaraderie. Olli went to put baby Tess in her bassinet.

Kurt asked Cole's permission to take Eva for a short drive around town. Cole told the young couple to go, but that they should be back before midnight.

After Kurt and Eva left, Olli and Cole went off to bed.

Later, lying in bed nearly asleep, Olli smiled in the dark when she heard Kurt bring Eva home.

On the porch Eva said a quiet goodnight to Kurt before she entered the house. She thought Cole and Olli were asleep, so was surprised when she heard Cole's voice boom out of the bedroom,

October 1929!

"Nice catch Eva!" And they all laughed. Eva giggled as she went to her room.

The next morning, after Cole went to work, Eva and Olli sat in the kitchen having morning coffee while Tess played on her knee. Her red curly hair shone in the sunlight that streamed through the window. Eva reached down and caressed the infant's soft halo of curls and told Olli how lucky she was to have such a sweet child. Eva secretly wished that one day she would have a child, and she had set her heart on waiting for Kurt to fall in love with her. She knew, already, she loved him. Hers had been love at first sight. She hoped the same magic had happened to Kurt.

Near noon Kurt stopped the long black car in the driveway leaving the motor running. When he came to the door her told Olli he planned to take Eva on a drive to Hood Canal and have a picnic before it started to rain, saying they would be back before dark. Olli told them to drive carefully.

Eva and Kurt spent his days off driving around the areas between Mt. Rainier, the Long Beach Peninsula and Hood Canal. Soon Kurt's days off were over and he returned to Portland. He promised to be back in thirty days.

Olli could see they were smitten with each other because they wrote every day. She knew it wouldn't be long before wedding bells rang. She also realized Eva was headstrong so if they were truly in love they wouldn't wait or ask for permission of family.

Eva gave Cole and Olli the news that she had taken a job in the local furniture store. She told them she would pay them rent as soon as she received her first paycheck.

Cole said, "No." But Eva insisted. She began work in town the following Monday.

After Cole had spaded the garden spot, it was planted and produced a splendid crop.

Olli and Eva canned every vegetable that grew large enough to be pulled, dug, or picked.

The garden yielded a wonderful bounty, so the two women

canned hundreds of quarts of food. The apple orchard gave an abundance of sweet apples which the women quickly made into apple sauce and mincemeat.

    In late October, Cole, Ben and John went deer hunting, bringing home plenty of venison. So Eva and Olli canned that meat as well, until the root cellar was filled with enough food to last until the next gardening season.

24
Nell

In November of 1932, just before Thanksgiving, Olli gave birth to a second daughter. She and Cole named her Nell. The blonde, green-eyed cherub had a jolly disposition and enchanting grin endearing all to her instantly.

Though Cole had wished for a son, as he thought about it, the girls being just a little over two years apart, both Olli and he felt how great it would be for these two sisters close in age growing up together.

Olli had to stay in bed a long time after Nell was born. She couldn't seem to get her strength back. Nonetheless, she felt she just had to help with the preparations for a grand Thanksgiving dinner.

Ben and Lena, John and Hilda, Wes and Mary and their babies were invited. Eva gave Olli any preparations that could be done sitting down. Eva understood Olli was not strong enough to have all the company that was coming, and worried about her older sister. But she was also excited that Kurt would be able to join them. He'd have a chance to more of Cole's family.

Olli peeled potatoes, made stuffing for the venison roast, while Eva baked pies and chose the nicest canned vegetables from the root cellar.

While the meal was being prepared, the three sisters-in-law watched over the young children. They listened to the great time the brothers and Kurt were having guffawing and telling stories of their growing up days, all the mischief they had done, supposedly without their father's knowledge.

The dinner was a complete success. Eva and Olli chatted as they cleared the table. The sisters-in-law did the dishes and put them away. The evening ended quietly as everyone gathered their sleepy offspring and departed, thanking Cole and Olli for the wonderful dinner.

Eva and Kurt said good night. Eva was saddened by the fact that Kurt was on his way back to Portland and she wouldn't see him for another month. But by Christmas, she and Kurt had eloped and moved to Portland where they set up house keeping with Kurt's mother.

Kurt's mother's house was large and opulent, and because Kurt had been staying there before their elopement, there wasn't much adjustment for him. However for Eva it was a different story. It was the first time meeting Kurt's mother, and Eva was clearly stepping into a life in which she had a lot of adjustments to make. Right from the start, the older woman seemed dour, complaining and critical of Eva's every move.

Eva wrote often to Olli, sharing her happiness with Kurt and her struggles with his mother.

For Olli the next few months blended into a busy routine of work and childcare.

Winter 1933 blended into spring, then summer into fall, deep into the Depression. But Olli and Cole and their family were doing well compared to so much of the country—and the world, roiling once again to the winds of war.

Olli missed having Eva and all her help. She and Eva kept in touch by writing every week. Olli felt the mood of Eva's letters showed living with Kurt's mother was not a happy or an easy thing for either her or Kurt. Olli felt bad that there was nothing she could do to help Eva.

Nell

Late one autumn afternoon Eva telephoned Olli's neighbor, Mrs. Valley, and asked her to give Olli a message. It was about Ma and Papa back home in Lynden. Grandma Lucy Warren, Ma's side of the family, had died. Ma wanted Olli and Eva to come home for the funeral. Being that Grandma Warren had always held a special place in both girls' childhood memories, Eva hoped Olli would join her in complying with Ma's wishes.

When Cole arrived home from work that evening, Olli told Cole the news. "Eva and Kurt are leaving tomorrow for Lynden," she said. "I really should go, Cole. I need to. Grandma Warren, she was always so kind to me—and Eva too. Kurt and Eva said they can pick me up on the way north tomorrow."

This request surprised Cole. This was the first time he'd heard Olli speak kindly or fondly of any of her family—other than Eva. Especially Olli being concerned for her mother's feelings, concerned enough to make the long trip just because her mother had requested her to be there. "If it means that much to you, Hon." He didn't know what else to say. "But what about the girls?"

Olli had not told Cole that earlier in the week she had also received a letter from her old friend Dweena, the Gordon's house cook, asking if it was possible for Olli to come to see her.

The Gordons were gone for a two week trip to San Francisco. Mother Gordon was going too, which would leave Dweena to care for Cal (now ten years old). The fact that they would be alone would give Olli a chance to see her son. Dweena thought time enough had passed and the opportunity was right. Dweena had readied Cal to expect to meet an old friend of hers who might stop by some afternoon; she told Cal she hadn't seen her friend Olli for years.

So Olli told Cole she wanted to go for the funeral, riding up with Eva and Kurt, then stay overnight and come back later the next day on the train. Cole was a little puzzled at Olli's request to come back on the train, but he did agree that she should go and be with her family at this time.

Olli went next door to Mrs. Valley's and called Eva, accepting

Second Son

her invitation to go to the funeral with her and Kurt. She also relayed her plans to stay overnight in Tacoma and return to Olympia on the train where Cole would pick her up at East Olympia station. She then telephoned Dweena to tell her she would see her and Cal the day after her Grandma's funeral. So the plans were made—with Cole none the wiser.

Early in the morning of the next day, a blustery, cold and wet fall day, Eva and Kurt pulled into the driveway to find Olli ready to leave.

Cole had gone to work and Mrs. Valley was caring for Tess and Nell. She told Olli not to worry about the little girls. She said, "It will be fun for Richard and me to have two lively little ones playing around the house and staying the night. Go be with your family and we will see you tomorrow evening."

Olli gave the girls quick hugs and kisses. She waved out the back window of the car as Kurt drove down the street toward Olli's first visit to the family farm since she had recovered from her breakdown and stay at the mental hospital nearly six years before.

On the trip to the farm the sisters chattered like it had been only yesterday since they had seen each other. Eva told Olli she and Kurt had moved to their own apartment and they were very happy to be on their own. The best news was that she and Kurt were soon expecting a baby, in September or October.

Olli laughed because she had the same news to give Eva. Cole and she expected their third baby in November. The sisters shed happy tears together.

It seemed Eva's life was turning out like she had prayed it would.

Kurt was a fast but capable driver. They arrived at the Jergensen Farm at noon. The services for Grandma Warren were scheduled for two in the afternoon—leaving time only for the usual family sharing of thoughts and grieving before all the brothers and sisters, Ma and Papa, and assorted neighbors wended their way in

Nell

a slow rag-tag caravan of cars to the cemetery where Olli's oldest sister Rose and Olli's baby Jenny were buried.

When the short graveside service for Grandma Warren ended Ma wanted Olli to walk with her to Jennie's grave, but Olli declined—telling Ma that she was tired. Her present pregnancy was giving her an upset stomach and she just wanted to go back to the farm.

The truth was that she couldn't pretend emotion that Ma would expect from her. That chapter of her life was closed. She didn't want to dampen her expectations of the next day—being as tomorrow held for her the opportunity to see her boy, her son Cal, which was as much the reason for her coming to Grandma's funeral.

Ma acquiesced with Olli's wishes, and they returned to the car where they awaited the other family members who aimlessly wandered around among the headstones—sharing hushed reminiscence as they walked amid the resting places of family and old friends.

As Ma and she sat in the chilly car, Olli became quiet and distant. Rain drizzled down the windows, coating everything with gloom that penetrated not only her damp coat but her very soul. She observed family members shuffling here and there, the dripping trees, the whipping tree limbs dancing in the wind. She wanted to shout at everyone to get in their cars and get out of this depressing place. Didn't they know she had a happy mission to accomplish tomorrow? Tomorrow she would see her first born child. A joy was awaiting her and she needed no more mourning and moping. Olli just needed to get away and leave the dead behind.

Once back at the farm the family prepared a huge pot-luck dinner. The neighbors had also brought additional dishes of food to add to the feast. The sadness which had hung like wet moss over everyone had vanished. Taking its place was laughter, jovial tales and good food. Then someone began playing a fiddle, quite melancholy at first, then banjos and guitars joined in along with

Second Son

the piano, one of the brothers playing happier tunes, until the house hummed, pulsed and rattled with a din that drove Olli outside and down the path to the privy in order to escape.

Near nightfall the crowd dispersed leaving Ma and Papa, Kurt, Eva and Olli sitting amid the clutter of food bowls and dirty plates.

Olli volunteered to begin the clean up, but Ma said that she and the sisters would take care of them in the morning. So she, Kurt and Eva were free to start home, because of the late hour.

Olli thanked Ma, saying she was weary and they really should be on their way.

Kurt and Eva agreed, so Olli gathered up their coats and things. They said their farewells to Ma and Papa and drove up the lane to the main road. Heading south they reached the outskirts of Tacoma, where Olli asked Kurt to let her out at the large hotel across from the Union Station. She said she was tired and had made arrangements to stay the night in Tacoma, and Cole would be picking her up in East Olympia at the train station tomorrow.

Kurt obliged her by driving her to the hotel. The doorman helped her from the car and carried her small bag inside to the desk. Olli watched Eva and Kurt drive off into the night; then she registered for her room. Once in her room she sprawled, unladylike, in complete relaxation on the soft bed. She pulled the bedspread over herself—fully dressed and drifted into a muddled sleep.

In the dining room the next morning Olli ordered a lovely breakfast. It was the first breakfast she hadn't cooked for years, so she enjoyed every bite and left the waitress a generous tip. She left the hotel and boarded the trolley to the Gordons.

Olli stepped down from the trolley, turned and walked toward the familiar place. The house looked the same as it did nearly ten years ago—proper, clean and fastidiously kept. She mused, "Strange how outward appearances can so disguise the inward workings of deception and greed." Olli wiped those thoughts from her mind as she stepped to the kitchen door and knocked.

She heard muffled rattles of pots and pans. The door opened

Nell

and Dweena, her dear friend, stood before Olli with arms outstretched. She folded Olli in her plump, sturdy embrace. Olli blinked a tear and smiled at her old friend.

"Olli, my girl," Dweena said joyfully, "please come in. You look so lovely...my, are you expecting?" She touched Olli's stomach. "Why, how nice for you and Cole. Come in, come in. I have a pot set to heat for tea."

For a long moment Olli clung tight to her old friend. She had difficulty holding back a flood of mixed tears. She was happy to see Dweena, with hopes to soon see Cal, yet sad for past experiences she'd had in this very same house years ago. Dweena helped Olli remove her coat, then she pulled a chair into place at the table. It clearly pleased the old house cook to be having tea in familiar surroundings with her sweet young friend.

After Dweena started heating the tea kettle the two women sat facing each other, holding hands across the table. Olli saw that Dweena had eased into the years with smile lines and a twinkle in her eyes, while Dweena saw a blooming, clear eyed young woman who had overcome more than her share of obstacles.

The tea kettle's whistle broke the silent bond of memories the two friends were sharing. Dweena prepared an aromatic brew and put cups, sugar bowl and cream pitcher on a tray with the tea pot. She poured two cups of tea and smilingly recited an old rhyme. "Two old friends, Two cups of tea, One for you, One for me."

Olli chuckled hearing the familiar verse she had heard years before, but under far different circumstances. When Dweena poured more tea; the kitchen door swung open and a happy, blue eyed, blond boy of ten burst in. He stopped short and flashed a warm smile.

"Hi, Dweena," he chirped. "Are there any more cookies?" Then seeing Dweena's friend had arrived, Cal came over to Olli and added, "Hello, I'm Cal Gordon. You must be Dweena's friend. She said you were coming to visit. I'm very happy to meet you." He held out a hand.

Second Son

Olli forced a smile, then in a calm voice said, "Hello, I'm Olli Brauer. I've known Dweena since before you were born. I'm happy to see you again. I last saw you on your first birthday, so you don't remember me." She took the boys a brief moment.

Glancing around as if on a cookie hunt, Cal said laughingly, "No, I guess I wouldn't remember that."

Dweena brought the cookie jar to the table and asked Cal to sit with them and visit. Cal accepted a few cookies and a glass of milk and sat politely across the table from Olli.

Olli couldn't take her eyes off her handsome son. She said, "I'm pleased you can stay a few minutes, Cal." Dweena wrote to me about how big you had grown. I see she was right. What grade are you in now? Are you a good student? Do you like school?" Olli began to ask question after question until she saw Cal's surprised expression. She knew he was wondering why Mrs. Brauer was so interested in him.

Off to the side, Dweena frowned quickly at Olli, warning her to slow the pace of her questioning. Olli caught the warning glance and declared, "My Goodness! Look at me chattering like a jay bird. I bet you're bored with this old lady and all her questions."

Cal had been taught good manners so he smiled and said, "You're not old, Mrs. Brauer, and I don't mind your questions, but I promised my buddies I'd meet them in the park, so I can't stay much longer."

Olli was aware that Cal was about to escape to join his friends, so she said quickly, "Wait a moment Cal. I have a small gift to give you to help remember me." She reached into her purse and handed her son a plain envelope.

He thanked her and opened it carefully, removing a thin silver chain that held a tiny gold baby's ring. Cal again thanked her as he looked from Olli to Dweena with a puzzled glance.

Olli quietly explained, "It was supposed to be a birthday present for you on your first birthday. I didn't have a chance to give it to you then, but I want you to have it now. Let me call it a belated gift. Maybe someday, if you don't loose such a small

Nell

object you will look at it and remember that we met and had a nice visit.

Cal's eyes twinkled, put the ring back in the envelope, folded it several times and thanked Olli for the odd gift. He promised to keep it in his special hiding place in the attic, above the unused room where years before a maid had stayed.

Olli quickly caught her breath, remembering that tiny room of hers, and smilingly told Cal she was happy that he liked the ring enough to keep it in his secret place.

Dweena cleared her throat and told Cal he should head for the park before his friends left him behind.

Cal nodded agreement, shook hands with Olli, grabbed a few extra cookies, shoved them in his pocket, and told Dweena he would be home before five.

After Cal rushed out of the door, Olli's face crumpled into a tear-stained mask. She knew her reaction was because she realized she might never see him again—she feared it.

Dweena poured each of them fresh tea, patted Olli's shoulder and said, "My Dear, I know there wasn't time for you to enjoy Cal, but I'm glad he stayed long enough for you to give him a gift. Was that his baby ring?

Olli glanced up and smiled and told Dweena how she had secreted it out of the nursery the night she'd been driven from the house.

"So, you've had it all the time? Mother Gordon had the gardener and the whole family nearly combing the lawn when the next morning she found the ring was missing from Cal's finger. The old woman thought it had slipped from Cal's finger during the birthday party.

They talked until Olli looked at the kitchen clock finding it was time for her to catch the trolley back to the train station where the train would take her back to her family.

She had lied and deceived Cole, the only time she'd ever done that, to be able to see her son, about whom Cole knew nothing. She convinced herself the short meeting and the gift she had given the

Second Son

boy was worth the deceit, and that Cal would one day remember her because of the ring, and question his adopted father about it.

As Olli prepared to leave, goodbyes were said and promises made between the two friends to write often.

A blustery wind was sweeping trees bare of their golden cloak of leaves. Olli stepped aboard the trolley, seated herself and stared at the colorful autumn scene on the trip down to the Union Station. Mixed emotions welled up inside her. Happiness, loss, remorse, regret; yet a swelling of expectation also engulfed her. She felt a twinge of shame at the ease with which she had lied to her beloved Cole. She wondered if she would ever be able to tell him of this trip, or most of all, her first son.

The trip south to Olympia took a little over half an hour. The train slowed for the East Olympia stop. Olli saw Cole patiently standing on the station platform. As she departed the train Cole sauntered toward her in his unhurried manner. He took her in his arms and gave her a bold kiss. As they walked to the truck he asked if she was all right. She smiled and assured him she was tired, but fine.

Olli told him about the grave-side services, the family and neighbors. She was happy she had gone. It pleased Ma and Papa to see her. The rest of her experiences she kept to herself.

The little girls were happy to have their Mama home. A loud line of childish chatter filled the house. Cole was relaxed and smiling. All was as it should be.

When she lay beside Cole that night listening to his peaceful breathing, she vowed to never lie about anything again. She knew her life had finally evened out. She and Cole were happy just having quiet times together while they awaited the arrival of—hopefully—a son. Little did either Cole or Olli imagine the change that was about to take place in their family, or the decisions that would have to be made.

25

Second Son

Olli and Cole loved their two girls—Tess three and Nell one—and delighted in everyday changes as they grew.

But unknown to Cole, Olli was beginning to feel something lacking in her life. She yearned for the expected child to be a boy. One to replace her first-born son who had been so deceivingly taken from her. She felt she needed a son to heal the hurt that, years before, had cut such a deep hole in her soul, leaving Olli with a feeling of loss which lingered secretly in her heart. The years had rolled by, but the emptiness remained. Olli had overcome the heartache over the death of her baby girl, Jenny. It was as though that segment of her life had never happened.

A few months passed, it was November now, and Olli's heavy pregnancy was nearly to term. She sat in her small, hardwood rocking chair reading to the girls. They lay on the livingroom floor, chins in hands, completely engrossed in the story Olli was reading aloud.

Olli's back ached in a familiar way that told her labor had begun. She stopped reading and put the book on the side table. She felt her water break.

The girls started to protest the end of the reading time, but Olli's expression was so serious, even in their youth they knew to listen to their mother and do exactly as she said.

Olli asked Tess to take her younger sister and go next door to

Second Son

the neighbors and have Mrs. Valley call the doctor and tell him to come quickly.

The girls jumped up and scurried quickly from the house, Tess helping Nell with her sweater as they ran across the yard. They were yelling as they approached their neighbor's door.

Mrs. Valley saw the two little girls running toward her front door, and knew it must be Olli's delivery time. She opened the door and quieted the chattering children as they told Mrs. Valley that Mama needed a doctor.

Mrs. Valley told her daughter, Leone, to help the children take off their wet sweaters and make warm cocoa for them. She then called Dr. Clancy. Leaving Leone with the girls she put on her raincoat and dashed over to help Olli.

In the neighbor kitchen, the girls were overly excited and rattled on endlessly. Leone sat them at the kitchen table and poured warm cocoa in pretty china cups. Leone said she knew their new baby was on its way. Tess told Leone they had to watch out the kitchen window. Mama had told them as soon as the baby was born if it was a boy she would ask Dr. Clancy to hold their new brother up in the bedroom window so the girls could see him.

When Mrs. Valley arrived Olli was on her knees cleaning the floor with a towel. Mrs. Valley scolded her and told Olli to put on her night gown and get in bed. Olli thankfully obeyed, and the older woman, after seeing Olli to her room, took over the cleaning task.

Familiar with the birthing procedure, Olli laid out a stack of towels and sheets, put on her clean nightgown and got into bed. She went through the motions as if in a trance. Her mind jumped ahead, knowing the pain that would come, but not knowing if her secret prayer for a son would be answered.

Her back pain became more intense. She was muddled in her mind and thoughts, hopes and longings for a boy child tumbled around in her head. Because this was her fifth child she could tell labor was definitely advancing faster than any of the others. She became anxious that the doctor wouldn't arrive in time, but as if on

Second Son

cue, Dr. Clancy entered the room. Olli's fears quieted. He washed his hands, examined her and immediately got ready to deliver the child, who seemed in a terrific hurry to enter this world.

Soon the child's lusty cry told Olli it was not only a healthy baby, but the answer to her many prayers. In her heart the light that had gone out, glowed and shone again. God had given her another chance. God had given her a golden-haired boy to replace the little boy who had been stolen from her. Cal, who was alive, but long inaccessible, who breathed and grew in someone else's house, this son was lost to her. But here was the answer to her pleading prayers. At that moment, she gave little thought to Cole, to his part in her new son's existence. Her mind told her only this boy was truly hers.

Dr. Clancy brought Olli back to her senses when he asked if she wanted to hold the baby—to which she replied an excited "Yes!"

Olli remembered somewhere in the muddled, pain-filled time before delivery she had instructed the doctor: if it was a girl Mrs. Valley was to wave at the window so the anxious little sisters would know the baby was a girl; but if the doctor held the baby up at the window of their parents' bedroom the girls would know they had a baby brother.

The doctor followed Olli's instructions. As evening began to darken the sky, and Nell and Tess kept a diligent vigil at the window seat of Mrs. Valley's kitchen, a bright light shown from the window at their house. Soon the doctor held their new baby brother up at the window.

At first the children were filled with awe, then they jumped and laughed. Leone clapped her hands with the girls in celebration of the much awaited baby.

After the doctor had gone, Olli wondered where Cole had gone.

A few minutes later Cole came quietly into the bedroom. "I've been over at Chet's house," he whispered as he sat carefully on the bed.

Cole smiled at Olli and gently touched her hair. Olli lifted the cozily-wrapped bundle from the pillow beside her and put the

Second Son

child in Cole's arms. "Cole, meet your son, Cole Lewis Brauer," she said. Cole Sr. flashed a wisp of a smile as he opened the blanket gazing in wonder at the cherub-faced, red-haired child. Olli's smile was as warm as a sunny day. She didn't have the look of a woman who had just given birth, but rather a live radiance glowed upon her face.

The sight of his son's face made Cole's heart leap with a feeling of holding a precious part of family linage, a continuance of name, with the red hair as a bonus of Cole's Dutch and Welsh heritage.

Cole placed the baby back on Olli's pillow, bent and kissed Olli tenderly on her forehead. "Thank you," he said simply, gazing into Olli's eyes.

Olli knew he was pleased with his son, but Cole could not know how much the boy meant to Olli. She hoped someday the time would be fortuitous to tell Cole this one secret story of her life. "The girls are spending the night at Mrs. Valley's," she said matter-of-factly.

Cole agreed that was a good idea. Then went into the kitchen and prepared a simple dinner for two of them of hot soup. Cole cleaned the dishes and kitchen, took a quick bath before he gently lay on the bed beside Olli and his new son. He lay close to Olli, covered only by a sheet. Sleep crept over them. They lay asleep with their boy child between them.

In the next few days Cole's brothers and their wives came to see baby Cole Jr. They each remarked at his size. He weighed nine and a half pounds and was a well-filled out newborn with a healthy pair of lungs.

Olli recuperated a short time after delivery. Her attitude was effervescent, more so than at the birth of Nell or Tess. She could barely put the baby in his basket. She cuddled and held him every waking moment.

The sisters-in-law felt Olli was being over protective of such a healthy baby. Olli didn't want anyone else to hold him.

Second Son

Two months followed the birth of "Cole Boy."

Eva and Kurt visited from Portland and brought with them their six month old baby girl, Georgia. She was a delicate, darling little creature, and everyone was completely charmed by her.

Eva wanted to hold Cole Boy. Olli gave the excuse that he needed his nap. She carried him into the bedroom and put him in his bassinet. Olli came back to the living room where Eva handed baby Georgia to Olli. Olli sat contentedly rocking the gurgling infant, cuddling the fair haired baby. She told Eva how small she seemed as apposed to Cole Boy. Even though baby Georgia was six months older than Cole Boy everyone saw that Cole Boy was nearly the same size as his older cousin.

It didn't seem to bother Olli when anyone mentioned his size. She just answered, "I love to hold Cole Boy. It seems he's always hungry. He's a growing baby."

The family could see Cole Sr. was worried at the heaviness of the child, but his opinion didn't seem to penetrate Olli's tight cloak of control around the boy. No one suspected the reason for Olli's over-protective manner with Cole Boy.

26

Cole Boy

May 1935.

Cole Boy was one and a half years old, Tess just shy of five and already in school, while Nell was two and a half.

Olli's spirits were high and her enjoyment of her everyday routine was amplified by the love she lavished on Cole Boy.

One mellow sunny day in September, Olli stood at the kitchen sink, washing dishes. Tess was in school, and Nell at the neighbor's. Cole Boy played happily on the floor.

In the back yard the orchard's branches were heavy-laden with yellow leaves that were beginning to flutter across the lower yard, revealing a bountiful harvest of winter apples waiting to be picked. Olli thought about canning and the job of picking the apples. She was busy with her thoughts when Cole Boy tugged her dress wanting her attention. She hummed a tune, wiped her hands on her apron, and picked up her precious son. He cooed and kicked his chubby legs. He was happy to have his mother give him hugs and warm kisses on his head of soft red curls.

Olli took the baby into the living room, and sat in the rocker, intending to let the baby nurse himself into his daily nap time. She leaned back to relax when a knock sounded at the door. It startled her. She hadn't heard anyone step onto the porch.She stood, placed her baby on her hip and opened the door.

Standing on the porch in a shaft of filtered afternoon sunlight stood a tall, handsome, white-haired man. For a split second she

Second Son

didn't know him. Then, like a bolt of lightning she recognized him. Her knees grew weak from sheer disbelief. She whispered in a dry voice filled with mixed emotions. "Papa. Papa, what are you doing here?"

He had grown old in the short time since she had last seen him at Grandma Warren's funeral nearly two years previous. She hadn't considered ever seeing him again. Yet, there he stood with hair as white as snow and a face softened with time.

Papa stood on the porch beside his large leather suitcase. He shuffled his feet and slightly hung his head. He held a sweat-stained felt hat in his hands, slowly turning it by the brim.

He cleared his throat before asking, "Olli Girl, may I come in?"

Olli hitched the heavy baby further up on her hip. She reached out and touched her Papa's hands. "Yes, Papa," she stammered. "Please come in."

Papa bent and picked up his suitcase and carefully stepped into his oldest daughter's livingroom. Olli watched as he made his way to the couch, placed the suitcase beside him and put his hat on it. In silence Papa slowly turned around taking notice of his sparkling clean surroundings. He seated himself on the couch and in a quiet voice said, "Olli Girl, you and your hubby have done real good here."

Olli still holding Cole Boy said, "Thank you, Papa, but how did you find me? And what do you...want?" Olli felt old resentment well up inside her until it filled her throat. She thought, here was her father who had made her leave home many years before. Her father who had sired a house full of offspring. He who worked only when he wanted to. Her Papa who was not a good provider for his large brood, nor a good husband for a worn out wife. This man, her papa, was like the proverbial grasshopper who played to forget his responsibilities. Who, so he wouldn't have to support them, pushed his offspring, one by one, out the door of the family home into the world, mostly ill-prepared for life.

Now here was Papa standing in hers and Cole's home, face

to face with his daughter, clearly wanting something. Something she didn't know if she was willing to give him.

Papa cleared his throat again. "Olli Girl, your Ma and I have had a lot of bad words between us lately, and I need your help. Ya see, Ma, has put me out of the house. I can't never go back, Girl." He hung his head as his voice trailed to a whisper. Olli saw tears in Papa's eyes.

Olli excused herself at this point to put Cole Boy down for a nap, giving Papa a moment to collect himself.

She came back into the room and sat in the rocker.

She didn't know how to reply. She didn't know what to say to him.

After a moment Olli said, "Papa I don't know what to do for you. I have two little girls, my husband Cole and baby Cole Boy who take all my time. We are just beginning to get ahead a bit now. What do you want from me?"

Papa looked her straight in the eye. His voice shook. "Olli," he choked, "I know I've not done right by you and your brothers and sisters, but I'm an old man, and your Ma got her dander up and kicked me out. Now I got no place to go. I want to stay with you for a while—if you'll have me."

Olli had a sinking feeling. She answered Papa as truthfully and calmly as she could. "Papa, I have to talk to Cole about this before I can give you an answer. He takes care of the decisions that concern our family. He'll be home by dark, so why don't you lie down on the couch and rest. I'll put water on for tea."

Olli made a pot of tea and returned to the living room with two steaming cups of the relaxing brew and a plate of homemade bread. Olli seated herself on the couch beside her Papa and heaved a quick sigh. "Well, Papa," she said, "After all these years, what on earth stirred Ma to the point that she tossed you out?"

Papa's face nearly released a twinge of a smile at Olli's question. He sipped his tea and said, "She and I just couldn't get along anymore. She wanted me to take steady work in town, and I tried, but it left me no time for things I wanted." He sighed. "Besides she accused me of messin' around with other womenfolk. Hell, Olli, I'm an old man now!"

Olli looked away because she knew in younger years his admiration for the ladies had been a very problem. In fact his appreciation of the fair sex had led Papa to the point of infidelity. It puzzled Olli why Ma had put up with it for nearly forty years.

Olli changed the subject. Papa and she sat discussing the family and old friends in the valley.

Tess came home from school with Nell tagging along from the neighbor's. They romped onto the porch like a giggling gaggle of geese and burst into the living room calling, "Mama, we're home." They stopped short when they saw Mama sitting on the couch with a strange old man. Tess whispered to Olli, "Mama what is that big trunk doing out on the front porch?'

Nell, being more outgoing in manner, spoke up, "Mama who is this man?"

Tess stepped out from behind Nell eyeing the white haired man, only to step back again when the old man smiled and winked at her.

Olli quietly said, "Girls, this is your Grandpa Jergenson. He has come to visit us."

The two girls smiled, curtsied and shook his hand and softly muttered, "How do you do?"

Papa's face brightened. A warm smile made his blue eyes twinkle. Immediately the little girls liked their Grandpa.

After the brief introduction, Olli suggested the girls run to their room and change into their play clothes. When they left the room they trotted down the hall, calling back, "Bye Grandpa." And giggled their way into their room.

After the girls had closed their door, Olli spoke to Papa in hushed tones. "I have mixed feelings about you being here. Up until now I have pulled myself out of the mess that my life was in, that is after I left home—and the time I spent back home after my stay in the hospital, you know, after baby Jenny died." Olli continued seriously, "Papa I've done well for myself, and I'm happy

Cole Boy

in my life with Cole and my babies. Cole doesn't know about some of my past, so I need your word that it must stay that way. Never a word from you about anything but family times."

Papa quizzed, "You mean you will let me stay if I promise not to talk about your past?"

"No Papa," Olli snapped. "The decision whether you stay or not will be up to Cole. The fact I don't want my past discussed is because I've never told Cole about the Gordons." Olli hushed as Tess and Nell came noisily into the living room.

At first the girls were a bit shy, but very interested in the big white-haired man. They were happy about a grandpa they had never seen before now. When Olli motioned them to sit, Tess chose the footstool, Nell being a bit more daring sat beside Olli's father on the couch.

Olli said matter-of-factly, "Girls, your grandpa will be here for dinner. In a little while I want you to put a clean tablecloth on the table, and settings for five, best plates and silverware."

The girls bounced from their seats and excitedly ran toward the kitchen saying, "We'll do it right now, Mama." They chatted about their new Grandpa staying for dinner and which of them would get to sit beside him.

Before Olli could speak further with Papa to finish her previous conversation, Cole's truck pulled into the driveway. Cole entered the back door calling, "Hon, I'm home."

Tess and Nell ran to Cole chattering together, jumping up and down, pulling him toward the living room. "Come Daddy and see who's here."

"Cole," Olli called, trying to make her voice have a joyful tone, "Come and meet my Papa."

Cole entered the livingroom and approached the tall elderly man who stood and extended his hand.

"How do, Cole." Papa's voice was uncertain.

"How do to you." Cole smiled and gingerly shook his father-in-law's hand. Cole's smile was genuine. He was happy at last to meet one of Olli's parents. "I'm pleased to meet you, sir."

Second Son

Papa Jergenson's smile slowly melted from his face like wax dripping from a lighted candle. He resumed his seat on the couch, cleared his throat and looked apprehensively at Olli, for her to explain to her husband this unexpected visit, luggage by the couch, trunk on the porch.

Cole puzzled at the furtive glances between Olli and her dad, but let the feeling pass.

Olli rose from the couch. "Cole, we have a few things to discuss after dinner. Papa will be staying for dinner and plans to stay the night. We'll talk about the rest when the girls are in bed."

At that moment Cole Boy woke from his afternoon nap. Olli asked Tess to run and get him from his crib so Grandpa could meet his grandson. Both girls scampered off to get their squealing, cooing baby brother, who at the sight of his sisters stood shaking the sides of his crib in anticipation of freedom and the forthcoming attention about to be bestowed upon him.

After a pleasant dinner of hearty stew, homemade bread and apple pie, Cole and Papa went to the living room while Olli and the girls washed the dishes.

Cole Boy bounced happily on Cole's knee, gurgling, as Papa and Cole talked men things like hunting and fishing adventures.

Olli bathed the girls and dressed them in their nightgowns. They begged for a bit more time to listen to Daddy's and Grandpa's stories before being tucked in.

Cole Boy joyfully splashed water putting on a perfect show of a happy infant.

Papa stood in the doorway and watched Olli lovingly wash and play with his cherub-like red-haired grandson. He wondered why he hadn't come to visit, or at least contacted her before this. He pondered to himself why it had taken his life with Ma being torn apart for him to find Olli and her family. Papa hung his head. His eyes rimmed with tears of realization, all the things he'd missed with his own brood, let alone his grand-babies. But, he mused, maybe, after Olli had talked with Cole about him staying with them, he'd be lucky enough to be accepted by the grandchildren.

He'd have time then to make amends for the past. Even after the way he'd treated her when she was younger—he *was* her Papa. Surely Cole and Olli would see that he was old and homeless and they would let him live with them.

He decided if he wouldn't be welcome to stay with them he could always go to Portland and see if he could live with Eva and her husband. One way or the other he'd find one of his girls to take him in and take care of him in his old age. He knew better than to go to any of his boys. The boys were on their Ma's side in the matter of him leaving the family.

Olli finished drying the wriggling baby and dressed him for bed. She handed him to Papa.

Papa Jergenson carried his grandson to the living room where he sat in the rocker. Cole Boy cuddled close to his grandpa. He found Grandpa's suspenders and chewed on his chubby fist and nodded off to sleep. Papa sat rocking the child while Cole and Olli excused themselves.

When they were in the bedroom Olli explained to Cole about the situation in which her Papa found himself. She told Cole her feelings of uncertainty of wanting him to live with them.

Cole listened, wondering why Olli was unwilling to let the old fellow stay. He seemed happy to be with his grand kids and the old man had talked about his love of gardening. He bragged about his ability with a one man saw and how he loved to cut wood and keep the woodshed full. He would be a help to them in that way. Cole liked the old guy and found all these things on the plus side for letting the old man live with them; and he could find no reason why they shouldn't let him stay. "Hon, after all, we have that attic bedroom where Eva stayed. And he'd be a real help for me with the wood supply for winter. He seems to love the kids. He could help with them too."

"Cole, it's up to you. You're the one who brings the money home. I think the situation may bring problems. But if you really think he'll be a help, I'll not object to his staying for a while. Knowing my Papa, I think we should set him a trial period."

Second Son

"Olli!" Cole sounded shocked. "I never thought you'd turn down your own father when he needs help. I think we shouldn't put any trial period or restrictions on him. I like him and I have no objections to him living with us. You wait and see. He will be a big help to both of us."

Olli accepted Cole's decision. "Maybe you should be the one who tells Papa he can stay."

When they came out of the bedroom they found the girls had crept out of bed and were seated on the floor at Papa's feet listening to one of his stories. Cole Boy was sound asleep on his grandpa's lap. Papa was deeply engrossed in the story he was telling. The girls sat with wide-eyed interest until he finished the tale. The girls clapped, jumped up and thanked him as they ran down the hall to their room, knowing Mama would scold them if they didn't immediately get into bed.

Olli took the sleeping baby to his crib. She left Cole to give Papa the news that he was welcome to stay as long as he needed. Papa Jergenson heaved a sigh of relief at the news, and shook Cole's hand. "Thanks," he muttered. "I knew my girl and her good husband wouldn't turn me out into the night."

Cole showed him the attic room where Papa's younger daughter, Eva, had stayed before she and Kurt were married. He helped Papa drag the heavy trunk into the house and tussle it, and the suitcase, up the narrow stairway to the attic. Cole left him to unpack and settle into the cozy, low-ceilinged room. Papa looked around at the clean chamber. "Not bad for an old man whose wife kicked his ass out." He whispered as his face wrinkled into a broad smile.

27
Guests

For a week it poured. Torrential wind-driven sheets of rain pelted down.

Olli would bundled Tess and Nell in rain coats and boots and sent them sloshing, respectively, the four blocks to school and next door to Mrs. Young, who loved caring for Nell whenever Olli need the help.

Papa spent most of the time secluded in his room. He told Olli he loved the solitude and the sound of rain beating on the roof above him. He was thankful there were no leaks to fix and no one to nag him into doing tasks which he hated.

Olli could hear the plaintive, familiar tunes from his fiddle slip down the narrow staircase during the gloomy afternoons. Papa sat in the warmth of the attic room and played songs that brought back happy memories from a time before the realities of life and growing up made Olli aware of her Papa's shortcomings.

Papa agreed with Olli and Cole about the chores that were expected of him, so two times a day he came down stairs, bundled up and went to the woodshed where he chopped an armload of firewood and brought it in and stoked the heating stove and the kitchen range. This kept the house snug and warm for Cole Boy, who was now toddling about on the floor. Olli loved having the kitchen range always heated and ready if she had baking to do. She was, in that respect, thankful for Papa's help.

Second Son

It seemed coincidental his wood-chopping times seemed to happen just before meal times.

Good meals were such a treat to Papa. Ma hadn't enjoyed cooking, most likely due to the fact there never seemed to be enough to cook for the number of mouths to feed and the meager supply of food or lack of variety of things. This was mainly due to Papa's small, part-time employment and his abundant time spent playing the fiddle.

Papa saw that Olli set a fine table and told her so every day. He bragged to Cole and often reminded himself how lucky he was to have such a fine cook for a wife. Papa seemed unaware that the abundant food that magically appeared on the table and never ran low came from fulltime labor on Cole's part—the man of the house. Olli knew that thought never entered Papa's mind.

Christmas 1935 came and went.

One winter afternoon Olli answered a knock at the door. When she opened it, she was surprised to see Ben and Lena standing on the porch holding their two little daughters. They each held a child in one arm and a suitcase in the other. Ben, for an instant, shuffled his feet and cleared his throat. Lena bent her head as if she was ashamed and ready to burst into tears. Ben stepped toward Olli. To greet her, he threw his free arms around her in a warm hug. "Well," he said, "I suppose Cole is not home from work yet. We hoped we could stop and see you for a little while." He smile was forced, tentative.

Olli looked over Ben's shoulder and saw Lena finally give into silent tears. She stood with slumped shoulders looking dejected and exhausted. Olli took Lena in her arms to comfort her. Lena's body shuddered as she tried to control herself.

"Hush, now Lena," Olli whispered. "You come in out of the cold and tell me what is the trouble." She smiled as she ushered them into the house.

The little girls, Amy, age five, and Alma, age three, held onto their mother's rain-soaked coattail as they shuffled into the warm house. Olli hung their wet coats near the heater to dry. She told them to make themselves comfortable while she checked on Cole Boy, who was taking a nap.

Olli, upon returning to the living room, waited as Ben started the conversation. "Olli, we've had a real bad time lately. I can't pay our rent, and we didn't want to go to Dad's again. I thought maybe we could stay with you and Cole until I we get back on our feet." He paused, hoping to see some kind of reaction from Olli. He saw none, so continued. "I'm sure if I worked in the woods with Cole, I could save enough to rent a place of our own soon enough. We've been stupid with our money. But I'll work hard to change that."

Olli doubted his words. She knew that Ben and Lena had been drinking again.

Ben went on with his plan. "Lena is willing to care for the kids so you could work with Cole and me if you want to. You're willing to do that, aren't you, Lena?" He questioned her with a look that told her she better say yes.

Olli smiled, broke into the thought, "I'm actually happy for now staying at home and caring for the family." Now that Cole Boy was walking, she really wanted to stay home. "Besides," She stated bluntly, "Cole makes those kind of decisions for our family now, so you'll really have to ask him." She decided it was time to clarify things a bit. "I guess you didn't know my Papa is living with us now. He came a few months ago. He staying lives in the attic bedroom. I would hate to ask him to move down to sleep on the couch. But, Cole will make the decision when he gets home."

Ben said, "I'm sure your papa wouldn't mind giving up his room, or mind the inconvenience, once he heard of our situation."

Olli turned and saw Papa standing by the kitchen door. Rather gruffly he asked, "Olli Girl, who are these folks, and what is this about me sleepin' on the couch so they can have my room?"

Olli quickly introduced Papa to Cole's brother Ben and his wife Lena, and the two little girls. "Ben and Lena are having a bit of a bad stretch. Cole would be home shortly and they will talk things

Second Son

over." She tried to smooth over the situation. "After Cole decides if his Ben and Lena may stay or not, we shall come to an arrangement satisfactory for all, I am sure."

"But for now," Olli said, "I'll fix a big pot of warm cocoa. We can all sit and enjoy this nice warm fire in the heating stove and get to know one another."

The two little girls smiled at that suggestion, as they warmed their backsides near the stove.

When Tess and Nell came home, they were a bit shy finding everyone sitting in the living room. But it didn't take long for them to reacquaint themselves with their younger cousins. Soon they talked their two cousins into going to their room to play with their new Shirley Temple dolls they had received for Christmas.

When Cole arrived home he was somewhat overcome with surprise to see his brother. He hadn't seen him for nearly a year, but it didn't take Ben very long to explain his plight, and it didn't take Cole long to solve the problem. "Of course you're welcome to stay," Cole said. "Ben, you and Lena and the girls can stay in Tess and Nell's room. Amy and Alma shouldn't mind sleeping on pallets on the floor in the same room with their folks. Olli and I will have Tess and Nell do the same in our room, so we won't have to disturb Grandpa Jergenson." Cole added, "I'm sure this will only be temporary, as you two will be back on your feet soon and out on your own again."

Papa heaved an audible sigh of relief that Cole had wisely preserved his much-cherished sanctuary in the attic. The only thing Papa could think that bothered him about extra folks being in the house was that there would be two more chattery, noisy children to listen to. He set his mind to ignore them.

After dinner every night he'd retire to his room and take his fiddle out of its battered case and quietly play his favorite tunes to cover the extra noise. Papa began that very night to do just that. Below, in the livingroom, no one heard a note he quietly played on the fiddle. The conversation of four adults was overridden by the happy jabbering of the chubby cherub, Cole Boy, and four little girls giggling and splashed in the bathtub. They played together like slippery eels in a cloud of bubbles, having the happiest time, like they had lived together forever.

After all the children were tucked in, Cole and Olli lay in their bed listening to the rain beat against the window. Olli smiled in the darkness. She whispered to Cole, "I feel like *The Old Woman In The Shoe*. She also had so many children she didn't know what to do."

Cole held her close and whispered, "Don't worry, Hon. I've got an idea blooming in my head that will solve a lot of problems, and we'll be okay."

Olli drifted off to sleep, confident that her loving and kind man had the situation well in hand.

On the first day of February 1936, Cole and Ben came home late from work. They looked at Olli and Lena like the cat who swallowed the canary. They had been up to something. Even Papa could see the two men had a plan or mischief of some kind up their sleeves.

After a dinner of stew and biscuits, Cole excused the children from the table. The adults sat enjoying coffee and conversation. Cole smiled at Ben. No longer able to withhold the mutual secret the brothers held, Cole chirped in a mirthful manner, "Next Wednesday we will be moving." He waited for a reaction. Everyone, except Ben, sat stark still and looked at each other. Papa pinched his foreboding-eyebrows together in a negative reaction, fearing to loose the sanctuary of his attic room if any changes were being planned.

Olli questioned loudly, "Why?" Lena bent her head as if in submission and said nothing.

Calmly Cole explained. "I've rented a big two-story, six bedroom house up on the mountain-view side of town. It has a full city block fenced yard, a workshop and garage, and a *huge* kitchen. I know you'll love it, Olli! And after we've live there a year, Mr. Wiley will let us buy it. Today Mr. Wiley talked with

Ben and me, and he had no objection to our two families and your Papa all living there together."

Such a living arrangement was more than common during the Depression years.

Cole paused a moment to observe the collective reactions around the table, observing clearly that the only person he'd have to convince was Olli.

"Hon," he said cautiously, "I already made the first month's rent payment this afternoon. I think we should all drive up and see the place."

Olli agreed, but felt it best that Papa stay home with the children.

So the next afternoon Cole, Ben, Olli and Lena went to look at the big house. On the short drive out of town and up the hill, Cole, in a continual line of prattle, sang the praises of his choice of domicile for the family. This attitude of her husband's gave Olli an apprehensive stone of doubt that rumbled in her stomach. She wondered if they could afford it.

Cole told the women how the kids could catch the school bus at the door, which was the only plus in favor of the change Olli had heard up to that point—until they turned down the street and she saw the white picket fence completely surrounding the large yard. At this, both she and Lena couldn't hid their smiles. *It was grand!*

They made a quick tour of the empty house. It seemed enormous compared to the small place into which they were now scrunched.

The kitchen came supplied with a harvester-table large enough to seat twelve. There were closets and cupboards everywhere. The living room was enhanced by a grand arch-topped bay window. There were two downstairs bedrooms, very ample in size, which pleased Olli.

Olli and Lena "OOOed and AHHed" at the size of the upstairs bedrooms.

Ben and Cole followed the women from room to room. They knew by the reactions they heard, the house pleased their wives.

Guests

When they were ready to leave, Cole made a bold statement for someone as easygoing, non-bragging and usually quiet-mannered as he. He looked around. He hugged Olli hard and blurted out, "I think, by God, I came up with the only solution that will solve all our family problems. I did okay, huh, Hon?"

Olli enthusiastically told him he had made her very happy, but inside her mind the wheels raced, wondering if the cost would be too much.

After dinner they told Papa and the children that everyone would have to begin packing boxes. The house was very nice, Papa would have his own room, and no one would have to sleep on the floor anymore. The children cheered! The kitchen filled with laughter and gleeful squeals from Cole Boy, who sat and banged a spoon on the tray of his high chair.

Next morning, with boxes scattered about the front rooms, and children scampering in and out, from house to fenced backyard, the move was complete. Bedroom distribution was quickly decided upon. The large front bedroom would be Cole and Olli's. Of course, Olli insisted Cole Boy share their room. The back room, down the hall would be Papa's, so he wouldn't have to climb the steep flight of stairs. It was quiet and out of the mainstream of household activity. Of the four rooms upstairs, Ben and Lena chose the large one at the back of the hall. Amy and Alma's room was next to their parents.' Tess and Nell would share the middle room, leaving one room as a play room for the children.

Papa was delighted with the arrangement.

Olli imagined where she would place the furniture in each room. She knew their present belongings would all fit in one room of the new house, but they could arrange things so everyone would be comfortable.

Ben and Lena had no furnishings and would have to buy beds and two chests-of-drawers.

Lena asked Ben for a small secondhand rocking chair and new bedding. Ben promised he'd do the best he could, but his promise to pay half of the rent would be first in priority.

Second Son

Olli became aware of a building excitement within her that slowly overcame her first feelings of misgiving she had harbored before seeing the house Cole had chosen. She knew he had done this to ease the crowded conditions in the smaller house. She also knew that eventually tension would have risen in the crowded little house with the two families and Papa cramped together. Cole would never turn any of his brothers away in a time of need; nor would she. She had already proved that to herself when first Eva came, then Papa.

Conversation continued long after dinner. All planned expenses were to go into a journal, monies to be divided so each family knew how much was their share of rent, utilities, and other sundry expenses. To Olli's surprise Papa offered a small amount from his pension toward rent.

Everyone spent a restless night. The excitement of the new house had everyone at high keyed anxiety to begin packing.

The next week was busy. Olli and Lena packed boxes. The four little girls and Papa helped by caring for Cole Boy.

Moving day finally arrived and Cole backed the pickup truck to the front door. After three heavily loaded trips up the hill to the new house, everything was transported, and the small house had been scrubbed clean. They were soon settled in the big new house.

The work had been hard, but as they sat at dinner they relaxed and enjoyed meat loaf and scalloped potatoes savoring it as if it were a King's feast.

The enlarged family sat at the huge harvester table and celebrated the new house. Everyone was happy about each family group having their own privacy. Olli could barely believe such luxury.

After everyone was in bed the large house no longer echoed the children's chatter and the clamor of unpacking. The children immediately fell asleep, but each adult lay awake for a long time into the night, unaccustomed to the quiet and the lack of audible human breathing. Instead, they lay listening to the hushed unfamiliar sound of wind in the chimney and creaking of the large house welcoming new inhabitants.

Olli and Cole crept into bed between crisp, starched sheets that held the scent of lavender. After the heaviness of sleep had descended over each room Cole and Olli finally felt free to be drawn to each other in complete private love making so intense their emotions were as rich and complete as during their honeymoon.

While they were in each others arms, Cole Boy, whose crib was in their room, roused and began to cry. He wanted to sleep with his Mama and Daddy.

Cole held Olli close and whispered, "Don't go, Let him go back to sleep. I need you near me tonight."

Olli loosened his arms from around her shoulders and slipped out of bed to bring the whimpering boy back to their bed. "Oh, Cole," she whispered, "he's afraid of the strange room. He needs me and it will be just until he gets used to things. I promise."

Cole heaved a disgusted sigh and turned to face the wall. Olli placed the active, whimpering child between them and pulled up the covers, which Cole Boy immediately kicked off.

Olli turned on her side and let Cole Boy nurse until he went back to sleep.

Cole's voice was barely more than a whisper, but Olli heard it plain enough. "I think it's about time you weaned that big fat kid."

Olli stiffened in silent protest, only to draw the child closer to her breast. She touched the soft curls on Cole Boy's brow and said softly, "Yes, I suppose you're right. I don't really have milk for him anymore anyway." She paused, then said, "I suppose I may as well tell you, I think I'm pregnant again."

Cole turned in bed facing Olli. "You're kidding, I hope." He muttered. "Or is this your idea of a joke? Lord, what will we do with another baby, with this house full to overflowing already with your Dad, Ben and Lena and their kids? I thought if I helped them by letting them live with us until they could get on their feet things would be okay. Hell, I may as well buy a dammed hotel."

Cole's unexpected reaction hurt her feelings. After all he was as much to blame for a baby as she, but Olli didn't say a word to him. She curled tighter to her precious sleeping baby son beside her. The child she loved so dearly. Silent tears welled in her eyes and ran down to soak her pillow as she drifted into a sad, exhausted sleep.

Two months later, at one o'clock in the morning Olli was awakened by a stabbing pain in her back. She roused from the bed and stumbled to the bathroom, where, when she turned on the light, she felt a warm rush of fluid surge down her legs. She saw, on the black and white tile floor, a brilliant crimson pool of blood. She grabbed a towel, placed it between her legs, then with a shaky voice she called for Cole.

Cole woke with a start and ran to her in a half awake state until he saw her. He was immediately alert, ran and grabbed a blanket from the bed, wrapped her in more towels, then in the blanket. He called Papa, whose room was the closest, and told him Olli was bleeding and he had to rush her to the hospital.

From upstairs Ben and Lena had heard the commotion and ran to help Cole put Olli in the truck. Lena told Cole she would care for the girls and Cole Boy. When Ben was outside helping Cole, Lena began to cry. She was five months pregnant, a fact she had kept to herself.

Cole and Ben drove the mile to the hospital in what seemed like less than a minute.

When they arrived Cole honked the horn of the truck. A doctor and two nurses rushed out of the emergency door and guided Olli into a wheel chair and took her directly to the operating room. The admitting nurse asked Cole the required medical information, then suggested that Cole and Ben wait in the waiting room.

An hour later Dr. Clancy approached Cole and Ben who anxiously awaited the outcome of Olli's emergency. He told Cole that Olli had lost the baby. The doctor said Olli had lost so much blood he felt it safest to keep her in the hospital for a few days. "She's is doing fine at this time, but she'll need to regain her strength which will take a short time of bed rest."

Cole thanked the doctor and asked if he could see her, but the doctor explained that she was still under anesthesia. "Why don't you come back in the morning. The nurses will have her in a hospital room, and she should be awake by then."

On the drive back home Cole told Ben how bad he felt about losing the baby because of the unkind way he had acted toward the news of her pregnancy. He felt he owed her a deep apology for voicing his objection to another child.

Ben understood the responsibilities Cole had taken on by giving him and his family, plus Olli's Dad, a place to call home. He told Cole how thankful everyone was that Cole had rented the big house so they would all have a comfortable home. He and promised Lena's help so Olli wouldn't have so much to do, especially while recovering.

Cole's mind was focused on Olli's condition, so really was not paying attention to what Ben had been saying, until he heard Ben say, "Maybe Lena and the girls and I should look for a place of our own, but I hate to leave you with all the added expenses."

As they drove in the yard Cole exclaimed, "Ben you don't have to move. This is your home as much as mine, after all, we're family. I'm sure things will all work out fine."

In the morning before going to work Cole and Ben went to the hospital. Ben waited in the truck while Cole went in to see Olli. She was lying flat in the stiff, high bed. Cole thought she looked like a thin young girl. Her face was drawn and her chalk-white pallor resembled the sheets on which she was lying. Gone was the gleam of spirit and ambition that had always shone from her eyes.

Olli became aware that Cole was in the room. She looked away.

He sat on the hard wooden chair he'd placed beside her bed and cautiously took her cool, thin hand in his strong sensitive ones. For a while neither spoke.

Second Son

Cole finally whispered, "Honey, I'm sorry about the baby."

Olli stiffened and whispered, "I thought you didn't want it, so why be sorry? Let's just forget it." She looked at Cole. In a voice that held a sharp edge of anger, she asked, "Well, how are things at the HOTEL?"

Cole released her hands and ran his fingers through his hair in gesture of exasperation. "Olli, please don't be so angry. That won't help things now." He changed the subject. "Things at home are fine. Cole Boy is being good for Lena. When I left he was playing with the four girls. They love helping Lena with him." He continued, "I want you to let all of us help you with the housework and Cole Boy. He's just getting too heavy for you to carry all day. Because you insist on doing everything that needs to be done it makes you too tired. We are all willing to help you."

Olli became snapped, "The rest of you be damned! Cole Boy is the only one who really needs me. I lost the baby not because I'm overworked. I lost it because it wasn't wanted."

Cole walked back and forth by the window, not really understanding this about-face he'd never before seen in Olli. Softly he said, "Hon, you know that's not true. Sure I was surprised when you told me about the baby, and I reacted badly. But you know in *your* heart there is always room in our house and in our hearts for another child. Always. As for needing you...the girls and I need you as much if not more than Cole Boy does."

Olli whispered as she flinched and turned away, "I wish you'd go now. I think I need a good hard cry, then I'11 be fine."

Cole caressed her hand gently. "Okay, Hon," he whispered, "I'll be back tonight. Don't lay and fret. Just rest. I'll see you before supper." He paused, bent and kissed her tousled hair and whispered, "I love you Olli." Then he left the room. As he closed the door he heard her begin to weep.

After arriving home, Olli spent a few days of bed rest. The children came in and climbed carefully onto the bed where Olli could cuddle and talk to them and read their favorite stories. Even Ben

Guests

and Lena's little girls were included in the bed full of children quietly enjoying being with Mama and Aunty Olli.

Olli was soon able to be up and about. While she had lain in bed she made lists of chores and little projects she felt needed to be done. Each day tasks were assigned.

As Cole and Ben came from work one evening, Cole looked a bit upset.

After dinner Olli asked what troubled him. Immediately Ben cleared his throat and announced. "Lena and I are expecting a baby in a few months, so we've decided to not add to the confusion in this house anymore. We are moving to our own place. We have found a nice little house a few blocks from here. I will still work in the woods with Cole, and Lena can come down and help you until our baby comes. I know that will break our bargain of help with the rent and utilities, but it is time we're on our own."

Olli saw that what Ben had said bothered Cole a great deal, so she interjected, "1 hope your decision to move had nothing to do with my loosing the baby. You shouldn't feel you have to go because you cause too much work for me. I like having family around, and my problem had nothing to do with anyone. It just happened."

But the matter was settled in Ben and Lena's minds. They had saved enough to get along meagerly and had made the decision to be on their own.

Olli had a feeling that they had been too confined because of the house rules. Cole had made it clear from the first day Ben had shown up at their door—no alcohol in the house. They had abided by the rule, but Olli saw they were craving their old way of life. She hoped after they moved, alcohol would not once again be a problem.

Ben and Lena moved the day before Easter Sunday 1936.

Olli had to admit the peace and quiet was great. Cole made breakfast for Papa, who chose to eat in his room that morning. The for the family, he made breakfast, put it on a large tray, and he and the girls sat on and around Olli's bed enjoying solitary family closeness. Cole Boy sat beside Olli on the bed. Olli loved it.

After breakfast Cole brought four large cellophane wrapped packages and placed one in front of each of the children and Olli. Olli flashed Cole an understanding smile. The children clamored on to the end of the bed and began pulling ribbons and crackling cellophane to see what treasure was hidden inside.

Tess received a large pink stuffed rabbit. Nell's stuffed rabbit was her favorite color, blue. Cole Boy's toy rabbit was yellow and made him giggle as he took it and ran around the room. Everyone laughed. The rabbit was as tall as the boy.

The girls ran to Cole and squeezed him lovingly. "Thank you, Daddy."

Cole handed Olli her gift. It was an expensive box of hand dipped chocolates. Cole handed her a lacy card and one long-stemmed yellow rose. He had written a note. It read, "To the one I love more than life itself. From your loving husband."

Olli's eyes glistened. She smiled at Cole. Her glance let him know her feelings.

For a week or more Ben and Lena were at their own house. Then they came to visit Cole and Olli.

Olli found their visit quite pleasant, knowing they had a home of their own to return to. In fact she was relieved to finally be down to a one family unit again, except, of course, for Papa.

Cole had also adjusted to the idea. Even he was a bit relieved that the house was nearly back to normal. It seemed that the Papa would always to be with them, it was a thing which puzzled Cole more and more. Olli had, over the years, told him bits and pieces of why she left home at the age of fourteen. It seemed strange to Cole, who came from such a devoted loving family, that Olli's papa had been so eager to rid himself of his family, and then to come after so many years and expect Olli to be obligated to give him a home, food to eat and a warm bed. Cole knew the old man felt no qualms of guilt, nor any responsibility. It was as if, because

Guests

Olli was his oldest daughter, she was obligated to let him live with them no matter how he had treated her in the past, as though he felt she still owed him allegiance and a safe haven for the rest of his life.

Papa had first agreed to help Cole, but as time wore on Cole could see what Olli called, Papa's grasshopper tendencies. He now did little, if anything at all to help physically or financially, which was something he would have to talk about with Olli.

Cole had always been in agreement about any family member that needed help if they lived up to their end of the bargain, helping with needed chores. His family had always helped one another—and not only family, but anyone in the community. The Brauer's were known to be a big, warm, loving family, and Dad Brauer would never have let the thought enter his mind to literally throw his children out of the house at such a vulnerable age as Olli's Papa had done.

Three of Cole's young brothers still lived with their parents. They all worked in the community and were single. They paid their way and helped around the house, because Dad Brauer's church work kept him employed for long hours. Recently Dad Brauer had developed diabetes, which slowed him down, so he especially appreciated the boys being at home to help. The fact was, Dad loved all his children, but seemed partial to the younger crop, which was his way of describing his three youngest boys.

28
1936

The spring of 1936 popped into full bloom. The weather turned warmer than usual. Olli felt strong and full of energy. Papa was asked, and complied to the request, to clean the flower beds. The girls planted daisies and pansies while Olli tended the overgrown rose bushes that were interwoven in the front gate trellis.

After a family discussion asking him to help more around the house, Papa was eager to help in the yard. He spaded a large area for an herb and vegetable garden behind the garage and built two rabbit hutches, for which he bought a pair of rabbits. The garden and rabbits became his project. He fed the weeds to the rabbits, then in turn used the rabbit manure to fertilize the garden. This cycle produced a bounty of vegetables.

Cole bought pellet food for the rabbits, but Papa fed, cleaned cages and did the butchering, at a time when the children were at school; he knew most children thought the bunnies too cute to butcher for food.

When the baby rabbits were large enough to handle, Olli allowed the girls to play with them, as she had done when she was a child. The girls brought them into the kitchen in a box, wrapped them in wash cloths and blankets. They also hand fed them carrots. The girls, of course, became fond of their pets and soon caught on to the fact that Papa had to kill some for meat—and chicken dinner wasn't always chicken. When they finally were told about the rabbit's fate they ran and hid and cried, and refused to eat chicken, just in case it was their rabbit playmates.

Just before Christmas, in the middle of the night, an earthquake woke the entire household. The shell of the house shook like the body of a huge loose-boned skeleton. The noise rolled and rumbled through the earth growling and violently shaking everything.

The children screamed, ran and jumped in bed with Cole and Olli.

Cole boy, as round and chubby as he was, climbed out of his crib and, dragged his security blanket with him and got into his parent's bed with the girls.

Olli was deathly afraid too, but managed to maintain an outward calm. Cole turned the light on in every room looking for any physical damage. There was nothing out of place, except three children who begged to sleep with their parents the rest of the night.

In the morning Olli was still upset. After the girls had gone to school and Cole Boy was playing in the living room, Olli told Cole she didn't want to live in the big two-story house any longer.

Cole laughed heartily at her attitude and told her she was not being rational or thinking clearly. "Olli, this house is sound and strong. That rattler of a quake never hurt a thing, nor anyone, and nothing was broken or even out of place. Besides, it would be silly to move from what I hope will always be our home, because of one earthquake."

Each passing day after the earthquake Olli became more paranoid about the house. She wouldn't allow the girls to sleep upstairs in their room. She put their beds in the corner of the living room. As a last resort she allowed no one upstairs.

Cole tried to console her telling her, insisting the house was a very sturdy building, and she was being silly to frighten the children by refusing to let them go up stairs for fear of another earthquake.

1936

One night at dinner Cole thought he'd mention, once again, that Mr. Wiley wanted to sell the big white house to them.

The girls were excited and shouted, "Yes! Yes! But Papa frowned. He knew how the house affected Olli.

Olli caught her breath at the thought of living in the big rattily house any longer, let alone Cole's suggestion to buy it. Cautiously Olli suggested, "If you want to buy property, then let's begin looking for a house with enough land that we can plant a huge garden, raise pigs, beef, rabbits and chickens. With a nice sized piece of land we can raise nearly all their own food, plus we would also have our own timber for winter wood."

Papa chimed in, "Olli, that idea doesn't sound half bad!"

Cole said, "That all sounds fine and good, but I'm no farmer. I work hard in the woods all day, Olli. How could I do that, then come home and take care of animals and chores? I think you're asking for too much."

Olli was silent, but her face had changed from enthusiastic planning to a staring stiff-lipped silence. Cole glanced at Papa. He could see Papa was in full agreement with Olli.

Papa gruffly mumbled, "Cole, I would be willing to help out on a place like that. It would give me something more to busy myself with than fiddling around with a few rabbits. We would have nearly no cost for food and we'd have our own wood to cut."

Cole could see his plan to buy the lovely big house was foiled, so he said no more on the subject.

29

The Farm

A few weeks later, Olli was scanning the local newspaper and found an ad offering a farm with thirty-two acres, two barns and a small house. It was five miles from town. The price quoted was three hundred dollars. She showed the ad to Cole after she had talked to Papa about it.

Papa told her it sounded like a bargain. Inwardly he mused, "I could finally have a farm I won't have to pay for, and I can meter out the jobs that I want to do, and Olli can do what she can, and the little girls can shape up and do chores too. Heck I'd be set for the rest of my days."

Cole decided the coming weekend they would drive out and look at the place, if for no other reason than to quell Olli and Papa's insistence on having a farm. Cole hoped it would be so rundown that Olli and Papa would have their minds changed. But if it was what they really had in mind, Cole would bend and consider anything to make Olli feel safe.

The winter weather showed its sunny face as the Brauers and Papa climbed into the old panel truck Cole had recently acquired. They made the short five mile trip down an unpaved road, through scrub pine trees, onto a prairie, blanketed with knee high grass. The dusty road wound through the tall prairie grass until a single lane road lead west and ended in the unkempt yard of the uninhabited farm. The barn was the prominent building, which was the only thing of value Cole could see. The house was about the

Second Son

size of a railroad freight car. The tar paper covering flapped in the breeze where it wasn't nailed to the outside walls. The front door looked as if someone had removed it from a chicken house and nailed it in place with leather hinges.

Olli didn't look at the house. She stood on the small mound behind the house and took note of the location of the water pump and a smaller barn and outhouse. She smiled at the sight of an enormous plowed garden that filled a small lower valley area down a slightly sloped hill close to the pump. She looked at Papa, knowing he'd be a better judge of soil than Cole. Papa looked pleased.

Cole considered the place with gloomy prospects. The house was miserable. So was the outside privy. There was no running water or electricity on the property either.

But Olli had put on her dream-hat which made her able to see a bountiful garden, a barn full of cows and calves and children running free and happy through the thirty acres of grass. The down-to-earth items such as the house, the inconveniencies of having to pump water and haul it up hill to the house, the long distance for the children to walk to the school bus, and the run-down condition of everything seemed to not affect her reasoning. Olli loved the place.

Cole could tell by the set of her jaw that she had already made up her mind, and Papa liked it too.

On the trip back home Cole, who had always been the one to make such decisions, had a feeling that, in the matter of a half an hour, he had lost.

The children were exceptionally quiet on the drive home. The girls were afraid. They could see their future on the lonely, run-down farm. They listened to Olli and Papa talking about the possibilities of owning so much land.

Cole knew by their conversation he had no longer any say in the matter. He would have the obligation of working a long time to pay for not only the farm but every stick of lumber, every bale of hay and every sack of seed that went into the place for the rest

The Farm

of his waking hours. But he kept quiet. His plans for something better for his family were washed away in the rush of ideas from Olli's and Papa's day-dreams.

The next day Cole drove out to the farm by himself to see if he could see anything of value, thinking he hadn't had an open mind the day before. There was a five-acre field of grass along the main country road and around the house. The barns sat back against the edge of a dense thicket of pine trees. The house was too small. That was the best thing to say about it. The front windows were the windshields from an old truck. There was no stove in the house. Just a black stovepipe and a hole in the side of the kitchen wall.

The wall studs and ceiling rafters were peeled fir poles covered with gray flannel paper. The dullness of the place discouraged Cole more than before. He was at the point of exasperation when he left.

When he drove in the garage back at the big house the two girls were sitting in the garage crying their eyes out. Cole asked them what was wrong and they, in one wail, said they didn't want to move. Cole hugged them tightly and said he'd talk to their mama about it.

When he walked into the kitchen he heard Papa make the statement, "Olli, Girl, when we get that place of yours I'm gonna need my own room. So the first thing to do is get lumber enough so's I can build me a lean-to on the end for my bed room to keep my things away from meddling kids."

Papa's statement stopped Cole in mid-stride. Olli also took offense to what the old man said, but she made no reply. Her back stiffened and Cole saw her jaw tighten.

Cole broke the tense silence. "I think both of you should know I haven't decided on buying that place yet. So neither one of you should start building personal rooms to keep meddling kids out of their things, or others planting five-acre gardens."

Papa and Olli stared at him as if he were a stranger. Papa was shocked Cole had talked to him in such a manner. But Olli, in her own way, was glad Cole had come in the house when he did, as she didn't want a bad scene with Papa.

Cole told them he went back out to look at the property and he'd talk over his decision after dinner. Nothing more was said about the statement Papa had made to Olli about the meddling children. Cole felt he'd deal with Papa's attitude on that subject when he and the old man were alone.

The next afternoon Cole took both of his brothers, Ben and John, with him on a second trip to look at the farm. He wanted their opinions, not so much on the house and barns, but wanted their opinions of the property. They took note that it was all well fenced, and two-thirds cleared into grassed pasture, enough to keep four beef cattle and two milk cows.

The large barn had been a sheep shed, which could easily be converted into a sturdy structure to store hay and equipment.

With the brothers' help, Cole began to overlook the needs of the place and see for the price, the land alone was a bargain. On the drive back to town Cole stopped at Mr. Watkin's office, who owned the farm, and left a large down payment on the property.

At dinner the conversation skirted around the subject of the farm until the girls cleared the dishes from the table. Cole then asked everyone to be seated because he had made a decision and he wanted everyone to know what he'd decided. "I went back out to the farm today and took a closer look at the land, fences, barns and timber. I've decided to buy it. I have made the down payment and we can move in as soon as possible."

Papa's mouth spread into a broad grin.

Olli jumped from her chair and gave Cole a hug and kissed him soundly, smiling and nearly giddy with excitement.

Cole was puzzled at their elation over acquiring such a large amount of work and self-imposed drudgery. He knew the house was nearly unlivable, the outside privy minimal, plus having no electricity nor running water were not what he wanted, but the price was fair for the land. If they did the improvement work as

The Farm

they could afford it, the move might prove to be worth it. Even though he wasn't a farmer. Olli and her Papa had great ideas and the know-how to work the place and make it a profitable farm. Cole knew he had made Olli and Papa happy when he told them to consider the farm, theirs.

For Tess and Nell it was another matter. They quietly asked to be excused from the table. Hand in hand the girls ran out to the garage, and climbed up on a pile of old tires in the corner. They held each other and cried as if their hearts would break. They loved the big homey house, the neighborhood, and their friends. They didn't want to move into the country. That night the two little girls cried themselves to sleep knowing they would soon be living in a cold, dreadful, dingy house that they hated.

Olli, Cole and Papa never knew how sadness like a heavy cloak had fallen on the little girls, as the three adults sat up until a late hour talking over the changes and improvements to be made; purposely omitting the mention of the added lean-to room for Papa until the last thing on the list. This quietly gave Papa a downgrading for making his previous statement about his grandchildren, who, he did admit to himself, had never invaded his privacy.

The day the Brauers and Papa moved from the big white house in town to the farm and its tarpaper shack with its too-small living space, the weather had done its usual springtime turn around. 1937 would be a hard year.

The sun was hidden. A gray cloud hung over them and released unrelenting, a torrential drenching rain.

Cole rented a covered trailer. The trailer and panel-sided truck were loaded and covered with a canvas tarp. Everything was drenched despite their efforts.

After the truck and trailer were unloaded at the farm, Cole told the girls they could stay at the new house while he returned to their beloved white house in town to gather the remaining odds and ends.

So, Cole, Olli, Papa and Cole Boy drove away in the truck leaving the two girls huddled together crying bitter tears. They sat on a pile

Second Son

of wet packing boxes in the cold dark house staring out of the rain-glazed windows. The interior of the house was nearly as wet as the exterior, because of the rain soaked boxes that were stacked inside.

It was bitter cold. No stove had been set up to warm the shack. The girls sat close to the windows watching for their parents return. The windows fogged over from their warm breath condensing on the cold glass. Spider webs woven in the corners of the window glistened with rain droplets. The sisters sadly sat waiting to hear the roar of the truck engine coming up the road. They could barely see through the rain.

The family was gone nearly two hours, so Tess opened a few boxes and found two warm quilts and wrapped Nell and herself in them to keep from catching a chill. In the center of the room, the roof was leaking into a galvanized wash tub. The blustery wind blew the tar paper covering on the outside of the house. The tar paper flapped noisily. The loose ends sounded like large bird wings beating against the walls.

A hole in the kitchen wall where the stove pipe was supposed to be, was letting both wind and rain chill and dampen the place.

It was nearly dark outside when the last box was unloaded from the truck. Papa previously had purchased two kerosene lamps which he filled with kerosene. He struck a match and lit the wicks and adjusted the glass chimneys. He placed each lamp on a secure box.

Everyone slowly looked around at the shadowy jumble of rain-soaked boxes. Not exactly understanding why, Cole began to laugh at the absurdity of the garbled mess at which he was looking. Finally, Olli and the girls joined in the giddy, infectious laughter after seeing the complete chaos stacked in the gloomy interior of the little house. Even Cole Boy clapped his chubby little hands, which brought more peals of laughter. Papa too, saw the complete absurdity and let out a few guffaws.

After everyone eased back into reality Cole and Papa cleared places to put the mattresses. Olli tugged damp blankets and sheets out of the wet boxes and made the beds.

The Farm

Everyone was starved. They hadn't taken time to eat since breakfast. Olli surprised them with a feast of jelly sandwiches, bananas and cold fried chicken.

They all sat on wet boxes in the meager light of the kerosene lamps. The food was good.

After a lamp-lit trip through the rain to the privy the girls were put in one bed. Cole and Olli tucked Cole Boy into their bed, and Papa gathered his few possessions near his bed. Exhausted, after listening to the rhythmic sound of the rain on the roof, the constant drip-splashing into the wash tub in the middle of the house beat a rhythm. Everyone fell asleep.

Morning dawned sunny, with a sharp chill in the air, accentuating the drab disarray in the small rain-dampened shack.

The children were roused from sleep by the clanking Papa and Cole made as they started a fire in the ancient cast iron heating stove. The men had placed the old stove at the far end of the room, then installed lengths of shiny black stovepipe into a hole in the side wall of the house. This task had been accomplished in a manner far more quiet than the wood chopping and banging of the stove door as the two men whispered and shivered until they began to see the humor of their attempts to be quiet, at which, they found themselves enveloped in raucous laughter.

Olli and the children also saw the completely ridiculous attempts of the men at being quiet. The family ended up with peals of laughter bouncing against the cold damp walls of the dingy room.

When the fire finally set to snap and pop, the roaring flames within the old stove radiated grateful heat throughout the room sending plumes of smoke up the chimney to be caught by the wind and carried across the greening fields and beyond to the pine thickets which encompassed the small desolate farmhouse.

Nell and Tess dressed Cole Boy—then a search began for his misplaced shoes. Nell finally found them under Cole Boy's pillow.

His chubby feet were icy cold, but he still made a game of having

Second Son

himself stockinged and shod. It finally took Olli's firm voice to quiet him down long enough for his sisters to accomplish the task.

Cole Boy, now two and a half years old felt he could do anything his sisters did, so he began opening boxes in the messy room. His attempts at helping made the piles of strewn items even more difficult to arrange. The girls complained until their mother found a large spoon and a pan, for a drum, and handed the delighted boy a toy that produced a nerve-racking, ear-splitting din keeping Cole boy occupied until Olli had prepared breakfast.

The top of the heating stove sufficed as a make-shift toaster. The coffee pot sat on one corner of the stove bubbling its friendly aroma into the room.

Cole and Papa arranged chairs around the stove while Olli buttered a stack of toast and poured six cups of steaming coffee. To Cole Boy's delight even he was given a cup of coffee mixed with milk. He liked being treated like big folks.

After the quick, warming breakfast Cole and Papa began placing the marked boxes in their designated areas.

Olli delegated the appropriate place for cooking items at one end of the room. Boxes of clothing were put near the back wall. After shifting things around, Cole and Papa assembled the iron bedsteads and struggled putting the clumsy cotton mattresses on the correct beds and cots in place along the back wall.

Olli took the blankets and quilts from the impromptu sleeping area of the night before and made the beds. She slipped clean starched pillowcases on the pillows and set them in place.

Immediately, Cole Boy climbed onto Olli and Cole's bed and began to jump and bounce.

Tess and Nell quickly snatched him from his chosen trampoline and busied him by unloading his toys into his small red wagon.

Arrangement of the boxed household items proceeded quickly after Cole and Papa nailed eight wooden apple boxes on the wall in the kitchen area. They nailed four wooden orange crates beneath the others, and put wide boards across the span between

The Farm

to serve as a kitchen counter top. The upper boxes were for dish storage. Olli was pleased with the makeshift cabinets serving the need until real cupboards were built.

By afternoon it was surprising how much had been accomplished. A large closet for the family's wardrobe was built on one wall. The girls unfolded and hung everything according to each person's belongings.

Olli stopped a moment. She pushed her fly-away hair from her face, and smiled as she looked around the once gloomy room. In a cheery voice Olli exclaimed, "You know, this is going to be fine. It will look pretty good as soon as I have time to sew curtains for the fronts of the closet and the kitchen cupboards."

Cole and Papa looked around, and rolled their eyes at each other. "Women and their ideas," muttered Papa. As far as the men were concerned they were settled in.

Cole said he couldn't afford to take off more than the two days he'd already taken, so he was up extra early the next morning. On his way to the woods he stopped in town at Ben and Lena's house to get Ben, who was working with him every day.

Time flew quickly. The frost and cold chill of early spring was replaced by greening fields full of buttercups and clover.

The girls rode the school bus everyday. They met all of their neighbor children and quickly adjusted to the routines of both school and chores.

Papa built a small three sided lean-to shed by the main road where the girls waited for the school bus.

Olli and Papa found some lumber in the barn. There was enough to construct a lean-to room on the west end of the house. This was Papa's room. It had a door to the main room and one to the outside, so Papa could come and go as he pleased without tramping through the house.

When Cole went to town Papa went along and bought enough lumber to build a roomy chicken coop. He bought chicken wire, nails and roofing.

Second Son

The next month, after Papa's small pension check arrived, he went to the feed store with Cole. Papa found the heady odors in the store aroused fond memories of the past. He had finished building the chicken coop, so he bought a bale of sweet smelling straw and a bag of chick feed.

The next trip into town, the feed store was filled with the sound of peeping baby chicks. The chicks were stored in cardboard trays on open shelves beneath warm lights serving as an incubator until they were sold. Papa bought fifty chicks.

The man at the feed store helped load the straw and feed into the back of Cole's truck, but Papa held the big box of chicks on his lap on the drive home.

Olli, the girls and Cole Boy heard the baby chicks peeping as Papa walked toward the chicken coop. They became excited, knowing what the big cardboard box held. On his chunky legs, Cole Boy ran jumping and squealing and begging Papa to let him see the baby chickens before his sisters. Papa stepped into the chicken coop. Everyone but Cole followed. Cole stood at the door watching his children's excitement build as Papa and Olli placed straw in a large galvanized wash tub. They opened the carton of chicks and placed them, carefully, one by one onto the sweet fresh straw. Then the children were allowed to hold the chicks. As the chicks were held the stiletto of shrill peeping increased.

Then a large burlap sack was placed over the top of the tub, and Papa told Olli to fill the red rubber hot water bottle with hot water, wrap it in a burlap sack and put it under the straw. This would keep the chicks as warm as if they were tucked under a hen.

Papa said, "At night, Nell and Tess can have the job of warming bricks on the heating stove, wrapping them in burlap and doing as Olli had done with the hot water bottle, to keep the chicks warm at night."

The chore of feeding and watering the brood also became the girls' job. Cole Boy stomped and screamed saying he had no baby chickens because the girls got all the fun things to do. After a few

The Farm

days, Olli allowed him to feed them even though he spilled most of the grain in the process. He was satisfied.

The addition of chickens to the farm made Papa feel his contribution toward the eventual increased food supply would be a great benefit, especially since the chore of caring for them was given to the children.

Cole, on the other hand, having never lived on a farm with animals to tend, felt the chickens were just another thing to be bothered with. He was convinced he would never be a farmer, whereas, Papa and Olli seemed to know the things it took to make a farm work. So he left it up to them.

Olli took the task upon herself to plant a garden in the low glen east of the house.

She tried spading the thickly matted prairie grass around the edge of the garden to enlarge the garden area into a rectangle approximately eighty by three hundred feet. She found it was a tremendous job.

Papa volunteered to help, but Olli was possessive in her task and told Papa, "The garden is mine. I'll be responsible for it from the time it's spaded until all the vegetables are canned for the winter."

It took Olli two weeks to spade, shake grass clods, rake and prepare the space for planting. It was early June by the time she had every seed in the ground. Then the weather turned blustery and rainy. The rain did its work in the garden. When the warm weather returned, the wonder of tender sprouts appeared throughout the length of Olli's first long-awaited garden. It was her pride reminding her of the lush gardens at her childhood home and more innocent times in Lynden Valley.

Within a week the garden was aflutter in the breeze with green growth bringing the promise of bounty. The girls wanted to help weed, but Olli insisted she would do it herself. Instead, she gave the job of watering to the girls. She found using the hand pump to fill the pails was strenuous enough for her, so carrying the pails of water to her precious plants was a job she decided she shouldn't do. The girls never complained unless Cole Boy followed them through the growing plants. He often trampled and broke the tender shoots, unaware he was destroying everything in his path.

Papa worked on the small barn. He added two stanchions, feed bins and two stalls where he scattered fresh straw. He mended the roof and repaired the barbed-wire fence making a corral in an area large enough for two cows.

Cole and Papa drove to a dairy farm in Skokomish Valley where they purchased two milk cows. The dairyman, Mr. Lutz, led the cows into a large horse trailer and delivered them to the Brauer farm for Cole. Olli and the children excitedly watched the cows being unloaded and put in the corral. Olli loved the cows from the beginning; even though she realized they would be a constant source of work for her. Papa had told Olli he would keep the barn and fence in good repair, but wanted nothing to do with feeding and milking the critters.

Olli needed the milk for the family's use, plus she knew any extra milk or butter could be sold to the neighbors. The monies from her milk transactions would be tucked away until she saved enough to buy a pig or two. Olli never wasted a particle of food. Whey or buttermilk would be used to feed the pigs. She had fully planned that in a year's time nearly everything the family ate would be produced on their thirty acres. Her determination was, at times, more prominent than her good judgment or even knowledge of how much more work she was piling on herself.

Olli's daily routine started before dawn lightened the summer sky. She milked the cows and poured the milk into flat pans to cool in a screened cooler box on the shady side of the house. Thick cream formed on top of the pans which had to be skimmed off and placed in a churn. Olli delegated the girls to take turns turning the crank, producing mounds of sweet fresh butter.

Papa built a strong pig house and pen, readying it for the pigs he knew Olli's determination would bring.

30

1937 to 1940

Tess and Nell, who had slowly succumbed to the excitement of life on the farm, hated to see the busy summer of 1937 come to an end—a time that would send them back to school. They had looked forward to helping Mama do canning and pickling from their very first garden. They were as proud of Mama's garden as Olli herself was. The garden had become the talk of the small farming area, enough so that one day the County Agriculture Agent came to see Olli. Their offer was to have her send samples of her beautifully canned vegetables to the state fair that fall.

Olli agreed, and she took blue ribbons on every thing she entered that year—and the following eight years! 1937 to 1945. The farm paid off after all.

Every year Olli canned one hundred quarts each of green and shelled beans, carrots, squash, peas, dill pickles, sauerkraut, spinach and tomatoes. Even wild mushrooms were canned, due to Cole's expertise in knowing a variety of choice wild mushrooms that he brought home from the woods.

Papa helped Olli dig a large pit in the hillside near the garden. Over it Papa built a snug insulated root cellar. When the shelves were installed, hundreds of jars of canned food were put on them, making the cellar look like store shelves stocked with a rainbow.

Cole was proud of how well Olli had done. She accomplished what she told everyone she would do. She made her garden, bought two cows, and the chickens produced enough to save a great deal of money.

Cole bragged to Ben nearly everyday while the brothers worked in the woods together.

Unfortunately Cole's zeal only caused Ben to become jealous of Olli's accomplishments. He told Cole that since he and Lena's third daughter was born Lena had lost interest in everything. The house was always a mess, and the children were never bathed unless he did it. Lena had stopped cooking anything except warming meals from a can. Her main problem was that she had gone back to drinking, and she used Ben's wages for alcohol instead of groceries.

Ben said he had been thinking of taking a job with the merchant marines for a year or two. He talked to his parents about it, and Mom and Dad Brauer were willing to let Lena and the babies stay with them so Lena wouldn't be able to drink and the little girls would get good care.

Mother Brauer's housekeeper Nanny, so long a part of the family, no longer lived with them. She said she had grown too old for housework and baby-caring, so she moved east to live with her daughter. But Mother Brauer said even with the three older brothers at home Lena would be a big help to her and she would love to have the little granddaughters playing around the place.

Ben said if he took the job that had been offered him he would go to Hawaii for at least a year. It looked to Cole as if Ben had already made up his mind. So, in late November Ben left Shelton to begin his new job. Lena and the three little girls moved in with Dad and Mother Brauer. Ben's absence left Cole working in the woods by himself, so Olli wrote to her brother Kyle, who said he'd be happy to come and work with Cole if he could bring his family.

The house was too small and cramped already, but Cole said they would build a room onto the house, if necessary, as he needed Kyle's help in his evergreen business. And Kyle wouldn't come without his wife and three children.

So plans were made to build a room on the house as soon as

1938 to 1940

possible. Both Cole and Olli knew Papa would never give up his room, even for one of his sons.

Olli was happy to hear Kyle and his family would be coming. In the interim, Papa could care for Cole Boy during the days until Kyle came, and Olli would work in the woods with Cole.

For the next week Olli rose earlier than usual to milk and care for the cows, make sack lunches for everyone, fix breakfast and make sure Papa had a list of things to do. Only then did she climb in the truck to go to work with Cole.

She helped pick evergreen sprays, bundle and carry them through the dense underbrush to the truck. It was hard physical work, but with each heavy bundle she knew the extra money would help build the added room on the house, buy two new pigs. She would also be able to buy Cole Boy new toys, for which he constantly begged.

Cole and Olli, returned each day from work shortly before dark. Cole ready to relax and Olli tired but ready to light the kerosene lantern and go to milk and feed the cows. She followed the same routine every night. She'd do the milking, cook dinner, pump and pack water up the slope from the pump to pour in a large galvanized tub which was heated on the green enamel cook stove. All this so the children could be bathed daily before they went to bed. After the children's bath, Olli put the evening milk in the cooler. She skimmed cream from the morning milk and filled the churn, ready for the girls to churn the next day. All the while, she hummed softly. It was her quiet time of the day.

One night the family was in the house awaiting Olli's return from milking when the house began to shake, rattle and moan, as if being shaken by an unseen monster. The ground heaved and roared like an oncoming freight train.

The stove pipe broke away from the heating stove filling the room with smoke.

The floor pitched, throwing Papa and the children sprawling on the cold linoleum.

Second Son

Cole grabbed the table, then the door sill and pushed his way out the door and down the pitch black path toward the barn. He saw Olli's lantern radically swinging as she ran toward the house. Her frightened voice quivered as she shouted, "Cole! Earthquake!"

The cows, mooing and bawling, broke out of the barn and ran into the dark pine thicket. Their cow bells and commotion added to the din of Olli's shouting and the children's screams.

The motion beneath their feet subsided as Olli, shaken and cold with perspiration, reached Cole as he raced toward the lantern light. He grabbed her arm, took the lantern from her hand and kissed her hair roughly, momentarily holding her. He knew how terrified Olli was of earthquakes.

"Are you okay, Hon?" he whispered hoarsely. He felt her body tremble, then she broke away running and stumbling toward the house shouting, "Cole Boy! Cole Boy! Papa, is Cole Boy alright?"

Cole ran to her and grabbed her hand to slow her pace and better see the path in the lantern's light.

"Hon," Cole stated, "Papa is with the kids. They're okay. Nothing is broken but the stove pipe. There is a lot of smoke. Papa and the kids are fine."

When Cole and Olli entered the smoke-filled house, three children were holding securely to Papa's pant legs, hesitant to release themselves from their grip on his overalls. They were frightened but safe.

Papa asked Olli to leave the door open to let the breeze blow the smoke out of the house.

Cole extinguished the flame in the barn lantern and relied only on the two kerosene lamps in the kitchen. He checked the fallen stove pipe.

Papa comforted the girls. Olli grasped Cole Boy to her heart and carried him on her hip talking to him in soothing tones to ease his fear.

Cole was puzzled why Olli had asked only about the safety of Cole Boy. She didn't seem at all concerned about the girls or Papa.

Cole asked Papa to help him straighten the stove pipe. It took a minute to re-adjust the pipe to its original hole in the wall so the smoke problem was solved.

When everyone calmed down, Olli, still carrying Cole Boy, remembered she ran from the barn, the cows had backed out of their stanchions and ran away.

Cole told her to stay with the kids while he and Papa went to the barn to retrieve the milk pails. They saw the cows had escaped into the thicket leaving tufts of hide and hair on the barbed-wire corral fence. They could hear the cows mooing out beyond the house where they were crashing around in the thicket. The two men decided it would be fruitless to make an effort in the dark to locate the animals, so they agreed to search the thirty acres in the morning.

Olli prepared a quick dinner of sandwiches, after the smoke was fanned out the door. The family went to bed early. Olli usually put Cole Boy in their bed between Cole and herself, but that night she rolled Cole Boy to the outside of the bed, so she could sleep cuddled tightly to Cole. He held her gently in his arms. She heard his breathing become a steady rhythmic murmur telling her he was exhausted and sound asleep. But Olli didn't sleep. She wasn't feeling well. She hadn't told Cole, but she knew she was nearly four months pregnant again.

She also knew she had been working too hard. This, plus the fright she'd had during the earthquake, she was sure caused her inability to sleep. She tried to relax but her stomach was upset and her back ached. The ache became more intense, becoming a gnawing pain. She was having another miscarriage, she was sure of it. Slowly she got out of bed and dressed. Then she woke Cole and told him she was ill and she feared the reason for her pain.

Cole was shaken and upset with her for not telling him about her pregnancy. But she whispered she had wanted to work to help pay for the addition to the house and the costs of another baby. Cole, thinking to himself, knew the reason she hadn't told him of the pregnancy was because of the way he'd reacted to the last expected child, which had ended in a miscarriage the previous

Second Son

year. In the big house in town they had room for a new baby, but here in the one-room shack there was neither convenience nor room for an infant.

Cole wrapped Olli in a warm quilt and carried her to the truck. He went back to the house and woke Tess, told her he had to take Mama to the hospital and she should get in bed with Cole Boy so if he woke he wouldn't be afraid.

Tess quickly obeyed her dad and whispered for him not to worry, she would take care of Cole Boy and tell Papa when he got up in the morning. She also took the responsibility to ask that Cole help Mama get well and not to worry about Cole Boy. Cole kissed his oldest daughter on the cheek, tousled her curly red hair and told her to wake Papa and tell him the circumstances. Then reconsidered and he knocked on Papa's bedroom door. Papa woke sharply when he heard the knock. Cole opened the door and quietly told Papa the situation. Cole added, "I don't know how long I'll be gone."

Papa said, "Things here will be fine, Cole. You just take good care of my girl."

Cole thanked him, then rushed out of the house into the chilly night.

Ice patches made the dirt road shine as he steered the truck down the lonely country road toward town. Cole honked the truck horn as he drove up to the emergency door of the hospital and called for the nurses to hurry. Olli was in severe pain.

The nurse helped her into a wheelchair and rolled her into the examining room. Olli didn't make a sound. Dr. Clancy examined her. He told Cole that Olli should stay until the pains and bleeding stopped—there was no stopping what her body had begun.

At two in the morning the doctor told Cole that Olli had been about four months pregnant and had miscarried, and she should stay a day or two to make sure there were no complications,

Cole asked Dr. Clancy if he could tell if the baby was a boy or girl.

The doctor looked at Cole for a moment, patted him on the

shoulder and said, "Cole, I don't see that it would help you or Olli to worry about that. The child is gone, there will be no burial services. It wasn't developed enough to qualify for such treatment. We are concerned only that Olli is cared for." Dr. Clancy added, "Olli works too hard. Since you folks moved to the country, she has taken on too much physical labor. She should slow down and take time to enjoy her family."

A touch of mirth flashed on Cole's face as he mulled over the doctor's advice. "Doc, he said, "since we bought the farm—Olli is obsessed with doing more and more, adding on, fixing up, and now she wants to build a huge bedroom addition, a fireplace, cottage windows and French doors. Heck! Doc, we don't even have electricity yet."

Dr. Clancy smiled. "Yes, I know, but she should take on one project at a time and quit working in the woods. She shouldn't be hauling heavy bales of evergreens to the truck; nor should she do the heavy farm chores. I know her, and she assumes if she works extra hard things will come her way. But, for her health, you'll have to convince her that you can work and be the provider so she can take it a little easier."

Cole shrugged his shoulders. "Thanks for everything Dr. Clancy. I'll try to talk to her. But right now I'd best go in and check on her and then get back home as soon as I can. With the earthquake, and now Olli loosing a baby, it has been a busy night." He shook the doctor's hand and thanked him before walking down the hall to Olli's room.

He opened the door to find Olli looking pale and weary, lying in the hospital bed. She was sleeping soundly. A nurse was in the room. She put her fingers to her lips indicating Cole should be quiet. In a whispered tone Cole asked the nurse if he could leave a note for Olli. The nurse handed him a pad of paper and a pencil.

Cole scrawled a quick note, folded and left it on the bedside table. Quietly he thanked the nurse then tip-toed out the door, strolled down the darkened hallway and out into the night.

On the cold drive home the truck headlights ate two holes

through dense clinging fog which had formed in the low-lying areas of the road. Cole was tired. His mind slipped from incident to incident, in sequence as they had happened the past evening. He began putting into category Olli's self appointed chores and vowed to help her in the barnyard. He would leave the milking to her, as she had a certain procedure. But he and Papa would take over stacking hay and lifting the heavy burlap feed sacks and carrying water for the animals. Cole's thinking flashed back to Olli during the earthquake, how her fear made her run toward the house in the dark. She had screamed so it seemed she was concerned only for Cole Boy's safety. Then, when in the house, she had carried the heavy, clinging child on her hip, hugging and cajoling to soothe him. He wondered if the action she demonstrated had been for her own feeling of safety as well. Why had she been so concerned with Cole Boy's safety and shown hardly any for the girls?"

After Cole arrived home, because everyone was still asleep, he slipped quietly into the empty narrow cot where Tess usually slept—she had moved into the big bed with Cole Boy.

Cole shivered because of the chill in the house. His mind danced in his exhausted attempt to sleep. His thoughts darted around, picking up bits and pieces of everyday happenings he had overlooked. He saw an unhealthy obsession forming in Olli's attitude toward Cole Boy. She didn't seem to care about anyone else's well-being. Now, with another miscarriage, Cole wondered if he should watch for more obsessive behavior from Olli about her spoiling Cole Boy.

Sleep finally caught and held Cole's thoughts long enough for him to slide into a deep slumber, freeing him for the time from a feeling of sadness and helplessness and a premonition about the future he couldn't explain.

Dawn broke on a cold, foggy landscape.

The girls woke to find Cole still sleeping soundly and Mania missing from the house.

Tess dressed Cole Boy while Nell called Papa to see if he was awake, only to find he had risen earlier and wasn't in the house. Presuming he was out in the privy, she started a fire in the wood stove and put on a pot of water to heat for oatmeal and coffee.

Tess, in hushed whispers, told Nell about last night and the trip that Daddy had to make with Mama, spelling words so Cole Boy wouldn't throw a fit and wake Daddy.

Hearing pots and pans rattling, Cole rolled over on the narrow cot and opened his eyes. He quickly remembered Olli's absence and wearily pulled himself out of bed, smiling to himself when he saw he was still fully dressed. He told the girls that Olli was alright. Then he picked up his chunky little son and held him on his lap telling him his mama wasn't in the barn milking the cows, but she had gone to see the doctor and she stayed to visit for a while.

Cole Boy shouted, "Where's my Mama?" He jumped down from Coles lap and began screaming. He ran to the door just as Papa came in the house carrying the full milk pails.

The door closed behind Papa. Cole Boy ran in circles pounding on the rough boards, wailing, "I want my Mama! I want to find my Mama!" He had clicked from a happy boy into a distressed wailing child.

Papa was gruff with him. Tess and Nell pulled him away from the door and tussled to take him to his Daddy so Cole could quiet him.

Cole picked up his screaming, wriggling child, took him to the bed and placed him on his lap. In a quiet easy manner and with his voice soft and soothing, Cole soon had Cole Boy listening intently as he told about the trip he and Mama had taken in the truck. He told him about the icy road and the pretty fog along the road. The boy listened more intently when Cole told him, "Son, when we go to get Mama from the hospital, you can ride in front and help Daddy drive the truck. How about that?"

This completely satisfied the child and he ran to tell Tess and Nell, with childish excitement, that he was going to get Mama home in a few days, and if they were very good they could go too.

Second Son

Papa grumbled as he strained the fresh milk before putting the pans of warm milk in the cooler.

Olli was home from the hospital about a week when—bag and baggage—Kyle, his wife Annetta, and their three children arrived. Olli was happy to see her favorite brother. To her surprise the children were well-behaved and enjoyed helping with chores. Annetta became a real blessing to Olli. A real camaraderie between the two women soon became evident.

The cousins were enrolled in school, so everyday the five children, in a chattering flock, trouped off to the school bus leaving Cole Boy to spend the day at home with Olli, Annetta and Papa. The little boy said he wished he was old enough to be in school too.

Just before Thanksgiving 1937 all awakened one morning to find a blanket of wet snow had fallen during the night. The road too dangerous for venturing out, so the two men decided to stay home and use the day to chop wood and do a number of small repairs on the barn and truck.

The school bus didn't arrive, so the children trekked back to the house. In the cramped quarters of the one room house all six children found quiet games in which to engage themselves. The harmony of the group surprised the adults who congratulated the children on the delightfully quiet day they had enjoyed together.

Olli and Annetta planned a special menu for their first Thanksgiving together.

The Wednesday before Thanksgiving a letter had came from Dad and Mother Brauer informing Cole and Olli, due to the weather, they couldn't come for the holiday. Inwardly Olli knew their absence was because of her recent trip to the hospital and all the added company who filled the small house filled to overflowing. She had written and told her in-laws how happy she was to have Kyle and Annetta staying with them, how much help they were to her and Cole.

Thanksgiving morning dawned cold and blustery, but having

her brother, his family, and Papa with them warmed the day for Olli. Annetta prepared most of the meal and engaged the help of Tess, Nell and her oldest boy, Cary. They peeled vegetables and kneaded bread for rolls while the three younger children placed silverware and plates on Annetta's lace tablecloth she had saved for the special Thanksgiving meal.

Everyone ate heartily and the children were proud of the job they'd done. The results were extravagant in comparison to the usual daily fare, and everyone got up from the table completely satisfied, full of food and warm feelings.

During the next two weeks snow flurries continued which meant no school for the children and no working in the woods for the men. These conditions made the small house seem even more cramped than usual.

The children busied themselves playing outside when the weather permitted. They made a snowman, came in and dried clothes and drank gallons of cocoa, repeating this hubbub routine all day. For them the days passed quickly.

It was Papa's habit and enjoyment to play his fiddle and tell stories for the children every Sunday morning. He also listened to the old radio which worked by hooking it to a car battery. The children knew Papa expected the group to be quiet when he listened to his favorite programs.

31
Infamy And Funerals

1941, the children were growing. Tess was 11, Nell 9, and Cole Boy 7. It was a good year for the Brauer farm.

One Sunday, December seventh, 1941, the radio program Pap normally listened to was interrupted by an urgent broadcast from the President Franklin D. Roosevelt. He announced the Japanese had bombed Pearl Harbor in the Hawaiian Islands, sinking a large part of the American fleet. The news broadcasters then said there were many dead and injured American servicemen.

America was at war. The wars in Europe and Asia had made their way across the Atlantic and Pacific oceans to the shores of the United States.

Just a few days passed before Cole's brother Ben and Olli's brother Kyle enlisted in the army. Ben was rejected because of poor eye sight. Lena and the girls still lived with Dad and Mother Brauer. Ben signed up again for a civilian construction company that went to Hawaii to begin contracted cleanup work, but he soon returned home at the request of the military in the Hawaiian Islands.

In the meantime Kyle asked Cole and Olli if Annetta and their three children could stay with them until he finished Boot Camp. He planned to enlist in the Army, then he would move his family close to where he'd be stationed. Cole and Olli agreed.

After Kyle left for military service, things were quiet. Annetta and the children settled into a somber, depressed existence waiting for word from Kyle.

Second Son

Cole and Papa had been talking for a week or more, and Cole announced that the time had come to begin building the addition on the back of the small one-room house. They decided on a large single room dormitory. It wasn't what Olli wanted, but she said nothing to discourage the promise of more space.

Early that spring of 1942, Cole and Ben worked in the cold rainy woods gathering and selling an abundance of evergreens, putting in extra-long hours to make enough money to build the needed space. Still in need of cash, Cole went to the bank and borrowed money to finish the much needed room. Cole's brother, John, was a cabinet maker in the local lumber yard and supplied the project with useable scrap lumber.

Much to Olli's approval the new room had large cottage windows across the back to let in the early morning light. The room, when finished, was divided into four areas by suspending blankets on clothes lines stretched from wall to wall. This created privacy, of sorts, which everyone rejoiced in.

Warm weather came early. The household overflowed with laughing children, garden planting, clothes washing, farm chores, dish washing and cooking for ten people.

Olli worked with Cole in the woods again to make wages to feed everyone. Papa stayed home and helped Annetta with those farm things that needing tending.

One wet evening when the chores were finished, the children settled down to a quiet time of school studies. Annetta was in her room where she had taken one of the kerosene lamps so she could read to Cole Boy and her youngest little girl, Connie, to keep them quiet while the other children studied.

Cole looked out of the front window and saw car headlights flash across the yard. Out in the muddy driveway an engine chugged to a halt.

Cole went to the door and opened it just as his brother John stepped onto the porch. John's face was white. Something was

Infamy And Funerals

clearly the matter. Grasping Cole's hand, he stepped over and stood by Olli's chair sadly shaking his head.

John hesitated, then in a hushed whisper asked if the children could go to their bedrooms. Cole motioned to the round-eyed, perceptive children. They obeyed by quickly going to Annetta's room to join the others and wait until the adults had been told the news.

John cleared his throat. "We just received news from Dad. He telephoned from Chehalis to tell us our three young brothers, Liar, Jessie and Carl, all had drowned."

Cole found a chair. In disbelief, he sat down.

Olli asked a hushed question, "How could such a thing happen?"

John explained the three brothers had gone fishing in the Cowlitz River for the run of Steelhead salmon. They didn't have a boat, so they borrowed one from an old drinking buddy. The friend saw them put tackle and three bottles of whiskey in the boat and warned the jovial trio that they didn't need the whiskey for bait, but the three pushed the boat into the river's current shouting for their friend not to worry. They'd be back before dark.

The rain and sleet were biting cold, so the brothers apparently imbibed most of the whiskey they had taken with them, leaving their spirits too high and their good sense lacking. The river had risen to a dangerous level due to unexpected rain and snow melt. The drunken trio took no notice of the swiftness of the water where they had ventured. The boat overturned. The next day, miles down the river, the boat was found—*empty*.

The boys' buddy, who had lent them the boat, felt something was wrong when his three friends didn't return. He alerted the sheriff's office. After the boat was retrieved, the sheriff, deputies and volunteers searched the icy stretch of roaring water.

The second day, after searching every eddy they found three bodies in a remote back water slough. That was when they notified Pastor and Mrs. Brauer.

John recounted the story Mother and Dad Brauer response:

Second Son

The two parents showed controlled emotion when the sheriff had given them the news of their three sons' drowning. The sheriff had asked Pastor Brauer to accompany him to the mortuary to identify the bodies. Solemn-faced with sadness, Pastor Brauer somberly placed his black hat on his bald head, bent over and placed a kiss on Mattie's snow white hair, then followed the sheriff out the door of the parsonage. As the door clicked shut, the usually controlled Mattie Brauer, as in slow motion, fell to her knees upon the thread-bare carpet, a wail not unlike a wounded animal spilling out into the cold day. She had lost her three youngest sons. Her boys, though grown men, were still her babies. God had wanted her three boys. He hadn't waited to take them until she had gone home to her maker. She had always prayed that she would go first to avoid the ripping pain that now tore though her soul. She was wracked by the loss of not only her boys, but the loss of her faith in prayer. The news drew Mattie to the brink of a loss of faith in God.

Mattie lay on the carpet, exhausted and numb. A quietness came over her senses as she drifted back to reality. Remembering she was a pastor's wife, she knew her husband would soon return. He, in his secure faith, would most likely have the last minute preparations for their sons taken care of before coming back to the parsonage. Mattie knew him so well. He'd be in his solemn, God-trusting frame of mind. He'd pat her on the hair and hold her like a hurt puppy. He'd never ask how the loss of her boys affected her, just assuming her faith in God, like a healing balm, would cover her pain and loss as it covered his own.

Mattie rose from the solidness of the floor. She felt older than her sixty years. She washed her face in cold water and combed her disheveled hair. On the outside she appeared normal; but inside she was alone and confused, needing to be held and reassured that God was right to take her three youngest sons—and that she was not to question His ways. She needed to know it was all right for her to feel anger. But when Dad Brauer returned home, just by looking at him Mattie knew she would have to work out her feelings by herself. She knew he was well collected, accepting God's will, and unable to imagine any other viewpoint but God's.

The following day, Dad Brauer conducted the burial services for his three sons. Half of the population of the town came to the small church to show respect for the family.

Dad Brauer gathered his remaining sons and his only daughter, Margaret, and held a short family prayer before leaving the church.

The grown children and their spouses came together with mixed emotions, knowing their pastor father accepted God's will. But they also saw through their mother's fragile shield. An invisible shield she held high when she knew anyone was watching. But pain oozed out and sat on the rims of her eyes when she felt no one was aware.

After the service, a large dinner was provided by the church family. The room smelled of spaghetti and carnations. The odors began to overwhelm Olli as she helped serve the food. She excused herself and stepped outside.

Olli was shaky and knew what her problem was. She hadn't been feeling well for the past few weeks, but had refused to tell Cole she believed she was once again pregnant. At home she hid morning sickness quite well by excusing herself on the pretext of outside chores whenever she felt ill. But the upsetting day and the stuffiness in the house, coupled with the smell of flowers and food, had brought on an emergency escape to the back yard where she was violently ill.

After the last two miscarriages she had an uneasy feeling about telling anyone for fear the circumstances would be the same. She didn't really want another child. The child within her womb and the two previous ones she felt were taken away because God knew Cole Boy was the answer to her prayers for a son.

The rain revived her so she quickly slipped back in the church kitchen door where a large group of ladies cleared up the dishes.

Second Son

The family lined up near the main door to thank everyone for offering condolences.

The men and their wives walked Mother Brauer across the yard to the parsonage. Everyone was lost in his or her own thoughts.

Olli and Lena led Mother Brauer into the bedroom. Lena hung her mother-in-law's shawl on the end of the bed while Olli helped the exhausted woman lie down. Olli plumped the pillows beneath Mother Brauer's head before offering her a cup of warm tea.

Mother Brauer gratefully sipped the calming liquid, surprised she crept out of the canker filled hole of sorrow in which she'd been lost. She found she was able to hold on to fragments of conversation and gestures of kindness shown her by her daughters-in-law.

At end of a long difficult day everyone took a large step away form the sadness and looked toward the rest of their lives. They all knew that life is a cherished and fragile thing possessed by each one.

Dad summed it up in his parting message to each son and their wives and Margaret as they prepared to leave. He said, "I thank God everyday for each of you and pray that you live your lives in a manner that makes Mother and me proud, according to God's will."

The trip home was cold for Cole and Olli. The constant rain slapped the windshield with an irritating chunk-squeak, chunk-squeak, of the wiper, smearing Cole's vision of the highway. The headlights cut thin holes in the inky darkness surrounding the weary travelers.

Arrival at home found Papa, Annetta and six children sitting around the kitchen table awaiting their arrival. The children were in different stages of nodding off to sleep.

Cole asked Tess and Nell to help Annetta put the young ones in their beds. The little ones toddled into the bedroom and were gratefully tucked into bed, content to know Daddy and Mama were home and safe.

Papa lifted the heavy sleeping Cole Boy and carried the overweight child, putting him in Cole and Olli's bed. Papa thought it such a foolish thing for a five year old to still be sleeping with his parents, but he'd found over time it was not his place to interfere.

Cole put the kettle on the stove while Annetta placed cups and butter and bread on the table. Talking to himself Cole muttered, "I think some hot tea to relax us will be a good end to a trying day."

Tea was a tradition that had eased many a crisis.

Olli was far beyond the realm of being tired, when she, Cole, Papa and Annetta sat down at the table. Olli poured the pungent brew, which was quickly savored, then sighed heavily, bent her head and began to sob for reasons far beyond those that the family suspected.

The next few months went by in the usual routine, and Olli unavoidably revealed the expected child, as she had expanded out of every piece of clothing she owned. Early in June, 1942, Olli finally forced herself to go to the doctor. Before leaving his office she was shocked and depressed when Dr. Clancy told her she was carrying twins.

"Oh Lord!" She moaned. "What am I going to do"?

Dr. Clancy said in an unconcerned voice, "My Dear, you will give birth to them and they will be fine."

Olli knew better. She wouldn't be fine at all, and she sobbed, "My house is brim full now. I can't work any harder."

Dr. Clancy knew her situation at home but assured her she was over-reacting. He consoled, "I'm sure the girls are old enough they'll enjoy helping with two babies. And Annetta will be a big help with the extra house work. Maybe you'll enjoy these babies more than you think."

In mid July Olli began labor earlier than predicted. Labor was long and difficult; nothing like her previous births. The reason was the babies were in breach position. Neither one was willing to give way for the other to be delivered. After twenty hours Dr.

Second Son

Clancy delivered identical twin baby girls. They were pronounced still born. They had strangled on twisted umbilical cords.

Olli was exhausted and hearing the babies were dead, she slid into a deep purple depression where she allowed herself to be encased in a self-woven veil of doom. There she dwelled for three weeks.

Cole came to the hospital everyday only to find her curled in that safe cocoon of her own making, not wanting to escape and face Cole and the bleak emptiness she would face, even with the fact she had sworn she hadn't wanted another baby. But loosing two at one time had scarred her heart.

Cole was heartbroken and afraid of Olli's mental condition. Dr. Clancy told him to speak to her gently and keep her involved in news of the family, which he did. Cole told Olli that Papa, Annetta, he and the children held special burial services for the babies. He told her the children had named the twins Daisy and Deana. He said the children picked lace baby dresses, and the burial site was on a little hill in a sunny spot in the cemetery.

Dr. Clancy realized Olli needed medication, which he prescribed, to bring her out of her melancholy condition. In a few days Olli was brought back to a quiet shell of herself, so the doctor declared she was well enough to be released from the hospital. She wrestled with the pain of going home, but when settled in her familiar surroundings, her spirits lifted. She found Annetta had cleaned and kept the house and all the children in a peaceful, easy order that calmed her misgivings about going home.

The subject of the twins came into family conversation only once, and Olli found the pain and guilt was bearable when she mulled things over in her mind and lay the past behind her. She rested a week in bed, then remembered a saying Ma had said to her during her early childhood: "Pick up your boot straps, Olli, and get on with what needs to be done." How true the thought rang through her mind—giving her strength she was unaware she held within her fragile frame.

The children, all six, Cole's and hers, Kyle's and Annetta's, had truly missed Olli during her time of absence from the house. Daily, after school work and chores were done, they happily gathered around her bed, sitting on the floor quietly visiting, drawing pictures and bringing her anything she needed. They desired the closeness of their mama and aunt.

No longer did Cole Boy did not demand the majority of Olli's attention. In fact he behaved himself unusually well.

One early August day Annetta received a letter from Kyle saying he would be home in a few days. He wouldn't finish Boot Camp or be sent overseas. He had been given a medical discharge because of asthma. This news surprised everyone, but secretly Olli was happy to know the extra family members would soon be moving into their own home.

Annetta was doubly happy and looked forward to seeing Kyle again soon. She could scarcely contain herself because she hadn't bargained to end up caring for hers children and Cole and Olli's three, plus having all the housework to do while Olli recuperated.

Annetta asked Cole to let her drive with him on his next trip into town so she could look for a house of their own and be ready to move when Kyle returned.

Kyle's return from the service was sooner than anyone had expected, and he gave Cole and Olli some of his mustering out pay in thanks for allowing his family a home while he was away. Kyle moved his family into a small, rundown house Annetta had located in the outskirts of Shelton. Kyle said he would still like to work in the woods with Cole. That news made Cole happy to know he'd have a partner again.

A week after Kyle's family moved out, the daily routine fell into place for Olli. She had rallied well since the loss of the twins.

32
August 1942, The Damned War

In late August, just before school began, the mailman honked. That always meant there was mail in the box at the main road.

Olli was busy plucking chickens in preparation for the evening meal, so she sent Tess and Nell down the lane to retrieve the mail.

When the girls handed the envelope to their mother, to their surprise, Mama stopped working on the half plucked birds and instructed the girls to finish cleaning the wet smelly feathered carcasses. Olli cleaned her hands, wiped them dry on her apron and took the letter, then went out the back door and slowly walked down the path to the barn. The girls looked at each other, puzzled, why Mama always went to the barn when she got an envelope from Tacoma.

Olli settled into the quiet sanctuary of the barn, sitting on a hay bale. She could smell the warm heady aroma of the hay mingled with familiar smells of the cows. The combination eased her anxious inquisitiveness as she tore open the envelope, knowing by the loosely written script the letter was from her dear old friend Dweena, still working for the Gordons. To Olli it seemed a lifetime had passed, but in the interim their correspondence had never ceased. Through the years Dweena had remained Olli's confidant and secretly kept Olli informed about the life of her first son, Cal. She never sent pictures that Olli would have to explain, simply writing about Cal's achievements in school and his steady growth into a handsome young man.

Second Son

    Olli had successfully kept those youthful years to herself, but always held hope that she could see again her first born son. However, she knew after all the years had passed, her hopes were dim of ever seeing him—due to unalterable circumstances. Besides, Cal had never been told another person was his true birth mother. Olli knew Mother Gordon's secret was never mentioned in the house after Olli was forced to leave her boy behind. Olli felt they could pass on the street and wouldn't recognize each other, because it had been nearly ten years since she saw Cal when she had gone to the Gordon's house the day after her Grandma's funeral. Cal was now nineteen.
    As Olli scanned Dweena's waveringly scrawled handwriting, she was aware Dweena was fast aging. She knew one day her friend's letters would stop. This would mean Dweena was ill or had passed away, leaving Olli with no way to keep in touch with her son's life.
    Olli read the precious paragraphs. Then a small spark of hope flashed before her eyes. Joy and expectation broadened her mouth into a vibrantly alive smile. The realization of the letter's message quickly turned Olli's outlook to joyful tears.
    She sat for a long quiet moment before carefully folding the letter. She tucked it in the front of her cotton dress, hidden close to her heart. She knew she had vowed never to lie to Cole again, but in this case she would have to bear the burden on her conscience alone. In time she would be able to forgive herself, but this deceit was necessary, she assured herself.
    She smoothed her hair and brushed her shaking hands down the front of her apron before stepping out of the barn and returning to the house.
    The children asked who had sent the letter. Papa would have inquired too, but he felt he knew it was from Olli's old friend, so he busied himself and acted as if he had no interest in it.
    Olli never told the family who sent the letters to her or what the contents were when she received letters from Tacoma, but the girls could tell when the post mark was Tacoma, Mama

was always cheerful after reading it, so it must bring her good news.

The rest of the day Olli's mind rolled plots and schemes around in her head. She had to make some sort of a plan to accomplish what Dweena had suggested.

When Cole came home from work, Olli had a special dinner prepared. The meal was eaten early and the dishes cleared away. Olli finally sat at the kitchen table and casually mentioned she'd been thinking of taking the children to Point Defiance Park in Tacoma, as a special treat before school started.

Cole was surprised at Olli's apparent good natured attitude. He thought after all she had been through during the summer it would give her a lift in her spirits, but said because he had to work everyday she should take the children on the bus or the train. He wondered if she felt up to the trip. She and the children became excited. Olli replied warmly saying she felt fine.

The children, overhearing the conversation, jumped for joy with anticipation of the adventure of a bus or train ride.

Olli said she thought the children would see more of the countryside if they took the short train ride from Olympia to Tacoma, then caught the trolley from the train station to the park. They could take a picnic basket and have lunch on the lawn near the rose gardens.

The children were excited about seeing the caged wild animals and cheerfully told Papa they would tell him all about what they saw and draw him pictures of their favorite ones when they returned home.

The plans seemed to be completed before any objections were forthcoming, especially from Papa, as he'd likely have to stay home and care for the chores.

Cole was puzzled at the sudden enthusiasm Olli showed, but agreed it would do the children good to get away from the farm for a day. So plans were made for Cole to drive them to town to catch a bus that would take them to Olympia to catch the train.

Cole asked about the cost of the trip and Olli said the cost was minimal. Cole didn't know Dweena had written the needed information in the letter which was hidden inside Olli's dress. He agreed that on the following Wednesday Olli and the children should make a day of it on their first train ride and a trip to Tacoma. This would be a special outing before school started.

After the agreement, the atmosphere in the dingy, gray-walled house brightened. The children noticed Mama hummed and smiled much more than usual on the days preceding their train trip. Mama had always said she was too tired to play games after her daily chores, but suddenly she was eager to teach them new games. The family sat around the kitchen table in the light of the kerosene lamps and shared camaraderie more mellow and happy than had been there for some time.

Olli found one of Cole's old army uniforms and expertly tailored a replica, in miniature, for Cole Boy to wear for the special outing. When he tried on the uniform he marched around saluting everyone, holding a hand-carved wooden rifle which Papa had made, so he could play soldier.

Cole thought he looked so cute and patriotic, he found the camera to take the boy's picture. Olli saw what Cole had in mind and quickly retrieved the camera from Cole telling him she wanted to get some special shots of Cole and Cole Boy together. She didn't include the girls in the impromptu photo session. Tess and Nell, unnoticed, disappeared into the house feeling left out and unconnected from the admiring circle that surrounded Cole Boy. Even Papa forgot about hurting their feelings.

In the afternoon, the girls having mended their mood of being excluded from the photo session, dutifully helped Mama plan a picnic lunch to take on the trip. As they talked they became excited about going, and soon returned to a happy mood.

Because of the war, due to gasoline rationing, the children hadn't had the opportunity to get away from the farm. Every trip in the truck had to be necessary, so an outing such as the one on which they were to embark was a very special treat. Cole saved ration stamps for extra gas for such trips. Cole was aware Olli

August 1942, The Damned War

didn't ask for much that wasn't really necessary, but the trip with the children seemed to have special meaning for her, so Cole did what he could to show his encouragement and to acknowledge he knew she needed time out away from the drudgery of canning and harvesting.

The morning of the trip finally arrived with much flurry and excitement. Olli and the children climbed in the back of the old panel work truck. Papa sat in his usual place in the passenger seat next to Cole.

In the back of the panel truck there were no cushioned seats, only two wide boards spanned from fender well to fender well. Olli and Cole Boy sat on the front board. Tess and Nell sat on the board in the back. With one hand they supported themselves by hanging onto handles on each side of the truck.

The truck rumbled and clanked down the dusty road. No one complained because they were off to catch the bus to Olympia on the way to their first train trip to Tacoma and Point Defiance Park, their first out-of-town adventure to outshine all other adventures.

The weather was as delightful as the high expectations for the day.

The bus delivered them to East Olympia where the train was quick to arrive at the station. Olli and her three excited children, picnic basket in hand, clamored aboard and were safely seated before the train was again in motion.

The trip lasted less than a half an hour. The locomotive chugged past Fort Lewis where Cole Boy counted tanks, jeeps, cars, cannons and soldiers. This excited him so much he had to be told to stop jumping up and down on the seat. He jabbered excitedly telling his sisters that everything he saw would soon be going to Germany or to fight the Japanese in a big war.

The train arrived at the huge domed station in Tacoma. The children were fascinated by the expanse of the place. They had never been in such a large building and were enamored with the polished pink marble floor and the glistening varnished benches. The overhead light illuminating the huge room made it sparkle

Second Son

with reflections from the benches and the crowd of travelers who scurried through the station. The children were quiet as they took in every aspect of the place. The hustle, bustle, comings and goings of people from every walk of life fascinated them also. It was a sight which three small town, country-raised children had never before seen.

Outside on the loading platform a long line of soldiers stood with duffle bags on their shoulders, waiting to board the train.

Tess, Nell and Cole Boy walked to the tall glass doors to watch the crowd. They saw a properly dressed older lady wearing a lovely blue suit and a hat with a curved feather. She had smooth leather gloves on her dainty hands. She strolled toward Olli.

Olli, without seeming to have acknowledged the woman told the children to sit on one of the benches near the door and wait for her to return.

The abrupt order from their mother was very unlike her usual manner as she never had left them with strangers; nor would she allow them to go to unfamiliar places. So, though puzzled, they sat on a large bench not daring to move until their mother returned.

The children watched their Mama follow the old lady until they walked nearly out of sight. They saw Olli clasp Dweena's frail hands and give her a swift kiss on the cheek.

In hushed and hurried conversation Dweena pointed to a soldier who stood in the line of men which slowly shuffled toward the train.

Olli opened the camera and clicked a picture, then the two women stood near a marble column on the boarding platform. Olli's eyes filled with tears as she watched a tall blond soldier step toward the train. Unknown to her waiting children, the soldier was Olli's first son, Cal, leaving for Europe to fight in the "damned war."

Cal, waiting his turn to board the train, glanced at the station and looked for Dweena. She told him she would be at the loading dock to wave goodbye. Cal scanned the area and saw Dweena and raised a hand to wave. Then he noticed Dweena's friend, standing

August 1942, The Damned War

with her. Cal was puzzled why Dweena's friend was also smiling and waving, then raising a camera to take a picture of him as he boarded the train steps. Cal remembered the slight blond woman. He had met her only one day ten years before, but remembered her because of the unusual gift she gave him. He had hidden the ring in his secret place, but retrieved it when he'd joined the army and had chosen it as a good-luck charm. He carried the silver chain and gold baby ring, because it seemed that it had meant a great deal to the woman, enough that she made a special trip to give it to him. Over time, Cal learned to live with the mystery of his adoptive parent's refusal to discuss his true parents, saying only they were both dead. A few years before he felt doubt creep in, and he wondered why the Gordons had shown little interest in his leaving for war. He wondered if his real mother stood with Dweena, watching as he stepped onto the train and into a future of heroism or oblivion.

Olli composed herself as best she could. She kissed Dweena quickly and returned to the lobby of the station where her future waited. She knew she had seen a part of her past life move away from her, maybe to be gone forever.

The children, on her return to them, saw tears in their mother's eyes. "What's the matter, Mama?"

Olli's quick response was, "It is so sad to see all of those young men going off to war."

Tess asked, "Mama, who was that old lady?"

Olli smiled and answered, "She is a very dear friend from a long time ago."

Olli picked up the picnic basket, gathered her children like a mother hen gathers its chicks, and they left the station. Tess and Nell clasped Cole Boy's hand and followed Olli out to the shiny green and gold trolley, which, to the children, looked like a magic chariot that would take them to Point Defiance Park. The trolley's bell clanged, and the trolley jerked and bumped its way up and over the top of a long hill toward the park.

The children, still perplexed by Mama's actions, never

mentioned the train station encounter again. It wouldn't even be remembered until years later when the girls would fit the puzzle pieces together.

Their day at the park was glorious. The lawns were warm, lush and green. The walkways were filled with young soldiers and sailors visiting with buddies or strolling with their sweethearts or wives.

Olli invited three young soldiers to share the homemade picnic she had prepared.

Cole Boy was a cute chubby child and the handsome young soldiers were impressed by the hero worship and admiration Cole Boy heaped upon them. He saluted them and begged to have his picture taken with them.

They laughed at his childish charm.

The three children and the soldiers played a game tossing a ball. Everyone had a good time, as if they had known each other forever.

The day came to a weary end. Olli and the tired but happy children took the trolley back to the train station, the train back to the bus in Olympia, the bus to Shelton, where Cole and Papa were waiting for them.

Tales were told and retold about the train ride. Cole Boy talked about all the tanks and guns, the trolley and zoo animals they had seen. The picnic had been fun with the new soldier friends they had met. When they arrived home everyone changed into their chore clothes and gladly began the evening routines. Olli milked the cows. Papa fed the pigs. The girls gathered eggs and fed the chickens. Cole built the fire in the stove and set the kettle on for tea. The old routine clicked into place so quickly the day seemed like a wish come and gone rather than a short-termed adventure with unexplained undertones.

33
The Attacks

Cole continued to supply evergreens to the Seattle and Portland distributors. Kyle worked everyday in the woods with Cole. Ben soon joined them.

The main florist and evergreen outlets in Seattle and Portland approached Cole about opening a processing station for the many types of forest products available on the Olympic Peninsula. If Cole consented, a number of independent pickers could bring their greens to be sorted, baled and regularly picked up by trucks owned by the big distributors.

Cole agreed to open his own evergreen shed and made arrangements for a bookkeeper, and officially hired Olli and Annetta to sort the greens. He painted a large sign that was nailed to a post out at the main road. Then Brauer's Brush Business was open and waiting for the local men who needed the services Cole was ready to provide.

Papa, Olli and Cole, Kyle and Ben helped build a lean-to on the back side of the house which became the sorting and storage shed for the new business.

The word spread quickly among evergreen workers and Cole's business began to prosper. He found many of his close neighbors were evergreen workers too, and they were likewise thrilled to be able to bring their greens to such a convenient deposit site.

Cole and Olli hadn't met many of their neighbors until the business opened. Chores, hard work, building and preparing the

Second Son

work shed, plus all the relatives who had lived with them, and Olli's illnesses, had kept them all too busy to become acquainted. The children, as children do, had met the neighbor children on the school bus and had become good friends with many of them.

The children back in school, autumn was busy painting the roadside hazelnut bushes and alder and vine-maple trees red and yellow, while the chores around the farm broke into full swing. Olli worked hard again canning fruits and vegetables, making pickles and sauerkraut, and butchering pigs and chickens to fill the food cellar with winter supplies.

Besides working in the sorting shed, Olli took on all the regular tasks involved in readying the family for winter. As some winters were harder than others, the food she prepared would be the only food supply the family would have because heavy snow sometimes made it impossible to work in the woods.

Every night Olli went to bed utterly exhausted but satisfied she'd done the best she could.

The neighbors came whenever Olli let them know there was a pig to butcher. They knew after the work was done they would be given a wonderfully-prepared feast and a generous portion of the pork, chickens, turkeys or rabbits to pay them for help with the butchering. Olli and Papa reciprocated the gesture when any neighbor also needed help. Some of the neighbors were poor and often appearing at the Brauers on Sunday, strangely, right at dinner time. They knew they would never be turned away, as Cole and Olli set more places at the table and fed anyone who appeared.

After dinner Olli was often asked to cut Johnny, Billy, or Ted's hair, as their parents couldn't afford to have a barber do it. Olli always obliged cheerfully and at times would sing silly songs to the grubby little children. This transformed a possibly demeaning situation for parent and child into a pleasant episode, where the singing spread through the group standing around waiting their turn for the clip of the scissors.

The Attacks

Cole was aware that Olli was overwhelmed by making herself available to anyone in need, never asking for anything in return. The only things she ever accepted were extra things for Cole Boy. But this year Cole planned to do something special for Olli for her birthday.

On the chilly November afternoon of Olli's birthday, Annetta and she were sorting evergreens in the shed when a large covered delivery truck pulled to a stop in the driveway. Olli went to the truck thinking the driver needed directions to a neighbor's address. Instead, the driver and his helper began to unload a very large padded box. They put it on a hand cart and tussled it into the dingy little house.

The driver handed her a slip to sign to prove the object had been delivered. He returned to the truck and backed out the driveway leaving Olli standing in the room looking puzzled.

Annetta came in from the shed. She was smiling with a mischievous glint in her eyes. "Open it," she said.

Olli stared a second, then stepped forward and pulled the padded cover from the object. She sank to her knees in weak surprise. Before her sat a shiny player piano. Her sheer delight shone in the tears that rolled down her face. "You knew about this, didn't you?" she gasped as Annetta patted her shoulder.

Annetta said, "It has been so hard for me to not mention this surprise. I'm happy it's finally been delivered before I gave the surprise away."

There was a large card attached to the keyboard. It was from Cole. As Olli read it, she took her handkerchief out and blew her nose and blotted her eyes still not quite believing what she saw. Olli was truly overwhelmed at such a thoughtful gift. She had talked to Cole many times about the times she remembered when Papa and Ma, her brothers and sisters gathered around the piano while Eva played, Kyle strumming his guitar, Papa making his fiddle sing, and Ma strumming her ukulele—the family singing

Second Son

along. Olli sniffled, her head hung low, as she asked herself where that wisp of memory had come from.

When Cole arrived from work he heard the faint trickle of melody pouring out of the house and knew the piano had been delivered. He wished he could have been at home to see the surprise in Olli's eyes which he knew would have been in the form of happy tears.

From that evening on, after chores, the family gathered around the piano as Olli ran her fingers over the ivory keys playing familiar melodies. Sometimes Papa joined in the music, playing his fiddle. The children absorbed the simple magic being performed as if they were in a mysterious presence holding a touch of the untold story of Mama's childhood.

It was after her birthday that Olli and Cole made the acquaintance of the Pomeroys. They were a middle-aged couple who began bringing their evergreens to Cole's brush shed for processing. James and Mary Pomeroy were from Alaska. They made regular visits to the Brauer's to bring their weekly bundles of evergreens. Sometimes they arrived at the time the family was absorbed in their music. The Pomeroy's would sit quietly and listen to music that spontaneously sprang from Olli's fingers rippling over the piano keys and Papa's well-rosined bow dancing tunes from his fiddle while Tess and Nell sang.

James enjoyed hearing Papa spin his Nordic tales of Northern Minnesota, his growing-up years with his immigrant Norwegian parents, brothers and sisters. Papa wove in wonderful fishing and hunting stories that held even the wiggliest child spellbound. Cole, in his quiet happy manner, loved to sit in his rocker and absorb evenings of music with his dear wife and family and friends—knowing his gift of the piano had been the catalyst which brought a blessed calm to his household.

James and Mary soon became the Brauer's best friends. They talked of events and joyfully passed times which slowly bound the two families together as fast friends.

The Attacks

After a year of their weekly visits, in early 1944, the Pomeroys decided to return to Alaska to visit old friends. The weekly visits with them were sorely missed by all.

James and Mary returned to Shelton in early spring and rented a small beach cabin on Oakland Bay. As soon as they unpacked all the boxes and settled in, Mary invited the Brauers and Papa for a visit and picnic at their house.

The invitation especially excited Tess and Nell when they saw the Pomeroy's quaint blue-shingled cabin, built partially on stilts. The front porch suspended out over the mud flat area of the bay. When the tide came in full, the water lapped in wet whispers at the under side of the porch. Early spring daffodils blossomed in random bunches in the tall beach grass which grew to the tidal mark on the beach.

While the children waited for food to be prepared, Tess and Cole Boy decided to take an adventurous walk up the lonely beach. In the cabin, Nell was fascinated watching Mary and Mama cooking in the kitchen that was built like a ship's galley.

Papa and Cole drove into town for a few needed food items Olli had forgotten to buy.

After they drove away, Nell, in her new sun shorts and blouse, tired of watching the women cooking, decided she would go to the beach to look for starfish. She walked toward the shore humming contentedly. Stepping onto the beach gravel, she heard James call for her to wait, saying he wanted to show her a wild mallard ducks nest in a small niche in the beach grass where a fresh water spring trickled to the bay.

James took Nell's small hand in his large, burly hand and led her down the beach—out of sight of the cabin and Tess and Cole Boy, who had walked in the opposite direction. James talked in hushed tones. He said to be quiet, so the duck wouldn't fly off her hidden nest. They came to a small stream. The beach grass and cat tails grew extra tall. James held Nell's hand very firmly as they stepped cautiously up the stream that was seeping toward the outgoing tide. He pushed a large clump of cattails aside and pointed to the duck's nest where a lovely camouflaged, brown speckled mallard duck sat so still on her hidden nest they could barely see her, except when she blinked her eye.

Nell was surprised when James picked her up in his strong hairy arms and spoke with a husky voice, "Let's sit here a while and watch the duck." He squatted down in the grass and pulled Nell's legs around his waist so she was sitting on his lap-facing him. He pulled one leg of her sun shorts to one side and slipped his rough burly hand up, into, and past her underwear until his grimy fingers touched penetrated her private parts. He smiled and whispered, "We'll sit here. It's okay, I won't hurt you, you're such a sweet little girl and I like to feel little girl's lady parts. I love you very much Nell. You make me very happy."

Nell's eyes filled with fear, then tears, as she struggled to get free. She whimpered as she pleaded, "Let me go, please. I won't tell. I promise."

James said fiercely, "Oh Nell, you must never tell anyone or they'd think you were a bad, nasty girl, so you must never ever tell."

Nell heard Olli call the children to come for dinner. She jerked away from James, but he put his dirty hand over her mouth in an attempt to keep her quiet. Then, thinking more clearly, he let her down from his lap, uncovered her mouth and told her to remember what he'd told her. Nell called back to her Mama.

"I'm here, Mama. I'll be right there." She clamored up the grassy bank of the narrow ditch. As she did, she saw Tess and Cole Boy running up the beach from the opposite direction.

Nell fell in the mud. She brushed it off as she tried to climb away from James. She knew she would have to explain about the mud on her new clothes, but she felt if she said anything besides finding the duck nest, things would never be the same with her parent's friendship with James and Mary. She went to the house

The Attacks

still brushing the mud from her clothes. She met Tess and Cole Boy as they reached the cabin door.

Cole and Papa drove in the driveway at the same time James appeared—walking up from the beach from a different direction than from which Nell had come.

Everyone enjoyed a great picnic. Everyone laughed at Papa's stories. Nell was quiet through it all.

While Olli and Mary did the dishes, the men and Cole Boy turned on James's new radio and listened to a comedy program. Nell asked Tess to go out to the privy with her. It started to rain, so the girls dashed out holding a newspaper like an umbrella over their heads.

When they reached the outhouse, Nell could no longer hold the tears that had been welling up in her throat. She was full of horror and shame as she told Tess what had happened. Her older sister held her and comforted her until the tears dried up. Tess told Nell that no matter what—she would have to tell Mama and Daddy as soon as they got home. Nell dried her eyes and waited until the redness in her face had vanished, then the girls returned to the house, both holding a terrible secret.

A week later Nell mustered up the strength to approach Olli and tell her what happened the day of the picnic. Olli listened, her eyes glared dreadful accusations. She snapped that Nell lied. A dead stillness filled the room when Nell finished.

Olli turned and faced the pale frightened girl, then in a voice Nell had never heard come from anyone's mouth, Nell cringed as Olli hissed, "Nell, you're lying. James is too sweet. He's a good person. He would never do such a thing to one of my children. You are a filthy rotten lying brat. And where did a daughter of mine ever hear of such things and dare to make up lies to hurt our friends? Shame on you Nell!"

Olli gave Nell strict orders to never mention what she had just told her. Such lies would make Cole upset and he would lose one of his best friends.

Second Son

Nell would do as her mother commanded her and would never told her father. She left the room in stark disbelief her own Mama would take such an attitude. Later in life, Nell would look back and realize why a lack of respect for Olli began festering at the moment her Mama called her a liar about something so disturbing to an innocent and trusting young girl.

The following week passed quickly. The night arrived again for the Pomeroys to bring their weekly truckload of evergreens to Cole for processing. When Nell saw them drive in the yard she inconspicuously slipped into her partitioned area of the bedroom, not wanting to come face to face with James Pomeroy ever again. She thought if she could stay hidden and out of sight and out of mind, no one would miss her.

After Cole had finished in the work shed he invited James and Mary into the house for coffee. Being unaware of the secret that Olli held from him about the molestation of Nell the day of the Pomeroy's picnic, Cole called the girls to come and sing.

Olli quickly obliged by sitting at the piano, but Nell hesitated to leave the safety of her bed, where she sat cross legged reading a book. After two or three requests Cole came to her room and told her she wasn't being very friendly to their friends and wanted to know why she was acting so contrary.

Nell wanted so much to hug her daddy and tell him about her fear and dislike for Mr. Pomeroy. But ringing in her ears she heard the man's growled warning as she'd been held in his grip, crouched in the muddy crevice on the beach. She also remembered Mama's warning hissed at her about her being such a liar, and that their friendship with the Pomeroys was in Nell's hands.

Nell submitted to her father's request and remained silent about the incident for fear of Olli's wrath. The two girls sang three songs before excusing themselves in the pretence of having home work to complete before dinner. Cole invited the couple to stay for dinner, which they did.

The Attacks

Cole said he'd drive into town for fuel for the truck before the gas station closed for the evening. He asked James to go with him and they'd be back before dark, thus giving Olli a chance to make dinner. James declined, saying he'd stay and help Papa with the early evening chores.

After Cole left, the women started preparing dinner. Papa went to the barn to do the milking. Cole Boy and Mary were playing a checker game, and again Nell retreated to her bed to resume reading her book.

Tess grabbed up the egg basket, remembering she'd forgotten to gather the eggs. She went down the path to the chicken house, where unknown to anyone, James followed, sauntering across the back yard. He went to the chicken house door, where he silently slipped inside. His presence there, so close behind her, sent chills up Tess' back and she gasped in fear, knowing what had happened to Nell. James closed his big burly hand over her mouth and reached for her, groping at her private parts as she struggled to get free. Tess hit him in the head with the basket and bit his hand hard enough to draw blood. She broke free and ran from the chicken yard. She slowed her pace as she entered the back door and ducked into the bedroom area and scurried to Nell where she grabbed her sister and whispered what had happened. The two upset youngsters held tightly to each other while Tess sobbed in silence.

Cole returned just as Papa brought in the evening's milk. All chores were put on hold when Olli and Mary called everyone to dinner. It took a few extra minutes before Tess controlled herself enough to join the family. She pretended to sneeze and blow her nose as an excuse for her red eyes and runny nose.

The girls excused themselves soon after dinner.

They did the dishes, then, on the pretext of being tired, they went to bed earlier than usual, having secretly decided not to tell Mama but wait until later and talk to Daddy about what Mr. Pomeroy had done.

Second Son

Two weeks passed. The Pomeroys told Cole and Olli they were moving back to Alaska to be near James's ill parents. They left with the secret untold. The girls were unsure of mentioning anything to Cole after the source of their fear had moved away.

Another month passed when Mary wrote Olli and Cole a letter. She explained that they had just settled in Sitka, found jobs and made some new friends, when James was arrested for molesting three little girls. Mary was sure he would be sent to prison. She would live with James's parents; she was so ashamed she would never write again to the Brauers. She didn't ask if Tess and Nell had been approached, or molested by James, but in her heart she knew the truth.

34
War's End

By mid-August 1945 both war fronts had dwindled to an end, the atom bombs finishing the war in the Pacific. The attention of the whole world focused on the news that the war was over. The rationing of gas was over also, along with the limits on foodstuffs, tires and wire for electricity installations—which had all been high wartime priorities.

It wasn't long until the Brauers were on the list for installation of electrical power. That fact alone was cause for celebration, and celebrate is what everyone in the United States did.

The Brauers were no exception. They invited all the neighbors to a big potluck dinner. The house was filled to the brim with folks who brought any food they could gather.

It was a memorable time for every guest, from the elderly, blind widow neighbor lady, to the shaggiest ruffian boys who, after dinner, lined up for one of Olli's hair cuts.

Mrs. Byers, who played the piano at church, took over Olli's position at the pump organ and played every song anyone asked for, while Olli finished the hair cutting chore. Tess and Nell swept the floor and carried out nearly a bushel basket of hair trimmings.

The gathering soon dispersed as the early twilight of the late fall gave signal for everyone to go home to do their own farm chores.

When the crowd had gone the quiet was a relief. The family sat around the kitchen table completely satisfied, with full stomachs and happy hearts. They had been able to do what they could to make a day of celebration that would be remembered for years.

After the last of the garden harvest was put in the root cellar, Papa, Cole and the children spent any free time during the next few weeks chopping wood and stacking it in preparation for the coming cold weather. Olli decided to go back to work in the woods with Cole, even though Kyle and Ben were still working with him. There were so many things that Olli wanted for Cole Boy. She knew unless she was willing to extend herself to bring in more income, her dreams of lessons and musical instruments for her much-loved son would never be within her reach.

Annetta came to the evergreen shed five days a week and did the greater part of the sorting and baling, while Papa cared for the majority of the chores. The function of the farm and brush business had begun to revolve around Olli's desires to give the best of everything to Cole Boy.

Papa saw it plainly and resented the overfed, pampered boy and the sway he had over his Mother. Cole was also aware that Olli was overworking herself to the point of exhaustion just to supply the boy with the lion's share of his selfish material wants. Cole became distant and sullen.

Kyle and Annetta silently watched day by day, seeing Olli work to the point of physical exhaustion to make and save enough money so she could satisfy Cole Boy's unnecessary wants, which he, even at his young age, had begun demanding from his Mama. Olli's brother, Kyle was puzzled at his sister's attitude toward the boy.

Olli was unaware that everyone she knew talked behind her back and murmured among themselves, and even talked to Cole about what they observed. They asked him what would finally happen when Cole Boy was a teenager with demands beyond the family's ability to provide. Cole could give no answer.

When Olli lay down, exhausted, at night, sleep didn't come easily. In the darkness she listened to the easy breathing of her family asleep around her. And as she listened, her mind raced and busily danced, building fantastic dreams of a great future for her special male child. Her beloved Cole Boy.

Olli had convinced herself Cole Boy was the most beautiful and talented of her children, to the growing neglect of her two daughters. With constant urging and enough money her son would become a great musician or person of public importance. Olli told herself Tess and Nell were pretty children and would not need as many opportunities to do well in life. The girls, Olli felt, wouldn't need an abundance of clothing and material things. All they needed was knowing how to care for a household. When the time came, they would find husbands who could provide for them.

Cole was more interested in each of his children getting a good education, to give each a better opportunity for their future.

Olli knew Cole Boy as a bright child, but she was not aware that her second son knew exactly how to get anything he wanted from his mama. Cole Sr. had nothing to say pertaining to the boy.

One rainy night Tess and Nell became fully aware of their mother's feeling toward them and her feelings for younger brother.

Cole had driven to town to see his brother. It was early evening and Cole wanted the family to go with him to see Uncle John. But everyone declined the invitation because evening chores had to be finished as the winter's sun was enveloped in heavy clouds and the night fell like a heavy curtain.

Cole left for town alone. He told Olli he would be getting home late.

Papa had gone to his room after his chores were finished. He loved the separation from the children so he could concentrate on reading the newspaper or playing his fiddle.

Olli and the children sat around the kitchen table. Their conversation had been light and ordinary until Cole Boy interjected, "Mama, I'm getting tired of taking violin lessons."

Olli frowned because Cole Boy had been taking lessons only six weeks. But Olli asked him what he would like do instead of playing the violin.

Second Son

Cole Boy gave his sisters a sly knowing glance, saying, "I think you should buy me a big set of drums so when I am older I will be the best drummer in the school band. Don't you think that's a good idea Mama?"

Olli smiled and readily agreed to his idea of being a drummer, saying it would be more fun for him and he would have more attention drawn to him. Olli never paused to think of the cost of not only the drum set but the cost of private lessons. She felt if he wanted drums he should have them.

Tess and Nell began with quiet objections reminding Mama she had promised Tess could take art lessons after school and Nell could take voice lessons.

Because Cole Boy wanted to play drums, the girls knew there would be no money for the promises Mama had given them about lessons. Their little brother had made sure he would be the first to get what he wanted.

Olli didn't see Cole Boy as others saw him. He was an over fed, over indulged, spoiled, irresponsible child. All Olli saw was Cole Boy's head of red curly hair and cheerful attitude. The fact was Olli still saw Cole Boy as her special gift.

Olli's secret child, Cal, was God only knew where. Did he survive the war or die on a foreign field? Olli wondered if she would ever know. No letters had come from Dweena for a long time to let Olli know anything about Cal, so Olli felt she had seen her first son for the last time when she'd seen him boarding the train in Tacoma. She assumed Dweena had passed away or was unable to write to her.

Tess and Nell decided to pursue further what Olli had just told Cole Boy, that is, that he could have a set of drums. They verbalized loudly how unfair Olli was to them. But Olli refused to see the girl's point of view.

Cole Boy began whining, pounding on the table, throwing himself on the floor kicking and screaming in a tantrum to convince Mama to give him what he wanted.

Then the girls shouted at Mama, telling her how she had spoiled Cole Boy.

War's End

The bickering continued until Olli's anger became beyond her control, because of the girls' continued objections.

Olli flew completely out of character and with a quick, sharp movement she jumped from her chair. She took a spatula from the counter and brought it down on the table top with such a force that the noise of it sounded like a rifle shot. The children's drawing paper, crayons and home work were strewn across the floor. The three arguing children's voices ceased as sharply as if the words had been severed with a knife.

Olli became so angry she flew into a rage and focused her anger on Nell and Tess. She shrieked, "You two, shut up! Since when do you dumb girls think you need anything more than you've got? You have a hundred times more than I ever had when I was your age."

Nell softly whimpered. She became afraid of her mama's outburst. But nonetheless continued her protest. "Mama you always let Cole Boy have what he wants. He is really spoiled. Tess and I never get anything extra even though we help you with anything you ask us to do. You never even say thank you. You tell Cole Boy how much you love him, but you never say that to us. Why?"

Olli turned to Nell with the threatening spatula raised above her head ready to strike her round eyed, frightened daughter. Nell showed stark fear, believing she was about to be beaten for talking to her mama in the way she had just dared to do. Nell had never seen Mama so angry.

Olli, still out of control, screamed at the girls. "How dare you question me or say bad things about your sweet baby brother? He is my very heart and soul. Cole Boy is the most important person in my life, and I'll give him what I want, when I want, whenever he wants it." Olli ranted on. "Cole boy is God's gift to me, to replace what was taken from me a long time before you were born. If I had to live my life over I'd only want Cole Boy. You girls wouldn't even be here."

Olli leaned with her palms on the table edge. She lowered her voice in a frightening manner that chilled Tess and Nell, and in a

Second Son

hoarse whisper she hissed through her teeth. "Did you hear me? I love Cole Boy. If I had a choice he would be my only child. I take care of you, but I'll never love you two like I love Cole Boy. I will give him the best of everything!"

Both girls rose from the table where they had been seated during their mama's tirade. For young impressionable girls of thirteen and fifteen, this outburst had crushed them. Their mama who usually was happy and even-tempered had shown them a rage within her that terrified them. They didn't understand where her rage had been hidden all these years; nor why such a tiny spark of contention had ignited her anger into a full blown tirade against them.

Nell and Tess grasped each others' hands, in unspoken agreement. With broken hearts they ran toward the kitchen door.

In the clamor to leave the house, Nell accidentally tipped over the chair in which she had been seated.

"Come back here and pick that up you squalling brat." Olli screamed. Her voice tore a hole in the blackness outside the house, as the girls stumbled down the back steps.

Their hands remained clasped together as they groped their way down the dark path to the outhouse. The outhouse became a strange, but available sanctuary for the sisters. They escaped from the extreme stress to which they had just been subjected.

Back in the brightly lighted kitchen Olli had quieted her demeanor and comforted Cole Boy. He knew he was really the cause of the upset he'd just seen, so he became quietly engrossed in coloring pictures in Nell's history book, knowing his action would be something Nell would have to explain to her teacher.

After the noisy episode of Olli's outburst subsided, Papa came out of his room. He poured a cup of coffee for himself and one for Olli. Papa tried to not be involved in family "To-dos" (as he called family disputes), but this time he had heard his daughter say things of which he disapproved, so he meant to have a few words with her. Papa motioned for Olli to be seated at the table opposite him. He placed the steaming coffee cups on the table, ignoring Cole Boy. Papa then seated himself heavily on a kitchen chair.

Olli glared defiantly into her Papa's eyes. In response, Papa scowled as he poured cream into his coffee, stirred the brew and gestured a second time for Olli to be seated.

She reluctantly slid onto a chair. She indicated with her eyes and body language the Papa should wait until she had Cole Boy leave the room to go to bed, but Papa cleared his throat and took a quick sip of coffee.

"Daughter," He began, "I think Cole Boy knows the outburst we all heard from you was caused by his insistence on having his own way, because he knows how to work you to get what he wants." Papa turned to the guilty face of his angelic looking grandson, who was very aware his grandpa was right.

Cole Boy dropped his eyes—then threw the remaining crayons to the floor. He'd never heard Papa talk to him or Mama in such a stern manner, so, to cover his embarrassment and get his mother's sympathy he began to cry.

Papa put out his hand physically halting Olli from going to the boy and hovering over him in an attempt to escape Papa's reprimand.

"Daughter," Papa warned, "don't think this child doesn't know and hasn't known for a long time the facts you just screamed at your two girls. He's a bright boy. Your feelings toward him and the girls have spoken for themselves without your outburst which has broken the hearts of your two sweet daughters."

Olli opened her mouth to object, but Papa put his hand up in a sharp motion for her to remain silent until he was finished speaking.

"Olli, Girl," Papa sharply clipped, "I'm ashamed of you right now. I'm just thankful Cole wasn't home, or you would have some heavy explaining to do to him. The fact of Cole Boy's being your gift from God to replace the boy that was taken from you, because I think that is part of your earlier life of which you have never told Cole. Right?"

Second Son

Olli snapped at Papa. "That is none of your business, so don't ever mention it again to Cole or anyone." As she paused, her eyes flared vengeance and she growled in a voice that was so out of character for Olli, that Papa hardly recognized it. "Let me tell you right now, Old Man," Olli threatened, "if I ever find out you have told Cole anything about that part of my life, I will kick your ass out of this house so fast your head will spin."

Olli stopped to take a deep breath before she continued. "Then, dear Papa, where the hell would you go for your free lodging and three square meals and your own room? Would Ma take you back? I think not. You never provided for her all the years you were married. All you gave her were nine kids and a house full of good old' boy times, stories and songs. Those make very thin soup, Old Man. If Cole wasn't the kind man he is, you would have been hunting for a place to squat a long time ago." Olli's tirade ended. She wilted to the table top with her head on her arms.

Cole Boy got up to run and comfort his mama, but decided against it when he glanced at Papa, whose deeply grooved eyebrows told him to keep quiet and remain where he was seated.

As these events took place in the kitchen, neither Olli nor Papa saw the headlights of the car as Cole drove into the yard.

After Cole parked the car and shut off the motor he heard sobbing coming from the outhouse. He called, "Tess, Nell, girls, are you in the outhouse? Are you all right?"

The girls heard Cole and whimpered, "Yes Daddy, we're here."

Cole quickly walked down the dark path. The girls met their Daddy and grabbed him around his waist for comfort. They were still sobbing as he leaned over and hugged them. They clung to his neck. Their tears soaked his shoulders.

Puzzled at the reason for their crying, Cole asked, "What has upset you? Tell Daddy."

Tess hiccupped and snuffed between sobs and tried to tell Cole how Mama had said bad things to them and how Mama told them she loved Cole Boy and didn't love them and wished she only had Cole Boy.

War's End

Tess gathered her feelings enough to calm herself down to explain. "We told Mama it wasn't fair for her to always buy things for Cole Boy. And now she promised him a drum set and said he could have what he wanted and Nell and I could do without the things Mama had promised before, so sweet baby brother could get all the attention because he's the baby of the family and the only boy. Mama said if she had her way Cole Boy would be her only child because he was God's gift to her." Tess released a long strained sob then asked Cole, "Daddy, why does Mama only love Cole Boy?"

Cole loosened the girl's arms from around his neck. He held each girl's hand and walked determinedly up the path. There was a chill in his voice, "That is something we are going to ask Mama about right now."

The atmosphere in the kitchen was quiet, stiff and uncomfortable when Cole brought his two unhappy girls into the static-filled room. Cole boy was sullen. Olli was ashen white. Papa looked disgusted.

"What the hell is going on here?" Cole snapped.

Papa stood up and excused himself. He went directly to his room, knowing he told Olli all he should say, so he left the peacemaking to Cole.

Cole Boy trotted behind Papa and crept quietly onto his own narrow cot. He pulled the blankets over his head. In the dark he lay afraid to hear any more cross words, especially when he knew they involved him.

Olli saw Cole was angry as she had ever seen him. She knew Cole only as a quiet, peaceful, loving man. But now she saw a fire in his eyes that she'd never seen before. She knew the anger was the product of her own making.

In the kitchen, Olli took her broken-hearted girls to the wash basin, where with cool water she cleaned their pink, swollen faces. She bent over each girl in turn and told them how sorry she was for her hurtful words. She kissed their cheeks and asked them to go to bed. "We'll talk about this in the morning when we all feel better." She said, "Good night."

Second Son

The girls walked over and kissed Cole, then walked hand in hand into the darkened bedroom and crept into the bed they shared. Neither said a word.

Olli poured a cup of coffee for Cole. They sat staring at each other across the table. Olli's face was as pale as a ghost. Cole's eyes remained sharp and full of rage.

Olli whispered hoarsely, "Cole, I'm sorry about shouting at the girls and saying things that I didn't mean. I'm not feeling very well, so I took it out on them. I'm sorry."

Cole asked sharply, "Why in hell would you tell our girls you wish you had only Cole Boy? Why would you say such a thing to our sweet girls and tell them you don't love them as much as the boy? What the hell got into you, woman?"

Olli twisted her hands and shook. "Look, Cole," she whispered, "I told them I was sorry and that I wasn't feeling very well. I'm sorry. It won't happen again."

Cole stared at her coldly before stating in a chilly monotone reply. "If you ever tell our girls anything like you did tonight, upset them this much, ever, you can take your fat, spoiled rotten brat son and your Papa, and find someplace to live where you can do as you want, and buy anything you want for the boy. Then, maybe, you'll be happy. I wish to God, you'd make up your mind what you want. First you wanted this farm. Then you work so hard that you put yourself in the hospital. The hard work you thrived on lost our twin babies, plus the other miscarriages. Now you're working in the woods again, and for what? To buy that spoiled brat whatever he wants." Cole shouted, "This has got to stop. STOP!"

Cole paused, took a breath and stated in a matter-of-fact tone, "This is the last time I want to talk about your attitude; whether you don't feel well, or not, for any reason. Get a hold on your problem with that boy. I don't want to hear any more about it now or ever. This is the last time."

Cole stood up and made his way to bed.

Olli turned out the lights and crept into bed beside Cole. He

War's End

turned his back to her. Olli felt a deep chasm slice through the bed. Silent tears rolled down her throat and filled her heart.

The following days and weeks, feelings rubbed like sandpaper until the grit disappeared leaving patchy spots of glossy bare feelings. The fine dust of forgiveness filtered through the family until a kind of smoothness returned.

The incident of Olli's favoritism toward Cole Boy flushed itself out of existence, never to be mentioned again. Cole Boy, young though he was, seemed to have learned enough from the experience that no more tantrums or demands reared their heads to antagonize his sisters. If he wanted something special he learned the fine art of timely suggestion. Then subtly he received what he desired without the knowledge of anyone but himself and his Mama.

Cole Boy kept a close eye on Papa and his daddy; to keep in their good graces he followed Papa around eager to help with chores. He found this tactic kept Papa and Daddy's wrath at bay.

Papa even took time each day to teach Cole Boy to play chess on Papa's prized handmade chessboard. Papa kept the game in his shabby old trunk where he also kept his amazing treasures ferreted away from prying children's eyes. But on special occasions—Papa would tell stories about his childhood. Each item in the trunk sprouted multiple memories he shared with his grandchildren.

Everyday Olli worked with Annetta in the sorting shed, sorting and packing evergreens. The work was much easier on her than working in the woods with Cole.

35
Papa

When spring 1946 came, Olli and the children tilled and planted the enormous garden. Papa watered it by hand. Cole Boy made a game of helping by pumping the water. The garden flourished, so when the time came to begin picking beans and peas, Olli sold the excess produce and the extra eggs from her laying hens. The county hospital paid well for the farm produce. She tucked money away for the purchase of more items for Cole Boy.

She had time to can and preserve every type of foodstuff that she could lay her hands on.

Cole Boy stopped riding the bus when he was sixteen. Olli bought him a car.

Finally Olli had learned to relax and take time to enjoy the neighbors. Even Papa enjoyed Olli's participation in things other than work. He loved hearing her humming happily as she busied herself doing things she enjoyed.

Papa hadn't told anyone, but for some time he hadn't been feeling well, especially after he'd physically exerted himself.

One morning while chopping wood he lost his breath and had chest pains.

Olli was home and was so thankful for the newly installed telephone. She called an ambulance and Papa was taken to the hospital.

The doctor told Olli and Cole that Papa had been lucky to have help so soon, as his heart was enlarged and he would need to go

Second Son

to a homecare hospital in Tacoma. Olli contacted Ma in Lynden and Ma insisted, after finding Papa was so ill, having him closer to the family and had him transferred to a convalescent home in Seattle, so they could visit him.

Olli thought it strange that Ma would want Papa close to the main body of the family after the eleven years he'd lived with her and Cole. Nonetheless Olli cleaned out Papa's lean-to room and put his meager belongings into his tattered trunk so he'd have his belongings with him.

Olli knew, as the years had passed, she and Papa had healed wounds left over from their early years. Time had passed quickly. Each one, like a bead strung on a string of struggles and pleasures, clasped together the feeling that each had done all they could to make life good.

Tess was twenty, Nell eighteen, and Cole Boy nearly seventeen, when Papa passed away in 1950. The funeral was held in Lynden. The family found Papa was well-remembered by his old friends and neighbors, and by the number of people who came to the service.

Ma said how sorry she was Papa was gone. She thanked Cole and Olli for caring for him all the years he'd been with them, even though Papa had lived the life of a carefree grasshopper, rather than that of an ambitious ant. She wanted Papa buried in the cemetery with their daughter, Rose and other family members.

On the way home from the services Olli was depressed and relieved at the same time. At the time she did not understanding her inner feelings, nor later, as the weeks eased past. She finally got hold of her feelings and told Cole the lean-to room that had been Papa's should be torn down and a large sunny window installed in its place on the south end of the living room. In doing so, the task brightened the spot where Papa's room had been.

Everyone decided it was better to have a sunny window in memory of Papa than to leave a dark room filled with shadows.

36

The Children Grown

Olli could barely believe how quickly the children had grown. The family unit was beginning to feel loose and uncertain, as the girls expanded their horizons and already been dating. Both had steady boyfriends and within a short time both were engaged.

Tess had graduated from high school two years previous. Nell was in her senior year of high school, but the promise was made that she would finish school and graduate before marrying, so Cole gave both couples his blessing. In June 1950 the two couples had a double wedding ceremony.

Olli said she felt sad and relieved at the same time and didn't understanding why—or did she? The girls being on their own paths to life left her free to do bigger and better things for Cole Boy.

There wasn't that much fan fare or to-do about the event, except it did give both sides of Cole and Olli's families a chance to finally have a mutual coming together for a celebration.

Tess and her husband Jake, in the army at the time, lived with Cole and Olli for a short while before Jake was discharged. They then moved to Philadelphia, where they lived with Jakes' parents in a grey-stone house in a rundown area of town. After their first child was born, Tess decided her marriage was unstable. She purchased a train ticket for herself and baby daughter Bonnie and traveled back to Washington, where she moved back home. Tess saved enough money to divorce Jake.

Second Son

Nell graduated, as she promised her parents, and a year later she and Elliot became parents of a daughter, Bliss, the first of four children.

Cole had closed his evergreen business and both he and Olli began working in town for a large forest product business. It was easier work without the hassle of keeping business books.

37
Cole

On a quiet day in October 1952, Cole took a day off from work and asked Olli to do the same, as he hadn't felt well and thought he should go to the chiropractor for the pain he had in his back and shoulder.

Olli felt as long as she had a free day at home it would be a good time to clean flower beds and rake the yard, readying it for winter. So while Cole was at his appointment with the chiropractor she accomplished the much-needed yard work.

The day was bright and brisk. The type of autumn day that gave Olli a real uplift in her outlook. Tess and toddler Bonnie were puttering about the yard helping Olli when Cole returned. He said he was feeling better.

Cole pulled Bonnie in the old red wagon around the yard. The toddler giggled and hung on the edge of the wagon as Cole pulled it in circles. Cole slowed his pace, then stopped and told Bonnie he was going inside.

Tess asked, "Daddy, are you okay?"

Cole nodded and replied, "Yah, I'm fine. I just need to go lie down for a while."

Olli followed him into the house. After he lay on the bed, Olli asked him if he was all right. He said he was fine, just a bit tired, so Olli went back outside.

Suddenly an ominous sensation came over Olli. As she started down the back steps, an uncanny premonition made her stop. She

Second Son

ran back into the house and called to Cole. She got no answer. She dropped her garden gloves and ran to the bedroom, knowing full well what she would find.

Cole was dead.

She shrieked and called his name, but he was gone. In the brief moment when the feeling of doom had engulfed her in the yard, Cole's spirit had slipped away to join his three younger brothers and his twin baby girls in a place beyond her understanding.

Tess ran into the house with Bonnie clutched tightly in her arms. She saw Olli standing, with head bent—patting Daddy's still hand. She saw the hollow grief-filled eyes of her Mama and knew that death had taken her beloved Daddy. She buried her face in Bonnie's hair and let the hot tears of grief and loss moisten her child's soft curls.

A long period of quiet engulfed the room before Olli loosened her grasp on Cole's hand. She stepped away from the body of her husband. For a moment she held Tess tightly about the waist, then calmly stepped to the telephone and dialed the number of Dr. Clancy.

"Cole just died and I need your help."

Within twenty minutes the doctor and the sheriff drove into the yard.

Tess called Aunt Annetta and Uncle Kyle. They came as quickly as they could. Then she called Nell, who immediately took her three babies to her neighbor's and asked if their daughter would care for her children and if one of them could drive her to her folks farm.

Everyone converged on the driveway about the same time that Cole Boy drove in from school. He saw the coroner and attendants from the mortuary as they carried Cole's covered body to the hearse.

Olli ran to Cole Boy, who began raging and pulling his hair in complete and utter grief. She grabbed him, barely recognizing her son. She held his flailing arms close to his sides, until Cole Boy realized it was his Mama who was beside him before he collapsed on a nearby chair. Olli and her son cried together, emotionally joined in their grieving.

Tess and Nell held onto each other and absorbed comfort from the closeness, knowing that Cole Boy couldn't handle the loss of his dad. This loss was a new mountain for him to climb. Thanks to Mama's hovering and spoiling him, he had never before been allowed to face life straight on. Now that the time had come, Cole Boy was not ready to assume responsibility.

During the next few days Olli remained in a trance-like state. All of the family and neighbors who attended the funeral were surprised at the full extent of grief Cole Boy displayed. He had always been such a Mama's Boy.

During the time at the mortuary and grave-side, Olli remained mute and distant, refusing any offers of help or condolence from anyone as she held tightly to Cole Boy's arm.

Tess and Nell stood beside Mama too, but it appeared to all observers that Olli had forgotten anyone's grief but Cole Boy's and her own.

The service ended and the mourners drifted away leaving Olli and her children alone.

❋

The next few weeks took on the motion of a slow moving stream engine. No ripples of excitement. No long conversations of any substance or importance. No movement toward acknowledging gifts or kindness shown during the time of Cole's death. Thus Olli and Cole Boy didn't have to accept the truth of Cole's passing.

Tess and Nell took on the responsibility of returning sympathy correspondence from everyone. They filled out legal papers so that Olli could receive financial help from the Veterans Administration and Social Security.

Olli finally adopted her own advice she had showered on her family over the past years and picked herself up by her boot straps, plodding from day to day, working at the farm chores without help from Cole Boy. He contended he had never done chores, so he didn't know what to do nor did he want to help.

Olli also returned to work in town at the evergreen business where she and Cole had built up. She tried to show that she could continue with life as if hers hadn't changed. But after two weeks, one afternoon, she collapsed at work. Her grief had suddenly rolled over her like an icy tide. Her cup had finally reached the overflow mark and she fainted, to awaken in a state of exhaustion, unable to function.

Her boss called Dr. Clancy, who came and examined Olli and wanted to hospitalize her.

Cole Boy was called at school. He became overly possessive and told the doctor he would take his mother home where he would care for her. Cole Boy arrived back home early that day, which puzzled Tess. Then she saw Cole Boy go to the passenger side of the car and help Olli walk into the house. Her Mama's face was blank, as if she was in some other place. Olli let Cole Boy lead her into the bedroom. Tess undressed Mama and put her in bed. Olli never spoke.

Cole Boy explained what happened, that he'd told the doctor they'd take care of Mama.

Tess was quite taken back, because she knew she was the only one living at home, except Cole Boy, who was close to graduating. So Tess alone would be responsible for the complete care of Mama, and she always hated to be around anyone who was ill. Especially because she didn't know what to do to ease Mama's grief. So she finally called Nell, living in town, and asked her to lighten the load of caring for Mama and the farm chores.

Nell agreed to have Elliot bring her before he went to work, three days a week. She had two youngsters, was six months pregnant and suffering morning sickness, but told Elliot she felt obligated to help Tess and Cole Boy.

Tess asked Nell to also care for her little girl, Bonnie, because Tess had a job in town. It was necessary that she keep working. They needed the money. That statement sat on the edge of truth.

Tess' main objective was to escape the care of her mother, the farm, and her own child at least three days a week.

So, Nell became the main caregiver while Cole Boy went off to school. Tess worked at a photography studio and saved all her money. The fact was Tess' job was the means to make it possible for her and little Bonnie to move to town.

Eventually Cole Boy talked to his sisters telling them he mentioned to Mama about the prospect of selling the farm, and how she finally had shown a spark of interest when Cole Boy told her the place was too much work for her. Plus he wanted to move away from the old memories the place held.

Olli sat up in bed and grasped his hands and said, "Cole Boy, if you think we should do that. Sell the farm. I'm through. I need a change to something that doesn't have so much responsibility. You are the man of this family now, so put the place up for sale and take care of all the finances. I don't want to have anything else to do with this place."

38

The Farm

So at the age of seventeen Cole Boy, puffed up by his own importance, told his sisters he would take care of selling the farm. As soon as he graduated he would take on full responsibility of caring for Olli. Tess and Nell would have nothing to worry about, because Mama would have Dad's Social Security, as well as their favorite son to rely upon.

In the weeks that followed Cole Boy found a friend of his Dad's who wanted to buy the thirty-two acre farm for $4,000—*cash*. Cole Boy thought it was a fair price. Little did he know the property was worth ten times that amount. He wouldn't listen to Olli's brother, Uncle Kyle, or his sisters. So the deal was struck with the new ownership to take place after Cole Boy's graduation from school.

Olli felt like a new person since her recovery from Cole's death. She thought Cole Boy could easily and maturely take Cole's place as provider. She was content in her knowledge that she could rely on her beloved Cole Boy caring for her well-being and taking the stress and problems from her shoulders. She convinced herself that all the giving and sacrificing she had made on Cole Boy's behalf throughout his lifetime had been the wisest thing she had ever done—despite the resentment she had taken from Cole Sr., Papa and the girls.

Cole Boy decided, before he and Olli moved from the farm, that he would sell the player-piano that Cole had given to Mama, his own violin, drum set and electric organ, plus Cole's work truck and the old sedan that Tess was driving back and forth to work. After all, the musical instruments were his because they were gifts to him from Mama; and therefore, he kept the money. The sale of both automobiles netted him a few hundred dollars more. He shared none of it with his mother Olli or his sisters, saying he needed the cash for rent and utility hook-ups when they moved to town.

Tess and Nell attempted a discussion with Olli about the "greedy and irresponsible way" Cole Boy was selling everything. But Olli cast aside their objections by telling them Cole Boy was now the man of the family. If they had any objections, they should talk to him. And so the sisters did. However, their interfering only brought on a childish temper-tantrum from Cole Boy.

The evening of "the discussion," Nell, Tess, Elliot and the three grandchildren left the farm in complete frustration. Cole Boy and Mama told them they needn't return if they didn't agree with Cole Boy's way of doing things. Olli told the girls she wouldn't need their help anymore now that their brother had taken all the pressure from her.

Olli was blind to Cole Boy's manipulation. She couldn't see he was stripping her of her independence and the respect of her daughters. Neither would she listen to nor could she comprehend her daughters' accusations about Cole Boy's greed and opportunistic behavior.

Olli's beloved son was like a cow bird chick hatched in the nest of a sparrow. He had literally kicked the opposition from the family nest and was gobbling up everything in sight. Like the loving mother sparrow who couldn't distinguish between her true fledglings and the greedy cowbird chick, so Olli kept feeding the largest and dominating child, feeding him until he had his fill of everything he felt was his—*which was everything*!

The two daughters walked away that night from Mama and their brother and into their own lives, leaving Olli and her precious second son unto themselves.

The Farm

One early June evening, 1953, Kyle and Annetta went out to the farm to see if Cole Boy needed help to move some 100 boxes of canned fruit and vegetables. Olli had refused to leave these behind when they had moved to town. Kyle estimated it would take two full truck loads to haul just the fruit, not counting the few remaining household goods.

The telephone jangled and interrupted as they began to load the pickup.

Olli answered it and spoke in hushed, urgent tones, pausing to tell Kyle the caller was their niece Elise, phoning from Elma. Elise and her husband had moved there years ago. It was a surprise to hear from her again after so long. Olli told Cole Boy and Kyle she wanted to take the call in the bedroom so their visiting and children's noises would not disturb her as she tried to understand Elise's emotional voice. Olli talked for a long time before hanging up phone down.

When Olli came from the bedroom, the tears in her eyes told everyone she was visibly shaken. She took a deep breath before turning to Cole Boy, Kyle and Annetta. "Please have the children go in the yard to play for a while. There's news from Elise the children needn't hear."

The children ran outside before Olli spoke again. She looked sad and shaken. Glancing at the ceiling before she spoke as if asking a higher strength to help her relate what Elise had told her. "William is dead," she muttered, "Elise shot him."

Those listening were struck dumb. Kyle told how his family had spent a few days visiting Elise and William at their isolated ranch not three weeks before. Everything seemed fine then.

Cole Boy stepped over and held Mama's hand, while in shock, she continued. "Elise shot him with his shotgun. She blew his head off."

Olli bent over in her chair and began to weep. Her hands shook so violently she grasp herself around the waist trying to subdue her emotions. She needed to tell everyone the events Elise divulged, leading to such a tragedy. Olli shuddered as she recalled the horrible account Elise had just related to her. "William had been drunk on the job again. He left work at noon. He told his logging crew that he was going home for lunch, and that he planned to kill his family. The crew all laughed at they consider nothing but 'drunken talk'. They ignored him as he stumbled toward his pick up. He always talked crazy when he was drunk."

Olli hesitated, then said, "William arrived home and beat the baby and the other four children and repeatedly raped Elise, calling her foul names. He hit her in the stomach with his fist, knocking her against the livingroom wall. Elise yelled and staggered to her feet. She got to her feet, held onto the frame of the door and screamed for William to stop! He kicked her into the bedroom where he beat and sodomized her for some time. The evening turned to night and the beating continued. Elise told me she begged William to let her to go to the bathroom. William growled, threw her to the floor, and told her to hurry back because he had something special in mind for her.

Olli took a breath, closed her eyes. Spoke softly. "Elise's mind raced for a solution to save herself and her five children from being killed. Fearing for her life, she staggered through the dining room slowly making her way in the dark house to the only means of escape she could find available. Instead of going into the bathroom she crept to the back porch, reached above the door and in the shadows her hands touched the cold hard steel of William's shotgun. She lifted it from its rack. In the pitch black room it was difficult to find the box of ammunition. Finally her fingers grasped the box. Shaking in the darkness, because she couldn't risk putting a light on for fear William would guess her intent, she quietly slipped two shells in the barrels. Then, she moved slowly toward the bedroom. The moon gave just enough light that from the doorway she could see William's naked, muscular body lying on the bed. William cursed, telling Elise to get back in bed. Instead she stood quietly in the doorway. William pushed himself up on one arm in a drunken attempt to get out of bed. He threatened to kill her if

The Farm

he got his hands on her. Elise raised the barrel of the shotgun. At that point William recognized the click of the mechanism as it readied to fire. He jumped up like a mad bull and came roaring toward her. She fired.

"Elise told me the acrid odor of gun powder tingled in her nose. She saw him fall backward onto the bed, twitch a few times, then...nothing. She said she blew face off. Elise said she fell to her knees and hung her battered head. She fainted. She said when she awoke, Amy and Terry were in the bedroom patting her face and hands to help revive her. The body of their father lay on the bed in the moonlight.

"Elise walked to the bed and drew a sheet over William's naked form, then she and her children left the tragic scene to go to the closest neighbor to call the sheriff. It was a mile, so Elise told the children to stay there, that she would return as quickly as she could. Barely able to see because of her swollen face, she tried to start the pick up truck, but couldn't. She'd flooded the carburetor. So she walked. She used the barn lantern to light her way down the road to the McCarthy's for help. When she finally reached the McCarthy's, they were shocked at her swollen face and blood-matted red hair.

"Mr. McCarthy called the sheriff. The sheriff had to drive thirty miles from Aberdeen. It took him over an hour, at which time the McCarthy's had cleaned Elise up and made her lie down on the couch. Elise held herself together long enough so she could tell what had happened.

"The children were still in shock when the sheriff returned with Elise to her house. The deputy and sheriff looked over the scene of the shooting. The coroner arrived just as the sun was coming up. They took the body out to his van.

"Elise said she was sure she would be taken to prison for what she'd done, but the sheriff took her statement, told her to get some rest, and left.

"Elise told me she went upstairs with her five children, put the two older boys to bed in their room, then took the three younger ones, pulling them into bed with her in Amy's room. She covered them with a warm quilt, and they calmed each other to sleep.

"Around noon the next day, the sheriff explained to Elise there would be no investigation and no inquest, due to the statements of William's fellow loggers about the previous day, plus the investigation of the crime scene. William's death had been classified a case of self-defense. No charges would be brought against Elise."

Olli shook her head, took a long breath and continued, "All this happened yesterday. Elise said she couldn't stay on the farm. She asked if she and the five kids could come and live here with Cole Boy and me."

Olli stopped talking and heaved a weary sigh. Finally, she added, "I told them no. I told her the farm had been sold. Cole Boy and I were moving to town, so I no longer had a place to care for any family members. I have no room, no money, no patience with family problems."

Olli was at the end of her rope in caring for homeless, moneyless brothers and sisters, their kids or any problem that arose. Cole Boy was the head of the house, and Olli had made her last decision. Olli had said emphatically! "No."

Cole Boy was happy Mama had solved the Elise problem, because he knew he couldn't have made such a decision so wisely or quickly.

On the other hand, Kyle and Annetta were clearly shocked hearing such a traumatic story, and, on top of it, that Olli had turned Elise and her children away in such a time of need.

39
Poor

After the moved to town, the weather turned cold. It was fall 1953.

Olli was stunned to find that Cole Boy had no money to have the utilities connected—and the house was electrically heated! Olli knew Cole Boys' purchase of the new sedan used most of the money from the sale of the farm. Nonetheless, she was disappointed to find the apartment would have to remain unheated until the beginning of the next month when her Social Security money arrived. It was like living in an ice box.

Olli caught a terrible cold that soon turned into the flu complicated by strep throat.

Cole Boy kept Olli as warm as possible by piling her bed with layers of blankets.

Nell's delivery of her expected baby had brought her and Elliot a third child, a daughter, Sarah. Their oldest girl, Bliss, was four years old, and their son, Casey, was eighteen months old. The three children kept Nell busy.

When baby Sarah was one month old, one early afternoon Nell saw Cole Boy drive his new car into the driveway and stop. She was surprised to see him as no one had seen him or Mama for nearly two months. They hadn't even come to see the new baby.

In fact, Christmas had come and gone with no family interchange during the holidays for the first time since Nell was born.

Second Son

It bothered both her and Tess. Mama had chosen to separate herself and Cole Boy from everyone.

Nell wondered if the move to town, and adjusting to never being invaded by family or neighbors, had made Olli retreat from reality in some way. Nell knew the holidays weren't the same since Daddy passed away. Tess and Nell agreed to give Mama and Cole Boy time until they wanted to join the family circle again.

Cole Boy stepped onto the porch.

Stiffly, Nell invited him in. But before she asked him to sit down, she inquired what had finally brought him to her house. She asked if he'd come to see the new baby.

Cole Boy was noticeably stressed. He told Nell that Mama was very sick and had been ill for over a month. He ask Nell to come with him, right then, to see if she could help Mama.

Nell explained she had no one to care for her children and didn't want to expose herself to anything contagious.

But Cole Boy pled with her. "Mama is very sick with a temperature of one hundred and four. I don't know what to do."

Nell made a phone call to Dr. Clancy, but he was on vacation. Nell tried her doctor and he was in. She explained the symptoms Cole Boy had described to her. "Mama had no money," she said. "She's too ill to get out of bed."

Dr. Clancy told Nell he would order a prescription to pick up at the drugstore. He told Nell how to care for her mother and the precautions to take in keeping her from bringing any contamination home to her babies. So Nell called her neighbor Dorothy and explained that she had to go help her mother and needed someone to watch the children until Elliot came home from work. Her friend came over immediately because of the urgency in Nell's voice.

Cole Boy drove Nell to the drugstore where she paid for Olli's medicine. Then they went directly to Mama and Cole Boy's apartment.

Nell dressed herself in a protective face mask, rubber gloves and one of Cole Boy's large clean shirts to use as a smock. She

Poor

found Mama incoherent with a high fever. She instructed Cole Boy to bring her a soft cloth and a bottle of rubbing alcohol, then to make some strong tea.

Olli objected to anyone but Cole Boy helping her, but Nell ignored her fevered objections and pulled down the blankets. She found Olli lying in her own urine and feces. She called Cole Boy to bring her a large cardboard box lined with newspaper to dispose of the infected bedding. Then she told him to bring a basin of warm soapy water for cleaning her up. She pealed off Mama's putrid smelling and soiled nightgown and tossed the bedding and gown into the box. "Cole Boy, be careful taking this out to the trash burner, douse it with kerosene and burn it."

Olli grumbled as Nell washed her with warm water. Nell rolled Mama's listless body onto clean fresh linen, then rubbed her entire body, face and hair with rubbing alcohol. This began to lower Mama's fever.

Cole Boy took the stinking box of soiled linen out while Nell redressed Mama in one of Cole Boy's shirts and placed clean blankets over her trembling form. Cole Boy brought a cup of warm tea to Mama. He had stirred honey in the cup as Nell instructed. Nell held Mama's head and helped her sip the tea. When Nell was sure Mama could hold liquid on her stomach, she administered pills from the prescription bottle, making sure Olli drank two more cups of warm tea. It was all Nell could do.

After a few hours Olli slept fitfully, but her temperature was down to one hundred, so Nell told Cole Boy to keep giving her warm tea and the pills every four hours. Cole Boy promised to care of Olli. He thanked Nell graciously.

On the way out, Nell gave her brother strict instructions, that if Mama couldn't get up to use the toilet, he was to get a wash basin for her to use as a bedpan. He would need to empty it immediately, then clean it, and use bleach to disinfect it. He must keep Mama clean and warm. Nell didn't question Cole Boy on why he had waited until Olli was so ill before letting anyone know about what was happening. Neither did she comment on the cold temperature in the house. Nor did she say anything about the fact Cole Boy was using the farm lanterns for light, and he had heated water on his old camp stove. She deduced that the statement about having no money was all too true. She knew that to reprimand Cole Boy would do no good.

Back home, when Nell got out of Cole Boy's car, there was no thanks from her brother; nor any explanation why he had waited so long to get help, or why he had no money left from the property sale. Nell didn't try to get any reasons from him. However, she did tell Cole Boy, if he needed her help again, he should call her, and she would do what she could.

She took a hot shower immediately, hoping to scrub away any germs that might endanger herself, Elliot or her babies.

When Elliot got home from work, Dorothy had phoned and told him where Nell was and why. While waiting for Nell to return home, he had prepared dinner, fed the children and saved Nell a warm plate of food. As she ate, Elliot was full of questions, especially why she hadn't made Cole Boy take Olli to the hospital instead of putting Nell and the whole family in contact with such a serious infection as strep throat.

Nell explained, "The reason was there was no money. Cole Boy had no idea how to cope with anything. I know Mama considers him the man of the house, but he's an immature, social cripple. Mama has always attempted to shield him from problems."

In the coming days, Nell went over frequently to care for Mama. Nell was always careful to use precautions when in contact with Mama, but each time she entered the apartment a terrible odor met her at the door which sickened her. At the end of the ten day period of medications Nell searched the house to find the origin of the odor, fearing it was a dead rat somewhere.

What she found: four boxes in the bathtub covered with a shower curtain. The boxes were filled with urine and fecal soaked sheets and clothing. She knew the mess was the accumulation of Olli's ten days illness. Cole Boy couldn't bring himself to touch or hand-wash the mess. When Nell confronted him with the putrid boxes, he told her it had made him sick to think of washing them. He had planned to take them to Nell's house for her to wash, but hadn't gotten around to it.

Nell sent him outside to the trash burner and told him to soak each box with gasoline or kerosene and burn them all, because she had no intention of taking that stinking mess to her house and contaminating her family with something he, long before, should have cared for.

Cole Boy reluctantly did what Nell told him to do and watched the foul smelling boxes of fabric, one by one, burn into a smoldering pile of ashes.

The first of the month came, Olli's Social Security money arrived, and Cole Boy had the utilities turned on. He no longer had to sneak pails of water from the neighbors at night for cooking and bathing Mama. He didn't have to use the camp stove to cook on, so Olli's food was at last more palatable. For food, Cole Boy used some of the one hundred boxes of home canned items Olli had insisted on bringing with them when they moved. These were their salvation, for otherwise they would have gone without food until Mama's Social Security money had arrived.

Nell was very aware none of the packing boxes had been moved or unpacked since Mama and Cole Boy's acquiring the apartment. Boxes were scattered throughout the two bedroom apartment, all unopened.

Cole Boy had made no attempt to unpack anything. The unmarked boxes were like an Easter egg hunt when anything was needed. Nell made an attempt to make a path through the jumbled mess so Mama could get out of bed and walk to the bathroom without having to wind through a path of boxes and likely trip. She told Mama that she was trying to coordinate things to make it easier to put things in their correct places. She also told her that she had Cole Boy had to burn the filthy sheets, blankets and clothing. At the news of the loss of sheets and blankets, Olli became very angry, yelling, "Don't you know those things cost money? Just because you and Elliot have a good income I suppose you can afford to do that sort of thing, but we don't have enough money to go out and buy new sheets and blankets. The least you could have done was take them home and wash them and bring them back clean. Not burn them all!"

Nell tried to remain calm. "Really, Mama, I wouldn't take that foul mess of germs to my house and contaminate the kids, especially the baby that you haven't even seen."

Olli retorted with a short, harsh laugh. "I suppose you think you are too good to help Cole Boy with something so dirty? Well you know how he can't stand smelly things like that. The least you could do then is offer to pay for Cole Boy's good shirts and my sheets and blankets."

All day Nell had been lifting heavy boxes of canned fruits. She stopped short and pulled herself into a stiffened position. Mama's last statement made her tingle with anger. She slowly put the box down, turned and looked coldly at Mama. She removed her apron and laid it on the couch. She called Cole Boy to come. "Cole Boy. Take me home," she ordered.

Cole Boy, seeing his sister livid with anger, played it cautious, asking, "Why? I might still need some help."

Nell said coolly, "Oh, my dear brother, you need help alright, but from now on it won't be my help that either of you get." She quickly put on her coat. "Take me home now," she demanded.

Leaving the house she called back to Mama over her shoulder, "Mama, I've done the best I can for both of you. I'm glad you're well again. I'll give Cole Boy some money to buy new sheets. But from now on you are both on your own."

Cole Boy hesitated and tried to explain to Mama that Nell didn't mean it. But as he got in the car, Nell told him forcefully she wouldn't help again, especially not after Mama expected *her* to pay for the mess *Cole Boy* had been unable to wash but rather had to burn. She said she would buy a few new sheets and blankets, but then she was through helping them.

Poor

He made a muffled attempt to ask her to come back again. But when they arrived in Nell's driveway, Nell hopped out of the car and didn't look back.

Cole Boy knew he was really on his own. He thought he could rely on Nell, but Mama had said the wrong thing and Nell was through. He knew he was on his own because Tess lived in Oregon, had a job and a busy life. Cole Boy hated to go back to the messy apartment, but he knew he'd said he'd be the man of the house and that time had come—again. This time he knew he couldn't expect any help, and he didn't know how to be what Mama wanted. He was afraid.

Ten months passed. Olli and Cole Boy received a letter from Cole's brother John telling them of Dad Brauer's death some weeks before. His burial had taken place in Chehalis. John had sold the house for Mother Brauer and moved her to Shelton to live with him and his family.

In the letter John stated the reason that Olli hadn't been notified before was that they didn't know where she and Cole Boy had moved. He would like to come and see how they were doing. Knowing that, Olli wanted to separate herself from all of Cole's family, for fear John would ask her to care for Mother Brauer. So she and Cole Boy decided to move to Port Townsend, thereby leaving Nell and Tess and their families behind, along with any criticism of their life from Coles' brothers.

That initial move to keep away from contact with the Brauers led to a continual dodging maneuver. And Cole Boy encouraged it to keep from answering anyone's inquiries about his sporadic work pattern and the squalid conditions his laziness had forced him and Olli to live in.

If it hadn't been for the home canned food Olli had insisted on carrying with them, the two would have starved there in Port Townsend. Being on their own, away from all family ties, Olli's soul began to feel heavy and unfulfilled. To her it was as if she had long roots dragging deep ruts in a mud of self-imposed

Second Son

poverty—always looking for a rainbow and a plot of land where she and Cole Boy could, unencumbered, ease their roots into a piece of ground, once more feel at home.

But such a place was never found.

Inwardly Olli knew Cole Boy wasn't capable of the responsibility. Olli had made a terrible mistake handing over to Cole Boy everything for which she and Cole had worked so hard.

They never unpacked over the next ten years.

They lived out of cardboard boxes in shambled shacks until their rent was overdue and the landlord was about to evict them. They would then move on in the middle of the night, Olli always feeling cheap and guilty for letting Cole Boy follow the same pattern over and over.

Ten years they lived in seven towns and moved fourteen times.

They found menial labor where Olli could work at the same place that Cole Boy chose. They picked apples and cherries in Eastern Washington, raspberries in the valley near Tacoma. Cole Boy seemed content with peasant wages; mixed with Mama's Social Security, he had all the money he needed.

Ten years passed. 1963.

Olli felt unwilling anymore to hand her money over to Cole Boy. But to keep him from leaving her, she praised his meager employment efforts, while she went without healthful nourishment, medical care and clothing. She remodeled all of Cole Boy's old shirts, jeans and underwear to fit her dwindling, thin body. Any new clothing purchased was for Cole Boy's ever expanding frame, while Olli wore the remnants of his old school wardrobe.

Olli finally grew ill. She had become thin and pale. They ate berries, beans and corn in season from truck gardens where they worked as pickers in the farm fields. They also dug and ate clams when they found an unguarded beach. They ate salmon in season, when they could illegally gaff them from available streams. Eating from the land, as they did, a balanced diet was impossible.

While they worked in the farm fields, they lived in a squatter's

Poor

shanty near the foot of Mt. Rainier. The season ended. Winter closed in. The rains came.

Days were dark and gray. The rain was the worst it had been in years. Enough so, that Olli slept in her oil-skin rain clothes because the roof leaked so badly over her bed. For months, the mattress remained cold and soggy.

Cole Boy ignored the deteriorating squalor.

For Olli it became the raw ache of regret.

Her health worsened. She never mentioned her painful feet, blurred vision or heart tremors. She knew if she complained it would be admission that she had done a foolish thing when she'd left her life in the hands of her beloved boy, her second son. She was sorry to admit he had no conscience, nor did he seem to have any feelings for her welfare.

Cole Boy never married. His immature idea of a woman was to find a few rich one-night-stands. With his chosen life-style, he would not have been a good man for any woman. His excuse to cover his own inadequacies: he claimed Olli was the reason he'd never appealed to women. He was sure Olli would think no woman was good enough for her beloved boy, so he never brought anyone "home to meet Mama." He wouldn't admit—far more likely—it was his obese body combined with the obvious lack of ambition that were the keys to his being alone.

Olli declined. She hadn't felt well for so long she couldn't remember when she had. There was no money to see a doctor, so she didn't know she had diabetes. She knew only that she was shaky, had pains in her legs and feet, her eyes were blurred and she was always hungry.

Years before, Cole Boy sold the car he had purchased with the money from the sale of the farm. With Olli's Social Security money he bought a used pickup. He was not working, so each night Olli drove the back roads with Cole Boy as he hunted, poaching deer all night.

Cole Boy knew a tavern in their neighborhood that bought all the venison he could supply. He never kept any meat for home consumption. He'd rather have the money, despite it being clear, he couldn't deny it, Olli was dwindling to a frail wrack of bones.

Each morning he took Olli home, then went to the tavern to deliver the venison. While he was there he ate steak, eggs and hash brown potatoes, never thinking about Olli. He took nothing home with him for his mother. Why should he? He never heard her ask for anything, and she didn't complain as long as she had flour for pancakes. Besides, she dawdled over the food she prepared like she was no longer interested in eating it anyway.

On the deer hunting trips at night Cole Boy kept handfuls of candy bars in the glove box of the truck so they were never short of snack material. Olli took delight in these as she ate three or four every night.

When they returned home early each morning Olli nearly fell into bed from exhaustion and heart tremors; but she never mentioned her condition to Cole Boy. She simply didn't want him to feel she was holding him back from the good money he received for the venison. She didn't want him to feel she didn't trust his decisions.

40
Clarity

The last time Olli's mind was clear enough to remember details of her whereabouts was the night she told Cole Boy she was too tired to go hunting. She decided she just wanted to stay home and sleep. This angered Cole Boy, so he stayed home too. They went to bed late. In the middle of the night Olli felt shaky and very hot. She got out of bed in the dark and took off her night gown. When she reached the bathroom door, everything went blank.

Olli had suffered a stroke. She lay unconscious and naked on the cold linoleum floor unable to move or speak. She lay there until after midnight. Cole Boy heard a thud in the hall and got out of bed to check on the odd noise. He turned on the hall light and found the frail, naked form of his Mama lying on the floor. She was grimed with urine and feces.

So shocked, Cole Boy didn't even think to cover her with a blanket. He checked her pulse to see if she was alive. Then he dressed quickly and drove like a madman to Olli's oldest brother's house, five miles away. He woke Ted and his wife and asked them to come to his house as fast as they could, because Olli was unconscious and needed help.

Ted and his wife were puzzled why Cole Boy hadn't taken Olli to the local hospital just two miles from his house. But they said nothing except that they would follow him home.

When Ted walked into the chilled house he was awestruck at

the sight of his sister's frail form sprawled out in human waste upon the cold floor completely covered and seemingly dead.

Ted grabbed a blanket off one of the beds while his wife wiped with a damp cloth Olli's motionless body. Ted then covered Olli and picked up her near weightless frame. He was horrified at his sister's frail, emaciated form.

Ted started to carry Olli to his car, but Cole Boy stepped in front of him, blocking the door.

"You're not taking her anywhere," he growled. "Put her in my truck. I'll take her where I know she'll get the help she needs."

So, Ted fearing for his sister's life if she didn't get care quickly, silently handed Cole Boy the tiny, deathly ill form of his sister. Cole Boy marched out into the cold rainy night, put his mother in the seat of the truck, never stopping to thank Ted for his help. He backed the truck out and drove off into the night, leaving Ted and his wife standing there helpless and stunned.

The two went back into the decrepit dwelling, cleaned the mess off the floor and put it in the garbage outside. They locked up the place and drove back to their own house. They called the local hospital to inquire if Olli had been admitted only to find she had not been seen.

Cole Boy drove through back streets until he reached the freeway where he turned south and drove at breakneck speed toward Shelton. His destination: Nell's and Elliot's house. He arrived there around six A.M., finding only his nephew and three teenage nieces, who were getting ready for school.

Cole Boy was told Nell and Elliot had gone to Reno, Nevada, on a three-day vacation. He turned to leave, when Bliss, the oldest daughter, who had wondered out to the truck, saw her Grandma Olli wrapped in a blanket and apparently unconscious. She yelled to her brother to call Mom and Dad at the hotel and tell them she was taking Grandma to the hospital.

Hearing this Cole Boy hesitated, but the other four kids insisted that he do as Bliss said. They yelled at him until Cole Boy gave in, so he and Bliss together drove Olli to the county hospital.

Clarity

Bliss held Olli's limp head in her lap, not daring to ask why her uncle had brought Gramma seventy miles to Shelton rather than taking her to the local hospital. His actions made no sense to the seventeen-year-old. She was soon to have the answer to that question.

When they arrived at the hospital, Bliss ran in the emergency door calling for help. Two nurses and a doctor returned to the truck with a gurney. The nurses lifted Olli carefully, placing her on the sterile conveyance and rushing her inside.

Cole Boy parked the truck and reluctantly joined Bliss in the corridor.

A nurse carrying a clip board approached and handing it to Cole Boy to fill the required information on Olli's medical history and medical insurance. Cole Boy backed away and sat in a chair in the hall, bowed his head, shoved the nurse away, held his head in his hands and began to sob.

Bliss put her hand on his shoulder as his huge body shook and shuddered like a lost soul. She turned to the nurse and took the forms and told her all she knew about her grandma, which wasn't much because of the long separation since she had last seen her.

When Cole Boy finally got himself under control, he informed the nurse he had no job, no money, and no insurance. The nurse told him not to worry because a social worker at the hospital would see to all of Olli's care until she was released. That news seemed to ease Cole Boy's mind. He waited for the doctor to examine Olli.

After receiving the urgent phone call from home, Nell and Elliot had driven top speed from Reno and arrived at the hospital about noon. Shortly after that, the doctor came out to speak with Bliss and Cole Boy. He told them Olli had suffered a massive stroke and was suffering from diabetes. She was so seriously ill she would have to be transported to the large hospital in Olympia for specialized care.

Elliot said he and Nell would drive her, but the doctor insisted she be taken by ambulance. Bliss and Cole Boy left the hospital and went back to Nell's house. Nell rode in the ambulance with

Second Son

Olli, while Elliot followed in his car so he could drive Nell back home after they heard if Olli would be all right.

The kids hadn't gone to school but stayed home. They anxiously awaited news of how Gramma Olli was doing. In the meantime they made a hot meal for Cole Boy and Bliss.

Cole Boy realized he was famished and wolfed down the hot food. He then lay down on the couch with the knowledge that Nell and Elliot had taken the burden off his shoulders. He knew they would do what he hadn't done, and so he fell asleep, his worries having been handed over to someone else. He slept peacefully.

At St. Johns Hospital, Elliot, being overly tired from the long speedy drive from Reno, stretched out on a couch in the waiting room and himself nodded off to sleep. Nell paced the hospital hallway until stress and exhaustion took over her mind. She leaned against a rain-streaked window and stared out over the rainy wind-swept parking lot. She barely noticed the trees outside shake and shudder, wind-whipped leaves dancing across wet pavement, sticking along the curbs and piling into a golden collage on car windshields. She watched the clouds part and the sun sparkle on rain puddles. She heard footsteps in the hall and quickly snapped back from her reverie and prayers.

Dr. Reiner asked the couple to follow him to his consultation office. Elliot rose to his feet, reached and held Nell's hand. The two followed the doctor. As they were seated in the office Nell wished fervently that her sister Tess was with them to hear about Mama's condition; from the doctor's demeanor she knew the news would not be good.

The doctor spoke softly. "Mr. and Mrs. Drake, Nell, your mother, is in a dangerous condition. She has had a severe stroke and is suffering from diabetes. I need some medical history. And an idea of how she's been living the last few years. She can't speak. I hope you can tell me what I need to know. She exhibits the worst case of malnutrition I have seen in my thirty years of practice." He paused, then asked, "Has she been living alone?"

Nell answered, "Mama has lived with my brother since our

Clarity

Dad died fourteen years ago. We haven't seen her much over that period. Maybe four or five times. The last visit was maybe three years ago. While we waited in the emergency area I made a call to Mama's oldest brother who lives a few miles from her. He said my brother, Cole Jr., hasn't worked much, if at all, so he and Mama have been living on her Social Security money my Dad left. Plus a few dollars from occasional seasonal vegetable and fruit picking jobs, I think.

"Uncle Ted told me all Mama had been eating was pancakes, syrup and candy bars, and it worried him, but my brother wouldn't listen, nor buy anything else, so they, more or less, ate off the land."

Dr. Reiner shook his head in apparent disgust, or disbelief. "I want you to know we are doing all we can to save your mother's life. But you must be prepared. Today she will either live or die. The next few hours will tell."

Nell hung her head as Elliot encircled her shoulders with his arms to comfort her. Nell spoke in a weak voice. "I feel so ashamed that I've neglected Mama. My brother, he has kept her from my sister and me. That's no excuse! We had no idea about her poor health until I talked with my uncle today. I wonder why, if he knew where they lived and knew how ill she looked, why didn't he write or call us so we could go and get her away from the terrible conditions in which my brother had her living. We would have. In a split second we would have. We would have," her voice broke, "insisted...she come and live with our family. If only we'd known."

Dr. Reiner saw how overwhelmed Nell was. Silently, he believed the son whom Olli lived with was guilty and ashamed of the care he'd given his Mother so he couldn't face his sisters to ask for help. This son clearly feared any scathing chastisement from the sisters.

Dr. Reiner spoke in a concerned professional tone. "Well, your mother won't have to return to that kind of life, nor will you or your sister be burdened with the constant care she'll require from

Second Son

now on. If she survives, as soon as she is able to be moved; I will place her in a convalescent home where she will receive post-stroke therapy, proper diabetic diet and medications. The convalescent home may be chosen by you and your sister. The Social Security she receives will be supplemented by the state medical program so her care will not encumber you or your sister financially. All costs for her care will be one-hundred percent paid in full."

The doctor continued in a sarcastic tone. "Of course it won't cost your brother anything either. This is the crime in this whole business. Your brother should be held responsible for everything. He should be ashamed of himself. By the way, why isn't he here with you?"

Nell shrugged. "He's never been good at accepting responsibility for any of his actions. He was the baby of the family, and Mama spoiled him all his life. After my dad died, Mama told Tess and me the story of her earlier life—which she had never told Dad. She was raped when she was fourteen. She had a baby boy out of wedlock. The little boy was taken from her. When Cole Boy was born she piled all her love and attention on him, thinking he was God's gift to her. Because of loosing her first son. To the neglect of Tess and me, despite six other dead children, Mama became obsessed with Cole Boy, figuring he could do no wrong." Nell exhaled, "Well, I guess he finally did something wrong. Very wrong."

Dr. Reiner nodded in silent agreement. He told Elliot and her to go home and he would call them as soon as Mrs. Brauer's tests came back from the lab, which would let them know if she would pull through this crisis.

Nell wanted to stay, but decided it would be better to go home. She would tell Cole Boy they would know Mama's condition and prognosis by that evening.

As Elliot drove the car into their driveway, both he and Nell were puzzled not to see Cole Boy's truck parked at the house. Upon entering, the found the four children crying.

Clarity

Bliss filled them in. "Uncle Cole Boy slept a few hours, then got in his truck and left. As he started to drive off, he called back, saying, 'Goodbye kids. I'm going where no one will ever hear from me again, because everybody will blame me for Mama being sick. I don't intend to stay around to pay doctor bills and listen to everybody's shit'." Bliss's eyes filled with tears.

The next day, Uncle Ted found a note taped to his car's windshield telling Ted to go to Olli's and Cole Boy's and clean the house out. "Keep what he wanted and trash the rest," the note concluded. Ted surmised Cole Boy was running as far away as Olli's last three Social Security checks would take him.

Cole Boy drove off knowing he was leaving his nephew and nieces saddened and confused. He wanted to get away from his sister and her family as quickly as possible so he wouldn't have to answer questions. He was sure Mama's condition was due to his neglectful inattention, but he didn't want to admit it. Not really.

He sped along the rain-washed freeway and found he was inadvertently headed for home. He debated if he should go tell Uncle Ted that Olli was in the Shelton Hospital where Nell and Elliot would take care of her; or should he simply find a motel room for the night. He decided to drive to Tacoma. He found a rundown motel off of the main highway and checked in.

After taking a hot shower Cole Boy wrapped himself in a towel and crawled, exhausted, between the sheets of the saggy bed, where he wracked his brain to decide where to go and what to do next. His mind raced along, searching for a direction to take. The flashing neon sign outside of his window hypnotized and numbed him until he fell asleep.

The morning brought more drenching rain. Cole Boy dressed in his dirty clothes and drove to the closest diner. He realized he hadn't eaten since Nell's kids had fed him 24 hours before. After he'd eaten he drove the streets aimlessly in a zigzag pattern until he found himself outside of Uncle Ted's house. He left the truck motor running, wrote a quick note and placed it under the car's windshield wiper blade. Then he sped away with no plans of ever returning.

Driving through rain washed streets, Cole Boy made one last stop at his house where he put his shotgun, rifle and ammunition on the seat of the truck next to him. A bundle of clothes, sleeping bag and camping equipment was stowed behind the seat. After having surveyed the house for anything else he might need to survive, he had decided the rest was all junk. It didn't matter that he had left behind all the family memorabilia: photos, wedding papers from his Dad and Mom, graduation and birth certificates. All he felt was freedom from the past.

He drove to the nearest freeway on-ramp and headed north.

A few miles south of the Canadian border he drove to a side road where he parked in a secluded parking lot behind an abandoned industrial building.

He wrapped himself in his sleeping bag and curled up in a cramped position on the truck seat and immediately fell asleep.

He slept through the late afternoon and through the night. Before daylight, clatter from a nearby garbage truck jarred him from his cramped sleeping quarters. He reared his heavy frame into an upright position behind the steering wheel, and before the veil of sleep had completely slipped from his eyes he started the engine and eased out onto the street.

He drove to the first fast food diner, ordered food, paid the waiter and left.

He found an inconspicuous dirt road and followed it into a thick wooded area for a mile or more until the underbrush along the roadside scratched the truck.

The road became non-existent at the edge of a swamp. He stopped the truck, got out and took inventory of his surroundings. He ate the food he bought. He then walked along the swamp's edge and found traces of a fire pit, assuming the area was occasionally used by hunters or poachers. He felt the remote area would be a good place for him to claim as residence until he had money to go where he had finally decided upon: Alaska.

Clarity

Cole was determined to make a complete change in his life now that he knew Mama was going to be well-cared for.

The idea of Alaska stirred excitement in his mind.

For the moment, he planned on finding a quiet, easy job nearby this hidden spot and stay the winter. He'd build a shelter to keep the rain out and eat in town, so heat was all he had to worry about. At least he wouldn't have to pay rent, and he could save any money a menial job would supply.

In the next few days Cole found a job that would suffice, with a small garage. He camped by the swamp for two months. Living in a frugal manner, his savings grew.

Since he'd made up his mind about his destination and his future, he bought maps of Alaska and read many articles that gave him a glimpse of the different areas. He decided he'd stop first in Sitka and feel out the job market there. If that didn't work out he'd head to Anchorage or check on the fishing industry along the Gulf of Alaska. Cole felt the Alaska-Canada Highway would be too rough a trip for his old truck, so he decided that when spring arrived he would sell it and fly to Anchorage where he would buy another vehicle.

One evening Cole returned to his swamp retreat to find his tent and camping equipment torn apart and scattered over the ground and thrown in the swamp. This was a shock to find everything he owned ruined, and he felt a real injustice had been done him. He climbed back into his truck, leaving his belongings in a shambles. He stopped at his job and ask to draw his pay. His adventurous trip to Alaska was to start a few months earlier than he'd planned.

When he reached the freeway, for some unknown reason, instead of going north, he drove south. He had no intention of going back to see anyone. He just had a hunch, or a premonition that the Alaska-Canada Highway would be a pretty dangerous stretch of road to travel with winter coming on, plus the fact that he would be traveling into unknown territory alone. He knew he would be smarter to make arrangements to fly.

Second Son

Cole headed for Seattle and Sea-Tac airport. He found a sporting goods store where he bought two of everything the salesman suggested that he would need for a new-comers winter stay in Alaska. He had the salesman make a compact roll of his purchases, including his shotgun, rifle and ammunition. Everything was rolled into a custom made rainproof duffle bag carrier that would pass airport regulations.

Cole found a used car dealership to buy his truck. The cash added to his savings, the money from the three social security checks of Mama's he had hidden away. He had quite a lump of cash. More cash than he'd had since he'd sold the farm right after Dad died.

He took a taxi to the airport and bought a ticket for the next plane to Anchorage. Arriving in Anchorage, he stayed a few days to look the place over. But he decided it was much too busy and more populated than he had anticipated. He wanted to find a smaller town where he could settle down into an unhurried job and lifestyle.

Cole wandered the taverns and local diners talking to anyone he could find who would supply information about local or nearby towns and chances for employment. One old timer, who called himself Copper River Ray, told Cole he'd heard of a cooking job that was opening up for the winter at a waterfront cafe in Cordova. Cordova was only 150 miles South-East of Anchorage by plane. The old man spoke of the mileage as if it was a hop-skip-and-a-jump away. Considering the miles from place to place in Alaska, Cole found the old man was right.

He took the shuttle van to the airport and bought a ticket to Cordova. As he left Anchorage he felt he had taken the right direction at last.

Arriving in Cordova, he asked the woman who drove the shuttle van from the airport where he could find the Fish Scale Cafe. She chuckled and asked how he knew of that place. He said he'd heard from an old timer that there was a wintering-over job for a cook there. The old timer's name was Copper River Ray. The

Clarity

lady laughed and said, "If anyone would know what's going on in Cordova, it would sure be Old Ray."

When they reached the waterfront it was dark. Cole made the parting statement to the driver. "This dark afternoon time is something I will have to get used to. I guess it being dark at three in the afternoon makes a person aware that they're in Alaska"

He sauntered along the waterfront past a cluster of weathered, grey fish canneries and hole-in-the-wall cafes and shanties. Because of the early afternoon darkness, he decided to find a room to rent for the night and resume his search for the Fish Scale Cafe the next morning.

It had been a busy week, and Cole needed to let himself adjust to the northern changes. He needed to relax his nerves and ready himself for the new adventure that was awaiting him.

Meanwhile, Olli's inner strength was trying to awaken her subconscious fighting spirit, to make her final grasp at emerging from the blankness filling her limbs and mind. In her subconscious she seemed to hear a long lost voice of Ma saying, "Olli pull up them boot straps and get on with it."

Olli opened her eyes and was aware of the bright light in the room. She saw the tubes hooked to her arms. She couldn't feel them, but she knew the tubes were her means back through a veil to reality. She blinked her eyes and tried to call for help. She knew she was warm and safe, maybe in a hospital.

A nurse who had been sitting at her bedside saw Olli's eyes flicker and immediately responded to her patient's attempt to communicate by firmly patting Olli's right hand. The doctor was called for.

Dr. Reiner came into the room. He leaned over Olli so she could see him.

"Well, He said cheerfully, "it is nice to see you've come back to us. My name is Dr. Reiner. You are in St. John's Hospital in Olympia where your daughter and her husband brought you. Do you remember Mrs. Brauer?"

Olli tried to tell him, "No," but she didn't recognize the voice and the jumbled sounds that tumbled out of her mouth. In panic she tried to get out of bed, only to find her left side wouldn't move. It was as if half of her had turned to stone. Muddled fear like she'd never known before nearly overwhelmed her.

Dr. Reiner quieted her with a gentle hand, and he didn't speak to her until he saw the glaze of panic had left her eyes. "Mrs. Brauer, you have had a stroke. And you have diabetes. We're giving you medicine to help both problems, so I don't want you to worry about anything. We'll do it all. You just lie there, relax, and start feeling better. The nurse will call your daughter and tell her you are out of danger."

Olli tried to say "Cole Boy." But again panic flooded over her like an icy wave as she realized her jumble of strange noises couldn't be understood.

Dr. Reiner patted her right hand again and told her to relax. What she was experiencing could be temporary and would likely disappear after awhile. He continued, "Your family will be back to see you tomorrow. I felt we should let you rest tonight and let our medical magic work its wonders. We'll see you get some warm broth and tea, then an injection to help you relax. I'll see you in the morning. The nurse will be with you all night and she's pretty good working with stroke patients. You're in good hands."

Dr. Reiner left Olli's chart and orders for her care with the nurse, then went to the nurses station to call Nell and let her know Olli had come through the crisis. He made an appointment to see Elliot and Nell the next morning before they visited Olli.

Olli received the warming broth and tea, which she found hard to swallow. The nurse gave her an injection and she slept like an untroubled child.

The following morning a different nurse was beside her, who fed her and cared for her personal needs including a warm, soothing bed bath.

Olli's right side felt the warmth of the soothing washing, but

Clarity

her left side felt nothing, so she deducted the stroke had affected her left side along with her ability to speak.

A tinge of self-pity caused hot tears to spring to the rims of her eyes, then she heard Nell and Elliot's voices in the hallway. She opened her eyes and hoped her feelings weren't evident.

Nell came in the room and leaned over and kissed her. The doctor had explained to them about Olli's problem with paralysis and the loss of speech.

Nell said, before Olli struggled to ask her about Cole Boy, that he had gone home for a while. She told Mama she had called Tess in Oregon and she would be driving up as soon as she could. She had also called Olli's family in Lynden Valley.

Olli grasped Nell's hand with her right hand and tried to mouth the words carefully asking for Cole Boy.

Nell guessed her mother's concern, so told her she tried to get in touch with Cole Boy by calling Uncle Ted's house. Olli would have to be satisfied with this. Nell said, "Mama, Dr. Reiner says you will have to stay here only until you're able to make another ambulance trip transferring you to the convalescent home in Shelton. You'll be just two miles from our house. That way the kids, Elliot and I can drop by to see you every day."

At that news the right side of Olli's face brightened. A wisp of a smile curved half of her mouth. She moved her lips the best she could to try and from the words "Thank you." She held Nell's hand in a desperate grip.

In time, Olli's condition improved enough that she was transferred to the convalescent home in Shelton. Soon a routine of visiting at least once a day delighted Olli, who realized she had been starved for family contact. But each visit prompted urgency of pleading eyes and jumbled verbal attempts to ask for Cole Boy. Olli longed to see him. She knew he had been gone since the night she became ill, but no one told her where he was or why he didn't come to see her.

Second Son

For Olli, the years strung out toward the edge of time with no word from Cole Boy.

No improvement came in Olli's ability to talk or walk. Her face showed the years by the hollow lost look pouring out of her eyes. But she had not stopped trying to ask after her boy. Her precious second son.

Nell and Elliot moved to Arizona because of a promotion in Elliot's work, leaving Tess and her grown married daughter, Bonnie, to take over the visiting routine.

Tess had married for the third time and was working fulltime. Having moved to Bellingham, she put Olli in a rest home near there.

The grandchildren grew, married and drifted away with family circles of their own, and Olli grew older and still more alone.

Cole Boy never came back to see her. No one spoke of him. Her precious second son.

Olli quietly passed away at age seventy-six, on an early November morning in 1983.

All the family tried to find Cole Boy to tell him of Olli's passing. But no one had a clue where to begin the search until Uncle Ted contacted the Maritime Union in Alaska, on the unlikely chance Cole Boy was in the state he had loved to talk about years before.

It seemed that Cole Boy had fallen off the face of the earth, until one day he showed up at the door of Uncle Ted's house in Tacoma. He had heard from the Maritime Union while he was fishing in the Gulf of Alaska. The notice of his mother's death came three weeks after her burial.

Cole Boy came back to Washington shortly after receiving the news, not because of regret or nostalgia, but because he had suffered a slight stroke himself.

And hoped to make some connection with any of his family. He learned Nell and Elliot had moved from Arizona back to a lake near Shelton. Both had been ill and were retired. Cole Boy decided to visit them and ask forgiveness for the mistake he'd made years

Clarity

before when he'd treated Mama so badly. He found his nephew Casey's name in the phone book, called him and asked him about where Nell lived.

When Casey and Cole Boy drove into the yard, Nell's resentment and hard feelings dissolved at the sight of her only brother, now an old white-haired looking man, though only 50.

Nell suddenly understood the biblical story of the prodigal son and the father's joy and forgiveness he had displayed at the appearance of his long lost son. That same feeling came over Nell as she rushed out of the door and pressed her tear-filled eyes against her brother's ample chest. At that moment all resentment vanished.

Cole Boy murmured, "I'm so sorry." Sad and happy tears mingled. They cried together.

Cole spent the afternoon talking about the past years that he had been gone. He told his sister and Elliot how he had traveled to Alaska and worked in a number of cafes and on fishing boats. He told them he had met a fisherman's widow who had four teenage children. She offered him a year-round job on her large fishing boat. First a cook and deck-hand, he then learned the tricks of the trade. When the four kids had left for college he fell in love with and married Dora. They hired an experienced crew and fished commercially until Dora became ill with cancer. They sold the boat and license to Dora's two older boys, who stayed at Cole's mobile home in Cordova, where Dora died. His stepsons and stepdaughters had grown to love Cole for his quick wit and good humor and the tender way he had treated their mother.

Cole had lost the hard edge of selfishness and had embraced his stepchildren as if they were his own flesh and blood. His life with his loving Dora had opened his eyes to his faults, and he had tried to undo the wrongs he had shone his mother by being kind and thoughtful to Dora and her family. They had changed his life.

But now he was alone, only wanting to see his sisters to tell

Second Son

them he was ill and desired their forgiveness for all his ignorant, childish years.

A year later, in 1986, Cole Boy's suffered the same fate as his Mama. In his early 50s, he was diabetic and had a severe stroke making him unable to speak. He passed away shortly thereafter at the same convalescent home where his mother had died.

Not long after Cole Boy died, Tess, at sixty-one years of age, suffered a stroke and passed away.

It was left to Nell to tell Olli's story of yearnings for lost sons: the first taken from her; the second son, spoiled and overindulged, who had left his mother dangerously sick and alone. In the fog of Olli's mind she had known her way of showing love and her need for Cole Boy had been squandered. Had he ever really cared? Nell told the story of Cole, Olli's loving and devoted husband, how he never revealed the secret behind Olli's mad obsession with her second son.

Nell knows the story well and understands the many facets of Olli's life. She saw the changes, knows the reasons, but would always be puzzled by the memory of her mother daily trying to ask for her precious second son.

A combination of circumstances left Nell—the only surviving member of Olli's family—to hold together the intricate pieces of her mother's complicated life, and to pass the story on to her children and her grandchildren. Nell knew her grown children should be told the story of their Grandma Olli's life, which inadvertently shaped the emotional state of Olli's only surviving daughter, Nell. She called her four children to a family gathering where she could share with them events that comprised Olli's seventy-six years.

Nell began to tell Olli's story. She told of each incident placing them as one would string beads on a silk thread. Each bead of information made Olli's life more intriguing to the grandchildren. Each child, overwhelmed by the hectic, depressing times which Olli endured—those things of which most of the family had known nothing—each grandchild now knew Olli's cheerful

Clarity

attitude had been held in front of her pain like a shield, to cover her disappointment and sadness about her first son, and to cover her broken heart that was never mended by Cole Boy, her beloved, precious second son, the second son who was nowhere to be found when Olli's life spirit drifted away to a kinder realm, her mind still calling for her lost, beloved second son.

As Nell spun the story, she carefully wove a basket of memories for each of Olli's grandchildren to carry home in their hearts. Each grandchild understood the reasons Grandma Olli held Uncle Cole Boy so close, and why that favoritism shown their uncle had caused Nell to never show favoritism toward any one of her own four offspring. Nell told her family she was lucky to sort out the pieces of her life that were wedged in her memory. She concluded with, "I wish only one thing, that Grandma Olli could have loved all of us and enjoyed being in our lives instead of holding so tightly to her obsession for Cole Boy, the son who was nowhere to be found when Olli's spirit drifted away. For Olli left this earth calling in her mind for her beloved second son."

Acknowledgements:

Special thanks to Holly Shepherd, administrator at Martha & Mary Health and Rehab Center, who recognized the potential in this story and recommended it to the "Senior Wish Project," a program sponsored by the Leadership Kitsap Foundation. Grateful acknowledgements to the members of the "Senior Wish Project"–Jennifer Allik, Brittany Bakken, Robyn Chastain and Sharon Purser–for granting Vernabelle's longtime wish of publishing her work.

Thanks also to K. D. Kragen, KaveDragen Ink LLC, for proofreading, editing, and manuscript layout, and above all being a trusted and caring guardian of this story from beginning to end. With Kragen's help, expertise, and perseverance, this story is now a treasured legacy of Vernabelle's life and a gift to be generously shared with her loved ones.

To my dear Friend Vicki who has been above & beyond supportive in trying times... I love you.
We have a mutual bond that not all people know. That's Forever

♡
Daryl

Vernabelle Rice
by Daralynne Fitzpatrick

Vernabelle Rice began life as Vernabelle Botts. Born in Shelton, Washington on September 12, 1933, she came from meager beginnings. She grew up the middle child with her older Sister Esther and her younger brother Charles. She and her family worked hard to put food on the table picking brush and working at a floral business.

Through her life she reveled in being a daughter, sister, wife, mother, aunt, grandma, great-grandma. She married her husband Darrell Rice when she was 16 years old and finished her senior high school year as a married woman.

She was amazingly creative in so many ways. She loved creating things with her hands *and* her mind. She was a seamstress, sewing clothing for her 4 children, quilting, and worked at a drapery business making draperies and upholstering furniture. She loved painting, oil painting being her favorite medium and creating wonderful works of art for her friends and family. She wrote stories, she wrote poetry ("She's a poet, don't ya know it, her feet are Longfellows.") and even put her poetry to music, playing her guitar. She loved singing and joined a choir group at her church, the First Christian Church, in Shelton, Washington.

She became the creator of a home for her husband Darrell of 61 years and their 4 children, Chris, Steve, Becky and Daralynne. She had an amazing ability to create meals from a limited pantry that became restaurant-worthy. One of the kids' favorites was what her children teasingly called Dog Poop Soup. A lovely zucchini and tomato stew (all ingredients grown in Darrell's huge garden). Another favorite was Dough Gods. Dough Gods are basically pan-fried bread dough, delicious with homemade, out-of-the-garden, raspberry freezer jam. Her creative mind couldn't make just plain pancakes... the pancakes were carefully poured into mouse-with-ears and rabbit shapes for four hungry children (and their many friends) to gobble down. When groceries ran quite low, she had the ability to make sugar and butter sandwiches seem more like a treat than a "This is all we've got today" meal.

Her love of laughter and love of her children, grand children and great-grand children were always apparent. She loved creating all kinds of things for them right down to the stories she wrote and the songs she sang to them while cuddling them. Her laughter was often and her attitude of "I'm fine" was always there.

In 1975, Vernabelle and Darrell relocated with their youngest daughter Daralynne in tow, to Montclair, California. Darrell's job changed and they were all sad to leave their home on Island Lake in Shelton, Washington, but a new adventure in California was what was next in Vernabelle's life. Leaving her other three children, Chris, Steve and Becky behind was hard for her. The three oldest children were all beginning their lives as adults, deciding to stay in their home town. Even though the change was a bit difficult, soon she became active in her church in Montclair and made friends quickly. She continued her sewing and quilting, and found a job at another drapery business, and she continued her painting.

Vernabelle and Darrell became "snowbirds" when Darrell had an early retirement. They sold their home in Montclair, California and bought a long travel trailer and a big Ford truck to tow their home into new adventures and new friends. They traveled back and forth to Washington State and Boulder City, Nevada for several years. They loved sharing their long walks in the desert with their dog Toto (Yes, he really looked just like Dorothy's Toto!) and in later years when Toto went to the big desert in the sky, they shared their walks and jack rabbit chases with McGregor, a lively Jack Russell Terrier. Vernabelle's love for dogs was always strong.

The big trailer they lived in slowly filled up with the treasures they found in the desert. Buckets of lovely rocks, some that they tumbled into shiny gem creations, some were left all natural. Some Vernabelle glued to wooden plaques and painted them to look like birds or some other of God's creatures. Collections of items found in ghost towns also found a home in their trailer. These treasures were tucked into every nook and cranny that they would fit in the limited space. Vernabelle had a knack for fitting something in that trailer when you really didn't think there was anywhere to put it! Funny thing is she could usually find it later, too...eventually. Creative organizing, definitely.

Throughout her traveling years, Vernabelle had a story idea developing. She finally began putting in onto paper, writing it in longhand, and taking her about 15 years to complete. She took creative writing classes while in Nevada and had guidance from her teacher and peers in her class. She wrote, rewrote, and refined her story. Then from the longhand manuscript, her friend typed out the manuscript on a typewriter. Thus, the book *Second Son* was born.

For health reasons, they decided to put down roots in Kingston, Washington, close to their daughter Becky. They got a lovely apartment with a peek-a-boo view of the water, yet were right downtown.

Declining health lead first Darrell, then Vernabelle into the loving care facility Martha & Mary's in Poulsbo, Washington, just down the road from their Kingston apartment. Martha & Mary's is large, beautiful facility that looks more like an estate than a nursing home. The staff and nurses quickly fell in love with the couple. Here Darrell and Vernabelle shared a room that Vernabelle referred to as their "apartment." The two were on a new adventure, and she liked leading sing-a-longs with the other residents. She truly enjoyed the staff and all the visitors that would bring their dogs in for pats and petting and knew each of the dogs and their owners by name. She even got her picture on the internet with the Kitsap Sun, the local newspaper, petting one of her doggie visitors!

It was here at Martha & Mary's that Darrell was asked if there was something he or Vernabelle had ever wished for. The *Senior Make-A-Wish Foundation* was looking for someone to do just that—make a wish come true.

Darrell told them, "Well, yes! My wife always wanted to have the book that she wrote published."

They submitted 100 pages to the committee and low and behold, her wish was going to be granted! Vernabelle and the entire family and their friends were ecstatic. Her story *Second Son* was going to become *A Book*.

On July 6, 2011, Vernabelle left this Earth with her husband by her side. Her family is eternally grateful to Martha & Mary's for making not only Vernabelle's wish come true, but her entire family. To hold this book in one's hands is to hold many years of love, work and creativity of a woman that fashioned a home, family, friends and many memories for many people. For that, we thank her. For the publishing, we thank *Make a Wish Foundation* and Martha & Mary's, as well as the fact that when Vernabelle left this world she was aware that her book was going to become *A Book*.